SOMETHING FABULOUS

PROSPERITY

Prosperity
Liberty & Other Stories
There Will Be Phlogiston

Other Titles

The Affair of the Mysterious Letter
Looking for Group

ALEXIS HALL

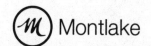 Montlake

Text copyright © 2022 by Alexis Hall
All rights reserved.

Published by Montlake, Seattle

www.apub.com

Amazon, the Amazon logo, and Montlake are trademarks of Amazon.com, Inc., or its affiliates.

ISBN-13: 9781542036290
ISBN-10: 1542036291

Cover design and illustration by Philip Pascuzzo

Printed in the United States of America

The person, be it gentleman or lady, who has not pleasure in a good novel, must be intolerably stupid.
—Jane Austen, *Northanger Abbey*

AUTHOR'S NOTE

Some linguistic choices are intentionally modern. Also, almost everyone in this book is queer.

Prologue

One had to own he was handsome.

That was what they said about His Grace, Valentinian Gervase Lorimer Layton, Duke of Malvern, Marquess of Ashbrook, Viscount Summersby, Viscount Cheverell.

But Miss Arabella Tarleton most certainly would not own it.

Of course, he possessed the requisite number of eyes (two, sultry green in colour, and rather heavy lidded), noses (just the one, straight and long, as if optimally designed for looking down), mouths (again, in the singular, wide, sensual, and framed by two brackets as if always on the verge of a deep and wicked smile), and limbs (four, each blessed by a certain strength and grace). But he could have possessed six noses, no limbs whatsoever, and a full three and twenty eyes, and Arabella Tarleton could have found him no more repulsive.

At this precise moment in time, he had arranged himself elegantly upon one knee before her and taken hold of her hand. His eyes gleamed at her through an unnecessarily lavish fringe of gold-tipped lashes.

She turned her head, entirely unconscious of the advantage such a severe angle was likely to bestow upon a neck that had, at least once in her presence, been described as "swanlike," and allowed the shudder in her heart to manifest in her cruelly captive body. It travelled all the way through her, stirring the artful little curls that clustered at her brow in what surely could not fail to be a piteously becoming fashion.

"Miss Tarleton," murmured the duke. "Are you quite well? The quail was rather rich at dinner."

She trained her eyes (these she had long hoped were luminous) upon the portrait that hung in pride of place above the fire, for she considered it a far superior sight to her suitor's disagreeable visage. It depicted Boudicca, her uncle's prize hog.

"Miss Tarleton?"

His lack of sensitivity did not surprise her. What could one expect of a man so advanced in age as to be approaching his thirtieth year? Who broke his promises as carelessly as snail shells. Who had even used the death of his own father as an excuse to cast off the friends of his childhood. She pressed her free hand to her brow in the hope this might stir the ashes of his withered and most likely dissolute heart. "It is not the quail, Your Grace. The quail does not rend my soul to tatters and cast it upon the monstrous pyre of land investiture."

"Well, that is fortunate," offered the duke after a moment's thought. He coughed slightly. "Miss Tarleton. Arabella, if I may—"

"Indeed you may not!"

"Forgive me. Miss Tarleton. I am sure you cannot be ignorant of—" He sighed.

Arabella's neck was beginning to ache, but, at that, she twisted herself into a pose of even greater severity. What right had *he* to sigh?

"Well . . ." His voice deepened, honeyed with a touch of mirth. "One would think my current position would speak for me. But, in any case, my dear Miss Tarleton—you know this would sound considerably better if you would permit me the use of your given name—my dear Miss Tarleton, I am come here tonight, with the blessing of both our families, to humbly ask for your hand in marriage."

She sniffed.

"I'm sorry, did you say something?"

She would have sniffed again, but then she recalled he had no delicacy of mind, and sniffing was somewhat unladylike besides. "I suppose you rehearsed that?"

"I certainly thought about it. I would not say *rehearsed*."

"Well, it is very shoddy." She tossed her head, slightly awkwardly given the angle, but she was not yet ready to abandon her attitude of Wounded Womanhood Beset by Misfortune, which—unlike the duke himself—had benefited from considerable practice before the mirror. "Especially since it is nothing more than a . . . a . . . wretched charade in any case, and you might just as well throw me across your shoulders and carry me off like one of those poor Sabine ladies."

The duke seemed rather startled, which allowed her to liberate her hand and nurse it protectively against her breast lest he try to violate it a second time. He came slowly to his feet, which was unfortunate because she had somehow forgotten how brutishly (and unfairly) tall he was. "I can assure you," he said firmly, "I have absolutely no desire to carry you anywhere, nor any intention of doing so. This coat would not abide it, and my valet would never forgive me."

Arabella had never been to London, so she had no idea whether His Grace was what her uncle would have called "one of 'em curst dandies." He certainly dressed like no man she had ever seen, and yet there was nothing explicitly extravagant about him. He favoured subdued colours and plain waistcoats, and his ornaments were minimal—merely his signet ring and a simple fob—but nobody could have mistaken him for a country squire.

While nothing would have induced her to concede on the matter of his good looks, his mysterious, sartorial splendour was undeniable. It intrigued and infuriated her almost equally, until she reminded herself that he was the defiler of her virtue and ruiner of her life, and then it merely infuriated her. When they were married (oh horrors), she would turn his valet to her cause—if nothing else, she had a remarkable facility for recruiting people to causes—and visit what reciprocal misery she could upon her husband by creasing all his cravats.

It seemed scant consolation.

"Have I offended you, Miss Tarleton?" enquired the duke when she did not speak. "If my proposal was insufficient, I can only apologise. Life affords one so little opportunity to hone one's technique."

In truth, Arabella had been slightly entranced by the pristine, intricate folds of the white linen at his throat, but she was a strong-willed young lady and she rallied. "There is no fashion, Your Grace, in which you could propose that would render it anything other than profoundly repugnant to me."

He blinked at her, his ridiculous lashes flickering. "I see."

"I see?" She went for another head toss, and it was considerably more effective this time. "Is that all you can say? Have you no shred of decency?"

"Oh, Belle." His voice dropped into that lower register again, the dangerously sweet one, and he held out his hand. She glared at it until it went away. "I know I would probably not have been your first choice of husband, but *profoundly repugnant* seems a little excessive. With a little accommodation on both our sides, I imagine we might deal together rather well."

"Accommodation!"

He rubbed his forehead—where a vein appeared to be twitching—and she was glad to see he was finally responding to the full and dire gravity of the situation. "Will you please stop repeating every damned thing I say in that tone of two-penny melodrama?"

She opened her mouth. Then closed it.

Two-penny melodrama! Truly the man was a monster.

"How dare you," she said, in stifled accents. "You buy me like a cut of meat or . . . or . . . a carrot . . ."

"Why, Miss Tarleton," he drawled, "you sell yourself too cheap with such similes."

Now she was too irritated even to head toss. "Then, like a rare and exquisite Sèvres snuffbox." She stamped her foot. "For heaven's sake, you beastly man, it does not matter what buying me resembles. The fact of the matter is you *are* buying me. And all feeling must revolt from such an abominable transaction."

He sighed again. "Feeling may revolt, or not, as the case may be, but it has long been the wish of our families to see our lands united, and as both our fathers are now deceased and you are of marriageable age, I would like to oblige them."

He took an impatient turn about the room. There was something about the way he moved that disconcerted her: grace poised on the edge of savagery, a panther in superfine. But when he stopped pacing and faced her, she took some pleasure from the fact there was a coldness in his eyes, and a tightness to his mouth, that suggested he might be disconcerted too.

With an elbow propped against the mantel, and one ankle hooked round the other, he looked almost as carefully situated as Boudicca, beneath whom he stood. "If," he began, "we must speak so vulgarly of trade, consider this. I will acquire no dowry, some convenient acres for whatever son you bear me, a wife who despises me and talks like the heroine of an inordinately bad novel. And you will be a duchess, one of the most powerful women in the land. Is yours not the better bargain? Surely the prospect must hold some appeal for you."

His words were ice water to her anger, and it fizzled away, leaving her small and miserable and—horrifyingly—on the verge of tears. "You are a man, Your Grace."

"Thank you for confirming that."

"I just mean . . . you could do anything. Be anything. And *this* is what you've chosen?"

"I think you will find," he told her, "that I have chosen to be exactly what I am supposed to be. You, on the other hand, appear to have fashioned yourself entirely from cliché."

5

"Oh." She would not cry. She would not cry. She would not cry. "How I hate you!"

"Which will not preclude your marrying me, my dear." He reached into an interior pocket so small and slim she would never have known it was there and twitched out a glossy handkerchief. "Come, dry your eyes. I am really not so terrible a fate."

She disdained his handkerchief, even if it meant a single tear slipped down one cheek. "How can you say that? My life is over. You might as well have killed me."

His hand clenched, for a moment, then slowly relaxed. "Both our lives are over. We may start them afresh together."

This gentler tone did little to ease her resentment of his previous words. Her fugitive tear plopped coldly onto the decorous décolletage that had long since been a battleground with her aunt, and she dashed it away with a fingertip. "That means little enough to you. You have already lived your life."

"My God." His sleepy eyes widened, startling in their sudden intensity. She was not precisely certain how she had, at last, managed to affect him, but she was fiercely glad she had. "Belle, I am eight and twenty. Hardly in my dotage."

She had no answer to such a deluded notion, so she sniffed again.

"If you must insist on crying, will you not take my handkerchief?" He waved it at her, and it unfurled in the firelight like a flag of surrender.

"If I were crying, which I am not, I would not touch your vile handkerchief."

His long, pale fingers folded it neatly and tucked it away. "Very well. I will not force my distasteful linen upon your virgin nose."

Arabella—whatever feelings she might once have entertained to the contrary—abhorred the duke on principle most of the time. But she was starting to learn she abhorred him most particularly when he was like this, brittle and mocking and cold, as if he did not take her anguish seriously at all. "If you are quite done with me, Your Grace, I believe I shall retire. While I still have the freedom to do so upon my own inclination."

"And"—he inclined his head slightly—"I will bear the happy news of our union to your aunt and uncle."

"I hate you," she reminded him.

"So I understand. You know . . ." There was something else in his voice this time, something softer, almost sad, but that was assuredly no concern of hers. "While you have no wish to be the wife of a hateful, doddering duke you barely remember from your childhood—though you rather liked me then, you know; we used to make posies together—I can also envisage a more rewarding future for myself than spending the next ten or twenty years shackled to a histrionic chit barely out of the schoolroom."

She pulled herself to her full height—all five foot four admirable inches of it—and gave him a look of magnificent scorn. Under different circumstances, she might have rejoiced for the opportunity to deploy it for, so far, it had not breached the confines of her looking glass. "Then perhaps I will contrive to relieve you of such burdens."

"Am I to find you floating in the millstream come daybreak?" His lip curled. "If you would care to wait until after we are wed, there is a fine brook that runs through Malvern Park. I believe there is even a willow grows aslant it."

Were there no depths to which he would not stoop? Now to ridicule poor drown'd Ophelia? She regarded him icily, just as he deserved, and delivered her answer so perfectly she half wished she had an audience to applaud for her. "I would not give you the satisfaction, Your Grace."

She turned, and it was a shame she was not better clad for sweeping. Her evening gown, while perfectly serviceable, and quite pretty, lacked for grandeur. Nevertheless, she did her best with what she was given, and she would not be sold like a carrot to a man with no respect for Shakespeare.

Let them own *that.*

Chapter 1

"Malvern?"

Valentine opened one eye, found the activity painful and the view unprepossessing, and, therefore, immediately closed it again.

"I say, Malvern?"

He opened his mouth with even more difficulty than his eye. Its interior felt both dry and sticky at the same time. He passed his tongue—which seemed to have died at some point during the night—across his lips and tried to remember how words worked.

"Dammit, Malvern."

Ah yes. Something like this: "No, thank you," he said politely, and buried his face in the pillow.

"Look, I'm sorry to wake you, but—"

"Not as sorry as I am."

There was silence. It was good. Valentine liked it and wanted it to continue.

"For God's sake, man. Are you soused? Would you care for some water?"

"No, I would not." This, Valentine was certain of. "I would care for you to go to the devil."

"Well, that's . . . very rude and not going to happen. Because I have to ask you something."

Valentine attempted to open his other eye. It reluctantly presented him with the hazy image of a young man standing over him, holding what was clearly a candle. This was not an auspicious sign. If it was dark enough to require a candle, it was too dark for the Duke of Malvern to be awake.

"I used to be mildly indifferent to you, Tarleton," he muttered. "Why this abominable betrayal of my trust?"

"Yes, well." The young gentleman—Arabella's twin brother, who went by the improbable name of Bonaventure and the even more improbable nickname of Bonny—sounded upset. And Valentine was upset at the volume of his distress. "I lied when I said I was sorry to wake you because I'm not. You deserve to be woken viciously and regularly. On account of being such a . . . such a bad person."

First the sister. Now the brother. Was there no peace for the . . . hmm. *Wicked* would have been putting it rather strongly. *Averagely virtuous?* "What are you talking about, Tarleton? And must you talk at all?" Valentine tried to move. Except it made his head explode, so he stayed where he was, twitching and whimpering.

Sometime later, finding Tarleton had still not done the decent thing and left, Valentine gathered himself and asked, "What in God's name happened to me?"

"From the empty decanter of brandy by your bed," Tarleton told him unsympathetically, "I suspect this decanter of brandy happened to you."

Valentine groaned. Then mustered his strength and rolled onto his back with all the grace and dignity of the Prince Regent trying to mount a horse. His body seemed altogether unimpressed with his behaviour and inclined to resist at any opportunity, but he persevered and pulled himself heroically upright.

Unfortunately, this caused fragments of last night to assemble themselves jaggedly in his mind—which, in turn, made him remember why he had chosen to take up with a bottle of brandy.

His relationship with the long-standing arrangement between the Tarletons and the Laytons had been rather akin to the relationship Damocles shared with a particular pointed and precariously positioned object. But his father had been right to suggest the match: it was an eminently sensible arrangement for both families, and Valentine's memories of Miss Tarleton had always been pleasant—a charming if shy child, he had thought with idle fondness. On the rare occasions he had permitted himself to think of his marital obligations at all.

Which may, in hindsight, have been an error. For Miss Tarleton had taken advantage of his absence to grow up exceptionally beautiful and unnecessarily peculiar. And, for no reason he could fathom, she appeared to hold him in deep aversion. Valentine was unaccustomed to being held in deep aversion—he was a duke, and if people held dukes in any sort of aversion, they usually only did so in private—and he found the experience unwelcome. As was her apparent conviction of his decrepitude.

Decrepit or not, a quick check of his current faculties, both physical and mental, confirmed that he was at least functional. Irked, possibly even vexed, but functional.

"Please," he drawled, "enlighten me as to the nature of the calamity so absolute and precipitous as to necessitate my being awakened at . . . I say, what time is it?"

Tarleton gave him a hard stare—or as hard a stare as could be expressed by a face so angelic. "It's four o'clock."

"Good God." Shuddering, Valentine fell back against his pillows. "Does the world even exist at such an hour?"

"Some of it. But please stop fussing. I need to talk to you about Belle."

Valentine arched the very tip of his brow—he rarely troubled himself to raise a full one. "Well, that makes a certain degree of sense, I suppose. Since she is assuredly both calamitous and precipitous."

This observation did not seem to please Tarleton. Both brows shot upwards as if in rebuke of Valentine's lack of brow-based theatricals. "Don't you speak of my sister that way, you shameless brute. This is your fault. She would never have done such a thing if you hadn't . . . done whatever you did to her first."

"I beg your pardon. I proposed marriage to her. As I believe it has long been expected that I would."

"Well . . ." Tarleton bristled like an affronted porcupine. "You must have done it wrong."

Was Valentine really being lectured on appropriate behaviour by a man who burst into other men's bedchambers at unspeakable hours? "I think," he said haughtily, "I know how to propose marriage."

"Show me."

"Tarleton, have you lost your mind?"

"I need to know what happened. I need to know *exactly*."

"You need to go away this instant and put your head in a bucket of water."

Tarleton did not, in fact, go away that instant and put his head in a bucket of water. Instead, he seized hold of the bedcovers under which Valentine was sheltering and yanked them onto the floor.

Thankfully, Valentine had slept where he had fallen and still in his clothes—thus sparing them both an intimacy for which they were not prepared.

"Propose to me." Tarleton plonked his hands on his hips. "Right now."

Valentine was unwinding the creased remains of his neck cloth. "You do know it won't be legally binding."

"I don't actually want to marry you." Tarleton—who must have been reading the same novels as his sister—stamped his foot. "You've clearly turned into an awful person. I just need to understand what happened to Belle."

First *decrepit*. Now *awful?* Such was Valentine's confusion that he crawled woozily off the bed. "She was behaving rather strangely all evening. I think it might have been the quail."

"It was not," returned Tarleton, his eyes flashing magnificently, "the quail."

Evidently, Valentine was going to get no peace until the young man felt himself satisfied. Though God knew what that was going to take. He had not precisely been delighted to renew acquaintance with his bride-to-be—especially when she kept referring to him as *repugnant*—but at least he was not expected to wed the brother. He positively pitied the poor woman who was going to have to spend her life with the lightning storm of wayward impulses given human form that was Bonaventure Tarleton. "If you say so."

"I do say so. That's why I said it. Now stop faffing around and tell me what you did. And don't leave out a single detail. Because I'll know."

"For the twenty-seventh time"—Valentine stifled a yawn, in a manner that any sensible person would have been devastated by—"I didn't do anything. We retired to the drawing room, I went down on one knee, as I believe to be traditional—"

"Go on then."

"You doubt my capacity? How infirm do you think I am?"

Tarleton's eyes widened. They were blue like his sister's. Just as bright and as disconcertingly pretty. "I never said you were infirm. You're very firm. Almost . . . excessively firm, really."

"I understand you're trying to be reassuring, but stop it at once." Flustered, Valentine sank to one knee. "I believe I did something like this."

There was a long silence—during which Tarleton subjected him to intense scrutiny. "Hmm," he said finally. "I thought you might have startled her somehow or made a mull of it. But, actually, that's not a dreadful start."

"'Not dreadful,'" repeated Valentine faintly.

"I mean, spoiled a bit because you look like you slept in a hedge, and your hair is all messy, and you haven't shaved—not that I object to a little stubble, but Belle's the fastidious type. It's one of the few things we disagree on."

"What is happening, please? I did not invite an assessment of my kneeling."

Tarleton smiled—and it was a strange angle for being smiled at. Valentine was used to people looking up to him. "Perhaps you should. You look delightful down there."

"Your sister was less than delighted."

"You must have been vile later. What happened next?"

"I might have taken her hand?"

Tarleton obligingly offered his own. He wore more rings than his sister. More rings than surely any one person needed to wear—unless they were at least part magpie.

"And then," Valentine continued, "I said, 'Miss Tarleton, I have . . . something something blessing of families . . . something something . . . honour . . . something something . . . wife.'"

"I'm assuming you didn't say 'something something' at the time?"

"Of course I did not."

"Always best to check. And then what?"

Valentine blinked. "And then what what?"

"What else did you say?"

"Well, nothing. I'd finished."

"You'd *finished*?" Tarleton's voice rose.

"This habit you have, of repeating everything I say. Is it hereditary?"

"This habit you have of sneering at everything—is *that* hereditary?"

It was probably a good time to rise. Not, Valentine reflected, that it had been a good time to kneel in the first place. "I," he murmured, "am not a villain in a tawdry romance. I do not sneer."

"Then what do you call"—Tarleton pointed with far more gusto than the gesture warranted—"that?"

"My face?"

"And"—another whirling of his fingers, the jewels refracting the candlelight into rainbow splinters—"this?"

"I have no idea to what you're referring."

Tarleton made a sceptical humphing noise. "You need to stop distracting me. What happened to the rest of your proposal?"

"What do you mean"—Valentine's reserves of sanity were fraying a little, as was his tone—"The. Rest. Of. My. Proposal?"

"The rest of it!"

Valentine was troubled to hear something like a snarl emerging from the back of his throat. "Tarleton . . ."

"You know, the bit where you told Belle she's the most beautiful woman you've ever seen."

"Why in God's name would I say that to her?"

"Well . . . well . . ." The young man seemed genuinely confused, his slightly retroussé nose wrinkling in confusion. "Because you're marrying her. And she *is* beautiful."

"Undeniably, but I do not see how it's relevant."

"You would prefer to marry someone ugly?"

"I would prefer not to marry anyone at all."

"And you said that?" exclaimed Tarleton. "To my sister? To whom you were proposing? *While* proposing?"

Valentine was getting a headache. On top of his hangover. He put his fingers to his brow and massaged it absently. "I didn't say it. I think it was mutually assumed."

Not to be outdone by physical expressions of dismay, Tarleton flung both his hands in the air, like a diminutive Prometheus defying the gods. "You did, at least, tell her how she'd filled your heart with laughter and your soul with joy, driven you to the brink of madness with desire, and made your life without her a vast and empty ache."

A pause.

"A vast and empty what?" enquired Valentine politely.

"Ache." Another arm wave. Valentine was starting to wonder if the entire family spent their lives in front of mirrors performing dramatic poses for an as-yet unrealised audience. "A vast and empty ache."

"If the ache is present, by definition it is not empty."

Tarleton was gazing at him much as his sister had the night before: with deep betrayal and burgeoning revulsion. Having apparently taken his fill of the bitter draft that was Valentine, he cast himself upon a nearby chair and flung an arm across his face. "What is wrong with you?"

This felt unwarranted. And somewhat hypocritical, coming from a man who clearly had many, *many* things wrong with him. "I have no idea what you're implying, Tarleton. My proposal was very polite and well reasoned."

"'Polite and well reasoned'?" Oh God, now Tarleton had gone back to repeating everything Valentine said. "Have you not read a single novel?"

"I don't see what that has to do with anything."

"Well, if you had, you'd know that 'polite and well reasoned' are not qualities people look for in marriage proposals."

"For heaven's sake"—Valentine tried, and failed, to keep the impatience from his voice—"if we lived life as though it were a novel, we'd spend all our time becoming embroiled in improbable adventures and spouting nonsense about filling our vast and empty souls with joyful aches."

"Yes," said Tarleton, "and?"

"Tarleton, nobody in their right mind would want any of that."

There was a long silence. Then Tarleton stood up, but only in order that he might further misuse the furniture by violently reoccupying it. "Now I understand everything."

Valentine sketched the most elegant bow he could manage, given the circumstances. "I'm gratified to have been of service. Do you think I might be permitted to return to bed?"

16

"Not really. I mean, I'm saying I understand. But it's still your fault."

The Tarletons were rubbing off on him. It was the only possible explanation for why Valentine—who prided himself on his exquisite manners and understated grace—crumpled to the floor and put his head in his hands. "What, for the love of God and for the last time, is my fault?"

"Why, Belle of course." Tarleton's voice had slipped into the mildly injured register of someone confronted by a sudden display of unreasonable behaviour. "She's run away."

Chapter 2

"She's what?" asked Valentine carefully.

Tarleton shrugged. "Flown the coop. Done a runner. Buggered off. Absconded. Exit, pursued by a bear." He paused. "She's gone."

"What? Has she taken leave of her senses? Why the devil would she do such a thing?"

"You know"—Tarleton shook his head in bemusement—"I have no idea. Oh, wait." His tone changed abruptly. "Maybe it's because she's having to marry you since your family thinks it's a good idea, and you couldn't even do her the basic courtesy of pretending you wanted her."

"It was not," offered Valentine mildly, "a basic courtesy she was inclined to offer me."

"So?"

"Courtesy is reciprocation."

Tarleton wore his hair a little longer than fashion dictated was appropriate—it swept in a romantic tousle across his brow and tumbled in equal profusion to his shoulders. Right now he was tossing it about in what Valentine supposed to be hauteur. "Courtesy is kindness."

"Kindness." Valentine felt his lip beginning to curl. Then remembered Tarleton's claim that he sneered and schooled his face into neutrality. "I see."

"Besides," Tarleton went on, "why should she have been courteous? She didn't owe you anything. It wasn't on her to make your unpleasant task easy for you."

"The unpleasant task is our joint responsibility. And it renders us jointly powerless."

To Valentine's surprise, Tarleton burst into theatrical laughter. Then leapt from his chair, seized a hand mirror from the dressing table, and thrust it before Valentine. "Are you aware of this man?"

"You mean . . . me? I flatter myself that I do have some familiarity."

"So, you know you're a duke?"

"Yes."

"And that you're very rich."

"Tarleton, I am not in trade. I do not discuss my finances."

"I'll take that as a yes. I could also point out you're an admired and well-established fashionable gentleman about town."

"On the subject of points, do you have one?"

"I do." Tarleton hurled the mirror aside—thankfully it landed on the rug so it did not smash—and then stood before Valentine with his arms spread wide. "Consider this."

"What exactly am I considering?"

"*This.*" A sweep of Tarleton's hand encompassed his whole body. "A delectable package of pocket succulence, admittedly. But untitled. Penniless. Mortgaged to the bollocks. Dependent on my sister to marry well so we don't end up servicing sailors on street corners."

"Would the sailors get a say in the matter?"

"I beg your pardon—I would be *very* well received by sailors." To Valentine's mild surprise, Tarleton's expression grew grave, his generous mouth pulling tight and his brows dipping into a pointy little frown. "The thing is, Malvern," he went on, "you don't know a damn thing about powerlessness. And, in most respects that matter, neither do I— but at least I know enough of what I have not to make a fool of myself."

Valentine eyed him. With his hair and his rings and his . . . everything. "I would strongly dispute that."

"Dispute all you like. We still need to go after my sister."

"To what end?"

"To . . . to the end of your doing a better job of proposing, of course." Tarleton flicked an imaginary speck of dust from his cuff—which was as fascinating as it was bizarre, for Valentine had never seen someone actually do that outside the pages of fiction. "Now that you have been appropriately instructed in the art."

There had been absolutely nothing appropriate about Tarleton's instructions. "I can imagine no power, be it in heaven or on earth, that could possibly compel me to address myself to anybody in so ridiculous a fashion."

"Malvern, you *have* to, or Belle will think you're irredeemable. You don't want to be irredeemable, do you? If you're irredeemable, you'll probably get shot or trampled to death by wild horses or . . . or *impaled on a spike.*"

This was far too much nonsense on top of far too little sleep offered in far too rapid a tone at far too intense a pitch. "Tarleton, you seem to be labouring under several misapprehensions, the most pressing being that—after the debacle of yesterday evening—I care a whit for your sister's delusional ideas."

"Oh, I know you don't care," retorted Tarleton, with another of his head tosses. "You made it very clear to everyone last night exactly how care devoid you are."

This was news to Valentine. He thought he had been perfectly civil—or as civil as one could be during a visit performed for the express purpose of discharging a matrimonial duty while the object of said duty sat opposite one, stabbing a quail repeatedly with a fork. "What were you expecting? Rejoicing?"

"I wasn't expecting you to be so . . ." And here Tarleton inter-rupted himself with a sigh, as if he didn't know what he was expecting Valentine to be or didn't wish to share it. "It doesn't matter."

"Indeed," Valentine agreed. "It does not."

For it *shouldn't* have mattered. Valentine's memories of Bonny were mostly of a roundish seven- or eight-year-old who had followed him around saying things like, "Belle's stopped speaking again" or "Belle says she's not coming out of the den" as if he truly believed nothing lay beyond Valentine's power to solve.

"In any case"—Tarleton was continuing with the air of a com-mitted continuer—"Belle's still your fiancée. That makes her your responsibility."

Rising from the floor, Valentine settled himself instead on the edge of the bed—intending to return to it fully the moment his nonconsen-sual visitor departed. "It was my father's wish that I marry her. Not that I involve myself with her imprudence."

"You're the one who made her run away."

"It was the realisation that life is not some great romance full of poetry and pretty flowers that made her run away. A piece of knowl-edge, by the way, that you would also do well to accept."

A long and heavy silence, emotions racing across Tarleton's face like clouds before the sun. It made Valentine weary just watching him. How could one person feel so much? "Why *shouldn't* life be romantic?" he demanded. "Why can't it be?"

"It is not a question of what life should or can be. It is a question of what it is."

Tarleton subjected him to a cold stare. "Which is what?"

"On this particular occasion: an arrangement between our families to mutual benefit. I see no value to any of us in pretending there is more to it than that."

There was another silence, just as long and heavy as the previous one.

"What happened to you?" asked Tarleton eventually. "Did your favourite puppy die? Have you not been cuddled enough?"

It was rare for Valentine to find himself lost for words. This was one of those occasions.

Tarleton sighed. "Never mind. If you won't help out of remorse or common decency, consider this: what my sister does reflects on you now. An escapade like this could ruin her."

"That is no concern of mine."

"Isn't it?" Those dreamy blue eyes raked over Valentine—it was disconcerting, the way they could be at once so soft and so intent. Thistle fluff and thorns. "Do you enjoy being whispered about? Laughed at behind your back?"

Something cold crept up Valentine's spine. His reputation was unexceptionable. Intimidatingly pristine. Vice, shame, folly slipping away as effortlessly as shadows from ice. But didn't that just make others secretly wish to see you besmirched? Damn it to hell—he had taken such care. Cultivated a life of ease and refinement, and absolute impenetrability, the passions and pains of other people a dance beheld through glass. He had gracefully eluded social climbers and fortune hunters, politicians and pleasure-seekers, shown consideration but never regard, indulged but never to excess, known the right place to be and the right time to leave. A true jewel of the ton: hard and bright and immutable. And yet it would come to nothing. All because of a silly girl with a head full of fancies.

Valentine abruptly realised he was quite annoyed. And it was not a pleasant sensation. Strangely exposing, as though someone had put a blade to his skin and was relentlessly peeling it back. This would simply not do.

"Where," he asked, with hard-won calm, "would she go?"

Tarleton shrugged. "Well, how should I know? She could be anywhere by now."

"So you're overflowing with insights into her emotional state, and opinion of me, but don't have the slightest clue when it comes to her actions?"

"She didn't choose to confide in me."

There was something . . . different in Tarleton's manner. A dimming of his eyes. The faintest droop to his shoulders. And Valentine found he did not like that *either*. "Does she normally?"

"Of course she does. We're twins. We tell each other everything."

"Tarleton, what are you—are you crying?"

"No." He brushed his face with his sleeve. "I just . . . it woke me up. When she left. The feeling of her leaving. And I ran to the window just in time to see the gig vanishing into the distance."

"I'm sure," Valentine heard himself lie, "she thought she was doing what was best for both of you."

Tarleton was too spare of vertical stature to pace effectively—it was more of an anxious bouncing. "She should have told me she was running away. I would have run away with her."

"Nobody"—Valentine's briefly renewed patience had already faltered—"should be running away at all."

Big eyes, still a little shimmery from unshed tears, fastened onto his. "It's the first time we've ever been apart."

Well, this was dreadful. Not only had Tarleton burst in on Valentine unannounced at an unseemly—nay, ungodly—hour and subjected his proposal to excoriating critique; he was now getting his feelings everywhere. And this, in turn, was giving Valentine feelings, mostly of discomfort. Which was not to say he didn't have emotions of his own. He just moderated them, as a man should.

Tarleton seemed to be waiting for something. And whatever he was waiting for, Valentine was rather dismayed to discover some part of him wanted to deliver it. So, in the absence of context, experience, or understanding, he did his best to do so.

"Pull yourself together," he said, in what he was sure was a bracing, encouraging, gentleman-to-gentleman kind of tone.

Unfortunately, Tarleton did not react as though braced or encouraged. Instead, he put his hand against Valentine's chest and started half stroking, half poking at him. It was probably the most disconcerting thing that had ever happened to him.

"Wh-what are you doing?" Assuredly a most dignified enquiry. Not at all a breathless squeak.

"I'm trying to work out what's happened to your heart." Tarleton pawed at Valentine's shirt. "Is it absent or damaged? Turned to stone by a wicked enchant—"

Valentine caught Tarleton's wrist. This was an even worse idea because neither of them was wearing gloves, and Valentine was not prepared for the reality of unadulterated Tarleton beneath his fingers. Mostly how warm he was, and how smooth his skin, the intimacy of bone and blood and the thrum of a pulse. Valentine let go abruptly.

"Once we find your sister," he pointed out, "you will no longer be apart. So I suggest you put aside your—"

"Natural human feelings?" suggested Tarleton.

"—and focus your attention on the matter at hand. Miss Tarleton is still your twin. You still know her." Valentine honestly couldn't tell if he was commanding or coaxing. "Think, man. Where would she have gone?"

To his credit, and from his scrunched-up face and pursed lips, Tarleton did appear to be thinking. "America," he cried.

"She's gone," repeated Valentine slowly, "to America?"

"Well, not immediately. It's quite far away."

"You astound me."

"So I suppose she'd be heading for Dover first."

And here Valentine had rather taken it for granted that she would have fled to a sympathetic relation or a nearby friend's house—from which she could have been straightforwardly, and nonurgently, retrieved.

"She's making for Dover? On her own? A young lady of quality with, as is becoming wildly apparent, no experience of the world whatsoever?"

"You see," Tarleton pressed him, "why I'm concerned?"

"As it happens I do. I'm relieved that one of you at least is blessed with some modicum of sense."

"I mean, she could be captured by pirates or highwaymen or . . . or vampires or anything."

"Forgive me, I spoke prematurely."

"Also"—apparently Tarleton was not done talking, but was he ever?—"I'm not completely certain she's alone. I think there was some-one else with her in the gig."

"Any notion who it might be? A lovestruck swain, perhaps?" *Lovestruck swain?* What was happening to him? Valentine had never used such language in his life.

Tarleton, however, seemed to find nothing amiss. "Unlikely. Swains are a bit thin on the ground round here. Trust me, we've looked. It's probably Peggy."

"Peggy?"

"Margaret Delancey—of the Devonshire Delanceys. She's Belle's best friend."

"And," Valentine wondered, "are they much alike?"

"Absolutely they are. They get on famously."

The severity of the situation was settling upon Valentine with the finality of a funeral shroud. "Oh, good God. They're doomed."

"So"—there was an unflattering degree of surprise in Tarleton's voice—"you'll come? You'll help get my sister back?"

"You don't feel rather a traitor to her cause in consigning her once more to a future with me?"

"I'm hoping a madcap chase across the country will bring you together."

"It is doing literally the opposite."

"In any case"—Tarleton shrugged—"marrying you is probably better than going to America."

"I'm flattered."

"You shouldn't be. They do terrible things to tea over there." Tarleton dived across the room, actually grabbing Valentine by the sleeve. "Now come on—we have to go."

Valentine glared at his sleeve. Then at Tarleton. Then at his sleeve again—though the young man resolutely failed to take the hint. "Go where, exactly? How are we to find them in Dover?"

"I'm hoping—if we move quickly—we can catch them on the road to Dover. They'll need to rest at some point, won't they?"

"Is there a hostelry en route?"

An eager series of nods. "Yes. Yes. The Wayward Goat."

Yesterday, Valentine's plans had included making a slightly reluctant trip to the country, proposing to the woman his father had wanted him to marry, and then leaving again as quickly as possible. And yet here he was, having been dragged out of bed at an unspeakable hour by a far-too-excitable young man, about to embark upon what would surely be a tiresome undertaking to retrieve his own bride. He was beginning to wonder if he had crossed some malignant spirit who had resolved to punish him for an inadvertent trespass. It was certainly the closest thing he could find to an explanation for his current predicament.

"Very well," he said, unable to shake the deep sense of foreboding that his acquiescence had occasioned. "Just give me a moment to get dressed."

Chapter 3

"When you said a moment"—Tarleton was standing behind him, weaving from foot to foot—"under what definition of *moment* were you operating?"

"I was operating under the definition of 'unit of time sufficient for me to get dressed.'"

"But you're taking *hours*," wailed Tarleton. "They'll be halfway across the ocean before we've even left your bedroom."

"A gentleman should never be seen abroad with an unsatisfactory cravat."

This inspired another little foot stamp. "Well, you won't be seen abroad. You'll be seen in Surrey, where nobody gives a damn."

"*I* will give a damn."

Tarleton made a noise like an elephant with a knot in its trunk. "I would never have taken you for a dandy, Malvern."

The censuring tone seemed slightly hypocritical for a man wearing seven rings—all set with different stones. "I'm not a dandy," he murmured, his gaze fixed on his reflection and the folds of linen he was manipulating with slightly less skill than usual. "Dandies believe in excess. I believe in moderation. I just happen to have standards. *Damn it.*"

Another failure. He cast the crumpled fabric aside.

"For someone with standards," said Tarleton, "you're not very good at tying your cravat."

"I'm not usually being *stared* at while I do it."

"Oh no. Am I cramping your style?" Tarleton's face was suddenly very close to Valentine's. "Well, guess what? I don't care because my sister is probably being forced to walk the plank right now."

Valentine turned his head, and they nearly bumped noses. "What do you think you're doing?"

"I'm creating an unpleasant environment so you hurry the hell up."

"You are *impinging* on my *person*."

"Then move your person's arse, and I won't be impinging on it."

"You know when I said I was mildly indifferent to you?" Valentine's eyes locked heavily onto Tarleton's—the strangest heat rolling through him in that moment. "I hope you realise you have comprehensively ruined that beautiful relationship."

The seconds ticked by, suspended like the single pearl that dangled from Tarleton's ear. Then Valentine found himself abruptly seized and spun, determined fingers beneath his chin tipping his head back.

"What—" was all he managed before Tarleton had flung a length of linen around his neck and was either trying to knot it or strangle him with it.

Valentine froze, half-mesmerised by the swift-moving fingers close to his throat, the graze of warm breath against his cheek, the way the tip of Tarleton's tongue touched the bow of his upper lip as he worked, how soft his mouth looked—

"There." Tarleton stepped back, with what Valentine considered a rather exaggerated air of accomplishment.

However, a glance in the mirror confirmed a serviceable mail coach. It was nowhere near as precise as Valentine, with time and the services of his valet, could have managed—besides which, he favoured the mathematical—but it would certainly do. At least for their present endeavour, since "chasing an impetuous fiancée you didn't want to begin with" seemed unlikely to have a dress code.

His hand went instinctively to the top of the knot to smooth it into place. Was that the warmth of Tarleton's skin that lingered on the fabric? And why would he even notice?

"Thank you," he said softly, relying on good manners to cover his confusion.

Tarleton, too, seemed momentarily off-balance, a faint flush painting the tops of his ears. "Coat. Greatcoat. Let's *go*."

The coat, however, proved something of an impediment, and Valentine found himself reduced to undignified struggling—even some small amount of flailing—beneath Tarleton's increasingly incredulous gaze.

"Can you not . . . ?" he asked, not even trying to contain his laughter. "That's your *own coat*. You can't get into your *own coat*."

Slightly out of breath, one arm twisted up behind his back and half into the sleeve, Valentine paused. "I usually have my valet."

"And yet you still didn't think to bring him with you."

"Well"—embarked upon another woolly battle, Valentine spoke without properly considering his words—"I didn't want to waste his time."

Silence.

"That is, because I did not intend to . . . make a lengthy visit. Not because . . ."

"I know," interrupted Tarleton coldly, "what you meant." Coming up behind Valentine, he made a valiant attempt to help him into his coat—but the cut of the garment, coupled with Tarleton's diminutive physique, rendered the task close to impossible. "Great gouts of hellfire. Is your valet a giant? A circus strongman?"

"On the contrary"—Valentine glanced over his shoulder—"he's perfectly average."

Growling with all the gravitas of a lapdog, Tarleton tugged again at Valentine's coat. "I may be but little, but I am *fierce*."

"Except right now you're failing to help a man get dressed."

"While you have failed to get dressed, full stop."

Valentine turned, once more almost colliding with Tarleton—who was clearly just an impinging sort of individual. "This is a sign from the universe. I shall have to return to bed."

"What?" Tarleton's hands were back on his hips. Their closeness, and the difference in their heights, meant he had to look up to meet Valentine's eyes—which gave him a slightly defiant air. "You're giving up already?"

"I can hardly leave the house in my shirtsleeves," pointed out Valentine reasonably. "No, I shall have to send for my valet. And most likely by the time he arrives, you will have returned with your sister and I will have achieved a decent night's sleep."

"Wait a minute—it's not my job to manage your marriage for you."

"I thought you said you *wanted* to chase down Belle."

"I do, but out of concern for her well-being. I need *you* to fix the damage of your god-awful proposal."

"You mean by lying to her. Professing sentiments I do not feel. Hasn't it occurred to you she might appreciate that even less?"

Clearly it hadn't. Tarleton's eyes fluttered, his golden lashes as long and lush as a woman's. "Don't you *want* to be in love with my sister?"

There was something at once so bewildered and plaintive in the question that Valentine let his voice soften. "Tarleton, I can't imagine being in love with anyone."

"Why not? I imagine being in love all the time."

"Yes. Well. Clearly you lack for diversion." To forestall further discussion on a topic that was as alien to Valentine as it was absurd, he attempted to strike a conciliatory note. "But your point is well taken. I owe your sister an apology, and I shall offer it as soon as the opportunity presents itself. For what little it may be worth, I truly never meant to make her feel dismissed or demeaned."

Tarleton bit his lip. "You know, I believe you. And that just makes it *worse*. Now give me five minutes—and don't you dare get back into bed—I'm going to find you a coat."

⟨❧⟩

"That," declared Valentine, having just about managed not to go back to bed, "is not a coat."

"It has holes for your arms and covers the body. It's a coat."

"It's barely even an object, and I will not be seen in it—not even in Surrey."

"Nobody will see it. It'll be under your greatcoat, and you could hide a water buffalo under there."

"Why would I want to hide a—never mind." Valentine, who had been waiting not precisely patiently in the stable yard, with the water buffalo–concealing greatcoat over one arm, now turned to leave again.

"But I found you a coat," protested Tarleton, and the genuine dismay in his voice halted Valentine in his tracks. "Please don't *abandon* us."

"I hate to harp on a theme, Tarleton: I'm not the one who ran away."

"But Belle wouldn't have done that if you hadn't been awful to her." Tarleton's eyes were . . . so big. So big and so blue. His mouth a trembling rosebud. "And now she's going to be murdered or kidnapped or *in America*, and I'll be *all alone*. Forever."

"Tarleton, please . . . I beg you. Stop having"—Valentine waved his hands—"feelings again. You'll be perfectly fine, I'm sure."

"I won't be *fine*," cried Tarleton, with such intensity that a nearby dog, startled awake, offered its own mournful howl. "How could I possibly be *fine*? My sister will be lost to me, I'll have no one, and nothing, in the world, and I'll have to sell the estate and go mad with grief like Ophelia and—"

"None of these things are going to happen. Give me the damn coat."

Tarleton beamed and held it out. "Here it is."

And now it was Valentine's turn to experience a lot of feelings—far more than he was used to, and certainly more than he was used to before six a.m. Irritation, though directed primarily at himself rather than Tarleton, for falling prey to such blatant manipulation. And, yet, at the same time a faint, undeniable thread of amusement, along with something more disquieting still. Curiosity, perhaps? Not curiosity? The sense of being—despite the hour—awake in ways he had not been for years.

Regardless, it was too late to refuse the coat. Thankfully, it fit—but then, being little better than a sack, it would probably have fit a gluttonous baboon. It did, however, smell strongly of . . . compost?

"Where, dare I ask, did you find this item?" Valentine nonetheless found himself asking as Tarleton readied his curricle—a rather stylish equipage, he was relieved to note, far more fit for purpose than the coat.

"There aren't many people of your height, you know."

"That doesn't answer the question."

"It gives context to the answer. Which is . . . it's the assistant gardener's."

"The *assistant* gardener's," repeated Valentine faintly. "I take it the gardener's wardrobe was not available."

"No, it was. You just wouldn't have been able to get into it."

"I see."

That conversation was going nowhere good. Valentine settled his many-caped greatcoat over his shoulders, which thankfully did conceal much of what lay beneath it. And then—after a minor altercation over who was going to drive, which Tarleton somehow won by pointing out that Valentine was the one who kept complaining of being tired and could very well run them off the road—they were on their way, a pair of matched bays whisking them along the main route to Dover.

For Valentine, it was altogether a very peculiar experience, both being the passenger in another man's curricle, and the bewildering set of circumstances that had led him to find himself in a position to witness Surrey by dawn. He supposed it was a fairly pretty bit of the country—the gentle curves of hill and dale, the inkblot clusters of trees against the horizon, and the fields, here and there, streaked purple with heather. The rising sun had rendered the sky a watercolourist's dream, rose-pink, and silver-grey, and burgeoning gold as rich as Tarleton's hair.

As for Tarleton, he turned out to be a very decent whip, too sensitive of his horses to treat them recklessly, or risk unnecessary theatrics. It was . . . a little surprising, considering both recklessness and unnecessary theatricality seemed to run in the family, but also reassuring. Valentine had little respect for men who did not respect their horses. Not, he hastened to remind himself, that it mattered whether he respected Tarleton or not. Bad enough that his father had inadvertently committed him to a lifetime with a beautiful idiot with ideas. The last thing he wanted was a connection with her twin as well.

Because Bonaventure Tarleton had grown up just as wilful and absurdly romantic as his sister. Just as stubborn and just as—in some peculiar way—charming. In fact, he was very probably *worse*. A thought that Valentine could neither account for nor justify. It was just a . . . feeling. A fretful animal presentiment of danger.

Or something else entirely.

Chapter 4

"Oh God, where am I?" An inordinately cricked neck and the dazzle of sunlight against his eyelids returned Valentine abruptly to consciousness.

"Asleep in my lap," said Tarleton.

Valentine jerked upright, blinking and mortified. "I . . . I . . . apologise."

"Don't worry. I was the one who woke you at four. Seemed only fair to let you catch forty winks."

The sky was a pristine blue, smooth as silk sheets, barely marred by clouds. "It seems," Valentine muttered, "it may have been more than forty winks."

"It doesn't matter." Tarleton grinned at him. "Besides, you're rather likeable when you're asleep."

"I . . . what?"

"You just lie there helplessly, looking all sweet and peaceful, and making little snuffling noises. Whereas when you're awake, it's nothing but sneering and mean comments."

"I do not sneer," Valentine insisted. Yet again. "And I am not *mean*. I'm . . . perhaps a little sardonic."

Tarleton shook his head decisively. "It doesn't come across that way. It comes across as though you care more about how you sound than how other people feel."

More nonsense. Maybe Tarleton was correct—and Valentine being insensible was better for both of them. "You can't go through life caring about other people's feelings. Where would it end?"

"I don't know." A delicate shrug, since Tarleton's hands were on the reins. "Maybe with being less mean all the time? You didn't used to be mean."

There was a pause. Valentine squeezed the back of his neck, stifling a groan as he felt the sinews catch and click beneath his fingers.

"And it's not true, though, is it?" asked Tarleton, abruptly. "That you go through life without caring for anyone?"

Valentine cast him an incredulous look. "Of course it's not true. There are those I care for. Deeply, as it happens. But—"

"Who?"

"Pardon?"

"Who do you care for?"

"Well, my mother for one. And do stop interrogating me, Tarleton. This is tiresome and absolutely none of your business."

"'This is tiresome,'" repeated Tarleton, in a lazy, self-satisfied voice, quite unlike his usual one. "'And absolutely none of your business.'"

"Is that supposed to be me?"

A sullen glance from beneath Tarleton's lashes. "Maybe."

"I see." Valentine was silent for a long moment, contemplating this new—and unmerited—assault on his character. Then flung his arms to the heavens. "Oh *nooooo*," he cried. "Everything is *terrible*. My sister has to marry an extremely rich and influential duke. How will we *survive* this *dreadful* fate? What will become of us, we poor orphan twins, with *nothing* in the world except our connection to one of the most powerful families in the land? Woe upon the house of Tarleton." It was at this juncture that Valentine realised exactly what he was doing and how utterly bizarre his behaviour was. "I'm sorry. That was uncalled for."

"I started it," admitted Tarleton, with unexpected generosity. "Although you know I don't actually sound like that."

"You don't?"

"Of course not. I'm far less restrained."

Valentine, surprised into laughter, put a hand to his mouth to stifle it.

And Tarleton, apparently equally surprised, glanced his way. "You should laugh more. It suits you."

"Eyes on the road, please, Tarleton. And I am not a hyena. And marrying me is far from the dreadful tragedy you both seem to have built it into."

"So you say, but the only points you ever seem to find in your own favour are that you have a lot of money and a fancy title."

"Given you have neither, it feels like a fair exchange."

Again, Valentine felt Tarleton's gaze, a strange weight to it almost, a warmth like breath or the brush of fingers. "And that's all you are?"

"It's all that's currently relevant."

Tarleton wriggled urgently, the requirement to drive a curricle visibly warring with his personal requirement to throw himself about in the most dramatic way possible. "God in heaven, have you no passion?"

"Passion for what?"

"I don't know. For something you believe in or someone you care abo—. Oh, what am I saying?" He sighed and steered them deftly to the side of the road. "We should stop for a while. I need to rest my horses."

"I thought you needed to find your sister before she was sold for a chest of doubloons on the Spanish Main."

"Yes, but I'm not going to kill my bays." Tarleton jumped lightly down from the curricle. "You can't do a good deed on the back of small cruelties."

"Would Belle agree, I wonder, when she's starving to death on a windswept moor?" And why, Valentine pondered distantly, was he needling the other man so? Yet he could not seem to stop.

"Of course she would. What use would my aid be to her if I'd made myself a terrible human being in the meantime?"

"I just," Valentine heard himself say, "don't see the benefit of passion."

Tarleton, in the process of unhitching his horses, didn't even look up. "I know you don't."

❦

Some minutes later, the bays were grazing peacefully, Valentine was gratefully stretching his limbs, and Tarleton was lifting a knobbly bundle from the depths of the luggage box tucked beneath the curricle's undercarriage.

"I didn't have time to raid the pantry as diligently as I might have wished," he remarked. "But we shan't go hungry on our rescue mission."

Valentine stared at him. "You expect me to eat off the floor?"

"Think of it as an . . . I don't know . . . *ad hoc* picnic. Everybody loves a picnic."

"I don't see the benefits of picnics," Valentine told him firmly.

"No passion and no picnics? What a dreary existence you live."

"My existence was perfectly adequate before you interrupted it."

"What do you even do for fun?"

Valentine gave him a cool look, the tip of a brow inching upwards. "I sleep until a reasonable hour and am helped into my clothing by my valet."

Shrugging out of his greatcoat, which was far less extravagant than Valentine's, Tarleton cast it to the ground. "Just sit down, will you? There's a pigeon pie here."

It would have been churlish, at this stage, to refuse. And, having been in no state to consider or acquire breakfast, Valentine was ravenous. Unfortunately, no sooner had he lowered himself onto Tarleton's coat and unwrapped the promised pie, followed by what looked like some kind of tartlet, shiny with syrup-drenched fruit, than a heavy buzzing began in the region of his ear. Whipping his head round, he beheld the largest, fuzziest bee he had ever encountered, bobbing drunkenly beside him, its legs occasionally catching in the strands of his hair.

The sound he made was extremely dignified. And with no diminution of his usual elegance, he adjusted his position on Tarleton's coat.

The bee transcribed a lazy oval. And then took up a new station, right in front of Valentine's face.

"Begone," he said, wafting in the bee's general vicinity. "Away with you."

The change in air currents seemed to confuse the bee, and it tumbled downwards, bouncing off the edge of the tart and then up again—colliding with Valentine's nose.

He leapt to his feet. "Good God."

Still buzzing in a low, faintly invasive tone, the bee ascended. Flew in a little spiral. And vanished into Valentine's hair.

"Where's it gone?" He rotated anxiously.

He could hear the bee, he could even sort of feel the bee—the vibration of its wings, or the brush of its fur—but he couldn't see the bee. And, somehow, that was infinitely the worst of all possible worlds. Further revolutions did not enable him to visually locate the bee, so he broke into a run, and then spun round. The bee spun with him, somehow evading his gaze, although its buzzing intensified.

"Leave me alone," cried Valentine, running and spinning, running and spinning, running and spinning. "Go away."

Tarleton was still standing by the curricle, with a loaf in one hand and a hunk of cheese in the other. "What are you doing?"

"It's after me."

"It's a bee. It doesn't have malicious intent."

"But . . . it . . . won't . . . stop . . . following . . . me."

"That's because you're being peculiar at it. Stop being peculiar at it, and it'll stop following you."

"I can't"—Valentine dashed past—"because then it'll get me."

"You are aware it's about *this* big." Tarleton made a shape with his hand to indicate the dimensions of the bee—which, to be fair, were still sizeable for a bee. "There's genuinely an upper limit on its capacity for violence."

"It's in my hair."

"It's not in your hair. It's just nearby."

"What if it stings me?"

"It's not going to. It's a bee. If it stings you, it'll die. It's aware of that. It's not going to suicide by duke." Shaking his head, Tarleton knelt down on the grass and began arranging his goodies. "It's probably a lot more scared of you than you are of it. Come and sit down, and behave like a normal person, and it'll probably get bored and go away."

"That hasn't worked with you," pointed out Valentine, reluctantly forcing himself to a standstill.

(The bee continued buzzing. It was definitely, absolutely, incontrovertibly in his hair now.)

Tarleton patted the ground. And, feeling as though he wanted to pull his head below his shoulders, Valentine tiptoed back across the glade to join him.

"It's still there," he said, having gingerly taken up a sort of nervous crouch on Tarleton's coat. "It's not going away."

Sighing, Tarleton leaned towards him. "Very well. I'll deal with it."

"Don't kill it!"

"Of course I'm not going to kill it. I'm not a bee murderer."

"You'll make it angry."

"Malvern." Tarleton's eyes caught his—held him for what felt like a blue forever. "For the last time, it's a bee. It doesn't have complex emotions."

A rush of air, Valentine flinching back with something that was certainly not a whimper, heat, and the scent of skin, half-sweet like strawberries, and then a blessed softening of the buzzing close to his ear. A moment later, and Tarleton was sitting back on his heels, opening his cupped hands to encourage—with a puff of air from between pink parted lips—the bee to fly off in some other non-Valentine-orientated direction.

Which it did, weaving a pollen-drunk path into the distance.

"It . . . it still feels like it's in my hair," muttered Valentine.

Tarleton reached out, his fingers light against Valentine's neck, and the vulnerable, bee-assaulted hairs that curled there. "It's gone."

"It was targeting me. Why wouldn't it leave me alone?"

"It must have thought you were a flower," Tarleton told him, smiling.

"I beg your pardon?"

"Mm-hmm." There was something in Tarleton's smile now. Something . . . intent, even a little wicked, for all the softness of that whimsical mouth. "It wanted to make love to you."

It was absurd because Valentine knew himself to be a man of the world. Nonetheless he gasped. "Tarleton."

"Bonny," returned Tarleton nonsensically.

"What?"

"Bonny. Short for Bonaventure. As in, my name. I'm getting tired of Tarleton this, Tarleton that. It makes me feel I'm at one of those boys' schools full of beatings and buggery."

"We are not intimates, Tarleton."

"Bonny."

"No. I refuse. That's an absurd thing to call someone."

Tarleton shrugged. "It fits well enough. We were born on a Sunday, you know. Belle and I."

"What does that have to do with anything?"

He smiled. "'But the child that is born on the Sabbath day is bonny and blithe and good and gay.'"

"That is a nursery rhyme. Not a directive as to nomenclature."

"Oh, Malvern." For some reason, Tarleton's smile deepened, a half dimple popping into existence at the edge of his mouth. "My reluctant flower. It's a good job you're such a feast for the eyes because otherwise you'd be *completely* unbearable. Instead of merely *mostly* unbearable."

Valentine had no idea how he was supposed to respond to any of that, though, thankfully, Tarleton spared him the trouble by passing him a bottle of ginger beer, a beverage he hadn't thought of since he was a child. He had forgotten the clean burn of it upon the tongue, the dance of tart and sweet—the way something so fresh on a warm day sent weariness scurrying away on rodent feet.

Chapter 5

For a while they ate and drank in silence, passing the bottle back and forth, lost in the pleasures of leftover pie, freshly baked bread, and the drip of sun-warmed cheese between the fingers. There was a little basket of peaches, too, each of them a drop of gold in a velvet skin that filled Valentine's mouth with the taste of summer afternoons.

"Tell me something?" said Tarleton, with his usual unerring instinct for ruining Valentine's peace.

Somehow, Valentine had stopped worrying about sitting on the floor. Now he was actually *lying* on it, his legs crossed at the ankles and his head propped against Tarleton's thigh, as he finished the last of the peaches and the sky rolled above him in cobalt waves, endless and serene and perfect. "What is it, Tarleton?"

"How can you not like picnics? Don't you own most of the north-west?"

"I manage my estates. From my library. With the assistance of my steward and my secretary. I don't go out in them."

"Why not?"

"I suppose I lack the Tarleton mania for running willy-nilly across the countryside." But Valentine, too, had been thinking in the quiet. He turned his eyes up to Tarleton. "Now you tell me something."

Tarleton looked genuinely shocked. "You . . . want to know something about me? I thought you didn't care about anyone anymore except your mother."

"This is curiosity. It's not the same thing."

But still, Tarleton beamed. "I'll make you a deal. Answer a question for me, and I'll tell you anything you want."

The sun and the peaches and the low hum of distant—emphasis on *distant*—bees must have lulled Valentine's sense of caution into a stupor because he heard himself say, "Oh, very well."

And, of course, Tarleton was ready immediately, like a panther ready to pounce. "Why did you come back? To propose, I mean. Why now?"

"Well, I . . ." Was this a trap? It felt like a trap. "That should be obvious, Tarleton. I had a duty."

"Yeeeeee-essss. But you didn't have a duty last year, did you? Or the year before that? Or, indeed, the year before that."

So a trap then. "That is between one and three additional questions, depending on whether we accept rising intonation as sufficiently question-like to constitute a question."

"They're part of the first question."

"You said one question. You did not negotiate for it to have parts."

Tarleton sighed. "Malvern, please. I don't understand, when you could have come back at any time, or not at all, why now. What changed?"

"Nothing changed."

The outraged "gah" of a man who felt himself tricked.

"No," said Valentine quickly. "I mean . . . nothing changed. Other than that I realised nothing was going to change. And that I had delayed too long already, waiting for or looking for or—I'm sorry, Tarleton, I don't know."

Tarleton was, once again, manifesting that curious and disconcerting intensity of aspect. "What did you think was going to change?"

"I *just said*," snapped Valentine, "I don't know. And you need not belabour your point: I know to have let so many years slip away was ill-done of me."

"We honestly thought you wouldn't return at all."

"I had a—"

"Yes. Yes." Tarleton's many rings flashed in the sunlight as he waved Valentine's words away. "You had a duty. But, do you really? It's never been a formal arrangement. Just something your father and my father hoped for. Uniting the lands and the name and so on and so forth."

"I cannot speak for your own principles, but honouring my father's wishes feels like a duty to me."

For no reason as far as Valentine could discern, Tarleton's eyes softened like a cloud-scudded sky. "Yes, I can see that. Were you very close?"

"Of course not. He was my father. Who is close to their father?"

"Umm . . ." Tarleton scrunched up his nose in a way that certainly wasn't endearing. "Elizabeth Bennet?"

"Nonimaginary people."

Now Tarleton was visibly pouting. "I don't know any nonimaginary people. I live in Surrey. And anyway," he rushed on, "why follow through on something for someone who means nothing to you?"

"I said we weren't close. I didn't say he meant nothing. He was my father. And this is what I have left of him." All, perhaps, Valentine had ever had: a sentimental dream from a long-vanished youth.

The pout disappeared. Replaced by deeply unnecessary sincerity. "Oh, flower. It's . . . surprisingly sweet of you to want to do this for your dad, but you know he wouldn't want you to be unhappy."

"I very much doubt," Valentine said, "that marriage to your sister will affect my happiness one way or another."

"Aaaand there you are." Bonny's tone had grown brittle. "I was wondering where you'd gone."

"What do you mean? I'm right here."

"Yes, but you'd started reminding me of who you used to be. Or at the very least who I used to believe you were. But thankfully, you caught it just in time, and now I'm back to thinking you're horrible."

"Tarleton"—it should not have rankled so much to be the subject of a constant barrage of Tarleton-twin dissatisfaction, but it did—"we were children when last we met. You should have had no sense of who I was. I certainly had none of you."

"A state of mind," Tarleton muttered, "you have carried into the present."

Valentine made an involuntary movement that was neither defensiveness nor discomfort. "Given that marrying into my family will save your own from ruin, is it really in your best interests to be questioning my motives?"

"No, you're right. Of course. I should just be flinging my sister at the nearest man like a string of sausages to a dog."

Probably Valentine should have suspected something amiss from "No, you're right." He made an impatient sound. "While I'm sure this fastidiousness on your sister's behalf does you credit, you realise there is nothing stopping you from making a successful match yourself."

"Ah," said Tarleton. Before falling silent for what felt like a long time. And then, "Was that what you wanted to ask me before?"

Valentine nodded. "You're . . . not wholly without merit to look upon. Of course, you also have many, many, manifest and undeniable flaws. But you possess a certain, I suppose, charm?" Valentine had somehow gone astray. He cleared his throat. "I'm sure there are women who will find you an agreeable husband. All you would need to do is find a rich one."

"Mmmrrrrmmrrggh," explained Tarleton.

"I beg your pardon?"

"As it happens, Belle and I have already discussed this."

A pause, which Tarleton allowed to linger, until Valentine asked him directly, "And what was your conclusion?"

"That I can't get married."

"Why not? It's hardly a complicated process."

"Well"—Bonny offered a nonchalant shrug—"it wouldn't be fair."

This was making perilously close to zero sense, even for Tarleton. "Fair on whom?"

"My wife, for one."

"Oh, come now. I know you're annoying, but you're not that bad."

"The thing is, flower, Belle and I both believe in marrying for love. And I don't fall in love with women."

Valentine tried to prevent them, but his eyes rolled of their own accord. "Putting aside, for the moment, your absurd obsession with love, you'd be surprised at the ardour an available fortune can inspire in the breast of the penniless."

"Not for me. Because," Tarleton repeated in unnecessarily strident tones, "I don't fall in love with women."

"You can't know—"

"I fall in love with gentlemen."

Valentine nearly swallowed his peach stone.

"Well, I say *gentlemen*," Tarleton went on, "but I more mean men in general. I had a rather delightful assignation with a gorgeous young redcoat once. And he wasn't gentle at all."

Very carefully, Valentine sat up. It felt quite important he be sitting up in that moment. "I . . . what are you telling me?"

"I'm answering your question."

"But I . . . I don't understand."

"You've eaten all the peaches, you rotter." Tarleton was peering disconsolately into the empty basket. "And I'm not sure what you don't understand. It's very simple. I can't get married because I couldn't love my wife. At least, not in the way she might want to be loved. I could definitely *love* her. I love lots of women. They're marvellous creatures. I just wouldn't feel romantic about her. Or want to have sex with her, and if I married someone and they didn't want to have sex with me, I'd feel a bit cheated, personally speaking."

The words swirled dizzily in Valentine's mind: a strange carousel of ideas that spun so brightly they were almost incomprehensible. "Yet," he said slowly, the words thick as sherbet in his mouth, "you do feel romantic about . . . about men?"

Tarleton, deprived of peaches, contented himself with picking the strawberries off a tart. "Not *all* men. Some men. The right men. And then there are others I am terribly, *terribly* interested in but not romantic towards in the slightest. Which I suspect is how most men feel about women: some you like, some you love, some you just want to get into their breeches. Well, petticoats."

"I . . . I don't understand," said Valentine again, helpless beneath this fresh informational onslaught.

A pause. And then Tarleton asked in a painfully gentle voice, "What don't you understand?"

"I don't understand . . . how it . . . how you . . ."

"I don't think anyone understands how they fall in love."

"Is there"—Valentine's tongue flicked across his dry lips—"something wrong with you, perhaps?"

"Look at me." Tarleton indicated himself with a flourish. "What could possibly be wrong with me."

"Well . . . falling in love with men . . . it can't be . . . be . . . convenient?"

Tarleton laughed, flinging his arms wide. "Love is not supposed to be convenient, my flower. It is supposed to be *transcendent*."

"Yes, but . . . I mean. Is it only you? Who is like this?"

"What? No. Of course it's not only me. How would that work?"

"I don't know." Valentine shook his head despairingly. "I don't understand how it works anyway."

Dropping to his knee beside Valentine, Tarleton impinged once more, bringing their faces together. "It works *the same*."

A long, long silence. "What is," Valentine ventured finally, "the purpose?"

"The purpose?"

"You can't conjoin property or procreate or unite your families."

Tarleton's look was almost pitying. "I know you think me a fool, but those all sound like terrible reasons to spend my life with someone. At least the man I choose, I will have chosen for himself alone."

"Isn't it"—Valentine swallowed—"wrong, though?"

"By whose reckoning?"

"Everyone's?"

A shrug. "When Adam and Eve ate the fruit of the tree of knowledge, they learned what was good, and what was evil, and how to tell the difference. I believe we know when we do wrong. We feel it. In our hearts, our souls, our conscience. And nothing I have ever learned or known or felt has taught me to believe that love is wrong. So no, my flower, it's not wrong."

"Oh," said Valentine.

Tarleton laughed. "You still look terribly—and if I may say adorably—confused."

"I . . . well. I am." He had not meant to sound so plaintive—but he did. Plaintive and lost, and far younger than his not-yet-thirty years.

"What can possibly be confusing you?"

"I just don't know what I'm supposed to do now."

"The same as five minutes ago. Which is help me pack up this picnic—and you *were* going to help me pack up this picnic, weren't you, not just sit there being aristocratic—and find my sister."

That made sense. And no sense at the same time. "Yes but, no but . . ."

"And all I'm asking," Tarleton went on, "is that when we do catch up with her, you give her a chance."

"She's put me to a great deal of trouble, but I will do my best."

Tarleton's eyes flew wide—their own perfect sky. "Oh, good God, no. What are you saying? She's fabulous, and you'd be lucky to have her. I mean, give her a chance to see you. The man I think . . . I hope . . . is still under all"—a rather disparaging hand gesture—"*this*. This cynicism and indifference."

"Tarleton, we've spent a handful of hours in a curricle, and I was unconscious for several of them. You are in no position to claim knowledge of me."

"And yet," he returned, "I have not stopped believing in you. Aren't I wonderful?"

The notion of Tarleton believing in him made Valentine's skin prickle with discomfort. In that moment of everything feeling raw and strange, it was too much like judgement. "You are incomprehensible. Both of you."

Tarleton sighed. "Be kind to Belle. Try to see her side of things. And if she still doesn't want you, have the grace to walk away."

"You care nothing for your own parents' wishes?"

"Our parents died in a carriage accident when we were less than a year old. I understand they were loving, joyful people. Why would they want their children to be unhappy?"

"And your estate?"

"You said yourself there's nothing like money to soothe over someone else's faults, and it may do the same for yours: I'd rather Belle had the choice, though. She has as much right to love as I do."

Valentine began wrapping up the admittedly rather scant remains of the pigeon pie. "I am offering your sister wealth and power, and all the security that they bring. Love offers only an inevitability of grief."

There was a pause. "Did you lose someone?" asked Tarleton, finally. "Someone you actually loved?"

"On the contrary, I have lived the most careful of lives."

But Tarleton, as ever, refused to let go.

"Then what are you afraid of?"

It was probably unavoidable given the direction of the conversation, but Valentine's mind had drifted back to those first few days in the immediate aftermath of his father's death. There had been so much to do for the estate, but he still remembered the dazed emptiness in his mother's eyes. "I'm afraid," he said, "of being bored and inconvenienced. So, as you may imagine, I'm currently terrified."

They cleared what was left of the picnic in not wholly comfortable silence and were on the road again in less than ten minutes.

"You know something," said Tarleton, with a sideways glance, "I don't think you're bored in the slightest."

And this time it was Valentine who chose not to answer. Because he was increasingly concerned his young companion might be correct. He was not, however, sure he liked it. After all, boredom was very safe and very familiar.

Chapter 6

"You know what we should do?" Tarleton didn't so much ask this question as announce it.

"Does it involve being quiet and self-possessed?"

The young man grinned. "That's one of the things I'm beginning to like about you, Malvern. Your groundless optimism. Of course it doesn't."

"Ah."

"But all teasing aside, we should stop at some of the inns along this road and make enquiries. Make sure we're actually on their trail. Not"—his eyes slid wickedly to Valentine's—"that I don't appreciate my jaunt to Dover with a man who would rather be in bed."

"On the contrary, Tarleton, I would rather be just about anywhere."

"Yes, yes, I'm annoying, my sister's not good enough for you, this is tedious. Do you need your watercolours, or do you trust the picture is clear enough to me?"

Valentine huffed out a sigh—half-amused, half-exasperated. "How do you imagine we are to make these enquiries? 'Hello, my fiancée-stroke-sister has run away under scandalous circumstances; she's yay high, believes she's on the stage, is about to irretrievably ruin her reputation; have you seen her, pray tell?'"

"Oh, Lord." Tarleton's face had fallen. "You're right. I . . . I didn't think that through."

"No? Really. You?"

"Need I remind you, flower"—Tarleton would have sounded a lot more dignified if he hadn't been pouting—"that I *saved* you. From a bee."

"To save someone requires their being in peril. As you pointed out at the time, I was not in peril."

"And yet you still ran around in circles, waving your arms and shouting."

"It was, I will grant," Valentine conceded, "an unfortunate moment in my life. But as you kept insisting there was no danger—despite the malignant persecutions of the bee, which I really do believe was probably rabid—I don't think you have any right to claim you rescued me."

"That's the thing about rescuing people," remarked Tarleton loftily. "Sometimes they're fleeing something entirely harmless, and others they're not even aware they're in need of rescue. Also, bees can't get rabies."

Valentine opened his mouth, then closed it again, coming perhaps too late to the conclusion that bee-related topics were not doing him any favours. And for a few blissful minutes they trotted along in something approximating silence.

Approximating because Tarleton was humming. Which soon developed into full-blown singing. As it happened, he had a pleasant tenor voice that would no doubt have delighted a fashionable drawing room. His choice of song, however, left much to be desired.

"Where the bee sucks, there suck I . . ."

"Tarleton."

"In a cowslip's bell I lie . . ."

"You are not amusing, Tarleton."

"There I couch when owls do cry."

"I'm going to push you out of this curricle."

"On the bat's back I do fly."

"Please—I'm actually begging you—be quiet."

"After summer merrily. Merrily, merrily—oh, I know. Let's say we're secret agents for the Crown."

Valentine nearly fell out of the curricle himself. "Pardon?"

"We can say we're secret agents for the Crown, and my sister is a French spy. And that way nobody will know she's run away from home."

"No," said Valentine slowly. "But they will think she's a French spy."

A sweep of Tarleton's hand. "Details."

"Also, do you really think if we were agents of the Crown, we would go around telling people we were agents of the Crown?"

"Well, of course we wouldn't," retorted Tarleton, stung. "But we could *insinuate* it."

"How? How would you insinuate it?"

"I suppose"—he seemed genuinely to be considering the matter—"I would say I was a person of no consequence looking for a young lady, and that it was imperative I located her for reasons . . . not related to national security at all."

Valentine covered his face with his hands. "Oh God, you're going to get us hanged for treason."

"Well." Tarleton wriggled huffily. "I don't see you coming up with any better ideas."

This was somewhat startling to Valentine. "I'm supposed to have ideas now?"

"Generally, flower, people do."

"My idea is, we go back to your house and I go back to bed."

"That's not an idea. That's a preference."

"Fine," Valentine muttered. "How about we stop at the next tavern; I say we've become temporarily separated from our party, and have they seen two young ladies pass by?"

There was a silence. "Are you sure you wouldn't rather let them believe we're secret agents?"

"Yes. I'm very sure I wouldn't rather have anyone believe that we're secret agents."

"What if you said that Belle has lost her memory."

"Why," asked Valentine, with icy patience, "would I say your sister has lost her memory?"

"Plausibility. It would explain how she got separated."

"Nobody is going to ask how we got separated."

"But what if they do? You need a story."

A story was very much the last thing Valentine needed. Between Miss Tarleton carrying on like the heroine of a gothic novel and her brother trying to force a love match from a perfectly tolerable arranged marriage, there was altogether too much story in his life already. "The story"—Valentine's voice exploded out of him at such volume that a flock of nesting sparrows took to the skies in fright—"is that we were on a fucking picnic—as evinced by *our fucking picnic things*—and we got fucking separated."

Tarleton was staring at him.

"I . . . I apologise. That was ungentlemanly of me."

"Ungentlemanly? That was terrifying. You looked like something from a mediaeval bestiary."

"I'm sorry."

"Like one of those illustrations of a manticore, or something, with the teeth and the severed feet sticking out of its mouth."

Valentine hung his head. His temper was . . . something he tried very, very hard to govern, and was always mortified when he couldn't. He did not even have the excuse of inheritance—his father had been, to the best of his memory, mild-mannered, and his mother, while passionate, rarely expressed it through anger. Which meant it was him, and solely him. A flaw running inescapably through him like a crack in a bowl.

"Arrgarrghh." Tarleton made the hand not currently on the reins into a claw and swiped at Valentine with it. "Do you like my impression of you?"

"Not especially."

Tarleton seemed to relent. "I'm just teasing, flower. You surprised me a little."

"You, by contrast, were being unsurprising. By which I mean, irritating."

"I suppose I must have been to have . . . unleashed the beast. You even said a naughty word. Several naughty words. Well, the same naughty word several times."

"Do you ever," Valentine asked, already knowing the answer, "let anything go?"

"Not as a general rule. I suspect losing one's parents suddenly, and at a young age, gives one rather a fear of transience."

Valentine's eyes widened. There was something, he was beginning to think, a little terrifying about someone who could be at once so indomitable and so fragile. It made him feel as though he was attempting to traverse quicksand. Emotional quicksand. Into which he was already sinking. "Tarleton, I . . . why would you tell me that?"

"I don't know. I suppose it's because I'm human, and I feel things, and I'm not ashamed of feeling them. You should try it."

Valentine gave a little cough. "We've seen what happens when I feel things."

"Now, I agree that was not ideal. Perhaps you could try feeling something that isn't being annoyed at me?"

"Such as?"

"They're your feelings, flower. Start small: it's a beautiful day. And you're in fabulous company."

"I feel," murmured Valentine, "an increasing concern that you are labouring under the misapprehension that it's appropriate to refer to me in that fashion."

"What fashion?" Tarleton gave him a look of studied innocence.

"You know very well what fashion."

"Until you say it, I will remain resolutely ignorant."

Valentine ground his teeth. "*Flower*, Tarleton. Stop calling me *flower*."

"But it suits you. And if you objected as vociferously as you claim, you would have manticored me earlier."

"It does *not* suit me. I am a duke. I am nothing like a flower."

"Is that so?" Tarleton was smiling—one of those smiles that seemed to hint at secrets beyond Valentine's ken. "Because in the right context, I'm sure you'd bloom like one."

Oh God, what did that mean? And why was Valentine suddenly too warm and too . . . looked at? Even though Tarleton wasn't actually looking at him. Just, somehow, seeing past everything he had so carefully constructed around himself as the years had passed. It was making him faintly dizzy. This whole-body prickling sensation, like a limb shaking off pins and needles.

"A . . . hostelry," he croaked, pointing at a cosy-looking building that had appeared just beyond a bend in the road. "I shall . . . I shall make enquiries."

"I really do think I'm on to something with the whole amnesia notion," insisted Tarleton. "Think how *romantic* it would be: two people, so desperately in love, yet driven apart by—"

But before he could finish—almost before the curricle had come to a stop—Valentine leapt to the ground and practically ran into the inn.

Chapter 7

"Any luck?" asked Tarleton when Valentine emerged again.

"I'm afraid not. Nobody had any recollection of two young ladies passing this way."

"Maybe they didn't stop. Belle is an absolute tyrant when she has the bit between her teeth."

Still too preoccupied to make the obvious retort—that such tendencies clearly ran in the family—Valentine simply climbed up next to Tarleton and sat in silence as they got underway again.

"She'll be at the Goat," remarked Tarleton after a while, although it was impossible to tell whether he was attempting to reassure himself or Valentine. "And we'll be there before sundown. This whole business will be wrapped up by bedtime, you mark my words."

A silence.

And then, "Tarleton?"

"Yes, flower?"

"Tarleton?"

"Still here. Been here all day. And will continue to be so."

"Tarleton, your . . . manner. Are you . . . are you flirting with me?"

Tarleton tilted his head quizzically. "Now?"

"In general."

"Well, yes. I flirt with everybody. If it's making you uncomfortable, I can stop."

It was. But also . . . it wasn't? "I am not accustomed to it. Especially not with another"—Valentine inscribed a nebulous gesture in the air—"personage of a gentlemanly persuasion."

"How can you be unaccustomed? Surely you must flirt with personages of a lady persuasion all the time."

"Of course I do not," snapped Valentine. "I am not a rake. And it would engender false expectation, given I am promised to your sister, and have been all my life."

"Strange how you would feel that way and yet leave us mouldering in Surrey for years."

Given that both Tarletons had responded to his perfectly civil proposal as though he had offered a monstrous insult, it did not feel like a good occasion to discuss Valentine's own long-standing uncertainties about matrimony. "I've been busy."

"Good for you. We've had nothing to do except dream." How Tarleton managed to deliver this sentiment in the tone of the utmost sincerity, Valentine was unable to fathom. But then he continued in a lighter tone: "We're not exactly drowning in winsome gentlemen out here, you know. I have to take what opportunities come my way, flirtation-wise."

"You mentioned a soldier," Valentine reminded him, unsure why this particular matter had lodged itself so thoroughly into the forefront of his mind.

"As I say"—Tarleton shrugged—"I'm open to opportunity. And, besides, you're the safest possible subject for a little light banter."

"Why? Am I not *winsome* enough for you?"

One of Tarleton's spring-morning laughs: bright and bold and heedless. "Oh, flower, you are *plenty* winsome. But you're engaged to my sister and don't think about other men the way I do."

"Nobody told me it was a possibility." Valentine suddenly discovered he was quite aggrieved. "Why has this never been brought to my attention?"

"It's not like that. It's just something you feel."

That did not improve Valentine's mood. "Then how did you . . . come to feel this way?"

Tarleton shrugged. "Belle and I, we had this . . ."

And then abruptly trailed off.

"You had this what?" demanded Valentine.

"I'm sorry"—he seemed to be actually blushing—"I've never spoken about this with anyone else before. I'm worried it might seem . . . peculiar."

"I don't know how to tell you this, Tarleton, but it is late in the day for you to be concerned about striking me as peculiar."

He tossed his head coltishly. "Well, I don't *care* about any of the other things about me you might find peculiar. This . . . this is important."

"I had no intention to trespass. Of course, you are under no obligation to confide in me."

Tarleton was quiet—an experience both strange to Valentine, and unsettling. He wanted to . . . he didn't quite know? Apologise? Something else entirely? Something that would bring the brightness back to Tarleton's eyes. The mirth to the rosebud of his mouth. Except, how did you do that?

How did you . . . make someone smile?

"I suppose it's probably best to start with my uncle," began Tarleton, his voice soft in the fading afternoon sunlight. Only to abruptly lose his way again and fall, once more, into silence. "You see, he . . ."

Valentine had never seen him so serious. "He what?" he prompted gently, fearing—in a misguidedly gothic impulse of his own—that some darkness lay within the family's past.

"He only"—Tarleton took a deep, shuddering breath—"he only owns books about pigs."

"He . . . what?"

"He only owns books about pigs. It was the sorest trial for Belle and me growing up."

"I see."

"Of course, he did his best—he'd always buy us something new whenever he went to town, but he's a country gentleman. He hardly ever went to town, and his taste was"—a profound quiver ran through Tarleton's entire body—"*grievous*. Let me see, we had a copy of *A Journal of the Plague Year*, *Thaddeus of Warsaw*, *The Vicar of Wakefield*, *The Little Female Academy*, and *The History of Sir Charles Grandison*, the most boring man in fiction."

"I don't recall Richardson giving it that subtitle."

"Well, he should have. Because it's true. We wanted *Clarissa*, of course, because we'd heard somewhere it was scandalous and about a rake. But all Uncle Wilbur could get was Sir Charles Boringson. Which is a book about someone who refuses to fight duels and won't stop talking about obedience to God and to society. Urgh."

"If it's any consolation," offered Valentine, "*Clarissa* is a book about someone who forces himself upon a woman over some two thousand pages. And then she dies."

Tarleton was gazing at him intently. "You've read it?"

"I have. And I do not recommend it."

"Well," returned Tarleton, with a noticeable lack of gratitude, "thank you for destroying my dreams."

"I was under the impression I was saving you from an unpleasant reading experience."

"Yes, but you have no idea how many times Belle and I have written *Clarissa*. And now . . . now you've spoiled it."

"With the truth?"

"Well"—Tarleton sighed—"I suppose Richardson spoiled it, really. But we had such hopes for that book. Our versions always ended happily, of course."

"Did you often write stories together?"

"All the time. We had to. Because even when we managed to get good books, they'd rather lose their shine after we'd read them a hundred times or more."

"Just out of curiosity, what do you consider a good book?"

"Oh, let me see. I mean, our uncle didn't always fail us dismally. There's *Udolpho*, naturally. And *Otranto*. Belle absolutely adores *Zofloya*. And I've always loved *Evelina* because you can't go wrong with a pure-hearted ingenue and a world-weary aristocrat, can you? And we also had *Clermont*, *The Castle of Wolfenbach*, and *The Female Quixote*."

"That latter novel? It didn't teach you anything? By any chance?"

"Not as far as I recall. We did have to rewrite the ending, though."

"You . . . rewrote the ending?"

Tarleton nodded vigorously. "Well, we had two versions of that one. One in which Glanville recognises that Arabella—the heroine, Arabella, not my Belle—is to be loved on her own terms and throws himself into the Thames to prove his worthiness. And another where Glanville realises he's truly in love with Bellmour and they run off together, and Arabella becomes a pirate."

"So, you not only . . . wrote books for each other, you rewrote them?"

"Yes. Sometimes we even . . . wrote ourselves into them. Ridiculous, I know. But that was when I realised just how badly I wanted to be Evelina."

"You wanted to be the eighteen-year-old daughter of a libertine?"

"No, silly. I wanted my own Lord Orville. And neither Belle nor I saw anything wrong with that."

"I see." Valentine did not see. "So you're saying that if I'd read more silly novels at an impressionable age, I, too, would have grown up with the understanding that . . . that there are choices?"

"It's not a choice to me, flower. It's who I am."

"Yes, but—"

"And by the time we were . . . ten? I think? Twelve perhaps? We'd invented a whole universe."

"You'd done what?"

Tarleton's face had grown soft and dreamy. Well, softer and dreamier than normal. Which was saying something. "It was called Arkandia, and the rules were different there."

"Well, so I would imagine," observed Valentine. "You'd made it up."

"That's the thing, though: we could be anything, do anything. A prince, a husband, a lover, a thief. We could fall in love, fall out of love, have adventures, overcome any adversity. My God, the stories we told. The lives we lived."

"Yes, but, you are aware that this is nineteenth-century England? That you *cannot*, in fact, be anything, do anything, or fall in love with anyone? For the world simply does not work that way, and it is . . . foolish, profoundly foolish, to hope or expect otherwise."

That made Tarleton's expression harden, and Valentine half wished he hadn't spoken at all—no matter how correct his words had been.

"Oh, go jump in the Thames, Glanville," Tarleton said, with one of his haughtier hair flicks. "You don't deserve me."

Chapter 8

An hour or so later, when the sky was rose-gold with the setting sun, they stopped outside a remarkably . . . adequate hostelry, built in the Tudor fashion—whitewashed stone, latticed windows, and a thatched roof. The painted sign, with its portrait of a rather devious-looking, devil-horned beast prancing on its hind legs, proclaimed it the Wayward Goat. They left Tarleton's horses and curricle in the care of the ostler and made their way into the taproom, Valentine almost banging his head on the low beams of the ceiling. He was, however, relieved to note that the room itself was well kept, the wooden furniture shabby but clean, and the brass fittings behind the bar gleaming cheerfully. It was an entirely respectable place for him and his fiancée to pass a night, in company with her brother and a female companion—surely the ideal conclusion to this unfortunate incident.

Strange, then, that Valentine still felt . . . off-balance? A kind of restless discontent, like having forgotten your pocket-handkerchief, or left the house with an imperfectly tied cravat. Perhaps it was some residue of the impulse that had driven him so deeply into his cups last night: this sense of a future he did not want pressing inescapably down upon him, when it was the same future that lay before nearly everyone of his rank. His bride, too, for all her silliness, was lively and beautiful. Tarleton was right. He should have wanted her. He should not have shirked his duty for two years.

He should not have been—

He should not have been afraid.

"What if we say," whispered Tarleton, "that you're having to flee her wicked uncle who has forbidden the match?"

Valentine paused. "Is your uncle wicked?"

"Of course not."

"Then don't you think it would be slightly unkind to tell people he is? Besides"—Valentine's brow did its lazy half twitch—"as you've pointed out several times today, I'm a very attractive, very wealthy duke. Who in their right mind would oppose matrimony with me?"

That earned him one of Tarleton's fierce little scowls. "I know I don't practice subtlety, but I *can* recognise it. Stop insulting my sister. And for all anyone's aware, you could be some kind of pervert."

In Valentine's experience of the ton, a dukedom compensated for any manner of personal failings. Nevertheless, it seemed important to make it very clear: "I am not a pervert."

"Isn't everyone, though?" asked Tarleton. "A little bit?"

"That may be true of you, but it is certainly not true of me."

"Really?" Tarleton was giving him a too-shrewd look. "There's nothing about you that's just a little bit peculiar to you? Like you enjoy having your shoulders bitten or the taste of yourself on someone else's lips?"

The air whooshed from Valentine's lungs. "Tarleton. We are in *public.*"

"And I'm talking very quietly."

"You should not talk about such things *at all.*"

Tarleton blinked—his ridiculous lashes a sheen of gold across his summer-day eyes. "Why not?"

"Because . . . because . . . they are not the sorts of things that are talked about."

"So, when you're with a lady, you perform in absolute silence? You don't ask her what she likes or what she wants? You don't tell her how good she feels or how exquisite she looks? How much you—"

"I am not having this conversation with you," growled Valentine. "Not now. Not ever."

A point he emphasised by pushing Tarleton aside and approaching the publican, who was polishing a glass behind the bar and seemed a bit surprised to have two of the quality having a sotto voce altercation in the middle of his establishment.

"Milord?" The man eyed him with a kind of wary deference. "Can I help you?"

"It's *Your Grace*. I am the Duke of Malvern, and I very much hope you can help me. We've become separated from the rest of our party—this gentleman's sister, and her female companion—and we thought, as the hour was growing late, they might have chosen to stay the night here rather than returning home. Have you seen the two ladies? Or do you know if they've passed through?"

"Not . . . not as I'm aware of, mi—You—Grace."

"I think you would remember them: one fair, and very beautiful, about twenty years old, the other dark."

"With curly hair," added Tarleton. "Quite tall?"

"They were travelling by gig."

"Pulled by a brown mare, with no distinguishing features."

"That's quite enough help now," Valentine said firmly.

But Tarleton had a dangerously thoughtful look on his face. "I did wonder at the time why Belle took Nutmeg instead of Moonbeam. Damn, I'd be so impressed with her if she wasn't causing such a fuss."

"Two ladies?" Valentine repeated, subjecting the publican to his sternest gaze, and hopefully smothering most of Tarleton's fraternal pride.

The publican shook his head. "I'm sorry, Your"—his attention flicked between them—"Graces, but I haven't seen two ladies."

Reaching into his pocket, Valentine was abruptly recalled to the fact the coat he was wearing was not, in fact, his coat. He had been intending to give the man a coin for his trouble but instead found himself offering a sugarplum, lightly covered in fluff, and a piece of string with rough markings on it that the assistant gardener likely used for measurements.

There was a long silence.

After a moment, the publican accepted the sugarplum with the air of someone about to send a stable boy for, in the best scenario, the local magistrate. In the worst, one of the doctors from Bedlam.

"I," began Valentine, "have become separated from my coat. Along with the two missing members of our party. What a day it has been for . . . for . . . ill-fortuitous separations." He attempted a light laugh. It did not come out well.

The publican was still regarding the sugarplum. "Right you are"— his voice had acquired a concerning note, not quite insolence yet, but definitely scepticism—"Your Grace."

"I assure you, this is an entirely plausible concatenation of circumstances." There were, Valentine was beginning to realise, few things less plausible than insisting something was plausible. He panicked. "Behold, my signet ring."

His signet ring was beheld.

"Of course," Tarleton offered, cheerfully, "you could have stolen that. Or murdered the duke and now be an imposter."

"I have not murdered or robbed myself."

"Also—I've no idea what the Layton family crest looks like, and I'm gentry. How is that supposed to mean anything to this poor fellow? He owns a pub."

"That's a good point," agreed the publican.

"What did I say earlier," asked Valentine, in a soft and deadly voice, "about helping? Please go outside *immediately* and ready the curricle."

The publican stroked his chin. "And what would the Duke of Malvern be doing in Surrey? And in my house? If there even *is* a Duke of Malvern."

"So"—Tarleton was already skipping backwards from the tap-room—"I'll be outside, readying the curricle."

Valentine turned back to the innkeeper. "I realise this is . . . that this absolutely regular situation may appear a little irregular at first glance. But I am the Duke of Malvern, and I am in Surrey to visit the Tarletons—because of a long-standing connection between our two families. You must have heard of the Tarletons."

"I know Wilbur Tarleton," said the publican. "He's a good man. Doesn't put on no airs and . . . graces."

"Well, that's his nephew. And I'm engaged to his niece."

A crash and a squeak from his side—a dark-haired youth apparently having knocked a couple of tankards off the bar.

"Do have a care," snapped Valentine, who was usually the most courteous of gentlemen, but had taken his day rather hard.

"Not to worry, young master." That was the publican, with the indulgence some seemed to naturally find towards the callow. He smiled encouragingly at the youth. "Now, is there anything else you and your sister'll be needing?"

"Oh." The stranger swallowed. "Well, B—b—*both* of us would dearly love a piece of the game pie. If—if it could be served in our room."

"The missus'll bring it right up."

Pulling his hat down over his eyes, the youth murmured his thanks.

"And for you, Your Grace?" asked the publican.

Valentine shifted uncomfortably, aware of the figure he was cutting, and the boy's scrutiny, even from beneath the shadow of his oversize hat. "Thank you, but no. I shall take my leave."

Drawing his greatcoat more firmly over the assistant gardener's coat, Valentine made his way outside, controlling his mortification by focusing instead on the deeply comforting thought that he would never, ever have to return to the Wayward Goat again.

Chapter 9

"You have a wonderful way with people," Tarleton said as they set off into the night. "The way you insisted he address you as *Your Grace* instead of *milord*—I thought that really won him over."

It was cold. The assistant gardener's coat was not as well made nor as warm as Valentine's own. He sagged lower in the curricle seat. "What does it matter? He's a man I will never have to see, address, or think of again."

"Do you actively want everyone to think you're an utter arse?"

"I don't want to be thought of at all."

A pause. "You . . . what?"

"I just want to live quietly, in my own way."

Tarleton huffed air through his nostrils with the air of a grumpy pony. "How can you call that living at all? I have spent the last twenty years being nobody to anyone but my sister, and it has been . . . it has been . . . oh, it is selfish of me to speak like this, because I know my aunt and uncle are kind, and I know Belle loves me, but I have *longed*—we have both longed—for more than the same walls and the same days. For the opportunity to live our own stories, instead of just reading other people's. I can't understand how you can possess so much and believe it worth so little."

"Perhaps," suggested Valentine, "it is because you are only capable of seeing walls when they are yours."

"As if you could not beat down any wall, if only you chose to try."

"Bonny"—Valentine was surprised by his own weariness—"please. I don't know why you have developed these expectations of me. I will make your sister a good husband, but I cannot be what I am not. I cannot . . . care as you do. And I have no wish to. And I'm . . . I'm tired. And cold. And I'm sorry to be so indifferent a man, but I wish you would have just a little mercy on me."

His words lingered in the silence, beneath the starlight.

Then Tarleton said, "No, I'm sorry. I'm worried about Belle, and I took it out on you."

"I . . ." Although the apology, and the reprieve, should both have been welcome, Valentine found he had nothing to say. "Thank you. I'm concerned as well. Do you have any idea where she might be, if not at the inn?"

"Maybe she went to another? But my bays are close to done for. And"—a sweet little smile, devoid of mirth of mockery—"so are you, it seems."

Valentine cringed. "I might have . . . overexpressed myself in a moment of . . . of . . ."

"Delicious melodrama?"

"Weakness."

Before Valentine had quite realised what was happening, Tarleton's whip hand had covered his. "Eeep, you *are* cold. I can even tell through my riding glove."

"I appreciate the second opinion."

"That's your 'I don't appreciate it at all' voice."

"Well, what were you expecting? I already know how I feel."

Tarleton gave his fingers a squeeze, enveloping him in smooth, skin-warmed leather. "I can warm you up."

"I would rather be cold than in a ditch, thank you."

"That's utter nonsense. I'm an excellent whip. Better even than Belle."

And, probably, Valentine would never have admitted aloud, better than he was—for Tarleton had a light, confident touch, and a natural sensitivity to his horses' moods. Still, he was released, and that was . . . that was a relief. Most certainly it was a relief. For all Tarleton had claimed Valentine was a safe subject for a dalliance, he was nevertheless uncertain that it was appropriate to allow another gentleman to take physical liberties with him. However generously they were meant. And clearly such gestures were a little uncomfortable for Valentine—despite his best attempts to be understanding towards his companion's eccentricities—for they caused his blood to flow too swift and hot through his veins. His heart to stumble.

"Why don't you put your hands in my pocket instead?" suggested Tarleton.

"Because that would be absurd."

He shrugged. "You won't be saying that when your fingers turn blue and drop off."

"They are mildly uncomfortable at worst." It seemed a good idea to change the subject. "What are we to do about your sister?"

"Well, I thought we could try the Old Cock, which isn't too far from here. Except now I'm starting to think that she wasn't at the Goat because she knew that I knew it was the most obvious place to go. And, since she will also know that I know to look for her at the Cock, maybe she won't be there either." His shoulders slumped. "Maybe she's somewhere else completely. Maybe she's on the moon."

"She is unlikely to be on the moon."

"Yes"—Tarleton seemed abruptly close to tears—"but she might as well be."

"Let's try the Cock," said Valentine, trying to sound soothing, and not entirely sure whether he had succeeded because it was not something he had ever been called upon to sound before.

"You don't understand. Belle and I, we know each other better than anyone else in the world. And she's using that against me."

"Yet you persist in wondering why I repudiate such connections."

This made Tarleton actually kick him in the shin. "*Not* what I needed to hear. Twinbond is *sacred*, Malvern."

Sacred? It sounded absolutely terrifying. To be so deeply known. To have your happiness entangled with someone else's. Your life shaped by them in unpredictable ways. And yet . . . was there not something terrifying, too, in days ordered to the point of interchangeable? Of an endless carousel of acquaintances who would never know you because you dared not let them. Something terrifying enough to drive one to Surrey, despite its being unlikely to hold answers either. "I apologise," he said only slightly tartly, "for my ignorance."

Tarleton sniffed. In the moonlight, his mouth was a tight, pale line. Given his apparent tendency to say just anything and everything as it entered his head, there was something about his quiet now that Valentine found oddly painful.

And he did not know what to do about it.

"Tarleton . . . may I . . . please put my hand in your pocket?"

"Only," came the swift reply, "if you call me Bonny again."

"What has that to do with anything?"

"It's the rules."

"What rules?" demanded Valentine, reassured his companion had been restored to his normal level of irksomeness, but also—perhaps inevitably—irked.

"The no takesey-backsey rules."

"Tarleton . . ."

"Bonny."

Valentine gritted his teeth. "Fine. Bonny. There. Are you happy now?"

By way of answer, Tarle—Bonny?—took him by the hand and tucked it gently into the pocket of his greatcoat. And Valentine had been entirely correct in his suspicion that it would be a peculiar, and not wholly easy, experience because it felt . . . yes, it felt intimate. This little space of secret warmth that curled softly round his fingers like a tongue. Not that he had any notion what such a thing would be like. Nor even where the idea had come from. Except for the sudden, too-vivid memory of the heat of Bonny's breath against his mouth when he had leaned in to capture that rabid bee.

It was, as Bonny had said, only an hour or so to the Old Cock—and in some strange, traitorous act against both their interests, Valentine found himself wishing the journey could last longer. Somehow, they had fallen through the cracks of time, caught in a silver haze between night and day, the world shadow-softened and star-dusted. They were, Valentine thought, nowhere and anywhen, and it was in the sweet no-ness of the moment that he curled his fingers safely in Bonny's pocket and let his head rest upon his shoulder. His skin smelled of the meadows where they'd eaten lunch, clean as grass, free as the sky. And sometimes the motion of the curricle would allow Valentine to turn his face slightly into Bonny's neck, where he felt against his cheek the nascent, fascinating roughness of stubble.

⟨§✦⟩

"Well?" asked Bonny as Valentine emerged from the Old Cock, which had turned out to be a slightly more upmarket establishment than the Wayward Goat and where Valentine had, thankfully, acquitted himself rather better. At the very least, he had not insisted upon a public viewing of his signet ring, nor had he offered anyone boiled sugar in place of legal tender.

He shook his head. "Nobody has seen hide nor hair of two ladies travelling together."

"I don't understand." Bonny ran both hands tragically through his hair. "Where could they be?"

Part of Valentine wanted to remind his companion that, earlier that day, he had made several suggestions, including abduction by pirates. But instead, he just said, "I don't know. I'm sorry."

Now Bonny had his face pressed into his palms. "I was *sure* she would want to go to America. But maybe not. Maybe . . . Wales? She could have headed for Wales."

"Why would she go to Wales?"

"Isn't that where druids are from? She might have wanted to become a druid."

Valentine very much wanted to return to the Cock. He glanced behind him to the dance of light on the cobblestones, thinking of a hot bath and a bottle of wine, a passably decent bed. "Do you happen to have any . . . ah . . . money? How about we take rooms for the night and readdress ourselves to the matter of your sister in the morning?"

"She's a person, Malvern. Not a matter. And she could be lost or frightened or in trouble or alone."

A tub big enough that his feet didn't need to hang off the end. Steam gathering on the surface of the water like the mists of Avalon. And a nice claret if they had it. Madeira if not. "That seems highly improbable. Not least because we know she's travelling in company."

Bonny gave a little gasp. "Of course—Peggy."

"Yes. Peggy. Of the"—Valentine tried very hard to hold on to his patience—"Devonshire Peggys. As you keep telling me."

"No but . . . God in heaven, I'm an *idiot*."

"I hope you're not expecting any arguments from me on this score?"

"God," said Bonny again, pressing the heel of his hand hard against his brow. "What is *wrong* with me?"

"I could make some suggestions."

Bonny removed his hand from his forehead in order to wave it at Valentine. "Stop trying to banter with me, man, and get back in the damn curricle."

In that moment, Valentine could not have been more horrified had he been Dante and Virgil had about-faced and started leading him back to the Inferno. "What? No. I . . . I refuse."

"I do not recognise your refusal."

Could you do that? Was that a thing you could do? And to a duke? "I'm not sure—"

"Seriously." Bonny pointed emphatically at the space beside him. "Get in. We're going to the Goat."

"But there's"—Valentine's gaze turned longingly to the building behind him—"a roast suckling pig in there."

"Jesus Christ himself, turning water into wine, could be in there. Belle is at the Goat."

"We were just at the Goat," Valentine absolutely did not whine. "Nobody had seen your sister."

"Wrong, wronger, wrongest. Nobody had seen *two ladies*. Now come on or I'm leaving you behind."

Which, given he had only his signet ring to his name, left Valentine with no choice except to climb aboard Bonny's curricle once more.

"I don't understand," he said, as the rattle of wheels over cobblestones travelled up through his legs and settled into some other regions, which were already not bearing the vicissitudes of the day with the equanimity he might have hoped for. "How can they be at the place we know they aren't?"

It was full dark now, requiring Bonny to give most of his attention to the road—his hands careful on the reins. "Because Peggy sometimes likes to dress as a boy. I don't know why I didn't think of it earlier."

The words individually made sense to Valentine. And yet still made no sense at all. "Peggy . . . likes to what?"

"Dress as a boy. It's why we should have been asking if anyone had seen a young lady travelling in company with a young gentleman."

"Is it Surrey?" Valentine wondered.

Bonny's gaze flicked his way impatiently. "Surrey?"

"Making you like this."

"I have no idea what you're talking about."

Valentine was feeling aggrieved again. Aggrieved and increasingly exhausted, in a way that was only partially connected to a day spent running around pointlessly in a curricle. "Men who want to marry men, and women who don't want to marry dukes, and girls who like to dress as boys."

"Yes," said Bonny decidedly. "It's Surrey. It's the mushrooms here. They make us true to who we are."

"M-mushrooms?"

"I'm *joking*, flower. This is just . . . life."

"But what can you possibly know of life? You've spent twenty years inventing stories about it."

"And yet"—here Bonny patted his knee—"it's still infinitely less confusing to me than it is you."

"I've just . . . ," began Valentine helplessly. "That is . . . everyone else has always seemed so . . . content and unquestioning."

Bonny gave one of his little head tilts. "Unquestioning about what?"

"How they should be or what they should do or who they should love. I suppose I assumed that . . . lacking such certainty was an oddity. Perhaps even a weakness."

"In my admittedly tragically limited experience," said Bonny gently, "very few people are as certain as they pretend to be."

"Perhaps." Valentine was in no way prepared to think about any of this. So he offered, instead, the faintest of smiles. "Or perhaps it is the mushrooms in Surrey."

Chapter 10

The Wayward Goat was as adequate as Valentine remembered from having been there but a few short hours ago. Perhaps, in all honesty, slightly less adequate, given the elegance of the Cock with its sandstone facade, classical geometries, and lack of a landlord Valentine had attempted to suborn with a boiled sweet.

Once again, they disembarked Bonny's curricle, leaving both horses and equipage with the ostler. And, once again, made their way into the taproom.

"Oh," said the publican, without enthusiasm, "it's you."

Bonny offered him a dazzling smile. "Yes. Yes, it is. You know how we asked if you'd seen two ladies earlier, one fair, one dark?"

"Aye."

"What if instead we were looking for a young lady—still fair, looks a bit like me, actually, except more female—travelling in company with a young gentleman."

There was a pause.

"Probably," tried Bonny, with the air of a man casting hazard dice, "her brother?"

The man's face cleared. "Well, why didn't you say so? A pair just like that came through this evening—and very amiable they were too. They're upstairs now."

Bonny let out a huge breath. "That," he declared, "is wonderful news. Isn't it wonderful news, Malvern?"

"They're upstairs?" repeated Valentine. "They're upstairs?"

There was a hand—Bonny's—curled about his elbow. "Let's be calm about this. We can have some of this delicious-sounding game pie, take a couple of rooms—"

"I've only got three rooms, and two of them are already taken," said the publican.

"—take *a* room and have a lovely, friendly, nobody-turns-into-a-manticore conversation in the morning?"

Except Bonny's words had blurred into noise, the events of the day splintering inside Valentine until they were nothing but edges. He had done his duty, hadn't he? He'd come to this bee-infested hellscape of a county to offer the protection of his name and fortune to a woman who had not only been ungrateful but had *fled* from him. As though he were an object of censure or disgust. Which had, in turn, forced him to rise early, borrow a coat from a gardener—no, an assistant gardener—and careen about the countryside after her in company with . . . with . . .

Someone Valentine couldn't afford to think of now. Or possibly ever. Bonny was too loud, too warm. He had too many opinions and far too many ideas. None of which, Valentine was certain, could possibly be as simple, or as easy, as Bonny believed them to be. But even if they were not—what did they nevertheless reveal of Valentine's own life? Especially the part of it that required him to be in Surrey, proposing to a woman who despised him, in the first place? It had all been bearable— he could have lived like that; he was sure he could—when he had not known that there were alternatives.

"Oh God, Valentine"—Bonny's voice seemed to be coming from some great distance—"where are you going?"

Up the stairs.

Two at a time.

He heard the rapid clatter of footsteps behind him. "I really think you should wait until—"

Valentine flung wide the door to an empty room.

The second door he tried was locked. But an unmistakably male voice called out in response to the thump of Valentine's shoulder against the wood, "I say, is that my pie?"

"Please"—Bonny was still attempting to catch him by the elbow— "think about this for a—"

Thrusting open the final door, Valentine did, indeed, rediscover his fiancée. She was naked on top of the bed, her shining golden hair thrown heedlessly across the pillows, while someone—clad in trousers and a loose lawn shirt—laboured diligently between her thighs.

The moments buzzed by like bees as Valentine's eyes, brain, and mouth singularly failed to connect to each other. He wasn't sure what he was seeing. Then he wasn't sure *who* he was seeing. Because Bonny had said Miss Tarleton had been in the company of Peggy . . .

Who, even if she sometimes dressed as a boy, was probably still a . . .

And Miss Tarleton was . . .

So they were both. And yet they were.

But how? And why? And what in God's name did it mean?

Was this why Miss Tarleton had fled him? To cast herself into wanton deviance with Peggy of the Devonshire Peggys? Or was she simply engaging in such behaviour now in the hope of dissuading him from his suit?

Which, frankly, was working. Even given his own disinterest in what he understood to be some of the significant aspects of matrimony, how could he be expected to wed a woman who . . . who . . .

"What," he managed finally, "is going on?"

This led to a flurry of motion, at least on Peggy's part—as she rolled away with a squeak, wiping her mouth with the back of her hand. Belle rose more languidly, pushing sweat-damp curls from her eyes and sauntering towards Valentine across the floorboards.

Which was quite a bit more naked woman than Valentine was prepared for. Or, indeed, had ever seen. Not knowing how he was supposed to react, he immediately stepped back—and collided with the doorframe, the impact of it knocking over a ewer and basin that had been somewhat precariously balanced on a nearby dresser. "What are you doing? Put some clothes on."

"Why should I?" The way Belle angled her head was suddenly familiar. Unexpectedly painful. "You own me anyway, don't you? It's nothing you won't see."

Valentine put a hand over his eyes. "That . . . that doesn't mean I have to see it now."

It was Peggy who darted forwards, flinging a blanket over Belle's shoulders and wrapping it tightly around her. She was tall and loose limbed, her face a little too strong boned to be pretty. Although, unlike his fiancée, she was mostly dressed, and so Valentine found himself looking at her instead.

"I've seen you before," he said.

Peggy nodded. "Downstairs. The first time. You nearly gave me a heart attack."

"I was under the impression I was looking for a lady."

"I am a lady," returned Peggy, without rancour. "Just . . . not all the time."

"Well, you may consider yourself fortunate you aren't a gentlemen because I would have called you out for"—Valentine discovered too late that he had no words for what he had just witnessed—"whatever you were doing to my betrothed."

"Whatever I was doing?" she repeated, laughing. And then, with an air of magnanimity, "But you may call me out if you wish."

At this, Belle gave a little scream and collapsed into a heap on the ground. "You monster. You beast. Is it not enough for you to demean me and pursue me, and strip my liberty from me? You would also *murder my friend*."

"I . . . ," began Valentine.

"He's not going to murder me," interrupted Peggy, looking affronted. "Have a little faith, darling. I can bag a rabbit at sixty paces, you know that. And he's a lot bigger than a rabbit."

Belle shuddered violently. "But then you will be a wanted woman, and we would have to flee the country lest you be hanged."

"I thought we were fleeing the country already?"

The rabbit comment had rather worried Valentine, as he had never picked up a gun in his life. "Nobody," he said firmly, "will be shooting anyone or fleeing anywhere."

There was motion from floor level. It was Belle, assaulting one of his boots, looking very much like a classical painting, with her tumbled hair and her bare white shoulders. "Please, I beg you, this is not Peggy's fault. Don't punish her for my wilfulness. I will . . . I will submit to your wishes. I will be your bride."

Valentine was in sore need of another decanter of brandy—though the last had served him ill. "You know very well they are no more my wishes than they are yours."

"You see?" Belle had now risen and was addressing her companion in more moderate tones. "You see what he's like? He claims he wants no part of me, and yet he has still hunted me down like a doe before the hounds over hundreds of miles of—"

"More like . . . thirty," put in Peggy, with far more gentleness than Valentine could have managed.

"It is not the distance. It is the *principle*. He neither wants me, nor will release me."

Valentine could have been in a hot bath right about now. Wait, no, he could be back in London, at his club, or at his home, with his valet just a summons away from helping him into any coat he preferred. "I understand that you have the lowest possible opinion of me, Miss

Tarleton, but I'm here because I could not allow a histrionic young woman with more hair than sense to run riot across the country, entirely unattended."

"Excuse me"—Peggy was giving him a hard stare—"I'm attending."

"You are certainly doing something," Valentine agreed coldly.

Belle whirled upon her companion. "Am I not vindicated? Are my actions not justified? He's an unfeeling brute. He even spoke derisively of Ophelia. Who *drowned*."

"Yes, darling"—Peggy attempted to settle Belle's blanket more firmly around her—"but she is fictional."

"What has that got to do with anything? It is through fiction that we learn to open our hearts. A man who cannot appreciate literature is a man who can appreciate nothing." Belle's disdainful gaze returned to Valentine. "How did you find me, anyway?"

At that moment, Bonny—who had been largely obscured by Valentine's body—gave a little cough. "Belle, I—"

Belle's eyes widened. Rather a remarkable feat as they were naturally wide to begin with. "Bonbon? Oh, Bonbon, you didn't. How could you?"

"I was worried about you."

"But," protested Belle, "I left you a note."

"Yes, and it said, 'I have gone. Please don't think of me. I love you.'"

She tossed her head. "I fail to see what was unclear about that?"

"Nothing was unclear. Except, how could you ask me not to think of you? You're my sister. I would do anything for you."

"Yet"—and here her eyes shimmered—"you have still betrayed me."

To Valentine's surprise, Bonny remained pressed to his side, almost as if he wanted shelter. "Belladonna, I would *never*. You know that."

Her lips—so like Bonny's in their softness, their sweetness—trembled. "Then what are you doing with . . . doing with *him*."

Valentine did not particularly enjoy being referred to simply as *him*, and certainly not in that tone of revulsion. But he was quick to realise that inserting himself into a conversation between the Tarleton twins would have been akin to rushing into the middle of a stampede of wild horses. It was in that moment his eye caught Peggy's—and she offered him a wry smile and the slightest of shrugs.

"I just thought," Bonny was saying, his hands clasped to his heart, "he deserved a second chance."

"You only think that," Miss Tarleton returned, "because you don't have to marry him. Because our family's future does not rest with you."

Bonny gave a sad little gasp. "You know I don't care about that. Or I do care . . . but not as much as I care about your happiness. And Valentine—"

"*Valentine?*" Both Miss Tarleton's look and tone were sharp.

"Malvern. His Grace. He's come all this way."

"All this thirty miles," Peggy reminded them.

"He still came." It was apparently time for a Tarleton foot stamp from Bonny. "That's romantic. Don't you think that's romantic?"

"No." Miss Tarleton offered a foot stamp of her own. "It is villainous. Chasing someone down when they have quite explicitly fled you."

"But," protested Bonny, "he's proving his devotion."

To Valentine's mind, what he was truly proving was a strong desire to go to bed and forget everything that had happened to him over the past day or so. It was not, however, the right occasion to share the sentiment.

Bonny was giving his sister pleading eyes. "Won't you at least hear him out?"

She scowled. "I heard him out last night. When he made it very clear to me what manner of man he has become. And, frankly, I don't know why we'd expect otherwise."

"He doesn't help himself," conceded Bonny. Which was not quite the ringing endorsement Valentine might have hoped for. "But I . . . I do believe there is . . . there is hope for him."

The expression on Miss Tarleton's face very much suggested otherwise. "No, you just *hope* there's hope. Do you think I didn't notice how many dukes there were in Arkandia?"

"It's a fantasy world. Fantasy worlds need dukes."

"And perhaps," retorted Miss Tarleton, "that's where they should stay. Because the fiction of a duke is likely to far exceed his reality."

"Please, Belle." Bonny's voice was soft as silk. So full of love that Valentine was slightly horrified. Such vulnerability could lead only to pain and . . . he did not want Bonny to experience pain. He wanted him to be safe. "Trust me in this. All you have to do is listen. And only for a moment."

Belle heaved a deep sigh. "Oh, very well. Anything for you, Bonbon." Her attention settled on Valentine again, her face hardening. "Well? What do you have to say for yourself?"

Valentine remembered what Bonny had told him. About what his sister was looking for. What she needed to hear. And not all of it would have been a lie: she was, indeed, beautiful. He would do his best—within the limits of his abilities and his nature—to be a good husband for her. Once he had an heir, he would even try to turn a blind eye to any . . . partialities she wished to pursue. That was freedom, wasn't it? Of a kind.

Except . . . he couldn't do it. He couldn't do any of it.

Because the only thing he felt right then was a hot desolate anger that gusted through him like the wind across desert sands.

What right had Arabella Tarleton to expect this from him? What right did she have to expect anything when she had caused him nothing but inconvenience? When she made her dissatisfaction with him so very clear and very public. When she had disported herself with her companion in a manner unbecoming of a lady, let alone an unmarried one. And no one had stopped for a moment to consider he might be equally miserable. Equally reluctant.

Equally . . . lost.

And he knew—he did know—it was wrong of him to hold her responsible for any of it. But he was—

He was envious. And ashamed.

All because she was absurd and silly and clearly thought she was the heroine of the sort of novels Valentine would never have admitted to reading. And yet still more honest, more courageous, more resolutely herself than he had ever been.

"Enough of this nonsense," he said. "We shall retire to our beds and, in the morning, take a respectable, highly visible breakfast, an occasion on which I expect you to be a lady, Peggy, and dressed like one."

Peggy frowned. "It doesn't work like that. It's not a switch."

"I don't give a damn. You will wear a dress or risk your friend's ruin."

"H-how dare you speak to us in this fashion." A valiant attempt at hauteur from Belle, but Valentine heard the tremble in her voice. "Who do you think you are?"

He glowered down at her from the cliff of his height. "I am the Duke of Malvern, and your husband-to-be. Which means you will obey me, madam, today, tomorrow, and for the rest of your life."

He had expected . . . he wasn't quite sure what. Theatrics of some kind. Most likely a vociferous condemnation of his character. But, instead, Belle was looking past him and towards her brother. And her brother—

Valentine was trying very hard not to see the expression of dismay on Bonny's face. The shocked betrayal in his eyes. The *disappointment*.

"Bonny," Miss Tarleton whispered, sounding very young, and very, very hurt. "I . . . I thought we were the same."

And then she cast herself onto the bed and started to cry.

Whatever was happening now was quite beyond Valentine—and he was already regretting it. Which added *pathetic* to the list of things he didn't want to be feeling, especially considering this was the closest he had come to getting through to his fiancée.

If making her weep like her heart was breaking could really be called "getting through."

Oh God, he ought to apologise. Except he didn't know how.

Because it was everything really, wasn't it? For his present behaviour. For his father's friendship with her father. For the death of her parents all those years ago. For being who he was in ways he hardly knew how to talk about. For being rich when she was poor. For being a man when she was a woman.

"I . . ." He swallowed. "I bid you good night."

Chapter 11

"What the devil was that?" demanded Bonny as Valentine half forced him back into the corridor.

Valentine's head was spinning, his stomach churning. And Bonny's voice was too loud, his body too close. "It . . . could have gone better."

"Could have gone better? You made my sister—the person I love most in the world—think I'm a monster. Who's trying to marry her off to a monster. For my own comfort." Bonny's fists thumped against Valentine's shoulders. "You complete . . . *arse*. Wait, I like arses. You . . . you complete something I don't like. Mustard. You complete jar of mustard."

"You . . . we . . . can explain in the morning."

This earned a Tarleton foot stamp. "In the morning? Damn the morning. After that little performance, I wouldn't let you near Boudicca."

"Well," murmured Valentine, "then she may count herself fortunate she died some nineteen hundred years ago."

"Boudicca"—Bonny's lip curled—"is my uncle's pig."

"I see."

There was a moment of silence. Too much and too little to say, tumbling like dust motes in the space between them.

Then Bonny sort of curled into himself, his fingers clutching at his hair. "God, what a fool you've made of me. Maybe you're right. I've read too many books. There's always good underneath, in the stories, if you just . . . learn to look for it."

"Bonny, please, I . . ." Suddenly Valentine could hardly catch his breath. He had always prized a kind of neutrality, in others and to others. But, somehow, the idea of Bonny losing faith in him was unbearable. "I . . . I will make it right. I'll apologise. I'll—"

It was at this moment that the previously locked door opened, and the occupant of the room stuck his head out. "Everything all right? I heard a bit of a commotion—good God, Malvern? Is that you."

Valentine froze. It couldn't be.

But, of course, it was.

"It *is* you," continued Sir Horley Comewithers, with what Valentine felt was unnecessary triumph. "Well, cover me in butter and call me asparagus. What the devil are you doing up the backside of Surrey? And why are you dressed like my gardener?"

"Sir Horley." Valentine offered an indifferent bow. "I'm staying with the Tarletons. As I'm sure you recall, I'm promised to Miss Tarleton."

Sir Horley was nodding vigorously, the mane of red hair that he was famous—or perhaps notorious—for flying around his head like a corrupted halo. "A Tarleton, eh? Of course, of course. Your father and their father. *Very close* at Cambridge, I've heard. But also very unfashionably happily married afterwards. I mean, until they both died. I mean, not together. Damned unfortunate business."

"Yes," said Valentine, "death is generally accounted unfortunate."

"Well"—Sir Horley grinned his slightly feral grin—"unless you don't like the deceased. Or stand to inherit a lot of land and money."

Tucking a hand behind his back, Valentine let his fingers press inwards, nails digging into his palm. "Why yes, had I been a little older, I'm sure I would have murdered my father myself."

"Malvern." A stagey gasp from Sir Horley. "You always did have the most macabre sense of humour."

"A consequence of the company I keep. Now I really—"

But before Valentine could make his escape, Sir Horley had turned his glittering green eyes upon Bonny. "Speaking of company, I'm sure this can't be Miss Tarleton."

"Not quite," Bonny said, with a ragged semblance of his usual manner. "But I don't look half-bad in a ball gown."

Sir Horley, who, Valentine was beginning to realise, was a striking man for all he was unbearably indiscreet, smiled winningly. "I can well believe it. How is it possible I have passed through this part of the country on many occasions, and yet never found time to appreciate it?"

A shrug from Bonny. "Having spent my entire life here, I'm not really the best person to ask about its attractions."

"That is because familiarity breeds contempt." Now Sir Horley was shaking Bonny's hand, lingering over it in a wholly unnecessary fashion. "But novelty renders all things beautiful."

Bonny had gone a little pink. "Oh," he said. *"Oh."*

Valentine—who did his best not to feel anything too intensely and had already had more than his fill of feelings in general—suddenly realised he had never liked Sir Horley Comewithers. That, in fact, he very actively disliked him. As one might dislike a woodpecker if one was a tree. Were there, he found himself wondering, any circumstances in which it was appropriate to poke an acquaintance in the eye in a hostelry in Surrey?

Unlikely.

But he was imagining it very vividly indeed.

In lieu of an eye poking, Valentine subjected Sir Horley to a searingly bland stare. "What are you even doing here?"

"I've property nearby, and now I'm on my way back to London. But"—he was still holding Bonny's hand; why was he still holding Bonny's hand; how long could it possibly take you to shake a hand— "I'd be more than happy to stay. Do a little . . . sightseeing?"

"Actually," growled Valentine, "we should retire. Mr. Tarleton, my fiancée, her companion, and I are intending an early departure."

Sir Horley sighed. "A shame. But I suppose I must bid you good night."

"And most likely farewell."

"Unless"—another of those too-intimate glances at Bonny—"you would prefer the accommodations in my room?"

It was all Valentine could do not to roll his eyes. "They're likely exactly the same."

"That's what you think, Malvern," returned Sir Horley, laughing. "That's what you think."

Bonny was silent as they went downstairs to secure use of the inn-keeper's final room. It did not last.

"Are you trying to ruin my life?" he asked, about a second after the door had closed behind them and he had thrown himself across the bed, much as his sister had earlier. "You've made Belle hate me. And that man outside was clearly a practiced seducer who was attempting to practice his seductions upon me, and I wasn't in the mood. You know, on account of Belle hating me."

Valentine sat down on the edge of the bed, exhaustion creeping up his spine, making his shoulders sag and his neck ache. "That man outside is the biggest gossip in London. He's nothing but trouble."

"He said I was beautiful."

The words *Well, he's not blind* nearly burst unbidden from Valentine's mouth. Followed by a kind of burgeoning panic that the thought had not only occurred, but had occurred so very naturally. That Valentine had slipped without noticing from assuming Bonny's beauty lay in the ways he resembled his sister to finding Miss Tarleton beautiful only because she resembled Bonny. "I think," he muttered, "I think you're letting your . . . predilections inform your perceptions. He was talking of the landscape."

To his surprise, Bonny let out a strange harsh laugh and rolled onto his side—presenting Valentine with his back and tucking up his knees until he was in the shape of a small, disconsolate comma. "I cannot countenance you right now."

It was a situation with which Valentine was not particularly familiar, but general civility suggested the appropriate course of action was to allow himself to be noncountenanced. "So," he heard himself saying, "that's what you find appealing, is it? An insinuating libertine with no regard for truth or decency?"

"Malvern"—the comma sighed heavily—"either he wanted to discuss the topographical features of southern England *or* he's an insinuating libertine. On this occasion—though not, I hasten to add, as a general principle—you cannot have it both ways."

"To call you a novelty was hardly flattering."

"Oh la," said Bonny, in what was clearly a mocking tone, "the bad man will take my maidenhead and leave me dishonoured. For God's sake, what part of 'I cannot countenance you right now' are you failing to comprehend?"

"I just think," muttered Valentine, "you could make superior choices."

"In case you need reminding, I'm not exactly drowning in them down here in the arse end of nowhere." Another sigh, even sadder than the last. "Every encounter I've contrived, I've had to initiate. And they've all been delightful in their own ways, but . . . it gets tiring. The uncertainties. I can't tell you how . . . how good it felt just to see honest, uncomplicated desire in someone's eyes. Except wait. No. This moment I have longed for my whole life—this perfect beautiful gift that fell unbidden into my lap in a pub on the Dover road—was *tainted*. Ruined. Worthless to me. Because I have irreversibly damaged my relationship with my sister. All because I trusted *you*."

The worst of it was that none of this felt untrue, or even—by Tarleton standards—exaggerated. All Valentine had been required to do was propose to his intended in a fashion that didn't distress her so severely she literally ran away, and then apologise to his intended for proposing to her in a fashion that had distressed her so severely she literally ran away. And yet on both occasions he had been too tangled up with—he hardly knew what. There was something wrong with him. That was the problem. There had always been something wrong with him. Some inexplicable splinter of *Not as he should be* he had driven deep inside. And was now working its way to the surface again in order to disrupt his life and the lives of anyone even tangentially connected to him.

Valentine put his head in his hands. "I apologise. I apologise with all my heart."

"Well, since your heart is about the size of a walnut, that isn't much consolation."

"I will fix this, Bonny. I promise you." The taut line of Bonny's spine yielded very slightly. And, encouraged, Valentine pressed on. "In the morning—"

This only made Bonny groan and pull himself in even tighter. "For pity's sake, Malvern. After what you said and did tonight, do you really think . . ."

"What?" asked Valentine, when he showed no sign of continuing.

"No." Liberating a single hand, Bonny flicked the air dismissively in Valentine's general direction. "Forget I spoke. I'm done helping you."

Valentine opened his mouth, then closed it again. And finally said, "Very well." Followed by, "What now?"

"Well, I don't know about you"—Bonny sat up and starting pulling off his boots—"but I'm going to bed."

First one boot, then the other, sailed over the footboard and clonked onto the floor. They were rapidly followed by his coat, waistcoat, stockings, and cravat.

"What are you doing?" asked Valentine, in some alarm.

"Unlike you, I'm not in the habit of sleeping fully dressed."

"That was"—Valentine shifted uncomfortably—"a single occasion."

Now Bonny's shirt sailed onto the floor.

"You do recall," said Valentine, "that I'm present."

Bonny was somehow managing to glare at him, despite doing something wriggly under the covers that suggested the removal of pantaloons. "So?"

"So . . . you . . . I . . ."

"For all I enjoy looking at you"—there was mockery in Bonny's tone, but more warmth than there had been previously—"you may rest easy that it's the limit of your appeal. Had I inclinations to woo a man, I would not choose one with no affection towards others of his sex, who was engaged to my sister, and with whom I was presently not at all pleased. I would also not initiate the matter by hauling off my garments like a sailor on shore leave."

"How . . . how would you initiate the matter?"

"My point: not it." Bonny's pantaloons landed directly at Valentine's feet. "And I really am done talking to you tonight."

"Yes. I . . . very well."

With nothing else to do, Valentine blew out the candle the innkeeper had given them, plunging the room into a greyish semidarkness. Then, shrugging out of his greatcoat and the assistant gardener's coat, he sat down on the only available chair to remove his boots.

"What the hell are you doing now?" came Bonny's grumpy voice from a mound of bedclothes a few minutes later.

"I'm removing my boots."

"Can you get on with it then? I'm trying to sleep?"

Twisting himself into an inelegant position, Valentine tugged again. "I'm *trying* to remove my boots."

"How do you function?" A soft flump from the bed as Bonny flung the covers aside and rose, indistinct but for the gleam of his skin.

"I have a valet—oh God, what are you doing? Are you naked?"

"No, I'm in full court dress."

Valentine's valet—a talented and devoted man, some fifty years of age—regularly knelt to help him with his boots. But it felt utterly different when it was Bonny, which did not seem at all connected to the impatient way that he yanked them from Valentine's feet. It was more the fantastical chimera of him, half-exposed, half-concealed, a man made of glimpses and dreams. Here the turn of his shoulder, there the line of his collarbone. The muscles shifting in his upper arms. The pool of shadow between his thighs.

"Your valet"—as Bonny rose and turned away, the moonlight through the thin curtains stroked his back with lover's fingers—"deserves a damn knighthood."

But Valentine was wordless. Senseless. Hopeless and adrift in the press of a hand cupped around his heel. He was worried he would never forget it. Never stop wanting it again.

"Come on then." Bonny, back in bed now, was resettling the covers.

"Wh-what?"

"Get your arse into bed."

Valentine was glad for the darkness, for it hid his expression. "Oh, n-no. Thank you. I'll be quite content in the chair."

"I've spent a single day with you, and I already know you will not be content all."

"I . . . I have no wish to impose."

Yet another of Bonny's expressive sighs. "Just because I'm angry with you doesn't mean I want to punish you. You don't have to sleep in the chair."

The area of Valentine that had spent most of the day on a curricle was already raising objections. "I'm fine."

"You won't be fine in an hour. You certainly won't be fine in eight. And I'm the one who'll have to deal with you in the morning."

"I . . ."

"Malvern, if you continue to act as though I'm going to violate you in the night because I enjoy intimacy with other men, I will throw your boots out of the window."

"That wasn't . . ."

But how could Valentine tell him that his fears lay somewhere else entirely? So he awkwardly shed the rest of his clothes and—modesty secured thanks to the voluminous folds of his shirt—insinuated himself gingerly beneath the blankets.

Bonny gave absolutely no sign he was even aware Valentine was there.

Though Valentine was terribly, terribly aware of Bonny—the fact he could just about discern the shape of him by the gathering of heat in the darkness between them, and the sound of his breath in the quiet room, something almost hypnotic in its ceaseless rise and fall.

His heart raced. He was too warm. The covers were too heavy. And there was a lump in the mattress digging into his hip. His foot was itchy. He wanted to sneeze but he couldn't. He felt like his hands had grown alien to him. He couldn't stop his thoughts—

"Bonny?"

"*Christ.* What? What is it now?"

"Does . . . does your sister feel as you do?"

"You're going to have to be a wee bit more specific."

"I mean, the way you feel about men. Does your sister feel that way about women? Is that why she—is she in love with Peggy?"

"Oh." To his surprise, some of the frustration faded from Bonny's voice. "Not . . . not exactly. Peggy's her best friend, other than me. But I don't think she's in love with her. I think she's more sort of . . . in love with Peggy being in love with her; does that make sense?"

Valentine thought about it. "Not really, no."

"I don't think she's fully aware of it herself."

"So"—this had been less illuminating than Valentine might have hoped—"she does not desire women?"

"She doesn't *not* desire them."

"Are you deliberately making this confusing?"

He'd made Bonny laugh. And, as much as Valentine disliked being laughed at, it was infinitely better than Bonny being angry with him. "Not everything has a simple answer, flower."

"Does . . . Peggy know?" asked Valentine, after a moment.

"Probably. She's no fool, and she's almost as close to Belle as I am. But I think she might think it's enough? For now. And I think Belle probably does too."

Valentine tried very hard to understand . . . anything. But it was all so beyond his experiences. The assumptions he had made about the world across nearly thirty years of living in it. "Do you think it's enough?"

"It's not my relationship, so I don't get to judge."

"Would it be enough for you?"

"No. But Belle is . . . Belle wants . . . that's the thing with being a twin, you know. You're never alone, but nothing is ever wholly yours. She wants something to be wholly hers."

"Just Belle?" said Valentine softly.

And Bonny made a sound, half amusement, half something much more naked. "Oh, stop trying to be sensitive. It doesn't suit you."

They lapsed into silence. One of Bonny's very cold feet had somehow found its way between Valentine's knees—and there it was apparently staying, making Valentine cold too.

"Bonny?"

"Yes, flower?" This time there was no irritation, just a kind of resignation.

"Would I . . . would I be in Arkandia?"

There came a sudden stillness in the space beside him. "Would you want to be?"

"Yes," he whispered. "But I don't know what I'd do there."

"Whatever you wished. That's the whole point."

"I . . . I don't think I know what I wish."

Now Bonny turned, from his left side to his right, until he was facing Valentine across the pillows—turning them into strange reflections of each other. Valentine felt the stir of Bonny's breath. Caught afresh the scent of his skin, sweet as honey upon the tongue. "There's still time for you to find out," he said.

And there, safely unseen in the darkness, Valentine smiled wistfully. Sliced a piece of truth from the core of his heart. "Only in Arkandia, Bonny. Only in Arkandia."

Chapter 12

Valentine woke to sunlight, to the discovery he was teetering on the edge of the bed with barely any blanket, and to Bonny, who had somehow taken possession of all the bed and all the blanket, and most of Valentine's person. He was still fast asleep, snuffling gently into the crook of Valentine's shoulder, his hair a fluff of thistledown, and the rest of him flung every which way like a wasteful starfish. He had an arm across Valentine's chest and a leg draped over both of Valentine's. A leg that was strong and soft and . . . bare against Valentine's own bare leg.

The heat between them was a clinging thing, a slick and supple thing, as intimate as the meeting of mouths. He could feel the yield of flesh and the press of muscle. The silky scratch of hair that allowed him all too easily to imagine how it might look: a whorl of gold on skin.

And now he was . . . good God he was. Abruptly, achingly, *unmistakably*. An occurrence, he was sure, a fellow gentleman would understand to be incidental rather than specific—but, then, what did Valentine know? He had never awoken with a fellow gentleman before.

And the fellow gentleman was stirring, all fluttering lashes and kittenish murmurs. Although for some incomprehensible reason, instead of drawing decorously away—as Valentine thought was probably appropriate behaviour under the circumstances—he was nestling closer. Which meant at any moment he would see, or touch, or otherwise become aware of Valentine's—

Half rolling, half heaving Bonny away, he scrambled out of bed and into his pantaloons.

"Mrf-urgh?" asked Bonny. "Mrrrh?"

The room was bright enough to suggest late morning if not noon. "Come, Tarleton. It is past time we were up."

"Nu-nrrgh."

Valentine's cravat was creased beyond salvaging, and the knot he tied it with an active abomination. He squinted at himself in the tarnished looking glass above a rickety chest of drawers and tried not to despair. Only yesterday he had been a polished blade of a man: exquisite, edged, and unassailable. Now he looked . . . tired, tousled, regrettably human. "You have no grounds to play slugabed when you imposed upon me at dawn only yesterday."

"Yesterday"—Bonny had opened a single eye, gleaming through the soft fringe of his lashes like a piece of sky—"I had cause."

Seating himself on the only chair in the room, Valentine began pulling on his boots. He was certainly not remembering how it had felt to have Bonny remove them for him yesterday. A man's hand laid upon him. A man neither servant nor family. "You have cause. Your sister will be waiting."

At this, Bonny gave an odd little laugh. "No she won't, flower."

"What? Of course she will. I instructed her last night: we would eat breakfast, then I would escort her home."

"And you just took it as read that things would happen that way?"

"Why would I not?"

There was a pause, during which Bonny made no gestures towards leaving the bed. "Has anybody ever denied you anything? I mean, *ever*?"

"I'm a duke, Tarleton. What do you think?"

"You know"—both Bonny's eyes were on him now—"I almost feel sorry for you sometimes. And then I remember what you're actually like."

"Will you please get up?"

Another pause. And then, in a tone of such mildness that it could only arouse suspicion, "Very well. For all the good it will do."

Whatever that gnomic little statement was supposed to imply, Valentine would receive no opportunity to address it—because his most pressing concern became Bonny, emerging naked from the blankets like Venus from her seafoam. If, that is, Venus had been quite differently made. Though perhaps not in so many particulars: for skin was skin and curves were curves, and what was supple and enticing was supple and enticing, and what was sweet and dimpled was sweet and dimpled. And as for what seemed rosy and interested—

"Like what you see?" Bonny put his hands on his hips.

Valentine, at once rosy himself, spun away. "Don't be nonsensical, Tarleton."

"Excuse me, I'm *delicious*."

"To those for whom it is possible to share your predilections."

Silence. Valentine took the opportunity to become very acquainted with the far wall. Then he heard the scuff of bare feet against the floor. Coming closer.

"Valentine . . ."

"Please," he said. Begged. "Won't you get dressed?"

There was warmth at his back, or the promise of it. It made the nape of his neck shiver with something terrible and desperate. But Bonny did not touch him. Only sighed. And his footsteps receded.

A small black beetle was edging along a crack in the wall. The wall itself was rough wood, splinter riven, and pockmarked with knots. Behind him came the chaotic rustling of a chaotic person getting dressed chaotically. Though Valentine had to admit, when he finally felt it was safe to turn around again, Bonny was looking considerably better put together than Valentine was himself.

Probably because he had lower standards in general, and thus the difference was less marked. As soon as Miss Tarleton had been returned to her family, Valentine was taking the longest bath of his life. No, he was having two baths. Maybe three. However many it took to wash away the events of the past two days.

Then he was going back to London and giving his valet a raise.

"What are you staring at?" Bonny had his hands on his hips again.

"I'm not staring. I'm daydreaming."

His cheeks went faintly pink "Y-you are?"

"Yes, I'm daydreaming of the life I shall have when I'm rid of you both."

"In case you've forgotten"—Bonny's tone grew abruptly cold—"you'll be married to my sister. That means you're *never* getting rid of her. Unless you're intending to murder her or something." He gasped. "My God, you are. You're going to murder Belle, you . . . you . . . *villainous knave.*"

"Whoever taught you two to read has much to answer for. But as it happens, I have no intention of murdering either of you, despite the fact no jury in the land would convict me."

Bonny rolled his eyes. "Yes, yes, because you're a duke."

"No, because you're very annoying." Reluctantly, Valentine picked up the assistant gardener's coat and dragged it over his shoulders. "In any case, I have decided Miss Tarleton and I shall enjoy a long engagement."

"Oh, have you?"

"It's for the best."

"Best for you, you mean. Since you'll be in London, pretending my sister doesn't exist, while we're still stuck in Surrey."

It was nothing but the truth. But over the course of two days, Valentine's future had gone from being unwanted to unbearable. And the only thing that was standing between the present moment and retiring to a corner of the room to weep was the fiction that anything might ever be the same again. "Well, you should have thought of that before . . . before—"

"Before," demanded Bonny, "we carelessly let our parents get killed? Before we made the strategic error of not being born dukes?"

"Tarleton, enough. We have matters requiring our attention."

"For the last goddamn time"—this last accompanied by a foot stamp—"Belle isn't a matter."

Valentine opened his mouth, closed it again, then turned and left the room—Bonny trotting meekly enough at his heels. He knocked gently on Miss Tarleton's door, conscious that Sir Horley was probably still lurking.

The man was an inveterate lurker.

No answer from within. A glance at Bonny was unhelpful, for he resolutely refused to meet Valentine's gaze.

Valentine knocked again. Less discreetly this time. "Miss Tarleton?"

Nothing.

"Perhaps," suggested Valentine, "she has already gone down to breakfast?"

Bonny yawned. "Perhaps."

"What is *this*"—Valentine found himself doing an uncomfortably Bonny-esque hand gesture—"implying? Do you know something that I do not?"

"How could I possibly when you instructed Belle yourself?"

When a third knock produced no different outcome, Valentine gave the door a tentative push. To his consternation, it swung gently inwards to reveal an empty room. And too much time with the Tarletons must have eroded his brain in some way because, for a split second, he genuinely entertained the thought that his fiancée might have been kidnapped.

If not by pirates then perhaps her own love-disordered companion.

But there were no signs of struggle in the room—he knew from direct experience that Miss Tarleton would struggle were she subject to any action that ran contrary to her will—just an open window and the sheets stripped from the bed. It was all quite peculiar.

"I am," said Valentine, "at a loss."

Bonny was leaning nonchalantly against the doorframe. "Are you, flower?"

"And somewhat concerned."

"I wouldn't be concerned."

"How are you so calm? Your sister has vanished under mysterious circumstances."

"Not so very mysterious."

"Tarleton, I insist you explain yourself immediately."

Somehow Bonny contrived to both sigh *and* roll his eyes. "She departed with Peggy in the early hours of the morning, probably on a rope of knotted-up sheets, through *that*"—a flourish—"window."

"What makes you so certain?"

"Well"—Bonny shrugged—"the sheets are missing, the window is open, and it's exactly what I would have done."

Put like that, it was obvious. Or obvious if one was willing to accept a world in which knotting sheets together and climbing out of windows was the sort of thing people did. Valentine, as it happened, was not willing to accept such a world. Unfortunately, he was beginning to suspect he might not have a choice in the matter. That choices, in general, were ebbing and flowing with what seemed like quite nauseating unpredictability. Possibility and impossibility, duty and desire, locked in an endless, unbreakable quadrille.

With far less elegance than he usually took care to display, Valentine slumped onto the bed. This was the second time, in two days, his betrothed had fled him in disgust. And all he felt was . . . betrayed. Betrayed for entirely the wrong reasons. He glanced across the room to where Bonny was still extravagantly lounging. It made Valentine want to . . . do something. Shake him. Yes. Definitely shake him.

"You knew this would happen," he said. "You knew that she would do this. And yet you did nothing."

Bonny proceeded with his lounge. "I have to say, that's the most magnificent pout I've ever seen."

"Tarleton, I am a duke. I do not pout. And, in any case, that's beside the point. Why would you rouse me at four yesterday to pursue your sister and allow me to slumber today in order that she might escape?"

"Yesterday I thought better of you."

That should not have hurt. Valentine should not have cared. "Without me, you could lose your estate. You will both be consigned to poverty."

Bonny's chin lifted stubbornly. "I would rather be poor—I would rather be just about anything—than permit you any say in Belle's life. You've made it very clear you care nothing for her comfort or her happiness. The way you talk to her—the way you talk *about* her, Malvern—I would not treat a dog like that."

That made Valentine draw in a sharp breath. He was renowned for his manners, his effortless social poise. When had he become a man who barged around inns and shouted at people? Overnight? Or had he always been a barger and a shouter, and just never known it? And what other things might he have always been? It was a train of thought he could ill afford. Not when his wife-to-be was, once again, publicly demonstrating her desire to not-be.

"I . . . I did not acquit myself well yesterday," he admitted. And it was hard to tell which was worse: the admission or the knowledge it was true.

"Oh?" Bonny gave him a look of exaggerated shock. "What could possibly have led you to such an outlandish conclusion."

"It had been a long day. This is a dreadful coat. I was . . . I was somewhat overset in general. And I did not anticipate the state in which I discovered Miss Tarleton."

"*Knocking* exists for a reason."

"She was in an intimate situation." It was not a comfortable memory. And the prospect of discussing it positively torturous. "With a person not her husband." A concern that had been bobbing like a dead salmon upon the current of Valentine's thoughts·chose this juncture to express itself. "Is she even still a virgin?"

Bonny made a sound somewhere between a squeak and a gasp. "What kind of a question is that?"

"A very relevant one from the man who will wed her."

"What is virginity, though?" asked Bonny, with the air of someone who genuinely considered the subject open to debate.

"It is the state one lives in before one is married."

"No, but really."

Valentine gave him a flat stare. "Yes, but really."

"Surely you don't mean . . ." Bonny stared back, something perplexed and searching in his gaze. "Valentine, are *you* a virgin?"

A kind of horrified heat rolled through Valentine. "That is hardly your business, Tarleton."

"Oh my God. How old are you? Thirty? Why aren't you *desperate* to marry?"

"I am eight and twenty," returned Valentine stiffly.

"Very much not the important part of that question."

Valentine tried to think of something cutting to say. But somehow he told the truth instead. "I have no notion."

And the next thing he knew, Bonny was on his knees in front of him. Had even taken his hand, which Valentine should have certainly resisted. But found he lacked the strength to. "My sweet flower. Is it the wedding night? Are you . . . apprehensive?"

"What?" lied Valentine. "No. Of course not."

Bonny was peering up at him, his lashes so perfectly gold, and his eyes so perfectly blue. "There's nothing to be frighted of or worried about. It's . . . it's a beautiful act. You just have to . . . to . . . talk about it. Go slow and gently. Take care of each other. If you'd only been honest with Belle, she'd have understood. In fact, she'd most likely have found it very attractive."

"Good God." Valentine wrenched his hand away. "I do not need advice on the performance of my husbandly duties from you."

"I think the fact you're referring to them as *husbandly duties* suggests you do."

"That is quite enough. We shall have no further discourse on the subject."

Sighing, Bonny sat back on his heels. "I wish you could be this man. For Belle, and for your own sake."

"What fresh nonsense is this?"

"I really could like you," Bonny told him, with the simplicity of a knife thrust, "when you're true. When you allow yourself to admit uncertainty. When you allow yourself to laugh. When you're not too afraid of feeling to care. And, you know, I think Belle could like you too."

Valentine swallowed. He was a duke. Dukes were neither pouting nor fearful. Nor any of the things Bonny had suggested. "I'm not afraid. I'm not afraid of anything."

"If you aren't afraid, why are you sabotaging your own marriage?"

"I'm not the one who ran away."

"Not physically," conceded Bonny. "But you did everything else."

It was entirely the wrong occasion to be regretting having let go of Bonny's hand. Not that Valentine could envisage a right occasion for it. "What do you mean?"

"I remember when your father used to bring you to visit. You weren't like this then."

"I was a *child*," Valentine pointed out.

"Yes, but . . . you were fun and kind. You let Belle braid flowers through your hair."

He had, and if he sometimes missed the simplicity of those days—a time with fewer questions and fewer expectations; when caring carried no meaning beyond itself—it did not feel prudent to dwell on it. "Again, I was a child."

"And then you grew up, and you left us here. And when you came back, you were so cold. And you only laughed to keep us out."

Valentine could hardly bear the hope in the bright horizon of Bonny's gaze. He was correct, of course—not in hoping; this was not a situation that allowed for hope—but the rest of it. It had not been Valentine's intention to drive Belle away, but it might as well have been, so marked had been his disregard. While he had long acknowledged it was his duty to marry, he realised now how little he had truly accepted it. Letting the years slip by, like a prisoner in denial of his sentence.

It was time to stop pretending. He had never been free, and he never would be. And what right did he have to mourn the absence of something so ephemeral when he possessed so much that was not? Wealth, power, grand estates, a centuries-old name, a loving mother. What was freedom, really? Candle smoke. Spring blossom. Sun gleam on swift water. Butterfly dreams, meant to fade with a fading day. And what would he have done with it—even had he possessed it? He'd had close to a decade to understand himself. To uncover the secrets of his own heart. And all he'd found was the same emptiness.

But he would put this right. He would fix what, in his cowardice, he had come close to breaking.

"I'm sorry," he said at last. "I'm sorry I am not the sort of man your sister would prefer me to be. And I will not pretend that this is more than obligation for either of us. But I agree I have been selfish. And I have not . . . I have not been kind."

"Well"—Bonny's smile was impossibly sad—"that's something, I suppose."

"I am not passionate, Bonny. Nor am I romantic. It is simply not in me to be those things. But I will be a better husband than I have given either of you cause to believe."

Bonny gave an unimpressed little murmur. "You have an appalling temper. And are *beyond* high-handed."

"I was raised to my rank. It is what I am required to be. But I will . . . curb myself, and my temper, for Miss Tarleton. She will have my fortune and the protection of my name. I will not stray nor shirk my responsibilities, and she may have her . . ." Valentine's pride balked—it balked terribly—but he pressed on regardless: ". . . liberty."

"You would do that?" Bonny asked, sounding somewhat startled. "For Belle."

Did he have much choice? He could weather the scandal of a broken engagement, for all he would have preferred to remain unsullied by gossip. But what of his father's dream? A single task left to Valentine from a man it was now impossible to know, impossible to make proud, and he would have failed.

And besides, if not Miss Tarleton . . . who?

"It would be . . . be," he tried, " a civility to me, were she to be . . . discreet."

Bonny's eyes narrowed suspiciously. "I can't tell if that means you're really trying to love her or have simply accepted that you never will."

A laugh clawed its way out of Valentine's throat. "You are impossible to satisfy. I have just capitulated in every way it is possible for a man to capitulate to the woman he will wed, and you are still inclined to view me disfavourably."

"Oh God, no." Bonny was shaking his head so violently it cast his curls into wild flight. "Not at all. I'm just made so very differently."

"In what fashion this time?"

"In the fashion of wanting someone who is mine to be mine entirely and singularly. But Belle does not feel the same way. And it speaks well that are you willing to compromise."

"As you have both been at pains to point out to me," Valentine murmured, "the fact I am marrying her does not make her mine."

"I mean"—Bonny wrinkled his nose—"except legally."

Valentine's head was spinning. It had been spinning for two days— except for brief interludes when the world had come, all too fleetingly, to rest. A basket of peaches as warm as the sun. His hand tucked into Bonny's pocket. Waking up in another man's warmth. "Well, perhaps that is not right either."

A pause, during which Valentine found himself subject to all manner of wayward impulses. It half seemed, in that strange, dreamy moment, like it could be the most natural thing in the world to stroke a fingertip down the slope of Bonny's nose. Or touch the perfect pink flower of his mouth.

"I will not find her without you," he said instead. "If you help me, I will . . . I will not drive her away again."

The perfect pink flower of Bonny's mouth twisted sceptically. "I suppose I can give you another chance. But you know the saying: 'Fool me once, shame on you. Fool me twice, shame on me.' You'd better not make me ashamed of myself."

"On my honour. Although I suppose you would not thank me for the observation that you require no assistance from me to look foolish."

Bonny tilted his head slightly. "No, I would not thank you for that observation. Also it rings a little hollow from someone who is literally begging for my assistance."

"Would we say I was begging?" asked Valentine dubiously.

"Yes. Yes we would."

"I am not the one on his knees."

"Oh, flower"—and here Bonny smiled up at him, dimples glimmering irrepressibly—"if you think a man only goes to his knees to beg, then—"

Chapter 13

It was perhaps inevitable that Sir Horley Comewithers would choose this moment to emerge from his chamber. "I say," he exclaimed, striking a pose of theatrical consternation. "Malvern, you sly dog. And with the door wide open too."

Valentine rose abruptly. "I have no idea what you're suggesting."

"It's true," added Bonny, hopping up as well. "He really doesn't."

"His loss is my gain." Sir Horley turned his greedy crocodile smile upon Bonny. "May I say, you were lustrous by candlelight, but you are radiant in the morning."

Bonny was nodding eagerly. "Yes. Please say that. Please feel absolutely at liberty to say that."

"Then"—slinking into the room like an alley cat, Sir Horley possessed himself of Bonny's hand—"you were lustrous by candlelight, but you are radiant in the morning."

"He thinks I'm radiant," Bonny told Valentine, who was in no need of a translation.

Whatever Valentine was feeling right now—some kind of, he assumed, social discomfort from two men acting so shamelessly with each other—he did not like it. "He's toying with you."

"But I like toys," put in Sir Horley. "Who doesn't? They're fun."

Bonny only shrugged. "Maybe I'm toying with him."

"Oh, are you?" Sir Horley's brows lifted. "What a wicked thing you are, playing with gentlemen's hearts."

Now Bonny's dimples were glimmering for Sir Horley. "Only a little wicked. In general, it's not gentlemen's hearts I like to play with."

This—whatever it was—had to be stopped. And Valentine was going to be the one to stop it. "Unhand Mr. Tarleton, you reprobate."

But for some reason, rather than cowing him as he deserved, this just made Sir Horley laugh. "Your fiancée, Malvern. Conspicuous, ain't she? By her absence."

"She . . . she has gone on ahead with her companion."

"Gone on ahead, has she?" Sir Horley inclined his head solemnly. "With her companion."

Valentine glared. "Yes. That's what I said. She's gone on ahead with her companion."

"Come on, man. You're among friends here."

"I am not among friends. I am with you and Tarleton."

Releasing Bonny, Sir Horley lifted his hands in a gesture of sur-render. "My apologies. I did not mean to diminish your connection."

The man was an arrant knave. "What are you talking about?" snapped Valentine. "I told you yesterday: I am here to visit my fiancée."

"Of course, of course. *Miss* Tarleton, I think you said?"

"My twin sister," offered Bonny, who appeared to be finding some-thing very amusing indeed.

Another solemn nod from Sir Horley. "Your twin sister."

"Do you have some kind of brain fever?" Valentine spun his glare to Sir Horley, then to Bonny, and then to Sir Horley again. "Why are you repeating everything anyone says?"

It was Bonny, however, who spoke next. "We do actually need to be getting on. And I am urgently in need of breakfast."

"Of course, of course." Sir Horley seemed to find it impossible to stop smiling in Bonny's direction. It was beyond unnecessary. "Don't let me keep you."

"I hadn't planned on it," Valentine told him. "Come, Tarleton."

He had meant to sweep out of the room, but Sir Horley—with an appalling familiarity—caught his arm midsweep, aborting Valentine's egress.

"One more thing, Malvern. If you'll forgive the presumption."

Valentine subjected him to his iciest gaze. "You should know I am not, as a general rule, inclined to."

"But I am learning new things about you all the time, my dear."

That sounded rather distasteful. Valentine went to a lot of trouble to remain as constant and mundane as it was possible to be. Also there appeared to be some sort of localised disease affecting travellers that led them to reject appropriate forms of address in favour of ill-chosen endearments. "I should hate for you to look foolish," he murmured, "were you to mistake yourself."

Sir Horley only laughed—the tone of it rather different from his usual horrible bray. It sounded unexpectedly . . . gentle? As if his aim was to reassure, though what he thought Valentine might need reassuring about was beyond imagining. "Believe me, I only like you better for them. But I simply must have a word in your ear. About this young man."

"Me?" Bonny bounced like a spaniel called for walkies. "What about me?"

"No," said Valentine.

"No?" Sir Horley blinked. "You mean, no, I can't have a word?"

"No anything. Tarleton is none of your business."

"Are you about to propose some manner of an indecent transaction?" asked Bonny. "Because I would be outraged by that." He fluttered his lashes. "Deeply, deeply *outraged*."

Another of those strange laughs from Sir Horley. One of his hands had come up to rest against his chest, and he looked, if anything, slightly soft eyed. "You must see, Malvern, what a gem he is."

"Yes," said Bonny. "You must see what a gem I am."

Valentine glanced at Bonny. "He's . . . a person? An adequate person, I suppose? If you overlook the fact he dresses like a magpie and won't stop talking."

"Oh, you two." Now both of Sir Horley's hands were pressed over his heart. "But seriously: do better, Malvern. This place is a veritable dive. Take him somewhere nice next time."

"I . . . I . . ." Valentine was genuinely lost for words. "Pardon?"

"Don't skulk around. It implies you're ashamed."

"I have nothing to be ashamed of," retorted Valentine.

Sir Horley clapped him vigorously on the shoulder. "That's the spirit. Try the Old Cock sometime. Wonderful baths, and the stable boys are superlative. Or I have a"—and here he held his hands up on either side of his head, crooking his fingers in a most peculiar fashion—"'hunting lodge' nearby. Very discreet. You'd be more than welcome to stay."

"To say I have no interest in staying at your hunting lodge"—Valentine drew himself to his full height—"would be to vastly understate my indifference to the proposition."

And then he shook off Sir Horley and proceeded with his sweep, wondering with some irritation why the man kept smiling so.

They were well past any hour that could reasonably be called breakfast, but Bonny—through pure persistence—managed to secure them a repast of bread and cheese. Although, to Valentine's mind, the bread could no more reasonably be called bread and the cheese cheese than the meal could be called breakfast. The former was tough and grainy, the latter sufficiently pungent to make his eyes water.

"It's like eating old stockings," declared Bonny, with every indication of pleasure. "Best cheese."

Valentine abandoned his attempt to cut a piece from the loaf. "You appear to be operating under some alien definition of the word *best*."

"You should eat, flower." Bonny picked up the bread, tore a chunk free, buttered it liberally, and passed it to Valentine. "Keep up your strength."

The butter was rich and salty. It softened the bread and tempered the cheese, and the combination was perilously close to acceptable. Especially if one was hungry, which Valentine discovered he was. "How are we to find your sister? Do you have a plan?"

"Naturally I do. I'm going to ask people."

"You're going to ask people?" Valentine repeated. "That's the plan? After I begged for your assistance?"

Bonny gave him a lofty look. "I thought you hadn't begged?"

"I . . . I . . ." Better to avoid that argument entirely. "Didn't Miss Tarleton leave in the early hours?"

"Yes, but she'll have needed the gig, which meant a visit to the stables. So we should start with the ostler."

"And he's just going to tell you, is he?"

"Of course. You must have noticed, I'm very charming."

They hastily finished what was left of the food and made their way to the stable yard. Valentine had only the vaguest recollection of the ostler from the previous night. It had been dark, and he had been very tired, and his posterior very sore. Daylight, however, revealed him to be young, broad-shouldered, and clad in an unnecessarily clingy shirt—the sleeves of which were rolled up to reveal brawny forearms, lightly dusted with brown hair.

Valentine did not like the fellow.

"Hello," said Bonny, bouncing up to him, all bright eyes and dancing curls. "Have you seen my sister? She left earlier this morning?"

The ostler had a piece of corn balanced on his lower lip. He removed it, his gaze travelling over Bonny in a fashion that seemed frankly lingering. "I might have."

"You couldn't mistake her. Looked like me? Accompanied by a dark-haired gentleman? They'd have been sneaking off in the most dramatic possible fashion."

"Maybe." The ostler's expression grew thoughtful. "Maybe I do recall something of the sort. About five o'clock it was."

"Did you happen see what direction they were headed?"

There was a long pause. The ostler was still staring at Bonny. His mouth twitched upwards. "I might have."

"I will, of course," Bonny told him, staring right back, "compensate you for your time."

"We are ourselves in something of a hurry," Valentine added.

Bonny's eyes flicked towards him in some irritation. "I can be *very* efficient."

"What did you have in mind?" asked the ostler, apparently oblivious to the interruption.

And Bonny placed a hand on the man's chest, going up on tiptoes to whisper something into his ear. Whatever it was, it seemed quite involved. "Or," Bonny suggested. And kept whispering.

"Well, young master"—the ostler gave a slow, satisfied smile—"you've got yourself a deal."

"Wonderful. Do you have . . ."

"Hayloft?"

Bonny actually gave a little skip. "Oh, you've no idea how long I've wanted to . . . in a hayloft." He waved a hand in Valentine's direction. "Give me . . . fifteen minutes? No, twenty. Half an hour at the most. I'll be right back."

Before Valentine could protest—and he was going to protest; he was going to protest vehemently—Bonny and the ostler had vanished into the stables together. This left Valentine in something of a quandary. Given his unfortunate relationship with the innkeeper, he had no wish to return to the inn. But nor did he wish to stand around outside, looking, particularly in the assistant gardener's coat, like some kind of malingering malcontent. Besides, in the typical fashion of an English summer, yesterday's clear blue skies had been replaced by sheets of sullen grey, promising rain.

Sitting gingerly on a low stone wall, Valentine wished for the pocket watch he had been in too much of a hurry to bring with him yesterday. He had no idea how long Bonny had been gone, but it felt like an excessively long time. And whatever understanding had been reached with the ostler was making Valentine increasingly uncomfortable. It was, after all, Valentine's fault that his betrothed was once again at large and in the wilds. That had nothing to do with Bonny.

And yet it was Bonny who—

What was he doing? Or having done to him?

Valentine—who once upon a time rarely bestirred himself from a gentlemanly languor—ran across the yard, heedless even of the puddles that splashed his once-pristine boots with mud. And from there into the stables themselves. Bonny's bays regarded him with mild equine surprise.

Then he heard Bonny, his voice raised in a kind of . . . musical warble that could have been distress. Valentine had never climbed a ladder in his life, but he practically flew up the one that led to the hayloft.

Where he beheld Bonny. Sprawled in the tangle of his clothes across a hay bale, his pantaloons around his knees, one booted foot flung across the ostler's shoulder, the other cast wantonly in the air. His member—and Valentine had no idea why it should arrest his gaze—was also skywards inclined, its tip pearlescent with excitement, and its base a cloud of shining golden hair. It was shocking the way something so lewd could also be so lovely.

The ostler was nestled low between Bonny's thrown-wide legs. His head came up slightly. "You taste like wild strawberries."

Bonny curled a hand into his hair and pushed him down again. "I bet you say that to all the boys."

"You know," remarked Valentine, "I have lived for nearly thirty years, and not once in all that time have I stumbled across other people in acts of . . . acts of *this*. And now it has happened twice in a row. Do you think it could be the company I'm keeping?"

The noise Bonny made in response was somewhere between *worrglffh* and *nrrghurgle* as he arched into a semiupright position. Which did little to protect his modesty and, in fact, only further flaunted his enticements: all the places he was softly made and gently curving, and the contrasting ones where he was . . . so . . . very . . . powerfully, gloriously hard.

And Valentine was, once again, furious. Though he hardly knew why. Just that the more he tried to repin his world into place, the more wildly—the more kaleidoscopically—it spun away from him. And, the truth was, it hurt. Too many colours, dazzling too sharply in eyes too accustomed to different hues. He had wondered how he was supposed to return to life as he understood it after the things Bonny had told him at their picnic yesterday. He had wondered again when he had found his fiancée in bed with a person who was only sometimes a woman. But, for all his wondering, it had still felt possible. What hope did *anything* have of ever being the same again now he had seen—

Now he had seen the way a man could glisten. The way he could both yield and claim. Now he had seen Bonny in reckless ecstasy.

"What in God's name are you doing?" he demanded.

To his credit, Bonny had the grace to look slightly abashed. "Well, I . . . I'm having my arse licked." He paused. "And very capably, if I may say so."

Valentine glanced from Bonny to the ostler, who had, at least, paused in his . . . endeavours. "Was this your arrangement?"

"Part of it."

"There's more?"

"With me, flower"—Bonny flung out a hand in a gesture of general enthusiasm—"there is always more."

"You would trade yourself? With this . . . *person*. For information?"

Untangling his legs, Bonny eased himself into a sitting position, his shirt slipping down to cover the only aspect of him Valentine had ever successfully managed to quell. "Why not? I'm the most valuable thing I own."

"What does that . . . are you . . ." Valentine was as much lost for concepts as for words. "Are you some manner of boy doxy?"

Bonny's eyes flew wide. "That is insulting in so many different directions I don't even know what to say to you."

"Is there a problem, milord?" That was the ostler, though it was unclear exactly who he thought he was addressing.

Valentine ignored him. "Get dressed. We're leaving."

"In case you've forgotten"—Bonny began pulling up his breeches, his attitude one of high dudgeon—"we still need information from this man."

"Then pay him for it. With money."

"I'm quite happy to just tell—" began the ostler, who was backing away from both of them with his hands raised in a conciliatory manner.

"I don't have any money," Bonny snapped, tossing his hair from his brow. "I'm impoverished, remember?"

"You are not wearing apparel provided by an assistant gardener. Surely you have some coins or notes about your person?"

Bonny did some further hair tossing. "I did. But I spent them to cover our room and Belle's room and breakfast."

"Then . . . then . . . give him one of your rings."

"My rings are *paste*. Do you really think I casually own rubies and diamonds and sapphires?"

"Why would you wear fake jewellery?"

"Because it's *shiny*. Obviously."

Valentine was breathing hard. Could feel the hot beat of his blood in his veins. Putting a hand to his forehead, he massaged his temples.

He was going to control himself. He was going to control himself *and* the situation.

"You." He gestured to the ostler, who stumbled obediently forwards. "I'm going to give you my signet ring. I don't recommend you attempt to sell it, because it will surely be assumed you have stolen it."

"Why are you giving it to him then?" asked Bonny.

"Be quiet," Valentine told him. "It's my surety."

The ostler glanced unhappily between them. "And I can't just go back to licking his arse?"

"No. Absolutely not." It took Valentine a second or two to twist the ring from his finger. And he felt strange without it, a little bit naked, but also a little bit lighter. "You will take this as a guarantee of my return. You see I find myself in, shall we say, challenging circumstances. But if you assist us now, you may be assured the debt will be repaid."

The ostler seemed less impressed by this than Valentine might have hoped or expected. "And"—he turned his large brown eyes upon Bonny—"we're not to—"

"No," Valentine said. "Under no circumstances. Now which way did they go?"

"North, milord."

That made no sense. "North?"

"Yes, milord. Along the road to Rochester."

Wait. It *did* make sense. "Of course," Valentine muttered. "Knowing they were pursued, they would not head to Dover directly but would naturally divert north in order to confound us. Knowing this, however, they would perhaps have chosen instead to travel south, thereby hoping to outpace us while we wasted our time hoping to outpace *them* on the road north. But Miss Tarleton clearly realised that I would foresee this eventuality and has thus gone north, hoping to evade us while we go south, hoping to catch her in the belief that she believes that we believe that she has gone north."

"I think," the ostler whispered, "there might be something wrong with your friend."

Bonny just pulled a face. "Tell me about it."

Chapter 14

Valentine dispatched the ostler to ready Bonny's curricle. Which left him alone in the hayloft with Bonny, and the memory of Bonny. The memory of Bonny with his head thrown back and his legs parted, and his mouth open in a delirious gasp.

"What"—Valentine caught him by the elbow—"was that about?"

Bonny immediately pulled away. "Excuse me?"

"What exactly," demanded Valentine, "were you trying to prove here?"

"I wasn't trying to prove anything. I was trying to get my arse licked."

This conversation had already gone awry. The problem was, Valentine had no idea what *not awry* would have looked like. "But . . . but why? To punish me or—"

He was interrupted by Bonny laughing at him. Laughing in an angry sort of way. "Flower, what happens to my arse has *nothing* to do with you. And is certainly not any sort of punishment for anyone."

"Then . . ." Something wounded had crept inescapably into Valentine's tone. Something he knew had no right to be there. "Why would you . . . why would you do . . ." He flailed a hand descriptively.

"Because I wanted to." One of those defiant little head tosses. "I like sex and I like being wanted, and I need no more reason than that. What does, however, need more reason is"—Bonny launched a descriptive hand motion of his own—"this."

"What?" Valentine offered an unconvincingly blank look. He knew he was behaving . . . strangely. That he had been behaving strangely for the past few days. Feeling too much and reacting too much, and only some of the time understanding why.

"*This,*" cried Bonny. "The way you're acting right now."

"Which is how?"

"Like you have some claim on me."

"I will not have you making a spectacle of yourself."

Valentine had not realised how cold blue eyes could be. Right now, Bonny's were positively arctic. "You know, a spectacle requires a spectator. If you saw something you weren't prepared to see, that's on you."

"And what of the ostler?"

"Oh no, he was definitely prepared to see what he saw."

Contemplating what the ostler might have seen was not conducive to either Valentine's mood or peace of mind. "You aren't the least concerned about what he might have thought of you?"

"He thought pretty damn well of me until you barged in like a jealous lover."

"I'm not jealous," Valentine said quickly. "I'm . . . I'm frankly appalled. That man is a servant."

"So I should only sleep with the landed gentry? Passing royalty?"

"You shouldn't be sleeping with anyone."

There was a long silence.

"Why?" asked Bonny finally. It was his sweetest voice, and Valentine knew him well enough by now to distrust it. "Why shouldn't I be sleeping with anyone?"

"You know why."

Another long silence. The loft smelled oddly sweet—fresh hay, and the faintest hint of Bonny. The ostler's observation regarding wild strawberries was feeling less fanciful with every passing second.

Then Bonny heaved a sigh. Some of the frost had faded from his eyes. But it had taken some of the glitter too. "You don't own me, Valentine. You don't get to decide what I do or who I do it with."

The problem with having started this argument was that Valentine had no idea how to finish it. There were ways out of it, but they would have meant . . . confronting something or admitting something, and that was already too many *somethings*. No, Valentine was committed. Stuck. And the only way out was through—even if through felt like its own catastrophe. "While you are with me, your behaviour reflects on me and reflects on your sister. If you wish to debase yourself, you may do so on your own time."

Up came Bonny's chin. "*Debase* myself? Is that really what you think about . . . about me?"

"I don't know what to think," said Valentine. Which had the merit of being the only true statement he had made for a while. "But this is supposed to be a rescue mission. It is not an opportunity to indulge in lewd shenanigans with anyone and everyone who catches your eye."

"So Belle is to have a fabulous adventure and I am not?"

Valentine narrowed his eyes—dangerously relieved for an opportunity to turn the conversation back on Bonny. "Is that what this is about? Do you want to find your sister or merely emulate her?"

"Wh-what do you mean?" The words usually rushed out of Bonny like poor-quality claret from a broken bottle. So the fact he hesitated now was telling.

"You're hurt that she left you behind," Valentine continued, not wanting to say any of the things he was saying but too scared to stop. "Even, perhaps, a little envious."

"I love Belle." Bonny sounded small. "I want her to be happy."

"That's not in question. Yet she still abandoned you. And you may make eyes at every degenerate from here to Dover, but it won't change the fact Miss Tarleton's life will take her places yours can never take you."

The strangest laugh broke from Bonny's throat. "Flower, I realise you didn't like what you interrupted. You don't want to say these things to me, though. You really don't."

"I'm only offering you the truth. There are stories that are not written and cannot be rewritten. And I'm afraid yours is one of them."

"This isn't truth. It's cruelty."

"Truth is like your bees, Tarleton. It is neither cruel nor kind. It simply exists."

Bonny gave a swift, desolate shake of his head. "You're wrong. You're so, *so wrong*. You don't understand bees. And you don't understand me."

"Then it is fortunate," said Valentine, ignoring the strange ache that was spreading through his heart, "that my acquaintance with both will be of equally brief duration."

There was an odd shimmer in Bonny's eyes, quickly banished behind the flutter of his too-long lashes. "You asked for my help. I was trying to help."

"If carrying on with stable hands is your idea of helping, then I think I shall be better off without your assistance. In fact"—Valentine careened onwards, his tongue a wild horse—"it is probably best for both of us if you stop helping altogether."

Whatever response to this Valentine had been expecting, it was not the quietness of an "I see."

"Do you see?" Why he was pressing the point, he didn't know. "There is to be no more helping, Tarleton. Never again."

"Believe me"—Bonny flashed him the oddest smile—"there will not be."

The silence that followed was less comfortable than it should have been.

"Good," said Valentine. "I'm glad we . . . I'm glad we have an accord. And if I spoke out of turn, I—"

Bonny was already whirling away. "We should go. Or we'll never catch Belle."

Which left Valentine with little choice except to follow him. But, the truth was, he had never felt less in accord with anyone than he did with Bonny just then. Probably Valentine owed him an apology—for the harshness of his words, regardless of their accuracy.

Normally *being right* would have been reassurance enough that Valentine would not have questioned himself. Now, though, it felt like merest trivia. The hollowest of comfort.

Because Bonny had been sunshine that morning. Dazzling. Irritating. Making every dull thing he touched impossibly bright. But waiting for Valentine in the stable yard, there was just a young man in rumpled clothes, with paste rings on his fingers, and eyes as grey as the drizzling sky.

ᘉᘏ⭑ᘏᘊ

Valentine, in his naivete, had believed yesterday would rank as possibly the worst day of his life. After all, he'd been awoken early, suffered terribly in the absence of his valet, and then been jolted through the highways and byways of Surrey in pursuit of the wayward fiancée he had later discovered in someone else's arms. He'd also been victimised by a bee, denied a bath, and had his entire world turned upside down and inside out courtesy of a . . . of a . . .

Of Bonny.

But at least there'd been the compensation of novelty about the whole experience. And he'd taken hope from the likelihood of its short duration. Unfortunately, today was turning out much like yesterday, with the added disadvantages of a nonspeaking companion and increasingly heavy rain.

The drizzle had softened him up, coming down with sufficient persistence as to be inescapable and taking him gently but inexorably from a state of being dry to very much the opposite. This had somehow felt far worse than the sudden saturation of a downpour. It was, instead, like being pickled in one's own discomfort. And then, of course, there'd been a downpour anyway. So Valentine was both pickled and drenched, the chill of the rain seeping deep into his bones as it ran in little streams from his hair and down his nose.

How long they'd been travelling he couldn't have said. Hours, he thought. Definitely hours. With occasional breaks to rest the horses and take a sip or two of execrable brandy from Bonny's hip flask. Valentine had tried, on several occasions, to think of something he could say to ease the silence between them. Yet each and every time he had faltered. And now he had lost track of his own wrongdoings.

He had said some things. Some things he should not have said. Some things he did not mean. But it was not really the *what* that mattered. It was the *why*. And he barely knew how to explain the why, even to himself.

Because you make me feel like a coward.

Because I have never known what it was to want before.

Because you are so beautiful it terrifies me.

Valentine's hands were cold again. But cold they would have to remain.

"This is no good," said Bonny eventually, with a glance at the ever-darkening sky. "We need to find shelter."

Glancing around, all Valentine could see were sodden fields and rain-bowed trees. "Where? Is Rochester far?"

"Half a moment: let me focus my Rochester-Detecting Mechanism." Bonny put on a show of sniffing the air like a sailor searching for shore. "Sorry, perhaps the weather is interfering, but for some reason I can't identify our relative proximity to a town I've never visited and have no knowledge of."

"Then," asked Valentine with impressive patience, "what are we to do?"

"We could look for some woods? Or a bridge, maybe?"

"A bridge? You want us to rest beneath a bridge? Like a troll in a folktale?"

"And your idea is . . . ?"

"An inn? A farmhouse?" Valentine peeled some strands of wet hair from his equally wet face, his tone becoming increasingly desperate. "A stable? Anything? Tarleton, we could die."

"This is England. If people died of rain, there'd be nobody left."

Valentine was going to argue. He really was. But he was too tired and too . . . sad. He was just too sad. "Please, can we at least attempt—"

"Is that . . . something?" Bonny pointed to a glimmer on the horizon.

"I wouldn't care if it was Titania and her entire fairy court. Let's try."

Bonny nodded, easing the bays into a gentle trot. Though somehow, during the conversation, through means imperceptible to Valentine, he had shifted position. Moved . . . closer. And now there was a steady warmth at Valentine's side, shining like that distant light, beating like a second heart.

It felt so good he almost wept.

And over the course of an hour or so, with the rain needle sharp and the sky roiling darkly like a wrathful god, the glimmer became a gleam became a glow. Then finally it was a cottage, jaunty and white painted, with a thatched roof and a scattering of outbuildings—including a well-kept stable, already occupied.

"Oh God," said Valentine, shocking himself with his own fervour. "We're saved."

Bonny was already jumping down from the curricle. "Can you talk to the owners—ideally without shouting at them or lecturing them? I need to take care of my horses."

Once again, Valentine was poised to defend himself. But then came the first rumbles of an impending thunderstorm, which made being *not outside* an even greater imperative than it had been previously. He strode—he assuredly strode, and absolutely did not dash nor scurry—up to the front door of the cottage and gave it a sound rap.

It was opened, with some alacrity, by a plain woman, in an equally plain dress, holding up a lamp against the dark of the evening.

"Madam"—Valentine sketched a bow—"do forgive the intrusion. Is your husband at home?"

Her mouth did something strange and slightly wicked, curling into the most private of smiles. "He most certainly is not."

Ah. "That is rather unfortunate. You see, we were on our way to Rochester when the weather took against us. And here you find us, in rather urgent need of shelter."

"And you wish to shelter with my husband?"

"N-no. No, of course not," said Valentine, laughing and blushing slightly. "But we are two gentlemen travelling alone, and I would not wish to imperil either your reputation or peace of mind."

"I appreciate your concern, but I have a rifle."

Valentine wasn't quite sure what to say to that. "Good for you, madam?"

"And," she added, "I live with a female companion who can act as chaperone should we become overwhelmed with passion for each other."

Valentine wasn't sure what to say to *that* either. So he bowed again.

"Come in." She stepped away from the doorway. "As it happens, you're not the first travellers to run afoul of the weather tonight."

"I . . . we . . . are most grateful, madam."

"And your friend"—she raised her voice to be heard over the rain and the wind—"may stable his horses round the back."

"Thank you," Bonny called in return. "You're an angel. An angel in grey. A greyngel."

The woman's mouth curved into its elusive smile. It became her, Valentine thought, for all she was otherwise unprepossessing. A shame she was not married—for she was clearly a gentlewoman—but unsurprising. "This way, please."

As Valentine stepped inside, heat rolled over him in waves, the pleasure of it enough to make him languorous. Even a little dizzy. He just about managed not to groan in sheer relief in a strange lady's hallway. And then became aware of the mud he was leaving all over the polished flagstones. "I'm terribly sorry. I appear to have brought the storm with me."

"I think under the circumstances you can be forgiven. You must have had quite a journey."

He nodded and explained somewhat piteously, "We've been travelling *all day*."

"A little time by the fire," the woman told him, "will do you the world of good."

The cottage was small and—it was impossible not to notice—somewhat shabby, but meticulously neat. An everyday kind of tragedy: two spinsters doomed to spend the rest of their days in a state of genteel poverty. Still, Valentine admired their commitment to making the best of their situation.

From the parlour drifted the scent of brewing tea. And it took most of Valentine's remaining strength not to tumble over the threshold like a man finding an oasis in a desert. Instead, he followed his hostess as decorously as he could.

"Angharad?" This she addressed to another woman, currently tending to a teapot. "Two more for supper, please. And how remiss of me. I've made no introductions. I'm Miss Fairfax, and this is my companion, Miss Evans."

While Valentine's sense of beauty had always tended towards the abstract, rather than the carnal, there was no escaping the fact that Miss Evans was extraordinary. A vision of Titian-red hair and golden skin, and eyes like the sort of cat ancient Egyptians would have worshipped. It made no sense that such a woman should be unwed—no matter how meagre her portion. Perhaps she had made some deleterious choices or been led cruelly astray. Not, of course, that it was his place to speculate what had brought these two ladies to such a sorry state.

"Thank—" he began.

Before a piercing shriek rent the air and a wild burst of lightning made the room crackle silver.

Arabella Tarleton, who had been sitting by the fire, combing through her wet hair, leapt to her feet. "It is *he*," she cried, pointing a chalk-pale and trembling finger in Valentine's direction.

And then she fainted dead away.

Chapter 15

With instinctive gallantry, Valentine stepped forwards to catch his fiancée as she swooned but was promptly elbowed out of the way by Peggy—into whose arms, instead, Miss Tarleton drifted quite exquisitely.

"How dare you try to touch her, you . . . um . . ." Apparently Peggy lacked her friend's knack for theatricals. "Varlet?"

Valentine stepped away. "Fine. I'll let her crack her head open on the hearth next time."

"Oh, you unfeeling brute." Miss Tarleton opened an eye. "Of course you would love nothing better than my incapacitation or demise."

"Demise," murmured Valentine, "seems too much to hope for. But given I have spent the last two days chasing you across the country, I would indeed welcome your incapacity."

Miss Tarleton uttered another shriek. "You see. He *admits* it. He has no shame."

"I'm terribly sorry." The general excitement had driven Miss Evans from her seat, but now she gave a little jump. "I was just thinking how splendid you look arranged in that fashion. Wouldn't they make the most wonderful painting, Emily?"

"Perhaps they'll be willing to pose for you," remarked her cohabitant. Miss Fairfax had just returned, having briefly quit the room, and Valentine was very much not delighted to observe she had brought a rifle with her. "After we resolve matters between our visitors."

Valentine decided to remain very still. "There is nothing to resolve. This is my fiancée. I simply wish to bring her safely home."

"I told you," cried Miss Tarleton. "I told you he would say that."

Miss Evans was nodding. "She did tell you he would say that."

"I confess"—Miss Fairfax showed no signs of relinquishing her hold on the firearm—"I did think it a little fantastical, and I would know. But this gentleman's arrival seems too great a coincidence."

It was hard to remain polite at rifle point. But it was also vital that Valentine did. "That's because it is not a coincidence. We had a misunderstanding. Miss Tarleton felt compelled to flee me. And I have come to . . . apologise."

"Apologise?" repeated Miss Tarleton, who had clearly recovered from her faint sufficiently to sweep about the room. "You wish to apologise? For imprisoning me? For threatening me? For attempting to force me into matrimony?"

"I'm not forcing you. I'm honouring your parents' wishes."

Miss Tarleton cast herself at Miss Fairfax's feet. "He is not, he is not. They knew not what manner of despicable creature he is when I was entrusted to his guardianship after their passing. He only desires my fortune."

This was . . . increasingly hard to follow. "You don't have any fortune," Valentine reminded her.

"I am an heiress. And he will do anything—*anything*—to possess me."

"Perhaps you should decide," Valentine suggested, "whether I am trying to possess you or your incredible wealth?"

Miss Tarleton burst into tears. *"Both."* And then, clasping her hands together, she turned her piteous gaze upon Miss Fairfax. "Will you help me? Please. I beg you."

Miss Fairfax and Miss Evans exchanged glances.

Which was not at all the reaction Valentine thought the situation warranted. "You must see this is nonsense."

Miss Evans shrugged. "It has happened. There are stories."

"There are indeed stories," agreed Miss Fairfax, with a somewhat wry look.

"And this"—Valentine wanted to make an emphatic gesture, then thought better of it—"is *only* a story. I am the Duke of Malvern. Miss Tarleton is not an heiress. Our engagement was arranged by our families and is of long standing."

Miss Fairfax was frowning slightly. Never a cause for optimism while in the vicinity of a rifle. "If this is true, why would Miss Tarleton run away from you?"

"I was," he conceded, "slightly rude to her."

Miss Tarleton put a hand to her brow. "He lies. He lies. He is full of lies."

"I mean"—that was Miss Evans—"how rude were you?"

"I didn't run away because he was impolite," Miss Tarleton cried. "I ran away because he is vile and cruel and trying to steal my fortune."

"That does sound more plausible," said Miss Evans. For all her beauty, Valentine was beginning to think he did not like Miss Evans. Perhaps she deserved her fate.

Then came the sound of rapid footsteps in the hallway, and the door opened to reveal a rain-soaked and dishevelled Bonny. "I'm so sorry. I tried knocking, but nobody answered. And then I heard shouting and so I—oh my God, you've got a gun. Why is there a gun?"

"Bonny." Miss Tarleton dashed joyously into her brother's arms. "This is Miss Fairfax and Miss Evans. They're my rescuers."

"They're being taken advantage of," Valentine growled. "Your sister has spun them the most absurd fable. Now will you please enlighten them as to the reality of the situation."

To Valentine's surprise, and increasing irritation, Bonny did not immediately speak.

And Miss Tarleton took the opportunity to cast him one of her haughtiest looks. "Absurd fable indeed." She glanced again at Bonny.

"Can you believe he tried to convince them he was the Duke of Malvern?"

Valentine gave an outraged gasp. "But I *am* the Duke of Malvern."

"It does seem a little farfetched." Miss Fairfax took a step towards him, the rifle disconcertingly steady in her hands. "After all, how many dukes are there in England? Perhaps you should have claimed a viscounty? Even an earldom."

"Miss Fairfax"—it was Valentine's most ducal tone, the one that cowed all who had the misfortune to encounter it—"for the last time, I am the Duke of Malvern. And you will regret crossing me."

Her eyes narrowed. "If you are the Duke of Malvern, your taste in coats leaves much to be desired. And where is your signet ring?"

"On my fing—" Oh no. Oh dear. Valentine quickly retracted his hand. "About that. You see, there was an incident. With an ostler. And—"

"Enough." Miss Fairfax had graduated from holding the rifle to brandishing it. "Sit down. At once. We must decide what to do with you."

Valentine stumbled backwards into the nearest chair, his eyes flying frantically to Bonny. "Bonny. Please. Tell them this is a misunderstanding. Tell them who I am."

"I would, but"—Bonny stroked his chin, affecting an attitude of great contemplation—"didn't you recently tell me I shouldn't help you anymore? Never again? Not ever?"

"I didn't envisage a situation like this arising," Valentine protested weakly. "How could I? I more meant . . . with ostlers. That you shouldn't help me with ostlers."

Bonny's gaze was cold and righteous. "Well, that's not what you said, is it?"

There was a fraught silence.

Finally broken by Miss Fairfax. "I confess, I have never held a man at gunpoint before. What happens now?"

"Secure him to the chair?" For most of the previous exchange, Peggy had remained quietly by the fire, her elbow propped on the mantel and a booted foot resting against the fender. "Your hands will get tired otherwise."

"They're quite tired now," admitted Miss Fairfax. "This is hard work."

"Wait. Wait." Valentine did not like the direction of the discourse. "I don't want to be secured to the chair."

But Miss Evans was already glancing about the room. "What can we secure him with?"

"Rope," suggested Peggy, who had chosen an abominable time to get involved. "Anything ropelike. Stockings in a pinch."

Valentine shook his head urgently. "No. Absolutely not. I do not consent to stockings."

"You are being held prisoner," Miss Tarleton told him huffily. "You can't consent to being tied up."

For some reason, everyone found this terribly amusing. And it was an odd moment for Valentine, being very briefly in sympathy with his wife-to-be as they exchanged impatient glances, wishing their companions would treat the situation with the gravity it deserved. Eventually, though, Miss Evans unhooked some of the curtain cords and passed them to Peggy, who set about securing Valentine to the chair. A task she performed with troubling efficiency.

"What have I ever done to you?" Valentine asked her plaintively.

Peggy glanced up from where she was tightening a knot at his ankle. "I'm helping."

"This is very much the opposite of helpful."

"Think what you will, but I have a strong preference for people *not* pointing guns at each other." She stepped away. "There. That should hold him."

Valentine very much wanted to make his feelings known with a supporting gesture, but, as it was, he was forced to rely on tone to convey his general dissatisfaction. "Of course it will hold me. I'm tied to a chair. You've tied a duke to a chair. I hope you're pleased with yourselves."

"Frankly"—Miss Fairfax gave him an appraising look—"I have no idea who we've tied to a chair." She turned the same look upon Miss Tarleton. "Is he really your wicked guardian?"

Miss Tarleton nodded vigorously. "Yes."

Peggy cleared her throat.

"No," Miss Tarleton admitted, hanging her head. "But he *is* trying to marry me against my will."

"I am not." Valentine gave the curtain cords a futile tug. "Well, I mean. She doesn't want to marry me now. But that's only because she's a silly girl who cannot see what will be good for her."

For some reason, this appeal to rational good sense did not please the company.

Miss Fairfax, who had at least set the gun down, crossed the room to stand by Miss Evans. "I'm beginning to see why she might be running away."

"Do you remember"—Miss Evan twined an arm about the other woman's waist—"when we ran away?"

That drew a soft laugh from Miss Fairfax. "I do indeed. My parents found us in a barn and dragged me home."

"But it didn't stop us running away again."

"No," agreed Miss Fairfax.

"And again."

"No."

"And again."

Miss Fairfax was smiling her secret smile. "I would have run away with you a thousand times. A million. I would have run away with you every day and every night." And then she leaned in and kissed her companion full on the lips. What a very strange friendship these women had developed. Perhaps it was the remote location. Or the fact they were jointly estranged from their families.

"Does . . . does this mean you will help us?" asked Miss Tarleton, who was now clinging to Peggy's hand.

There was only Bonny who stood apart, gilded by the firelight, his hair drying in wild curls. He was oddly still, and small for someone given to such extravagances, the look on his face unexpectedly sorrowful, full of naked longing. The moment he realised Valentine was watching, he turned away.

And suddenly Valentine didn't care about rain or hunger or being tied to a chair. All he wanted was for Bonny to smile. To smile forever. To smile for him.

Chapter 16

"Of course we'll help you," Miss Fairfax was saying. "Though I'm not entirely sure how."

Valentine gave another futile tug at his bonds. "I think you've done more than enough helping already."

"I mean"—Miss Fairfax continued as though he hadn't spoken—"we can't keep him tied to a chair forever."

"Can you keep him tied to a chair for a bit, though?" asked Miss Tarleton, before Valentine could get a word in. "While we make our escape?"

A thoughtful pause. "Wouldn't that make us kidnappers?"

"Yes," said Valentine. "Yes, it would."

Miss Tarleton's eyes got very big and very blue. Valentine had seen Bonny's eyes do something very similar. "Please? If we left at once, we would at least have a chance of escaping his hateful machinations."

"You can't leave now. It's a dark and stormy night." Miss Fairfax paused, her head tilting slightly. "'A dark and stormy night.' I wonder . . . is that something?"

"No," Miss Evans told her. "Definitely not."

"Then what about"—Miss Tarleton now turned her pleading eyes upon the company—"if we murdered him?"

Miss Fairfax frowned. "I'm already uncomfortable with the possibility I may have kidnapped him. Do you not think murder would be worse?"

"It would be quicker," explained Miss Tarleton. "If you kidnap someone, then you're stuck with them. But if you murder them, you're done."

Once again, Valentine was not enjoying the direction of the discourse. "You will not like it, Miss Tarleton, if you murder me."

She fixed him with a cold stare. "I daresay you'll like it a good deal less."

"I don't think we should murder him." That was Bonny, who was in the process of removing his soaked-through greatcoat. "I don't think he deserves to be murdered."

"But," enquired Valentine, with a certain degree of resentment, "he does deserve being tied to a chair?"

Bonny's gaze was as cold, if not colder, than his sister's. "Yes. Very much so."

In the silence that followed, Miss Evans lifted a vase of wildflowers from where it had been perfectly adequately residing upon a sideboard and placed it instead between Valentine's knees. "I'm sure he could be quite decorative with a little work."

"I'm not decorative." Valentine gave an outraged squirm. "I'm a person. And this is altogether ridiculous. Let me go."

It was Bonny, in the end, who returned the flowers to their more proper place. "One can be decorative *and* a person. Look at me."

Valentine could have pointed out that he'd done nothing *but* look at Bonny for two days. Look at him. Sit and sleep beside him. Feel the rhythms of his breathing. Live beneath the endless skyscape of his eyes. Except no. What would it have meant if he had? What use would it have served?

"One thing is clear," said Miss Fairfax finally. "Nobody can leave tonight. And we have guests."

The curtain cords were beginning to abrade Valentine's wrists, so he was obliged to stop pulling at them. "I think you'll find, madam, that a detained guest is a prisoner."

She shrugged. "We can debate semantics later. For now, we'll need towels and a fresh pot of tea and some of that wonderful stew Mrs. Baxter made for us."

"Hmm?" Miss Evans blinked. "Sorry, I was just thinking . . . decoratively."

Now Miss Fairfax was kissing her again. Which seemed as unnecessary as it had previously been perplexing. "Sweetheart, do come back to earth for a little and help me take care of our visitors. You may decorate them after, if you wish?"

"I am not to be decorated," said Valentine.

But, in the flurry of activity, nobody was listening. In fact, he became rather irrelevant to proceedings, as a kettle was placed over the fire, towels were retrieved and shared, and steaming bowls of stew were passed around. It was altogether a peculiar, and not entirely pleasant, experience—for all that Valentine never sought attention, he was used to having it as a natural consequence of his wealth and status. Worse still, his attempt to suborn Bonny, who had brought him a warm towel, had been soundly rebuffed. He had point-blank refused—*refused*—to untie Valentine and made some unamusing comment concerning the impropriety of untying a person who one's host had gone to the trouble of tying up.

The towel, though, *that* Valentine had to admit was very welcome. As was the careful way Bonny tucked it round him, brushing the wet hair from his brow, and banishing the raindrops that were still clinging to the back of his neck.

Meanwhile, Miss Evans had cleared a table of papers—why two women living together would need that many papers, Valentine had no idea—and dragged it over to the blaze so that everyone could huddle round it while they ate. The unexpected thought crossed Valentine's mind that firelight could be very kind. It swept away the shabbiness of the room, leaving only its cosiness. The small details—the wildflowers that had briefly decorated Valentine, the embroidered cushions, an open book resting on the arm of the sofa—suggesting a space that was not only lived in but loved.

It gave Valentine the oddest sense of disquiet. Tied to a chair or not, he was relieved to have some shelter from the storm that was still raging with sufficient violence to rattle the shutters. And there would not have been space for him around the table anyway. But watching the others—Peggy braiding Miss Tarleton's hair, Miss Fairfax with head upon Miss Evans's shoulder, Bonny punctuating some story with a needlessly exuberant use of his soup spoon—was like watching a painting.

A world someone else had dreamed up and laid before him.

Except they all lived and breathed and talked and laughed and hoped and felt. He was the one who sat, still and silent, trapped in his unbelonging.

Maybe *he* was the painting. Maybe he always had been.

"Oh." Miss Fairfax gave a little gasp. "Mister . . . um. I'm sorry, what do we call you?"

"Your Grace," Valentine said.

In this instance, the firelight was not kind. For it revealed Miss Fairfax rolling her eyes. "Very well, Your Grace. Can we offer you some of this Irish stew? I'm sure it cannot compete with the delicacies bedecking a ducal table, but it is quite nice."

Bonny's spoon once again pierced the air like a narwhal's horn breaking the ocean's surface. "It's *delicious*."

"And how do you propose I eat it?" Valentine attempted to look down his nose at five people simultaneously. "With the power of thought?"

"We could untie one of his hands," suggested Miss Evans.

But this inspired a fresh shriek from Miss Tarleton. "Please don't. You don't know what he is like. He is cunning and will stop at nothing to—"

"Arabella." Miss Fairfax cut her off gently but firmly. "You do not need to spin us tall tales to make us listen to you."

Miss Tarleton was silent for a moment. "I'm sorry," she said, in a voice unusually devoid of theatricality. "Everything is so much more bearable if you can convince yourself that you're in a novel. Real life is banal. Even its cruelties. Neglect and disregard and circumstance and powerlessness." She gave a bitter little laugh. "Give me ghosts and haunted moors and lost legacies and wicked guardians it is always possible to escape."

"However banal his wickedness"—Miss Fairfax cast a glance at Valentine—"it is clear enough this man frightens you."

Now it was Valentine's turn to roll his eyes. "She is most certainly *not* frightened of me. I have given her no cause."

"Beyond your pursuit of me?" asked Miss Tarleton. "And your determination to marry me irrespective of my feelings on the matter?"

This was infuriating. Mainly because it was deeply, deeply unfair. "I've offered you my name and my fortune and a future in which you will want for nothing. Clearly, I'm a monster."

The look Miss Tarleton slanted at him was that of a wild thing at bay, wary and defiant, before she quickly glanced away again. "He has said terrible things to me."

Valentine's eyes were beginning to ache from the demands of expressing so much scepticism. "Oh, for God's sake."

"When I told him of the unhappiness it would cause me were I to be wed to him," Miss Tarleton went on steadily, "he suggested I go drown in the brook at Malvern Park."

Four heads turned his way, wearing various expressions of incredulity and distaste.

"She . . . she brought up killing herself first," Valentine explained. Although spoken aloud, it was far from the stalwart justification it had been in his head.

Miss Tarleton folded her hands on the table, looking suddenly young and uncertain, in that abominable fashion that seemed unique to the Tarleton twins. "And only yesterday he demanded his right to my unquestioning obedience. I cannot live like that. It will destroy me. It would destroy anyone."

Put like that, it sounded unfortunate. And made Valentine more than a little uncomfortable. "In my defence, when I said that, I was very angry."

Miss Fairfax and Miss Evans were exchanging glances again.

"I think," Miss Fairfax said finally, "you and your protector should leave in the morning. We will decide what to do with this gentleman then."

"Will you—" began Miss Tarleton eagerly.

"No, we will not murder him."

While it was true that Valentine would never previously have counted *stew* among his preferred dishes, the scent of it—all rich and wholesome—drifting through the room was making him grumpy. "Of course," he said, "he might conveniently starve to death."

"Oh dear." Miss Fairfax wrung her hands. "I hadn't realised tying someone to a chair was going to prove so complicated."

Stew bowl in hand, Bonny rose and crossed the room to Valentine. "I can share."

Valentine glared at him—because it was far easier to blame Bonny than blame himself, and to be angry rather than ashamed. "Alternatively, you could put a stop to this nonsense."

"How?" asked Bonny, with a spuriously innocent look.

"By accepting your point has, once again, been well made and well taken, and explaining the situation. Please."

"But you claimed"—Bonny wagged his spoon—"you didn't want my help ever again. And, frankly, I don't feel like giving you my help right now. Except to have some stew, because you shouldn't go hungry."

Valentine closed his eyes for a moment. When he opened them, he was still in the parlour of two strange women. Still tied to a chair. Still being beheld with distaste by two Tarletons. Still very much not having a terrible dream. "When I said I didn't want your help . . . I spoke imprudently."

"And the other things you said?"

Valentine swallowed. They had been worse than imprudent.

But before he could begin to address them, Miss Tarleton elbowed her way sharply into the conversation. "What did he say to you?"

"Oh, you know . . ." Bonny shrugged. "That because I am a gentleman who favours gentleman, I will never be happy or loved or—"

There was a surge of motion from the table. Followed by another surge that turned out to be Peggy seizing Miss Tarleton before she could descend upon Valentine.

"I shall kill him myself," declared Miss Tarleton. Who had managed to lay hands on a knife—albeit only a butter knife, so she would likely have found more success attempting to spread Valentine on toast than murder him with it. "My brother knows more of happiness or love than a man like you could even begin to imagine. All he needs is someone worthy to recognise it."

"Belladonna, it's fine. It's fine." Except, in that moment, Bonny sounded so unbearably sad. He turned to Valentine with a trembling semblance of a smile. "So. Stew?"

Glancing from the bowl to the spoon in Bonny's hand and then to Bonny's face, Valentine shook his head firmly. "Under no circumstances. I cannot imagine anything more demeaning."

"Then starve"—Bonny was already turning away again—"with dignity."

"I intend to."

Which, with hindsight, was not quite the devastating put-down Valentine had intended for it to be.

Considering he was tied up, recently drenched, surrounded by people who thought about as badly of him as it was possible to do, and deprived of stew, dignity was about all Valentine had left to him. And he felt he did a more than reasonable job of maintaining it over the course of the evening. He kept his own counsel and tried to distract himself with thoughts of happier times.

Of hot baths and beautifully fitted coats and an extremely competent valet. Of long lie-ins and exquisitely prepared meals. Of being universally regarded with admiration. And even, perhaps, a little awe.

Except that life—his life—hadn't gone anywhere. He would likely be returned to it in a matter of days. And—given how recent events had gone—a failure to his father's memory but free of marital obligations. Free to continue as he had always done. Yet, somehow, the thought brought him little comfort. And his attention kept being drawn irresistibly back to the group by the fire.

"How about," Miss Tarleton was saying, "we play a game to pass the time. I simply adore games."

That, thought Valentine bitterly, was self-evident.

Bonny sprang from his chair. "Me too. Me too. There's perishingly few games you can play with two."

"Hello," put in Peggy. "I exist."

"Or *three*," Bonny amended hastily. "But you always say we form alliances against you."

"Well, you do."

It was apparently Miss Tarleton's turn to deploy the Tarleton pout. "We can't help ourselves. We're twins."

"What kind of game did you have in mind?" asked Miss Fairfax before the situation could devolve into a squabble.

"Any game." Miss Tarleton bounced up beside her brother. Then gave a little gasp. "What about charades. Can we play charades?"

Bonny bobbed about fervently. "Can we?"

Two sets of eyes grew jointly large, blue, and pleading. Valentine had never seen people so happy to be trapped in a cottage during a thunderstorm, nor so excited at the possibility of parlour games with a couple of strangers. It gave him the oddest pang, remembering what Bonny had told him of their stories and secret worlds.

"No." That was Miss Evans, who clearly had a heart of stone. "I'm sorry, but no. Charades is fatal to my happiness."

Miss Tarleton looked crestfallen. "How can charades be fatal to anyone's happiness?"

"Because Emily comes up with the most impossible things and then gets angry *with me* when I have no idea how to decipher them."

Miss Fairfax glanced up from whatever she was writing. "They are not impossible. And as my life's partner, my wife in all but paper, you should understand the way my mind works."

"I know you better than I know my own soul," protested Miss Evans. "But you are *terrible* at charades."

Miss Fairfax put down her pen with an irate clack. "I am not terrible at charades. I am a *writer*. I have a unique capacity for them."

"Dearest, no." Miss Evans was shaking her head in some alarm. "No. I love you. But no."

"Perhaps," suggested Miss Tarleton slyly, "you should try us with one of your charades, and then we can decide whether you or Miss Evans has the right of it."

Miss Evans uttered a wounded howl.

Miss Fairfax, however, gazed at the twins with approval. "What a wonderful idea."

"You have no notion what you've done." Groaning, Miss Evans sank into the nearest chair and put her face in her hands. "I would run onto the moors, except we don't live near any moors and it's rather cold and wet out there."

There was a momentary lull as Miss Fairfax prepared her charade, the twins standing before her like foxhounds awaiting the view halloo. Peggy, meanwhile, had gone to lounge by the fire. And Valentine tried not to be perturbed by the fact she was still in trousers. To tell himself it was none of his business.

But he could see her *legs*. They were right there.

Miss Fairfax cleared her throat. Then, with great ceremony, delivered the following: "Who murdered all the chickens."

"Um," said Bonny. "Pardon?"

"Who," repeated Miss Fairfax, "murdered all the chickens."

The twins stared at each other in puzzlement.

"I warned you," Miss Evans told them. "You can't say I didn't warn you."

Miss Tarleton and Bonny formed a sort of huddle, fragments of their whispering occasionally catching Valentine's ear:

Who murdered all the chickens?

Does "all" perchance refer to a whole word?

Could the answer mean some variety of chicken?

So then "who murdered" would be . . .

Could it be to rearrange the letters?

But the letters of what?

The word "who"?

"Wait," cried Bonny. "I have it. If we rearrange the letters of the word *who*, we get the word *how*, and how murdered would be some manner of weapon, I suppose?"

Miss Tarleton immediately chimed in. "So that means it's a breed of chicken that is also a weapon. Like . . . like . . . the Sussex poniard."

"Belle, darling"—Peggy glanced over—"that's not a real chicken."

"It might very well be."

"But it is not," Miss Fairfax informed them loftily, "the correct answer."

Once again, Miss Evans lifted her head. "Please stop trying. This will be something that makes sense only to Emily."

"Some other form of chicken then?" persisted Miss Tarleton. "The venomous brown. The spotted bardiche. The lowland slaughter hen."

Peggy was laughing helplessly. "Stop inventing poultry."

"I think"—Miss Fairfax glowed smugly—"I shall have to tell you the answer."

Miss Tarleton emitted an unladylike yelp. "No. I'm sure I shall hit upon it eventually."

"Tell them, Emily," said Miss Evans. "Tell them, for the love of God."

"French exploding bantam!" cried Miss Tarleton.

"The solution . . ." Miss Fairfax let the pause linger. "Is . . ." More lingering. "Claudius."

"Is that," enquired Valentine, since nobody else seemed to know how to break the silence, "some kind of chicken?"

Miss Fairfax subjected him to a withering look. "Of course not. He's a character in *Hamlet*."

"Hamlet's uncle?" Valentine blinked. "That Claudius? What on earth does he have to do with murdering all the chickens?"

"Do not—" began Miss Evans.

But it was too late. "Because, Your Grace"—Miss Fairfax was glowing again—"he committed murder *most foul*."

Silence descended like the guillotine.

"I don't know what to say," offered Bonny finally.

"I think," Peggy added, "some corner of my soul has withered and died."

Miss Evans rose and put a hand on her shoulder. "Best never to think or speak of this again."

"What is wrong with you all?" Miss Fairfax was regarding them with an expression both wounded and disbelieving. "That was an excellent charade."

"And I love that you think that, Emily," said Miss Evans.

Something strange was happening to Valentine. Maybe he was unwell. Maybe he was developing brain fever from having been out in the rain. But before he even understood what was happening, he was laughing.

He was laughing without reason or gentility. Laughing so hard it made him weep. So hard it hurt his throat. The sort of laughing that came tearing up from somewhere deep and impossible. Somewhere that should have been—that needed to be—locked up tight. Somewhere that had made the joy almost indistinguishable from pain.

Chapter 17

"I'm beginning to think," said Miss Fairfax, as Valentine gasped for breath, "it might not have been a good charade."

Bonny was kneeling in front of him. "Flower? Are you all right?"

"Y-yes?" Valentine's eyes were full of water. His voice little more than a rasp. "Yes. It was just so . . . just so . . . terribly unamusing."

It was the first time Bonny had smiled at Valentine all day, and it pierced him like sunlight. "You are very, very strange."

"It takes one to know one," Valentine told him primly.

And then Bonny—still smiling—brushed a tear from the corner of one of Valentine's eyes. The motion was too deft, and Valentine was too tied to a chair, for the touch to be anything other than fleeting. As light as petals upon the breeze. But it still shivered its way through Valentine's whole body, a flicker of heat and motion, a stranger's skin that did not, in that moment, feel strange.

"Perhaps we should not play charades," remarked Miss Tarleton, flinging herself into a chair. Valentine had no idea why nobody in that family could just sit down.

Miss Evans threw a cushion towards Miss Fairfax. "Now look what you've done. You've ruined fun for the young people."

"I think you'll find"—Miss Fairfax threw a piece of scrunched-up paper back at Miss Evans—"that the problem here, as ever, is your failure to appreciate my genius."

"I hope you're not implying we're anything like what's-his-name. That Lebeau fellow."

"Who's the Lebeau fellow?" asked Bonny, immediately curious.

Miss Evans waved a dismissive hand. "A critic. He writes for *The Monthly Review*. He called Emily's last book 'sensationalist drivel fit only for ladies and the simple minded.'"

"Which would have stung more," added Miss Fairfax, "had I not sold three thousand copies on the first day."

From where she was ensconced by the fire, Peggy gave a low chuckle. "Long live ladies and the simple minded."

Miss Tarleton was now gazing raptly at Miss Fairfax. "You're a writer? How marvellous. I have always wanted to be a writer, but it involves so much *work*."

"A peril of the profession, I'm afraid," murmured Miss Fairfax.

"Have you written anything we would know? I do hope it's not virtuous?"

Miss Fairfax's lips twitched. "I disapprove strongly of virtuous books. I think they're bad for the mind. Though I don't actually write under my own name—I sound too much like a spinster aunt, and not enough like a spinner of lurid horrors."

It was hard to conceive a state of raptitude that existed beyond the raptness Miss Tarleton had already manifested. Somehow she achieved it. "Oh, Miss Fairfax, I love lurid horrors. We grew up so deprived of them."

"Well"—Miss Fairfax's pale face had actually gone a little pink— "I'm . . . that is, I write as . . . it's nothing really. But you might—"

"She's Ambrosia Blaine," said Miss Evans.

Miss Fairfax nodded. "Yes, my last book—"

But she got no further because both Miss Tarleton and her brother had erupted into wild screaming.

"*The True and Shocking Confessions of Sir Willoughby Harkness,*" they chorused.

Valentine opened his mouth. Then closed it again. That he had devoured the book, in the privacy of his bedchamber, was a secret he preferred to keep. Even from the author. Even if part of him was desperate to ask whether the vengeful shepherdess truly was Sir Willoughby's illegitimate daughter, or whether that had been a devious fiction concocted by the monks.

Miss Tarleton pressed her hands to her chest. "We were desperate for a copy. *Desperate*. But Uncle Wilbur wasn't able to find one, so he brought us Richard Bradley's *A General Treatise of Husbandry and Gardening* instead."

"Are the confessions *very* shocking?" asked Bonny, breathlessly.

Miss Fairfax nodded. "They are soul-curdlingly shocking. And the printer sent me several spare copies, so you may have one, if you wish."

Both twins were nodding so fervently it was a wonder their heads didn't fall off. "We wish."

"I think"—Miss Evans peered under the table—"there's one under the wobbly leg here."

"Under the wobbly leg?" repeated Miss Tarleton, falling to her knees and rescuing the book—at some peril to the table. "How could you?"

Miss Fairfax shrugged. "Well, one must make one's work useful to oneself somehow or other. But, how about another charade? I think I have the perfect—"

"No." The response was universal.

"Oh." She looked crestfallen.

"Perhaps"—Miss Tarleton guiltily closed the copy of *The True and Shocking Confessions of Sir Willoughby Harkness*, which she had already begun reading—"we could play a different game?"

"Yes," Bonny agreed. "What about . . . do you have a copy of Dr. Johnson's dictionary? We could play the Dr. Johnson's dictionary game."

Both Miss Evans and Miss Fairfax looked perplexed. "I don't think we know that one."

"Well"—Bonny offered a slightly embarrassed smile—"I don't think it's . . . known exactly. It's more sort of a thing you can do with a dictionary."

"I'm beginning to suspect," said Miss Fairfax, "that you two must have had a very interesting childhood."

"Oh no," returned Miss Tarleton, "we didn't at all. Why else do you think we were reduced to finding things to do with a dictionary?"

Miss Evans had gone to an overstuffed bookcase in order to retrieve a battered copy of *A Dictionary of the English Language*. "How is it played?"

Once they were all huddled around the table again, Miss Tarleton explained. And, since Valentine had no other way to either occupy himself or pass the time, he listened. Of course, he had no wish to join in, for parlour games were exceedingly childish. And—he remembered—he neither knew nor cared for any of these people anyway.

The game required the appointment of a Dictionary Master and/or Mistress—who was responsible for choosing a word and noting down its definition from the book. Everyone else had to come up with their own definition. And apparently one "won" by either identifying the correct definition or convincing others yours was correct.

Bonny went first, selecting *lucubrátory*, and then reading out the following definitions: "A small ornamental pot," "composed by candlelight," "composed by candlelight," "in an amorous mood," "greasy like the Scots."

"Well," said Miss Tarleton thoughtfully. "This hasn't quite worked because we have two definitions that are identical, and usually when that happens it's the correct answer."

Miss Fairfax frowned. "Of course it's the correct answer. Surely everyone knows what *lucubrátory* means."

"Darling"—Miss Evans leaned in to mock-whisper—"not knowing what the word means is rather the point of the game."

"But it's obvious. It's from the Latin: *lucubror*." A pause. Then, "Have I ruined another game?" wailed Miss Fairfax.

Bonny grinned. "To be fair, this round came preruined because Peggy always says 'small ornamental pot—'"

"Well, someday," muttered Peggy, "it may very well be a small ornamental pot."

"And," Bonny went on, "'greasy like the Scots' is Belle's attempt to subtly deceive us by being rude like Dr. Johnson."

By popular agreement, they passed the dictionary to Miss Fairfax, who selected *vaginopennous*. This time the definitions were: "A small ornamental pot," "a portmanteau term of abuse," "having the wings covered with hard cases," "a species of mouse native to the Americas," "a type of musical notation."

"That was not me," cried Peggy. "Someone is attempting an elaborate bluff at my expense."

Bonny nodded. "Yes, it's Belle."

"It is not," insisted Belle. "But"—she waved her finger in the air—"if Peggy did not suggest the ornamental pot, then it must—on this occasion—be the correct definition."

Miss Evans shrugged. "Makes sense to me."

"No"—that was Bonny—"it's definitely Belle."

Valentine cleared his throat. "I believe the correct answer is the one about the wings?"

"Who asked you?" snapped Miss Tarleton, glowering. "Can we gag him?"

Being tied to a chair had quickly ascended to the top of Valentine's list of Bad Things That Had Happened to Him. And he had absolutely no wish to see it surpassed by being tied to a chair and then gagged. "I'm sorry. I didn't mean to—I'm sorry."

"No, it's—" Bonny started. "You can . . ."

Was that warmth in his eyes? Or pity? Either way, Valentine wanted none of it. Or, at the very least, didn't deserve it. "I hardly think so." He took a deep breath. "Frankly, I don't know what possessed me. If you don't know what *vaginopennous* is, that's entirely your own misfortune." If he hadn't been tied up, he would have pointedly turned away. As it was, he contrived to look loftily in a different direction.

"My apologies." It would have been easier—better—if there'd been anger in Bonny's tone. Instead, there was only a kind of wistfulness. "I keep hoping you're someone you're not."

Miss Tarleton put her hand over his. "He's not, Bonbon. No handsome duke is coming to save us, nor ever was. Our fate is our own."

"I am *trying* to save you," Valentine grumbled. "You keep running away."

"Your Grace"—Miss Tarleton's tone abruptly lost its warmth—"being married to you would be no rescue."

"Because being married to you would be a veritable picnic."

"Argument?" asked Miss Fairfax. "Or game?"

"My turn, I believe." A fluttering of pages as Miss Evans commandeered the dictionary. "And the word is: *gabion.*"

The scratch of pens upon paper. A thoughtful sigh. A poorly repressed giggle. Valentine wasn't sure what he would have written—since he didn't know the word, he would have needed to come up with something convincing to fool the others. Gabion . . . gabion . . . gabion.

Sir Horley. You, sir, are a gabion . . .

That sounded plausible. Gabion: a person of low moral character. Would that make Bonny laugh? Would he guess it was Valentine's, the way he always recognised his sister's?

More papery noises. "Let's see then," said Miss Evans. "Gabion: 'A wicker basket which is filled with earth to make a fortification or intrenchment.'"

Who had come up with that? Miss Fairfax perhaps? Personally, Valentine preferred his own definition.

Another slip was unfolded. "Gabion: 'An ornamental pot.'"

A few soft chuckles.

A third slip: "Gabion: 'An ornamental pot.'" Then the fourth: "Gabion: 'An ornamental pot.'" And finally the fifth: "Gabion: 'An orn—' Oh, for heaven's sake."

And by now everyone was laughing.

Well. Everyone except Valentine. After all, these weren't his friends. And it was their game and their joke. And Bonny had been right and wrong at the same time—because it was starting to feel as though the problem was less about who Valentine *was* and more about who he wanted to be.

Who he wanted to be was a man who made Bonny smile and flirt and shine. A man who knew how to play. Who wasn't just this composition of duty and decorum, and of distance carefully maintained. He wanted to be the man who could chase the shadows from those blue-forever eyes.

Unfortunately, he had no idea *how*.

If it was even possible. What it would mean if it was.

Chapter 18

It was a long evening, and Valentine's thoughts were wayward. But there was something lulling too. In the rhythm of the rain, the heat of the fire, and the laughter as the game became increasingly ridiculous. Exhausted by the travails of the day, and his own wonderings, he must have dozed a little, for when he next looked up, Bonny was in the process of carrying his soundly sleeping sister up to bed.

The dictionary was still on the table, but the people had dissipated somewhat. Miss Fairfax was writing, Miss Evans was sketching, and Peggy posed somewhat self-consciously before the fire.

". . . make the most splendid gothic hero," Miss Evans was saying.

Peggy brushed a glossy lock of hair from where it was inclined to fall across her brow. "Wouldn't I need a dark and terrible secret?"

Glancing up from her papers, Miss Fairfax nodded. "That would be traditional."

"It seems," Peggy remarked, "like it would be a lot of work. Having a dark and terrible secret."

A thoughtful pause. Then Miss Fairfax offered, "Perhaps you could be one of those gothic heroes who acts as though they have a dark and terrible secret and then, when you reach the final chapter, leaves you with an unmistakable feeling of, 'Oh, is that it?'"

"How about"—Peggy's expression grew quizzical—"not that type either."

Miss Evans's pencil scratched gently at the paper. "But you don't object, I hope, playing the hero for me?"

"Not at all."

"You would make an equally delightful heroine."

Peggy shrugged. "Hero. Heroine. In an ideal world, one would be both."

It was at this juncture that Bonny returned, closing the door gently behind him before he cast himself Tarleton-style onto the sofa. "Poor Belle. She's had a rough few days."

She'd had a rough few days? She hadn't been chasing herself.

"You're welcome to stay a little," said Miss Fairfax. "If you wish."

"I would love to"—Bonny heaved a sigh—"but I doubt Belle will agree."

Peggy nodded. "Yes, I'm not an expert on running away, but I do think Belle would argue the *running* part was critical."

"Where are you running to?" asked Miss Fairfax.

"The Americas."

Miss Fairfax spluttered into her tea. "You know you can have a life together, for example, not in the Americas."

"I'm not sure we're going to have a life together exactly," said Peggy. "But something will come about."

"What does that mean?" Miss Evans had momentarily paused in her sketching.

"Just, Belle isn't a forever kind of woman. I'd be a fool to think she was." Peggy shrugged. "And, for all I know, she'll probably get to Dover and then want to do something else entirely."

"What if she doesn't?" That was Bonny.

Peggy considered it carefully. "Then . . . I suppose I'll be in the Americas." She glanced over at Bonny. "Have you two declared pax?"

He shuffled miserably. "Oh, you know how she is. It's all or nothing; with me or against me; everything is the end of the world."

"Indeed." Peggy's sympathetic tone was belied by her expression. "Because that's certainly not like anyone else I can think of."

Bonny's hand flew to his brow. "Slander. Outrage. Impugnation."

"You are at odds?" enquired Miss Fairfax. "Arabella didn't mention that—only a fortune and a wicked guardian and possibly ghosts? I think there were ghosts."

Miss Evans nodded. "I remember ghosts. And a highwayman?"

"Well, there are none of those things," Bonny told them. "Just the mousetrap of circumstances. And a mistake on my part that felt like a betrayal."

"She betrayed you first." Valentine hardly knew he was about to speak until he'd spoken. "She was the one who left."

The look Bonny turned on him was infinitely weary. "Oh, flower. When you hurt someone you love, you don't keep score."

"She'll forgive you," Peggy said. "You know she will."

"I know." Bonny's voice had gone terribly small. "But I should have trusted her. Instead of . . ." He trailed away, his meaning all too clear.

Peggy toed idly at the grate. "Come on, Bonster. It's hardly your fault the fellow turned out to be the most colossal arsehole."

That made Valentine gasp. He had not behaved in line with his usual standards, certainly. But the circumstances had been extraordinary. "I feel," he told them, with all the wounded dignity of a man tied to a chair and then called names, "the magnitude of my arsehole has been somewhat exaggerated."

There was the sort of silence Valentine never again wished to experience.

He shrunk into his bonds. "That . . . that did not quite come out correctly. I would appreciate it greatly were we to pretend I did not exist."

They all turned obligingly away.

"Valentine may not be my fault," Bonny finally went on, "but *I* am my fault. And I was . . . I think I was jealous."

Jealous? Valentine suddenly started existing again.

Miss Evans reclaimed her pencil. "It's normal enough to be protective of our family members."

"This wasn't that." Tucking a knee under him, Bonny had retreated into himself a little. "I mean, it sounds so romantic, doesn't it? Marriage to a duke you've been promised to since birth."

"Wait a moment." Miss Fairfax's head came up. "He *is* a duke? Truly?"

"Maybe," admitted Bonny, wincing. "Kind of. A little bit."

Miss Fairfax turned wide eyed to Miss Evans. "Oh my God. We've tied a duke to a chair. Is that treason? I think that could be treason."

"No, no"—Miss Evans waved her free hand dismissively—"it's only treason if it's royalty."

"I wish," muttered Miss Fairfax, "I felt more reassured by that."

Bonny stole a little peep at Valentine. "But you can see what I mean, can't you? If you didn't know he was a colossal arsehole."

Valentine wasn't entirely sure what Bonny was driving at, but he felt it was to his detriment that both Peggy and Miss Fairfax were shaking their heads.

"I'm afraid I'm simply not fashioned to see such things in gentlemen," was Miss Fairfax's judgement. Whereas Peggy's was, "The problem with me is, once I've seen an arsehole, I can't unsee it."

"I can see it," offered Miss Evans. "From a purely aesthetic point of view."

"And of course," Bonny continued, "I don't want anyone to have to get married when they don't want to. But it's . . . it's hard when you can't have something that other people do."

Miss Fairfax rose and went to Miss Evans, resting her hands lightly on the other woman's shoulders. "It's less important than you think it is."

"You would say that." Miss Evans tilted her head back, smiling up at Miss Fairfax. "You don't believe in God. You heathen."

Miss Fairfax leaned down to kiss her. There was, Valentine was concluding, something more than a little suspect in the way these two women lived. "Technically, my love, a heathen belongs to a religion not recognised as such by a different religion. I am an atheist. But our relationship does not require an external authority to make it real. Nor"—she glanced towards Bonny—"would any you chose to embark upon."

"I know, I know," said Bonny, a touch impatiently. "It's more the principle. And the fact it's how the stories always seem to end. When mine never can."

Miss Fairfax regarded him steadily. "The stories end with love. That's what is important."

"S-sometimes I wonder . . ." Bonny gave a little sniff. "Sometimes I wonder how I am to even have that."

"Time?" Miss Fairfax's tone was unusually gentle. "An open heart. A little luck."

Peggy nodded encouragingly. "And all that flirting you do can't hurt."

"That's true." With a visible effort, Bonny straightened his shoulders and blinked the shimmer of tears from his eyes. "I am a very dedicated coquette. Are there lumberjacks in America? I feel I would be very appreciated by lumberjacks."

"There are lumberjacks in England," Peggy pointed out.

One of Bonny's most determined head tosses. "Well, I want to meet the American kind. So, I'm coming with you tomorrow."

"Bonbon . . ."

"It's already agreed. Belle's my sister. She doesn't want to marry Valentine, and I can't say I blame her. There's nothing for us in England anyway. If she's running away, I'm running away with her."

At this, Peggy swallowed a growling sound, flicking her fingers in a gesture of exasperation. "Look, I'm aware she's in a snit. But she knows you love her. You don't have to prove that by doing everything she asks."

"Neither do you," Bonny said simply.

To which Peggy had no answer.

Valentine, however, had many questions. "Am I to understand that you are now *also* proposing to flee overseas?"

"I am." Bonny's gaze was cool. "And I don't quite see what business it is of yours."

To be honest, Valentine didn't either. But it felt as though it ought to be. To lose one Tarleton would be a shame. To lose two—actually that might be a blessed relief. Or so it should have been. But the thought of Bonny being in some unknown and distant place, with or without lumberjacks, was well-nigh unbearable.

"No," he said, in a strangled voice. "You can't. I forbid it."

Bonny rolled to his feet, heaving a sigh up from his soul. "Flower, when will you learn? I am no more yours to command than Belle is."

"But . . . but . . ."

"But what?" Bonny's tone had softened unexpectedly. "But what, Valentine?"

How could Valentine even begin to answer that?

Crossing the room, Bonny rested his hands upon the arms of Valentine's chair. He was too close. His eyes far too intent. Far too hopeful. "Is there something I haven't considered? Something I'm not aware of? Some reason I might want to stay?"

Valentine's throat had closed up.

"Well?" Bonny's breath was warm upon Valentine's lips. "Is there? Could there be?"

"No," Valentine said.

Miss Fairfax cleared her throat. "This is all very well. And yet we still have a duke, tied to a chair in our parlour."

"Can't you keep him?" Bonny asked. He walked away from Valentine as if nothing had happened. As if Valentine was dust.

Truthfully, he felt like dust.

"Keep him?" Miss Fairfax did not seem overly enamoured of the notion.

Not enamoured of it himself, Valentine gave the curtain cords a yank hard enough to make the wood creak. "Keep me?"

"Just for a couple of days?" Bonny suggested. "Or even a day. That would let us make our escape."

To give Miss Fairfax due credit, she was clearly as inexperienced at having a captive as Valentine was at being one. "What are we to do with him?"

"You will let me go," said Valentine, very softly. "Immediately. Or I shall have the law upon you."

Miss Fairfax cringed. "You must forgive me, but that rather discourages me from allowing you liberty."

"For the last time"—Valentine gave another frantic pull, his wrists burning as the fabric rubbed, and his voice rising despite his best intentions—"I am a duke. I am a duke. I am a duke. You cannot do this to a duke."

"Direct experience suggests otherwise." For all the bravado in her words, Miss Evans had taken a step closer to Miss Fairfax.

"What do you want?" demanded Valentine, as the arm of the chair began to splinter. "Whatever you want, I can give you. Name your price and I shall see it met."

But Miss Fairfax was shaking her head. "I already have everything I want. Now can you please stop struggling? I'm concerned you're going to hurt yourself or—"

The crack of breaking wood rent the room. And Valentine lurched sideways like some kind of monstrous creation, half man, half chair, waving his newly freed arm wildly.

Someone screamed.

"Let's not do anything ra—" began Peggy.

At which point Valentine collided with the wobbly table. It was a ferocious battle: chair versus table, all legs and arms, shattering teacups and wood crashing against wood, with Valentine thrashing somewhere in the middle.

"Oh no," cried Miss Fairfax. "My teacups. My table. That's my favourite chair."

Valentine was still fighting with the furniture. "Damn your chair, madam. All the way to hell."

"I really think you should sit down." With the air of one approaching a wounded beast, Peggy was inching slowly towards him.

"I *am* sitting down," Valentine roared.

He made a positively herculean attempt to extricate his chair from the table, flailing with an arm that, while mobile, was still securely bound to a heavy piece of wood. And he flailed with such uncoordinated vigour that—when Peggy stooped to assist him—she was struck across the ribs with what amounted to a mahogany cudgel and sent sprawling backwards onto the rug.

Valentine froze. "Did I . . . dear God. I'm so sorry. Are you—"

"Get away from her."

Turning his head as best he could, Valentine discovered Miss Tarleton standing in the doorway, holding the rifle that he very much hoped he had seen the last of earlier.

"I . . . ," Peggy wheezed. "I'm . . . I'm fine."

Miss Tarleton—who was clad only in a borrowed nightgown—waved the rifle with alarming gusto. "He struck you."

"Let's not shoot him, though." To Valentine's great relief, Miss Fairfax extricated the gun from Miss Tarleton's grip.

"Can you sit up?" Leaving her now-scattered sketches, Miss Evans knelt down by Peggy. "Are you hurt?"

Peggy wheezed again. "Winded. Probably have a . . . an alluring bruise."

"You could have a broken rib."

"Don't . . . think so. Know how it feels. Fell into a cow once."

"I really am," Valentine began, "most sincerely sorry. It was not my intent to—"

He fell silent abruptly as Miss Fairfax—freshly armed—advanced upon him. "With all due respect, Your Grace, and you may interpret my use of that particular phrase in whatever fashion you prefer, I think we've had quite enough of you for one night."

Valentine would have protested. But he was, in that moment, not inclined to disagree. It was partially the firearm. Partially the fact he was—in all honesty—sick of himself.

"Bonny, can you untie him, please? Angharad, the spare blankets in the upstairs cupboard? Can you fetch them?"

Miss Evans vanished at once. Bonny hesitated.

"You're not going to hit me with a chair, are you?" he asked.

Valentine shook his head meekly. "I assure you I am not in the habit of hitting anyone with . . . anything."

"Apart from just now?" Miss Tarleton was less shooting daggers from her eyes than she was shooting bayonets. "When you did?"

What followed was an altogether sober affair, with Valentine striving to offer as little threat as possible while Bonny undid the knots securing him to what remained of Miss Fairfax's chair—all under the watchful eye (and rifle) of Miss Fairfax herself. Given that Valentine had spent most of the evening desiring his liberty, it was uniquely painful to finally obtain it under the present circumstances. Though, he had to admit, probably not as uniquely painful as being smashed in the midriff by a man strapped to a blunt instrument.

When the chair-Valentine emancipation operation had been completed, he was given a lamp and the blankets Miss Evans had retrieved, and then guided, at gunpoint, into the kitchen. He went quietly. It seemed very much for the best.

"I'm afraid," Miss Fairfax told him, "you're going to have to spend the night in the cellar."

Valentine blinked. "In the where?"

"In the cellar. It's quite clean."

"*Quite* clean?"

"I don't see you've left us much choice."

"You could"—the desperation Valentine caught creeping into his voice was real and mortifying—"tie me to a chair again?"

Miss Fairfax was not moved. "You are clearly not to be trusted with being tied to chairs."

"I would be on my best tied-to-a-chair behaviour," Valentine pleaded.

"I think we would all feel a lot more comfortable if you were locked in the cellar."

Valentine hung his head. "I would not feel particularly comfortable."

"I'm afraid your comfort has about as much priority to us as other people's has to you."

Once again, Valentine wanted to protest. But what could he say? He had not been required to think of anyone except himself for . . . well. Now he considered the matter, his entire life. It was perhaps understandable he had not formed the habit. Understandable. Not defensible. "How long must I remain in the cellar?" he asked instead.

"Just for tonight. We'll let you out tomorrow, when the others have departed. And hope, I suppose, that you do not have us arrested."

Ah yes. He had a hazy, chair-rage-swamped memory of threatening them with the law. "I will not have you arrested. I . . . you are being very kind. To the Tarletons."

Miss Fairfax shrugged. "It began as kindness. Now we've met you, it seems more like basic humanity." She gestured with the rifle. "Down there, if you please."

So Valentine descended the narrow stone stairwell that he presumed led to the cellar. At about the halfway point, he was struck by a fresh though. "Are there," he wondered, "are there spiders in the cellar?"

"Some, but you have the lamp. I doubt they will trouble you."

She was wrong. Very, very wrong. Because Valentine would be very, very troubled. "I am not, ah, overly fond of spiders."

"Then should one form a tendre for you, be courteous, and let the poor creature down gently."

That was not quite his meaning. But it was difficult to demand acts of spider-related compassion from a woman whose favourite chair you had recently destroyed. Especially when you had also, albeit inadvertently, used part of the recently destroyed favourite chair to bludgeon a guest. Without further appeals to Miss Fairfax's mercy, Valentine continued his journey to the underworld. Putting his shoulder to the cellar door, he shoved it open and then stepped into the room beyond.

The door closed behind him almost immediately. It was made of such heavy wood that Valentine heard neither the key turn in the lock nor Miss Fairfax walking away. There was just stone and silence. And the pool of fragile radiance afforded by his lamp.

This was not . . . it was not ideal.

Chapter 19

There were definitely spiders in the cellar. Valentine hadn't seen one, but he knew they were there. He could feel them in the darkness, twitching their long legs, watching him with their many eyes. What if one of them crawled on him? Worse, what if one of them crawled *into* him. That happened, didn't it? He had read something or heard something. About how spiders would go in your mouth or into your ears or up your nose and spin webs inside you and hatch baby spiders until they burst out of you and you *died*. Thinking about it, that last bit seemed somewhat implausible. But the rest of it? If a spider crept into his mouth while he was sleeping, then he would wake up with a *spider in his mouth*. And that was the worst thing he could imagine. Worse even than being harassed by a bee or tied to a chair.

As far as cellars went, Valentine was blessedly low on comparative experiences. But Miss Fairfax had been correct in her assessment that this one was *quite clean*. It contained a variety of the sort of thing that, Valentine assumed, cellars contained: sacks and crates and barrels, trunks of who-knew-what, disused furniture, old easels and piles of manuscripts. Yet all was neatly stacked into corners, and while the air had that stagnant quality one associated with being underground, it was neither dusty nor damp.

There was also a narrow window set high into one of the walls that, when Valentine stood on a box to peer through it, offered him an ant's-eye view of a cobbled path and the stables beyond. He wondered if, the next time the House was in session, he ought to raise the matter of the penal system. Being imprisoned was dreadful.

If he stood on the very edge of the box, and pressed very close to the wall, his view became more generous: he could see a corner of sky, what looked like the edge of a stream, and perhaps the beginnings of the tree line. The storm had abated, leaving a world like polished crystal: skies of silver and indigo, forests of celadon green, even the cobbles somehow turned lustrous beneath the rain.

Valentine watched for a long time, even though there was nothing much to see. Just the distant flicker of the stars and shadows stirred by the wind. He wondered if this was what Bonny's Arkandia looked like. Full of brighter colours.

Colours as bright as Bonny himself.

Eventually, he pushed three chairs together—still no spiders; they must have been biding their time, waiting for him to show weakness—and made a sort of . . . *bed* seemed too charitable a term . . . made *something* with the blankets, which had been offered in great profusion. Almost completely mummified, and precariously balanced, Valentine settled down to wait out the night. And, if necessary, mount a defence against spiders.

Sleep ebbed and flowed around him in tides, sometimes submerging him, sometimes merely lapping at him, until it was difficult to tell when he was awake and when he wasn't, when he was dreaming and when he was merely thinking. And always of the same impossible thing. The same impossible man. So much laughter and so much sorrow in eyes so full of light.

⟨✦⟩

Voices and the clatter of hooves outside nearly jolted Valentine off his chair arrangement. Stiff limbed and bleary eyed, he staggered to the box and scrambled up to the window—where he saw Peggy and the Tarleton twins readying their equipages for departure.

He fumbled with the latch and managed to get the window partially open, going up on tiptoes so he could call out, in a voice more tragic than he had intended, "Bonny? Bonny!"

Bonny gave a little jump and spun round. Then spotted Valentine. Who absolutely did not have his face pressed to a cellar window like a dog denied a trip to the park.

"It's going to be fine," he said, crouching down so he could get as close as possible to eye level. "The ladies will let you out soon enough."

The cellar was grey. But Bonny was gilded by the morning. Valentine gazed at him helplessly. "Are you really going? To America?"

Bonny shrugged "Maybe? Who knows? At least it's an adventure."

"It's a terrible idea. You've got nothing."

"We can live on our wits."

"And you're not overendowed in those."

Bonny's fingertips brushed the glass between them. "Take care, Valentine. You'll be back with your valet before you know it."

"I . . ." Valentine bit his lip. It was probably lack of sleep, but he couldn't think past the churning in his stomach and the tightness in his heart. The wet, heavy feeling in his eyes. "Don't," he whispered. "Don't."

Bonny leaned in, looking genuinely confused. "Pardon?"

Dammit. Valentine tried to find his voice. "Don't go. Don't leave. Don't leave me."

"My sister—"

"I'll do better. I'll make it right. I'll do anything. Please."

"Flower . . ."

"Please."

"Come on, Bonbon." That was Miss Tarleton, who was already climbing into the gig. "Stop dithering. Adventure awaits."

Bonny glanced over his shoulder. "Yes, yes, I'm coming."

"Bonny." Valentine put his own fingers to where Bonny's still rested against the glass. "Something could happen to you. I'll never know. I can't—"

"I'll write," said Bonny, too quickly, looking almost as distraught as Valentine felt.

"It's not enough. I can't . . . I can't lose you. There can't be a world that has you in it that is not mine."

Bonny had gone pink to his ears. And the laugh he uttered was nothing but uncertainty. "Wh-what are you saying?"

"I didn't know." The glass was warming slowly against Valentine's skin, but it was borrowed warmth, taunting and inhuman. "I didn't know."

"My God." Bonny was staring at him. "Are you possessed? What happened to you in that cellar?"

"Nothing. I mean. Everything. I mean, stay. I need you to stay. Won't you stay?"

There was a strange stillness to Bonny in that moment, his eyes locked on Valentine's face, his fingers an unreachable promise on the other side of the window. "I can't," he said finally. "It's . . . it's too late. Wait, what am I saying? It was always too late. You were always my sister's." Scrambling to his feet, he stumbled away as though Valentine had become—perhaps had always been—monstrous. "I have to go."

"Wait," cried Valentine. "Please."

But Bonny didn't wait. He didn't even look back. And Valentine need not have watched—need not have tortured himself—but he did. He watched Bonny's curricle until it was nothing but a pinprick in the distance. And then the horizon swallowed it whole.

Bonny was gone.

And Valentine . . . and Valentine hardly knew. Even the spiders temporarily seemed of only passing concern as he sank down onto the floor beneath the window, folded his arms across his knees, and buried his face in them. He knew, in some vague way, he was hungry.

Exhausted. Overwrought. Which probably meant he wasn't in a fit state to rationally assess his circumstances.

But everything felt unutterably and unbearably broken. Cracks through the eggshell of his life. A promise of light that was, in fact— had been all along—nothing but the sky falling down.

It went without saying he was going to be a laughingstock. His wife-to-be had fled overseas. That was not the sort of event likely to reflect well on anyone, and the fact it was Valentine—who had always presented himself as untouchable—would probably only make it more satisfying. More repeatable. More consumable. Complacency finding its just reward. A handful of days ago, this would have been a crisis. The notion of becoming the subject of ridicule and speculation would have appalled him. In all honesty, it was still far from pleasant. But it seemed . . . small. Very small.

Especially compared to the immensity of desolation that was sweeping through him now, raging like a sandstorm across what Valentine had always believed to be the arid plains of his heart. How in God's name did people endure this? Such longing and uncertainty and hope? The latter, in particular. Even in the midst of loss, it was there, buried deep. This thorn of terrible sweetness: eyes on his eyes, a hand in his hand, a body curled around his in the vulnerability of sleep. The voice that called him "flower." So many things that had once seemed so fundamental to others and so incomprehensible to him. What did it mean?

What could anything mean, now Bonny had left him?

Then came a tapping upon his window. And, looking up, there was Bonny. For a moment, Valentine thought he had lost his mind. It made a perverse kind of sense that he might—in moments of profound dismay—hallucinate Tarletons.

The Tarleton in question made a gesture of nebulous theatricality, which was enough to get Valentine back onto his feet.

"What are you doing here?" he asked, climbing onto the box.

Bonny pulled a none-too-encouraging face. "Making a terrible error in judgement, probably."

"You . . ." Whatever Valentine had been about to say was momentarily lost in a tangle of disbelief and delight. "You came back."

"Yes." Bonny seemed somewhat rueful. "Yes I did."

"Why?"

"Because . . . well. Because you asked me to."

Could it really be that simple? Could anything? "I didn't," Valentine admitted. "I begged."

A slow, unusually tentative smile was softening the curve of Bonny's lips. "I didn't quite understand at the time, but, honestly, I only needed you to ask."

"Noted." Heat was licking at Valentine's very bones.

"I mean"—Bonny, too, seemed slightly flustered, though he quickly rallied—"you should also feel free to beg. As much as you like. For anything. Anytime."

Valentine cleared his throat. "I would prefer to keep such behaviour to a minimum."

"Shame. It was kind of irresistible."

Impossible, as ever, for Valentine to know how to respond to that. "Do you think I could perhaps be let out of the cellar now?" he asked instead.

"I'm sure"—Bonny's gaze was speculative—"you could fit through this window."

"Why would I want to fit through the window when there's a perfectly serviceable door?"

"Well, you'd need Miss Fairfax to let you out. And she promised Belle otherwise. At least for a little while."

"Couldn't you explain, though?" While Valentine was a duke and, therefore, did not whine, he was nevertheless aware that his tone was not as unwhineful as it could have been.

"What would I say?"

"That I'm a duke and—"

"You know, there are some situations where *duke* is not the answer?"

Valentine had only recently begun to discover this. It still perplexed him. "Would your word not be reassurance enough?"

"Reassurance of *what*?"

"That there has been a mistake and it would not be wrong to release me."

"Valentine . . . my flower . . ." Bonny's sigh would have wilted daffodils with its suffering. "I've already abandoned my sister today. My twin. The other half of my soul. Please don't make me go and tell two lovely sapphic ladies about my worrying taste in gentlemen."

There was a lot to address here. "Two what kind of ladies?"

Bonny glared at him. "I came back for you. You can climb through a window for me."

"Door or window, my departure will be observable regardless."

"Yes, but this way it'll look like you escaped on your own."

"I *will* be escaping on my own," pointed out Valentine, "since you don't seem inclined to actually help."

"I'm helping. I'm giving you moral support and"—the flutter of golden lashes—"motivation."

"How are you giving me motivation?"

Flinging his hands towards the sky, Bonny struck a pose. "I *am* the motivation." Then he abruptly grew uncertain. "I . . . was right to return? You do want . . . you do want me?"

"I am not in the habit," Valentine said stiffly, "of begging for things I do not want."

And just like that Bonny was all smiles again.

"I am, however," Valentine continued, "uncertain that I'll fit through the window."

Bonny's fingers flickered, entirely unconcerned. "Of course you'll fit. You'll just have to wriggle a bit."

Valentine was about to explain, in no uncertain terms, that he did not wriggle. But perhaps, for Bonny, he did? Pushing the window open as far as it would go—which was not as far as he would have liked—Valentine hooked his fingers onto the ledge and pulled himself up. This turned out to be more difficult than it appeared, for it required the sort of upper-body strength that being a duke who sparred fashionably but only occasionally with Jackson did not, in the natural course of things, provide. Eventually, though, he managed to get his head outside. Followed by his shoulders. Followed by—

Ah. No. Just his shoulders.

"Bonny," he said, scrabbling and kicking. "Bonny, I'm stuck."

Bonny rubbed his chin, thoughtfully. "You should try removing some layers."

"How can I remove some layers? I'm halfway through a window."

More by blind panic than luck or judgement, Valentine managed to yank himself back inside—though it tore a long rent in the arm of his coat, and the sudden and unexpected absence of resistance when the window frame at last deigned to release him sent him tumbling backwards off the box with a crash.

"Are you hurt?" Bonny's anxious face appeared above him. "That was quite the tumble."

As it happened, Valentine *was* hurt. Except the injury was to a region he did not feel it was appropriate to discuss publicly. And his most pressing concern was the very real possibility that loud, unexplained noises from the cellar would have attracted the attention of the household.

As if to lend credence to the thought, he caught the faintest suggestion of movement from the floor above.

"Oh my God." With alacrity rather than grace, and at some detriment to the wounded area, Valentine leapt to his feet. "They're coming."

Bonny, who, if nothing else, could be counted upon to lend drama to any situation, gave a little scream. "Quick. Quick! Give me your coat and overcoat."

Without really stopping to consider any of the infinitely more sensible alternatives, Valentine stripped to his shirtsleeves and bundled the rest of his clothes out of the window to Bonny, who was regarding him in evident concern.

"Can't you take off anything else?" he demanded.

Valentine blinked up at him nervously. "Well, yes. But at that juncture, I'd be as good as naked."

"I wouldn't mind."

"I would mind. I would mind very much."

Casting a frantic glance towards the door, Valentine was sure he could hear footsteps. Which was to say, he was sure there were footsteps in the same way he was sure there were spiders: dreading the possibility of them.

"Is there," Bonny suggested, "some sort of butter or oil stored down there?"

"Maybe? Why?"

"You could rub it onto yourself."

"What on earth would be the benefit of that?"

"Lubrication. It'll help you"—Bonny did a sort of *whoosh* with his palms—"slide through the window."

Was getting stuck in a window worse than getting through a window, but being covered in butter afterwards? Regardless, Valentine had no time to debate the issue because the door opened, admitting Miss Fairfax and Miss Evans and, perhaps more significantly, the rifle.

"Good heavens," exclaimed Miss Fairfax, immediately throwing a hand over her eyes. "He's undressed."

"More to the point, Emily"—that was Miss Evans—"he's escaping."

Butter or no butter, it had very much become a now-or-never situation. Valentine raced across the room, scaled the box, and launched himself through the window. Once again, his own shoulders proved something of an impediment to his progress, but without the added bulk of his outer garments, a series of lizard-like wriggles propelled him on.

"I suppose we should stop him," remarked Miss Evans.

"Should I shoot him?" asked Miss Fairfax.

A longer pause than was comforting when you were partway through a window, with elements of your body presenting a far too accessible target. "Perhaps not? A shot duke may prove even more troublesome than a kidnapped one."

"What," pondered Miss Fairfax, "if he were to become wedged?"

"Then at least we won't have to worry about him escaping."

"True. But I'm not sure I want to live with a wedged duke as a permanent feature of my cellar?"

By an extraordinary effort of will, and some further wriggling, Valentine forced an arm free. For a moment or two he was left grasping at nothing, but then Bonny seized his hand and began to—

Well. *Pull* would have been Valentine's preferred description. Unfortunately, it was far closer to *heaving*. An impression not aided by Bonny's bulging eyes and reddening cheeks, and the fact he was making an *uhnhggghhh* noise as he dragged Valentine across the wet cobblestones like some potatoes he was taking to market.

"We could use his legs to dry linen?" suggested Miss Evans, in defiance of Valentine's vigorous attempts to use the legs in question for purchase against the wall. Although, in practice, what he was mainly doing was attacking the air and dislodging the occasional pebble.

Another unflattering expenditure of effort on Bonny's part, coupled with a wild flail from Valentine, and he was almost through. Which was to say, his head, shoulders, torso, and some portion of his abdomen were through. His posterior was opposed to the notion in its entirety: that is, both the entirety of his posterior and the entirety of the notion.

"Breathe in," whispered Bonny urgently.

That was not going to help. Although Valentine's attempt to explain came out as "Neeeeerrghhhhh." He managed to wriggle his other hand out from under him and applied it to the window itself, on the assumption it would be easier to induce the window to open more than it would his body to be a different shape.

The window responded with an ominous creak.

"Is he going to break our window?" asked Miss Fairfax.

"I think," confirmed Miss Evans, "he's going to break our window."

"Madam"—Valentine forced himself a few inches farther—"I am a duke. I assure you, I will recompense you for any . . ." The creaking of the window had intensified to a kind of low, wooden groaning. ". . . damage . . ." Now a crack as part of the frame split down the middle. ". . . caused." And, finally, a splintery explosion as the whole frame detached itself from the wall.

Followed by Valentine himself, who was propelled like a cannonball from what was left of the window, straight into Bonny, flattening them both to the cobbles.

"Oof," said Bonny, dazedly. This close he was a summer-day haze: all shades of milk and honey, soft and sweet and perfect. Perfectly beautiful.

Valentine sucked in several rough breaths. "I'm so sorry. Are you hurt?"

"You think you're the first gentleman to have cast himself upon me?"

"Do they normally cast themselves that hard?"

For some reason, that made Bonny grin. "Depends. But don't worry, flower. I'm well cushioned."

"I . . ." Despite having been recently propelled from a window, Valentine was conscious of the strangest, dreamiest sensation. Of being caught within the dewdrop of a moment, suspended upon the leaf of eternity. "You . . ."

"You broke our window." Miss Fairfax was peering up at them through the gap Valentine had left behind him. And then, "Bonny, is that you?"

Bonny gasped. "Oh no."

And the next thing Valentine knew, he had been detached, rolled away, and pulled to his feet, his coat and overcoat unceremoniously dumped in his arms.

"Quick," cried Bonny. "Run. Run away."

"They've seen you now. There's no poi—"

But then Bonny grabbed his hand, and Valentine lost his words to warmth and skin and Bonny. He was right, of course, that there was no point running. But run they did—still hand in hand, out of the stable yard and onto the road, and from there over a stile and across the green-gold-dappled fields. With Bonny's laughter dancing upon the breeze like sunbeams upon still water.

Chapter 20

Bonny had left his curricle by the side of a quiet country lane and his bays contentedly grazing in a nearby glade. And it was here that he finally released Valentine's hand (something Valentine did not require) and allowed him to rest (something Valentine very much did require). He couldn't recall the last time he'd *run*, either voluntarily or in obligation, and Bonny—for all that he was a generously proportioned young man—had an impressive turn of speed.

They flopped down together upon the daisy-dotted banks of a nearby stream, and Valentine was so relieved to no longer be in a state of running that he forgot to even protest at sitting upon the ground. For a moment or two, they were silent but for Valentine's attempts to pretend he was breathing less hard than he actually was.

"Those ladies," Valentine said finally. "I'm beginning to think . . . I have the oddest suspicion . . . when you said . . . could they be, perchance, like . . . like you?"

Bonny widened his eyes. "Like me?"

"Yes. Do you . . . do you think it's possible they feel about other ladies the way you feel about other gentlemen?"

It was the most outlandish notion, but Bonny appeared to give it consideration nonetheless. "You know something, flower, now you mention it, I think they might."

Valentine did his best to digest this. Then he drew his knees up, hid his face in them, and burst into tears.

It was some while before he became aware that Bonny had put an arm around his shoulders and was asking him—in a faintly horrified voice—what was wrong.

"Nothing," Valentine said. "But would you be so kind as to go away? I mean, just for a little while."

He felt Bonny nodding. "Mm. Yes. That sounds like a wonderful idea. This is me, going away, leaving you crying in the middle of Kent."

After a while, Valentine felt constrained to observe, "You haven't gone away."

"Did you really think I would, my ridiculous flower?"

"You shouldn't . . . I don't want"—Valentine gave an undukely sniff—"to be seen like this. Also," he insisted, "I'm not crying."

Bonny thumbed the tears tenderly from Valentine's cheeks. "Of course not. But, let's say, in the throes of some private delusion, I thought you were: Why would that be?"

There was no reason on earth for him to explain. He wasn't even sure he *could*. All he had to do was reestablish some sort of control over the tumult of his heart and the turmoil in his mind. Tell Bonny it was nothing. A moment of weakness. A moment of foolishness. But the past few days had stripped him somehow, as if all his defences and certainties—everything he thought he understood, believed, took for granted—could be stolen from him. Or left behind. As easily as the coat that was still probably draped across the chair in the guest bedroom at Bonny's uncle's house.

"I . . . I don't know," he blurted out. "I just feel so . . . it's all so . . . and I said *awful* things to you."

"Oh, flower." Having dealt with (some of) Valentine's tears, Bonny smoothed his hair away from his brow. "You do rather have a tendency in that direction."

"Of s-saying awful things?"

181

"Mm-hmm."

"But I don't," Valentine protested. "Or I didn't. Not until I met you."

"See."

"What? No. I didn't mean it like that."

But Bonny was laughing. "And that temper of yours? Is that my fault too?"

"I used to be in better command of myself."

"Did you, though?" Something of Bonny's amusement remained, but his voice had softened. Accrued an almost unbearable warmth. "Or did you just ignore your feelings until they exploded out of you?"

Valentine offered the coolest look he could manage in the wake of his weeping. "Dukes don't have feelings, Bonny."

"Liar."

And before Valentine could dispute the topic further, Bonny had taken his hand and brought it to his lips—as though Valentine had fallen into some mediaeval fairy tale where, far from being the noble knight, he was the damsel in the tower. But then, perhaps if knights had spent more of their time kissing other knights, being kissed would not be solely the purview of damsels in towers. "I don't like having feelings," Valentine muttered.

Except he was lying again. Because some of his feelings—the ones that moved across his skin like moonlight over water in response to the brush of Bonny's mouth—were . . . enticing. Extraordinarily enticing.

"You can't live without feelings," Bonny told him.

"As it happens, I managed perfectly well."

"But weren't you bored?"

"No. It was comfortable and peaceful and . . ." Unfortunately, the cloak of Valentine's old life had grown threadbare indeed. And he was too raw to pretend otherwise. Trembling slightly, fearful of another onrush of tears—and fearful of something of far greater magnitude—he curled slightly in Bonny's direction. Then broke entirely and pressed his face to Bonny's shoulder. "I'm so very sorry. I shouldn't have . . . I never believed—"

Bonny said nothing. Just made the softest, most soothing of noises and petted Valentine's hair.

"I called you a degenerate." They were words Valentine had already uttered and uttered directly to Bonny. But this time they had to be dragged out of him, jagged and bloody. "I said you would never be happy or loved."

"I can't lie," Bonny murmured, "I was quite hurt. But then I thought about it, and I realised you weren't really talking to me, were you?"

"What do you mean?"

"Oh, Valentine"—Bonny sounded perilously close to laughing—"you'll work it out one day."

Truth be told, Valentine wasn't sure if he was ever going to understand anything ever again. Somehow, he had gone from living a perfectly ordinary life—one where his status went without question, and nobody pointed rifles at him—to crying in a field in the arms of the most oversetting man he had ever met. A state of affairs that was at once so terribly wrong and so terribly right that Valentine had no idea how to cope with it. Apart from with a fresh burst of tears, no more welcome than the last.

"I . . ." He tried to explain but had neither capacity nor insight enough to do so. "I am not myself."

Bonny drew him in a little closer. "I'm not sure it works that way."

"No." It was hard to shake your head decisively when in the throes of mortifying emotion, but Valentine did his best. "This cannot be me. I . . . have been overcome by circumstance. I've been awoken at ungodly hours, terrorised by insects and women, tied up, incarcerated. In a cellar. I haven't eaten, or bathed; I've barely slept. I don't have my valet. I'm . . . I'm probably traumatised."

"Far be it for me"—Bonny's mouth curled into one of its most mischievous shapes—"to be the moderate one, but don't you mean . . . *a bit upset?*"

"Traumatised," said Valentine firmly.

There was a longish silence. Or as close to silence as it was possible to get when there were birds chirping in the hedgerows and a stream tinkling by.

"So you think *this*"—Bonny gestured between them—"is emotional distress?"

Valentine opened his mouth, then closed it again. It did not seem as though there was a good way to answer that question. "What else could it be?"

"I might have some idea."

A stillness had crept between them. And into Bonny a wariness that Valentine instinctively disliked and knew to be his fault. Because he'd done it again, hadn't he? Said yet another awful thing.

"Bonny, I—"

Before he could finish or, indeed, had barely managed to start, Bonny had set a hand over his mouth. "No. Don't say anything. At least, don't say anything yet."

"You have to understand," Valentine explained. Or rather, "Oohfftoonnersfff."

"What I understand," Bonny told him, eyes alight with sudden confidence, "is that you asked me to stay, and I believed in what you were feeling then. Or I wouldn't have come back."

Valentine offered a further muffled demurral.

"Don't worry." Bonny finally removed his hand, but it was only so he could leap to his feet and fling both his arms wide. "I shall address your trauma."

Well, that sounded dreadful. "Address my trauma?"

"Take care of you." Leaning down, Bonny deposited a kiss upon Valentine's anxiety-creased brow. "Then we can see how you're feeling after."

None of this made any sense to Valentine. But Bonny was already cantering towards his curricle, with his curls streaming behind him like the ears of an excited beagle. And so Valentine had little choice except to trail disconsolately after him.

"Did you pay any heed at all," he asked, "when I told you I didn't like feelings?"

Now Bonny cantered past him, heading back the way he'd just come, balancing an empty preserves jar from their previous picnic and what smelled like a freshly baked loaf. "Not in the slightest. Feelings are wonderful. And I want you to have lots of them. Especially about me."

"Then you will be gratified to learn"—Valentine kept following him—"that I have many feelings about you. I feel you are annoying. And chaotic. And loud. And—"

"Hold this, please." Bonny shoved the bread into his hands. "And stay here for a moment."

For some reason, Valentine stayed, cradling the loaf to his chest as tenderly as if it were the first food he'd encountered in twenty-four hours. Which it was. "Why? Where are you going? What's happening."

"Breakfast is happening." Bonny gave him a radiant smile. "Watch."

And with that, he was off across the glade, slowing to a gentle walk as he approached a distant tree, about which Valentine now realised with some sense of trepidation bees were busily clustered. The epicentre of their clustering was a hollow in the trunk, and it was towards this that Bonny—who was clearly deranged—made a . . . well . . . beeline?

"Bonny," Valentine called out to him. "Common sense dictates you move away from bees, not towards them."

Bonny did not take Valentine's advice. He was close to the tree now, a hazy figure, surrounded by a cloud of amber and black.

"What are you doing?" Valentine demanded. "I don't feel good about this. I'm feeling quite unhappy."

For someone with all the poise and patience of a sparkler, Bonny was moving with astonishing care. Not cautiously but with a kind of smooth and steady grace. Not remotely a normal reaction for someone near quite a lot of bees—but beautiful, in its way. A thought that lingered too long and too easily in Valentine's mind. Until it was comprehensively banished by the realisation that Bonny was . . . surely not . . . reaching into the tree?

The tree full of bees.

While the bees themselves crawled freely over him, up and down his arms, and across his shoulders, getting muddled in his hair. So much so that when he turned around, he was . . . mostly bees. A Bonny-shaped swarm.

Now walking—and buzzing—towards Valentine.

Who was very, very tempted to run away screaming, had it not been for the concern that such behaviour might make the bees go for him en masse.

"Bonny," he said, as calmly as he could. "I'm assuming you're aware of this, but you're covered in bees. And I'd really rather you weren't." He swallowed. "You know. Covered in bees."

As Bonny drew closer, however, the bees seemed, of their own accord, to depart. They hovered about him for a while before wending their way back to the hive. Which meant he was almost completely bee-less again by the time he was standing before Valentine. He was smiling, because he was Bonny and he was always smiling, and holding out the once-empty jar, in which now a piece of carefully broken honeycomb was slowly dripping its sun-gold bounty. "Sweets for the sweet."

And, once again, Valentine felt like the damsel or the knight. Honoured. Tended. Helplessly and heart-meltingly *romanced*. "I . . . I'm not very sweet."

"To me you are."

Valentine gazed at him. For the first time allowing himself to see and feel and dare to want without question, obstruction, or compunction. It was too much, in exactly the same way that Bonny was too much. And he could not get enough of it. "To me," he said, "you are a miracle."

Then he stepped forwards and kissed him. And Bonny's mouth blossomed like springtime under Valentine's, full of eager heat and endless promises, leaving upon his tongue, as sure as a brand, the taste of wild honey.

Chapter 21

It was Bonny, in the end, who drew away with a little squeak.

"What's the matter?" asked Valentine. "Was that bad? Did I do it wrong?"

Bonny shook his head. "N-no. Not at all. But . . . but Belle."

"I am by no means an expert, but should you really be thinking of your sister on the occasion of my kissing you?"

"That's the whole point: I *wasn't* thinking of her. Valentine, you're still engaged."

It was true. But Valentine's capacity to care much about anything beyond the softness of Bonny's lips against his own had been largely obliterated. "Miss Tarleton may well be on a ship bound for America by tomorrow."

"Oh, but don't you see"—Bonny flapped his arms excitedly—"if she knew about . . . about *this*, then she wouldn't have to go anywhere or do anything."

"She wouldn't?" Valentine asked, more confused than ever, but willing to take Bonny's word on almost anything if it would precipitate more kissing.

"No. It would fix everything."

"In which case, may I kiss you again?"

Bonny intercepted Valentine's mouth with his hand. "Certainly not. It's . . . it doesn't feel right. When it's behind Belle's back."

Through the haze of being hungry, tired, and as full of sparks as the air before a storm, it was hard for Valentine to focus on very much. Although, given what Bonny had told him of his sister, this did make some kind of sense. Valentine had given her no reason to trust him, or his intentions after marriage—even if he promised her, as he had promised Bonny, that he would not restrict her freedom or attempt to impose his will upon her. But if she knew that it was Bonny he liked? More than liked. Desired. Could he offer her any more surety than that? Any better safety?

And to think he had so dreaded the prospect of marriage, and everything he had thought it had meant. Perhaps the possibility of happiness was not so outlandish after all.

He gave a little nod. "I understand. What should we do?"

"Well"—he was gratified to note that Bonny's gaze kept drifting to Valentine's mouth—"we should finish addressing your trauma. And then we go after them. If we push hard, we should catch up before they reach Dover."

"Kissing you was very helpful," Valentine told him.

Bonny lifted his brows provokingly. "And how are your *feelings*?"

"Immeasurable. But I will admit, unrelated to trauma."

Settling himself on the bank again, Bonny removed the now somewhat squashed loaf from Valentine's grip. "Breakfast can only make things better."

Valentine had sat on the ground so much recently it was beginning to feel almost normal. Kneeling next to Bonny, he watched him tear a piece from the bread. "Where did this come from?"

"From Emily and Angharad and"—Bonny jerked a thumb over his shoulder—"that tree there."

The tree surrounded by bees. The tree Bonny had blithely stuck his hand in. "How did you do that?"

"I don't know. I think I just trust bees and bees trust me."

The honey was like no honey Valentine had ever seen before. Dark golden in the jar, it looked almost translucent when poured—and it poured as easily as light, leaving silver spirals upon the bread. "You weren't worried about being stung?"

"I've never been stung. Not by a bee anyway." A dark shadow settled momentarily upon Bonny's features, his nose wrinkling in resentment. "Wasps, though. Wasps can die in a fire."

As far as Valentine was concerned, they were both black-and-yellow flying creatures, somewhat less malignant than spiders—not counting the individual bee that had assaulted him—but still far from welcome in his world. "I'm not sure there's much to choose between them."

Bonny stared at him. "Oh my God, I can't believe I kissed you."

"That reminds me. About the kissing, I—"

"Valentine, bees are miracles." The slightest of pauses, the tip of Bonny's nose and his cheeks turning pink. "Just like me."

"You know"—Valentine's gaze followed the bread and honey that Bonny was waving around—"I really am *quite* hungry."

Bonny pulled his hand back. "Tough. You can't have any food until you admit that bees are wondrous."

"That's actual torture," Valentine pointed out.

"No, it isn't. I'm just encouraging you to embrace my view of the world by depriving you of sustenance."

"That's still actual torture," Valentine pointed out.

"But Valentine"—Bonny's eyes got big and round and pleading—"bees are the best."

It crossed Valentine's mind that, had this been a legitimately coercive situation, his resolve was putting in a pathetic showing. But what did it matter? He was already conquered. "Fine. Bees are the best."

"But," Bonny persisted, "do you understand *why* they're the best?"

"You love them. That is more than enough for me."

Bonny hid a smile behind honey-glistening fingers. "I give you credit for being adorable."

"Thank you. Am I permitted food now?"

"But you also lose credit for clearly not knowing anything about bees."

"Very well." In that moment, it was so easy to surrender—especially when it felt nothing like surrender. Stretching out on the soft grass, Valentine laid his head in Bonny's lap and stared at the blue-struck midmorning sky. "Tell me about bees."

"Well, they pollinate flowers and make honey."

"Bee neophyte though I am, I had worked out that much."

"But don't you think that's magical all on its own?" asked Bonny. "That this one creature does so much good in the world? They give us more flowers—can't go wrong with that—and one of my very favourite things."

He brought the piece of bread to Valentine's lips, and undignified as it was, Valentine was hungry enough to take a bite without complaint. The bread was fresh enough and soft enough to almost melt upon his tongue, and the honey was the sweetest he had ever tasted—as if whatever was served at the breakfast tables of the ton was some poor facsimile of something far bolder and far freer. Something that was supposed to be taken in a field, direct from the fingers of the beautiful man who had collected it for you.

". . . communicate with each other by dancing"—Bonny was still talking—"*and* they're all fuzzy and cute. If you ask me, bees are a very good argument for the existence of God."

"Not the watch and the watchmaker?"

"No." Bonny sounded very sure, as he passed the bread to Valentine and tore off another piece for himself. "That's about order and industry. Bees are a belief in universal benevolence. If I wasn't me, I'd want to be a bee."

The food was so very welcome, the honey itself so intense, that it had left Valentine feeling almost drunk. "If you were a bee, I would not object to your chasing me."

"I . . ." Bonny broke off, gazing down at Valentine with an unreadable expression. Then he grinned. "This is so strange; I feel like I'm in a fairy tale right now."

"A fairy tale? Why?"

Blushing a little, Bonny stroked a finger down the length of Valentine's nose. "Well. Look at you. And you're in my lap. I have a duke in my lap."

"Are you sure I'm a duke?" Valentine asked. "I don't think I've ever mentioned it."

Bonny's delighted laughter almost made the leaves dance with shared amusement. "See. I knew you were in there. I *knew* it."

"Maybe I just thought I'd rather be the man you saw than the man who I believed I had to be?"

"Or," Bonny suggested, "I broke the curse with my kiss."

"I was not under a curse."

"If you say so."

Bonny sounded far from convinced, but Valentine had been distracted by a more important issue. "About the, ah, the kiss. I would like to discuss that further, if you are amenable."

"I think"—now Bonny seemed to be checking an imaginary diary—"I have a window available in my very busy schedule for a kissing forum."

"Now?"

"No, three weeks on Tuesday. Yes, now."

Now had seemed like a good idea in Valentine's head. The reality of it, though, was intimidating. He took another bite of bread, stalling for time.

As well as an imaginary diary, Bonny also possessed an imaginary pocket watch. He drew it out and studied it. "I thought I was supposed to be getting a kissing forum. Where's my kissing forum?"

"It would help," Valentine told him, "if you could stop referring to it as a *kissing forum*."

"I'm sorry"—Bonny was clearly not sorry—"but nobody has ever invited me to a postperformance review before."

"Well, maybe that's because it wasn't their first kiss."

The words *first kiss* hung a moment in the still air. Then broke like a flock of sparrows and were gone.

"That was your first kiss?" Bonny asked.

Valentine shifted uncomfortably. "Not my first kiss. Obviously I've kissed people. I mean, I've kissed my mother. I mean, I've kissed my mother as one would kiss a family member. I've kissed my mother appropriately."

"Thank you for clarifying. Otherwise it would absolutely have occurred to me that you kissed your mother inappropriately."

"I think it would be for the best if we stopped talking about my mother."

Bonny nodded solemnly. "Probably a good idea."

"In any case," Valentine continued, "it was my first kiss of a . . . a . . . how would you define it? Romantic and carnal nature. And I would like to ascertain it was correctly delivered."

To his surprise, and mild irritation, Bonny said nothing. Only gazed down at him with a frankly absurd expression. "I'm your first kiss."

"I've just said that."

"I'm your first kiss."

"Are you suffering from some kind of head injury?"

"Valentine"—Bonny's expression had grown no less absurd—"that's such . . . such a beautiful thing."

Valentine was conscious of heat creeping to his cheeks. "You are reading far too much into it. I've never wanted to kiss anyone in that fashion before."

"Because you did not know there were other men like you?"

"No," said Valentine slowly, and with a vague sense of dread that perhaps he was going to be peculiar even by the standards of people who were peculiar. "I have never felt that sort of inclination towards anyone, man or woman."

Bonny's eyes were round. "Really? You've never seen a succulently be-arsed redcoat saunter by and thought—"

"No."

"And what about if you imagine someone? The most tempting person you can possibly conceive of?"

"I have no interest in conceiving of someone. I can see you." There was a long silence. It felt more like a thoughtful silence than an unpleasant one. But it made Valentine nervous, nonetheless. "I did warn you I was not a passionate person."

"You seemed passionate enough earlier."

Valentine sighed. "Only with you, Bonny."

"Clearly," Bonny declared, "I am magnificently special."

So it was true then. Even among people like Bonny, Valentine was something . . . else. "Clearly."

"Oh, flower." Apparently, Bonny had caught the note of defeat in Valentine's admission. "It doesn't matter."

"Doesn't it?"

"Why should it?"

It was hard to explain: just a nebulous sense of other. Of unlikeness. Of being twice removed.

"Everyone experiences everything differently," Bonny went on, as if Valentine had managed to articulate exactly what he was feeling. "What's wrong with being someone who gives your passion to few? Rather than someone who gives your passion to many?"

"What if I never meet anyone else I am inclined to give my passion to?" asked Valentine, wanting to be consoled and yet fearful of it at the same time.

Bonny beamed. "Then you'll be stuck with me for a long time. Possibly even *forever*." Before Valentine could lament such a terrible state of affairs, Bonny disentangled himself carefully and leapt—much less carefully—to his feet. "Anyway, now that I have seen to breakfast, it is time to deal with bathing."

"How is that going to be possible?" Valentine rose reluctantly, shaking grass from his greatcoat. "We're in the middle of nowhere."

Bonny just sparkled enigmatically. "Follow me."

"That's not an explanation," Valentine pointed out. "That's a direction."

But he followed regardless. Of course he did. He suspected some part of him would want to follow Bonny anywhere.

Chapter 22

"That's not a bath," Valentine said, a few minutes later. "That's a lake."

"It's not a lake," protested Bonny. "It's a pool. *With a waterfall.* It's beautiful."

Valentine assessed the situation. It was, he had to admit, quite beautiful, although *waterfall* was rather a strong descriptor for what was, at best, a small cascade: just the stream tumbling between some rocks and into a pool so overhung with trees that it gave the water a green glaze like a glass bottle, where sunlight danced upon its surface in dapples as big as sovereigns. "How do we know it's safe?" he asked.

"Safe?"

"Yes. There could be anything in there."

"Like what?" Bonny was already tugging his boots off.

Valentine racked his brain for any information related to marine life. Wait, was it even marine if it wasn't the ocean? "I don't know. Eels? Angry fish?"

"Angry fish?" repeated Bonny, dragging his shirt over his head, having already shed most of his other garments.

Which rather put Valentine's pond-based concerns into perspective. "Bonny, forgive me for mentioning this, but you seem to be taking your clothes off."

"Of course I am. They'll get wet if I don't."

"Yes, but"—Valentine had spotted the obvious flaw with the current plan—"then you'll be naked. And I don't know how I will feel about that."

Now only in his pantaloons, Bonny plonked his hands on his hips. "Because we're both men?"

"Because I may very much want to kiss you again."

The sound of someone removing his pantaloons and drawers became the entirety of Valentine's world as he hastily covered his eyes. Then the rustle of footsteps upon grass. And finally the brush of lips against the corner of his own.

"I thought," he said in a rather stifled voice, "we were not to kiss until your sister was . . . was aware of our . . . our . . . kissing."

Somehow, Valentine *felt* Bonny's smile. It was almost unendurably intimate, being able to tell the shape of someone's mouth just from its closeness to your own. "Yes. One of my sillier ideas."

Before Valentine could respond, Bonny had bounced away. Opening his eyes, with some sense of urgency, he caught a flash of curves and creamy skin, and then Bonny had plunged into the pool with a wild splash.

He resurfaced in a sparkle of water droplets. "Come in. It's lovely. There's no eels, and the fish are content and even tempered."

"How are we to dry ourselves?" Valentine didn't even know, at this point, what he was really objecting to, other than some nebulous sense that he was not the sort of person to leap spontaneously into unknown bodies of water. Although he had also believed he was not the sort of person to go around kissing other men.

"You see that big yellow ball up there?" Bonny pointed at the sky. "It gives off heat. It's amazing."

Still, Valentine hesitated.

Bonny gambolled naiad-like awhile before calling out, "You've been complaining about the lack of bath for days."

"A bath is more than mere saturation in water."

"Oh?"

"It's"—Valentine waved a self-conscious hand—"an *experience*."

"So's this."

Probably they could have debated the relative merits of indoor versus outdoor bathing for some time, but having spent a night in a cellar and the previous night in a less than salubrious inn, Valentine's bath-related needs were becoming as much practical as aesthetic.

"What if someone sees?" he asked. "A lady or something."

"Then she'll be scarred for life. Come on, Valentine."

Valentine waited until Bonny was distracted by the waterfall—he was standing beneath it, with his arms flung wide, letting the water rush over him in flurries of white froth—then hastily disrobed and tiptoed into the pool.

It wasn't as cold as he'd feared, but it was colder than he was used to. Colder than was likely to be flattering to parts of his anatomy he was not accustomed to caring about other people's reactions to. But the water itself was almost perfectly clear—and contained neither eels nor, as far he could tell, fish of any temperament—and there was something unexpectedly pleasing in causing his own ripples. In parting the smoothness of the water with his body and feeling it close coolly around him as he moved. In the pale blur of his feet against the pebbles below.

Valentine had just reached, at a cautious half walk, half swim, the centre of the pool when he was attacked. Bonny surged out of the water, wrapping himself round Valentine like an amorous octopus.

"Err," said Valentine.

They were eye level with each other, and Bonny was grinning. Up close, all that joy, it was like looking into the sun. "I can't believe you like me."

"If it's any consolation, neither can I."

By way of reply, Bonny kissed him. And Valentine wondered when he was going to get used to kissing. If it would ever feel like an ordinary thing, as it seemingly did, or could, to others. But he wasn't sure he wanted that either. There was too much magic here, and he had never allowed his life to admit the possibility of magic before. Had never felt its lack. Or, if he had, convinced himself he was not made for magic.

And yet, he felt it now. Travelling through him, in sparks as innumerable as stars, in the lightest press of Bonny's lips to his. In the suggestion of heat upon the current of his breath. In the way they floated together through the water, skin to skin and thoroughly entangled, as though they were one creature. Valentine could have drowned in that feeling, as blissfully as a sailor surrounded by a siren's song. And it made him wonder how he was to survive its loss. To move through the world enclosed with his own flesh, alone as he had never before recognised.

Eventually Bonny drew back.

"The kissing forum," he said a little breathlessly, "has concluded its business and prepared a report."

Valentine blinked. Then swallowed. "Oh?"

"Yes. The kissing is adequate. Fit for purpose."

"I . . . I see. Well. Good. I'm glad to hear it."

For a moment, there was nothing but the spill of the water. And then Bonny was laughing and laughing. "You silly flower. The kissing was *lovely*."

"You wouldn't prefer to be kissing someone with more kissing experience. Like"—Valentine had no idea why he was pursuing this line of questioning because it could surely lead nowhere good—"say, Sir Horley or an ostler."

Bonny held his gaze for a long moment, his eyes catching "No. I would rather be kissing you. The man who doesn't want to kiss anyone but me."

"To be fair," Valentine said, "I think that's more about my nature than it is about you."

"Well, yes, but"—leaning in even closer, Bonny nipped at the edge of Valentine's jaw—"let's pretend it's a little bit because I'm so very fabulous."

That was hard to dispute. "You are indeed somewhat mythical."

"So . . . ," Bonny insisted, ". . . very . . . fabulous."

And, with that, he licked Valentine's nose and splooshed off to play beneath the waterfall. At first Valentine simply watched, admiring his beauty and lack of self-consciousness alike, the chaos of water droplets as they sparkled hither and thither upon his skin. Eventually, though, he turned onto his back and let himself drift. Tried to, somehow, be as free as Bonny. And it was—just then—good to be weightless. A little form-less, his sense of his fingers and toes fading into the lapping of the water.

It was not, in any sense, like a bath. A bath cocooned one. Took one away from . . . things. Whereas this—the sky, the sun, the private currents of the pool—made you inescapably part of them. Cautiously, Valentine spread his arms. Imagined the play of light and shadow upon bare skin. The wave of his hair like weeds upon the water. Possibilities unfurling all around him. And for a little while, he was nothing but horizon.

Chapter 23

Afterwards, they lay on the bank, finishing the bread and the honey and air-drying—as Bonny had overestimated the power of the English sun, even on a warm day. Bonny was on his back, his hands folded behind his head, and Valentine lay on his side, propped on an elbow, so he could look at him.

"What are you staring at?" asked Bonny, opening an eye.

Valentine touched a finger to Bonny's lips, marvelling at the still-fresh memory of kissing them. "I'm thinking of the things I said. I—"

"Oh, flower, I told you. Forgiven and forgotten."

"N-no. I mean . . ."

Now both of Bonny's eyes were open. "All those times you told me I was irritating and unreasonable and had read too many novels?"

"Well, you *are* irritating and unreasonable, and you *have* read too many novels."

An outraged sound spilled from Bonny's mouth.

"But," Valentine went on hastily, "you're also like nobody I have ever met before."

Bonny looked no more mollified. "I'm not sure that's the winning compliment you believe it to be."

This was clearly not going well. "Forgive me. I'm as new to this as I am the rest of it."

"You're new," Bonnie asked incredulously, "to *not completely insult-ing people*? Ye gods, you must be popular in society."

"I'm a duke. I'm popular by default. But, the truth is, I rarely encounter anyone I—"

"Don't want to completely insult?"

Valentine gritted his teeth. "You're making this harder than it needs to be."

"Saying something nice about someone isn't hard at all."

"I'm trying"—the words came out a frustrated snarl—"to tell you that I think you're . . ."

"Irritating?"

"Yes."

"Infuriating?"

"Yes."

"Impossible."

"Yes," yelled Valentine. "Impossibly sweet and impossibly kind and impossibly inclined"—he was still yelling—"to see good where I would not even think to try. You make me laugh when I am not given to laugh-ter. You make me question things when I am not given to that either. You make me feel in ways I have never felt before. You are your own adventure and you are . . . beautiful." Abruptly aware of his volume, Valentine lowered his voice. "So beautiful that my throat clenches and my stomach flips when I as much as glance at you, and I wonder how the world turns when such wanting exists within it."

There was a silence so long it was a wonder they did not find them-selves in autumn. Bonny had gone the reddest of reds—and he was red everywhere, his cheeks, his ears, the tip of his nose, his throat, and across his chest. "I . . . I don't know what to say."

Valentine cleared his throat. "*And* you're annoying."

Bonny was still being inexplicably quiet.

"As am I," Valentine conceded. "Annoying."

That seemed to stir Bonny from his daze. "Yes. But you're worth it." He caught Valentine by the wrist. "And you really think I'm beautiful?"

"No. I only said it because I am a committed rake who wishes to kiss you again."

Bonny just stared at him with big, hungry eyes.

"Of course I think you're beautiful. You know you are. Sir Horley told you, I'm sure that ostler told you, and, for that matter, you've told me yourself on several occasions."

"Yes, but"—Bonny squirmed—"it's different coming from you."

Valentine gave a lofty nod. "I am the only person amongst that group with some level of taste."

A pause. Then, "So . . . flower."

"Yes?"

"I know you're new. And I enjoy the"—a wave of Bonny's free hand—"carnal antagonism."

"The what?" asked Valentine, appalled.

"It's what's been happening. Don't worry about it for now. What's important here is when you tell me I'm beautiful. I need that not to be the part of the . . . of the other thing. Not," Bonny added hastily and a trifle defensively, "because I'm not aware for myself. But it's harder to believe, sometimes, from others. And you in particular."

"And my wanting to kiss you doesn't already communicate that?"

"Rationally, yes. Of course. But"—thoughtfulness settled upon Bonny's brow—"you're right. I've read too many books. Words matter to me."

"Then," Valentine told him, "you are beautiful. But what did you mean by 'me in particular'?"

"Well . . ." Bonny sat up, tucking a knee under him and—in what was clearly an effort at self-distraction—flicking water from his curls. "I suppose because you look how men are supposed to look?"

"Which is what?"

"Oh, you know. Tall, chiselled, square of jaw, smouldering of eye, et cetera, et cetera."

While Valentine had been nebulously aware he was considered handsome, he had never quite known what to do about it. Grown increasingly taunted by it across the years. What, after all, was the use of being pleasing to the eye when he had found in himself only an obscure hollowness? A well of waiting and searching and wanting but never finding in which he had drowned a little deeper with every day that passed. "Surely," he said, "there are many ways for men—for anyone—to look?"

Bonny shrugged. "Theoretically, yes. But I'm short. And, not to put too fine a point on it, squishy. And . . . there's a lot of me to go around."

It was Valentine's first instinct to remark that now his attention had been drawn to these matters, he intended to seek out someone nonsquishy, posthaste. But Bonny had already made it very clear that it would not be—in this context—the correct response. "I would not," he tried instead, "have you look other than you do. However that may be."

"Points for trying." Bonny gave his knee a consoling pat.

"That was not intended as a platitude."

"I could be different. Belle's a sylph, after all."

The conversation was proving harder to navigate than Valentine was prepared for. "What does Belle have to do with anything?"

"We're twins, remember. We're the same."

"You are *similar*," Valentine suggested, "because you have lived similar lives and have similar temperaments. But you are not some ill reflection of her, nor she of you."

Bonny's expression was unreadable. "Belle looks like a heroine, though."

"And you look like you. Which, to my mind, is infinitely preferable."

At last Bonny smiled, animation returning to his face like daybreak. "It's probably infinitely preferable to me too. Being a heroine is hard work."

"Oh?"

"Yes. It takes effort and self-denial and lots of other things I'm not good at and don't care about."

Valentine considered this. "Are heroines required to be sylphs then?"

"As a general rule."

Valentine considered this too. "That seems limiting."

"I agree. We should be in charge."

"Technically I am in charge. Not that anyone has raised the issue of heroine volume within the House of Lords."

"I don't think"—Bonny's voice shook with laugher—"women like it if you refer to their *volume*."

"Noted. And, in any case," Valentine went on decisively, "your beauty has little to do with the shape of you. It is about the whole of you."

Now Bonny was definitely laughing. "You said *whole*."

"Yes? And that's a subject for mirth, why?"

"Never mind. We can get intimate with *my whole* on another occasion."

"And yet you are still amused. I thought you said this was not a subject for badinage?"

"I've changed my mind."

Valentine heaved a put-upon sigh. "You are very unappreciative of my efforts to soothe your concerns."

"Actually, I find laughing at you very soothing."

"So I should not go on to confirm that—irrespective of its insignificance in the intricate tapestry of my attraction—I find you quite physically captivating?"

Bonny's eyes flew wide. "No, no. Confirm away."

"Are you sure? Because it seems like you'd prefer to keep laughing at me."

"*Valentine.*"

Valentine turned his head to hide a smile. Not many people used his given name—now he thought about it, just his mother—but there was still something inescapably Bonny-ish about how he said it, especially when he was exasperated: a certain singsong rhythm like someone pushing a wheelbarrow over the summit of a hill: *Val-EN-tine.*

Overcome by the strangest comingling of desire and affection, he put a hand upon Bonny's knee. The skin was remarkably smooth there, warm as a sun-touched pebble. "I . . . ," said Valentine. "I've forgotten what I was saying."

The blues of Bonny's eyes had darkened like damp silk. "I think I'm getting the picture."

"God. Oh God." With a helpless groan, Valentine pressed Bonny back onto the grass and kissed him—a rough entangling, full of still-unfaded wonder, and something new and urgent that beat hotly inside him, relentless as a heartbeat. Vaguely he was aware of one of Bonny's legs flung over his hip. Fingers tangled in his hair, pulling him closer. Whatever had seized him—was consuming him—was assuredly mutual. Which should, he thought in some wild way, have appeased him. Except it didn't. It only made him want more. More of everything. Of the physical sensations, yes, of hands and mouths and bodies fit together. But mostly more of Bonny: the catch of his breath in his throat, the way he bucked up in welcome, the pressure of his naked thigh.

Valentine had never pondered overmuch on the rudiments of passion. He had assumed it was embedded in what one experienced. Now he was beginning to realise it was about what you shared. That it was neither given nor taken but built between you in trust and pleasure and hope. A willingness to bare the truths of yourself. This was not the sort of thing to come easily to Valentine—indeed, he had carefully constructed his life around avoiding it. With Bonny, though, it felt worth trying. It felt like it would have been impossible not to.

"Good heavens," he murmured when the requirement to breathe forced him to draw back.

Bonny gave a shaky laugh. His mouth was swollen, as red as wild strawberries.

"Are you . . . was that . . ." Valentine hardly knew what he was asking.

"Yes," Bonny said, somewhat impatiently. "It was. And you don't have to worry, you know."

Realising he had been atop Bonny for quite some while, Valentine awkwardly de-Bonnied and rolled onto his side. "I'm sorry. I don't have parameters for how this should be. And I don't wish to transgress. Or prove myself nonproficient beyond the expectations of my inexperience."

There was a brief silence. "So you're worried you might do something and you won't know if I like it?"

Valentine gave a relieved nod. "Exactly."

Another pause. Then, "Kiss me," Bonny told him.

Valentine kissed him, and Bonny melted into him, crooning softly against his mouth.

"That," he explained, "was me liking something. Now do you want to see me not liking something?"

"Yes?" A wariness had crept into Valentine's tone. He had the creeping suspicion Bonny was not taking him wholly seriously. As usual. "If you don't mind?"

Bonny gave him a cool stare. "Stop doing that, please. I don't like it." Then he smiled. "It's not complicated."

"I see your point," Valentine conceded, somewhat reluctantly. "But perhaps I, too, have read too many books. And would value words as encouragement as well as discouragement."

To this, Bonny did not hesitate. "I see your point. And, uncertain or deliberate, tender or ardent, I love how you kiss me. If we did not have to catch my sister, I'd gladly spend all day kissing you."

"Would it be so dreadful"—already, Valentine reflected, not an auspicious start to a question, but it was too late now—"if your sister went to America?"

"Well. Yes. Because then she'd be in America."

"But she seems to want to go there?"

"Only," said Bonny rather mercilessly, "because she wants to get away from you." He sidled close to Valentine again. "Please? And not just because I don't want Belle having adventures without me. She's very . . . determined? But she still has no money. And she doesn't know a soul."

Even before there'd been honey and bathing and kissing, Valentine had found himself somewhat lacking in resilience when it came to Bonny. The fact he was here at all, and not in bed, and that there *had* been honey and bathing and kissing was testament to that. But he was also beginning to know him. His pride and his uncertainties. His loneliness. His loyalty and his fierce love. As for what that burgeoning knowledge did to Valentine, how even the recognition threatened to unpick the knots of his heart . . . he could worry about that some other time.

For now, he simply rested a hand against the curve of Bonny's jaw and drew their faces together. "And, as you've mentioned on several occasions, she could very well be menaced by highwaymen or captured by pirates."

There was a flash of something like gratitude in Bonny's eyes. "Exactly."

"Shall we leave?"

"Yes . . ." Bonny dragged out the word until it sounded more like demurral. "They have a head start, but they only have the gig. And if we were to strike directly for Dover, we could very well cut them off upon the Canterbury road."

A smile threatened Valentine's lips. "That is where *they* are going. But where are *you* going?"

"Where I am going is, I think we can afford to linger just a little longer?"

It was probably the longest Valentine had spent naked in his life, certainly the longest he had spent naked *and outdoors*. But the pool was secluded, the morning warm, and the company far too tempting. "And kiss?" he heard himself ask, with all the poise and delicacy of a youth at his first dance.

Although, for once, Bonny was merciful and did not laugh at him for it. "And if there's anything else that takes your fancy."

"What manner of anything else?"

Bonny's eyelids drooped. His gaze turned distinctly sultry. And it made Valentine feel far too hot. "My hand on you? My mouth? Our cocks pressed together. Whatever you were yearning for these past couple of days."

"Mostly," Valentine grumbled, "I was yearning for you to be quiet and sensible."

"That's the most blatant falsehood I've ever heard."

"I know." Valentine sighed. "But my yearnings are not yet experienced enough to be specific."

Bonny pulled Valentine's face to his and pressed their mouths extravagantly together. "I'm sorry. I'm moving too fast. Pushing you too hard. You might not have noticed, but it's a teeny tiny little flaw I have."

The moment Bonny released him, Valentine glanced away. "I'm disappointing you."

"No." Bonny sealed the declaration with a kiss. "No, no." Another kiss. "Never."

"If I had only known it was possible for me to feel this way, I would have—"

"Would have what, exactly?"

"Practiced?" Valentine flapped a hand vaguely. "Somehow?"

"With people you didn't want? That sounds like the opposite of a good idea, flower."

"You've managed."

"Yes, but I've wanted everyone I've, err, practiced with. Even if I didn't want them in the way I want you."

"I see." Truthfully, Valentine didn't see. It was hard for him to imagine how it would feel to be with someone, as he was with Bonny now, if he did not know them. Was not profoundly irritated, and fascinated, and disarmed by them. And once this would have seemed like a flaw or some weakness in the way he was made. Now he was not sure. "So," Bonny went on cheerfully, "you're just going to have to accept it: you're mine, Valentine. Entirely mine. And we will build a world of kissing. Which is world enough for me."

Valentine tried to say something, but the words were stuck in his throat, muddled in his breath, which meant all he managed was a noise. A naked, somewhat mortifying noise: gratitude and affection; the recognition of being seen, and seen generously; of wanting to offer the same in return.

"You," he managed at last, "are a terribly possessive young man."

This earned a careless shrug. "I did warn you."

"And you're . . . you're quite certain I am worth possessing?"

"You're a duke, aren't you?"

"Yes, but—"

"I'm teasing." Bonny's tone softened. "If I didn't think you were worth possessing, do you really think I'd have been encouraging you to reconcile with my sister? I just"—he'd started to blush again—"never imagined you might be for me."

"If it's any consolation," Valentine told him, "neither did I." It was an odd moment for the image that had been lurking in the back of his mind to elbow its way to the forefront of his thoughts. But it did. And suddenly Valentine could think of nothing else. "Actually I . . . there is something."

"Anything."

"What the ostler was—that. I want that."

"You want me to lick your—"

"No," he said quickly. "The other way. I want to do with you what he was doing."

"Oh." Bonny's eyes were wide. His mouth had fallen open slightly. "Oh, flower. I did not see that coming either."

Chapter 24

"Is there a technique?" asked Valentine.

"Not . . . not as such." Bonny sounded rather breathless. "Just do whatever . . . whatever seems appealing."

Valentine surveyed the gorgeously undulating landscape of Bonny laid out before him. In response to Valentine's request, he had rolled onto his stomach, spread his legs, lifted his hips, and . . . presented. It was the sort of impulsive action Valentine should have expected. But it had left him dizzied regardless. "Are you sure you are comfortable?"

"My arse is in the air, Valentine. There's a limit to my comfort."

"You seemed quite comfortable with the ostler."

"Yes, except I didn't care about the ostler. I didn't care what he thought."

"But"—mustering all his courage, Valentine ran a shaky hand over the swell of Bonny's buttocks—"you know what I think. You also know, there is no one I've met with whom I have contemplated something like this. Let alone yearned for."

"And," said Bonny, quivers in his voice and dashing across his skin, "that's incredibly seductive in abstract. Right now, it feels like a lot of pressure. Plus, you're staring right at . . . right at a part of me I've not really had much opportunity to examine for myself."

Leaning closer, Valentine let his breath play where his hand had previously. "Oh, Bonny. You are beautiful. And you are beautiful here."

"Good to know."

"It is like," Valentine whispered, "some secret valley, where you are pink and supple, and ever so lightly stippled with pale-gold hair. And in the heart of it there lies the bud of some hungry flower that wishes to bloom beneath my—"

"*Val-EN-tine.*" Bonny's astonished squeal ricocheted from rock to rock before finally fading. "What are you *doing?*"

"I am describing what I see."

"You are not. You're . . . you're waxing poetic *about my arsehole.*"

"I thought," Valentine murmured, "you might be curious. Since you said it was an element of your body you were not familiar with."

"I'm familiar with it. Just not visually."

"So." Valentine skated a fingertip gently down the silken furrow between Bonny's cheeks. "You agree then?"

"A-a-a-gree?"

"That your arsehole is a hungry flower."

Bonny made a lovely, raw sound. "What is happening? What are you doing to me?"

"You told me you like words."

"Not about my—not about my—"

The rest was lost because Valentine had kissed him. Openmouthed. Directly where he'd just described. Bonny tasted of heat and of himself, and Valentine kissed him as he had his mouth: with all the tenderness and eagerness and passion he was still learning to express.

Bonny's reaction was gratifying, his hands clawing at the grass and his knees sliding wider—blatant invitation in the curve of his spine.

Valentine lifted his head. "How do you agree now?"

"I agree," Bonny wailed. "I agree. My arsehole is whatever you say it is. Only do that again."

"A hungry flower," Valentine reminded him. "Oh—is that why you've been calling me *flower* all this time? Because I'm an arsehole?"

Bonny wriggled his posterior encouragingly in Valentine's face. "No. It's because you're pretty and needed a good pollinating. Although given your reaction to my arsehole, if I *had* been calling you an arsehole, clearly it would have been a compli"—Bonny's voice shot up at least an octave as Valentine circled him with the pad of his finger—"*ment.*"

"It's true." To the touch, Bonny was soft and warm, still wet from Valentine's kisses, and already yielding. "I like your arsehole very much."

"It . . . it likes you too."

"I can tell." Valentine pressed his finger down lightly. Felt Bonny's full-body twitch. "It's trying to kiss me back."

Bonny clasped his heads over his head. "And you're trying to murder me."

Laughing, and increasingly comfortable with the notion that, perhaps, the only right way to do what they were doing was the way that pleased them both the most, Valentine lowered his head again and set to an earnest exploration of the man so generously offered to him. He let Bonny play guide—or, at least, his responses, for Bonny himself quickly passed the point of lucidity, reduced instead to shudders, gasps, and needy squirms.

His moans alone were their own language. He had a kind of low rumble, almost a purr, when Valentine traced a slow vertical path between his cheeks. For Valentine's lightest kisses—little flutters of his lips against the places he was beginning to recognise were the most sensitive—Bonny reserved a series of higher-pitched yips. And as for the deeper kisses, the ones where Valentine plied him lingeringly with lips and tongue, for these the sounds would spill from him in an unbroken, blissful stream.

When Valentine had suggested . . . asked for . . . admitted that this was something he wanted to try, there had not really been opportunity for him to ponder the reality of it. Mostly it had been the visual that had arrested him—how gorgeously wanton Bonny had looked sprawled across a hay bale. That, and a somewhat shameful wish to stake a claim of his own against any past and future ostlers. What Valentine had not considered, however, was the pleasure it would bring him.

The way his body would stir for Bonny as it stirred for no one, and rarely even stirred for himself. Entirely unlike the usual urge for release that seemed, in the moment of its passing, an infinitely banal juxtaposition of flesh and fluid. No, this was something else entirely. A bright piece of wonder that danced from Bonny to him and back again as though they together completed some greater pattern that Valentine could never have understood alone.

It was the intimacy of it too. Of knowing how Bonny felt beneath his mouth. How hot he was, how soft and strong and slick from Valentine's tongue. What made him cry out and what made him lose his voice entirely. The quiver of his thighs in the moments of his wildest abandon.

"Oh—my—oh—" said Bonny, a new urgency in his voice. "I need to—Valentine, I *have* to touch myself."

Reluctantly, Valentine drew back from what had rapidly become his new favourite pursuit. "Touch yourself?"

"Yes. My hand. On my cock. Now."

"I can do that for you—"

"No. Nonononono. No." Bonny twisted and shuddered emphatically in the grass. "You keep doing what you're doing. And I'll . . . I'll see to this."

Peering between Bonny's legs, Valentine beheld the object of contention. It was flushed and heavy, and recklessly glistening. "Are you sure? Your cock is very lovely too."

"Oh God. Is it a hungry flower?"

"No," Valentine conceded. "It's more of a"—he contemplated it further—"bejewelled sceptre, crowned with pearls."

Bonny made a squawking noise that Valentine chose to interpret as approving. "Fine. Fine. But listen. Valentine. Listen. I'm going to put my hand on my . . . my pearly sceptre, and you're going to do that thing with your mouth . . ."

"To your hungry flower?"

"Yes. To my—to that."

"Which particular thing?"

"The one where you . . . where you . . . all the angels of heaven . . . where you *suck*. And then wriggle your tongue just, y'know, *inside*."

Valentine was taking mental notes. "Yes. And then?"

"And then I'm going to make a really loud noise and come absolutely everywhere?" Bonny pulled in a desperate breath. "All clear."

By way of answer, Valentine pressed a kiss to one of the little dimples at the base of Bonny's spine. And then Bonny's whole body arched, his arse lifting higher as he flattened his shoulders to the ground for balance and reached a hand towards his cock. Valentine felt, rather than saw, the moment it happened—the reaction that travelled like a ripple up Bonny's spine and down his legs. What followed was a blur of sensation—Bonny's heat pressed against him, the clumsy rhythm of his pleasure, and the accompanying monologue of "Oh God" and "Fuck yes" and "Like that" and, finally, "Don't stop don't stop don't stop." It culminated, as promised, in a loud noise—a rough and beautiful cry that echoed through all the empty places in Valentine's heart—before Bonny collapsed onto the grass with the aplomb of a dying hero in an opera. And there he lay, still shaking, giggling helplessly, his breath coming in great gasps, as if even indignity delighted him.

Eventually, he pulled his knees together, lowered his arse, and flopped onto his back. His cock—not that Valentine was staring . . . well, perhaps he was staring a little—was beginning to soften, though it was intriguingly swirled with the remnants of climax.

"How's my sceptre?" asked Bonny. "Bejewelled enough for you?"

"I would say bedewed. Would you . . . that is . . . may I . . ."

"What? *Oh.*" Bonny gave a shuddery laugh. "B-be my guest."

So Valentine lowered himself to his elbows and gently furled his tongue over the head of Bonny's cock.

"You, flower"—one of Bonny's hands came to rest upon his hair—"are *such* a dark horse."

Glancing up, Valentine risked a smile. "Every part of you is sweet."

"Of course it is. I've told you so myself on several occasions. Now come up here so I can kiss you."

Valentine came up there. And was kissed. And also cuddled, in a fashion that brooked no refusal. Bonny pinned him with a leg, much as he had when they'd shared a bed, flung an arm across his chest, and settled his face firmly into the crook of Valentine's arm.

"Now," he said, "it's your turn."

There was a part—one part in particular—of Valentine that was frantic for attention. But the rest of him was . . . uncertain. Yes, he was literally naked; yes, he had just bestowed a very intimate service upon another man; but the thought of being *given* pleasure, even by Bonny, felt like a very different sort of exposure. One he was, perhaps, not ready for. As much as he also craved it.

He swallowed. "I don't . . . I'm not. Do you mind if we . . . ?"

"Whenever you're ready." Bonny flashed him a bright grin. "Just know I can't wait to assess the strength of your sceptre with my mouth and the eagerness of your flower with my fingers."

"You . . ." Valentine was obliged to pause and clear his throat. "You will find them quite amenable to your attentions, I'm sure. But I . . . can we . . . may we stay like this? For just a little longer."

Bonny gave an immense, leonine yawn. "If we didn't have a prior engagement to chase down my sister, I'd say we could stay like this forever."

"You are aware," Valentine told him, "that there exists a midpoint between forever and never, everything and nothing?"

"Moderation, Valentine, should be taken only in moderation."

A statement Bonny punctuated with another yawn. He did not, however, fall asleep, as Valentine thought he might—instead he just contrived to nestle himself even closer, and stay there, eyes half-closed, in comparative stillness. The sunlight gleamed on his curls and danced in flecks of gold upon his bare shoulders, and he smelled of clean skin and fresh pleasure. Sweet and wanton both, and clasped in Valentine's arms in perfect contentment.

And Valentine had somehow made it happen. The hitherto-unimaginable mysteries of carnality laid as bare to him as Bonny was. And with them the understanding that everything he had assumed . . . believed . . . feared . . . belonged in the same sphere and therefore could not belong to him, either, did not. Love, sex, friendship, kindness, laughter: they were all stars to be strung in constellations of your own making.

"Oh, Bonny," he whispered. *"Et in Arkandia Ego."*

Bonny pressed a kiss to the side of Valentine's neck. "No, flower. This is real life."

"It's—"

"Good Lord," exclaimed Sir Horley Comewithers, emerging from the tree line. "Imagine meeting you fellows here. I was told this place was rather private."

There had been too many occasions, over the past few days, when Valentine had been obliged to question his sanity. This was another one. Or else he had fallen into some kind of waking nightmare.

Except, no. Sir Horley Comewithers was very much the genuine article. And standing right there.

Realising that any sudden moves would likely generate more attention than the reverse, Valentine edged discreetly away from Bonny. "Good morning."

Sir Horley beamed. "Well, good morning. One of my horses threw a shoe—damned inconvenient. But then I was fortunate enough to meet this rather lovely blacksmith"—he gestured to the flowing-haired, muscular gentleman at his side—"and he's helping me get acquainted with the local area."

The blacksmith gave a nod.

"Mr. Tarleton and I were just leaving," said Valentine, firmly.

Sir Horley's smile took on that toothy, foxy quality that Valentine distrusted. "Let me guess. You've still misplaced your fiancée."

"I haven't *misplaced* her. She just doesn't happen to be here."

"Here"—Sir Horley gestured—"at this romantic spot with the waterfall and the wildflowers? Where you've been—"

"Bathing," explained Valentine. "As gentlemen do. With their gentlemen friends."

Bonny offered a decisive nod. "That is *exactly* what is going on here. Gentlemanly bathing. Between gentlemen friends."

"Ah, yes." With a wistful sigh, Sir Horley clasped his hands. "Gentlemanly bathing. Between gentlemen friends. Reminds me of my days at Eton. And Oxford, now I think about it. Good times."

"Well, I was tutored at home. And"—Valentine stood, mustering what little of decorum, and his clothes, remained him—"we really must depart."

"Not on my account," insisted Sir Horley. "Stay, my dear chap. Let us share the, ah, the bounties of nature together." He glanced up at his companion. "What say you to that?"

The blacksmith nodded, his eyes—Valentine noticed—lingering on Bonny, who was putting his garments on far too slowly for Valentine's comfort.

Sir Horley was still smiling. "He's a man of few words but exquisite action. I've never seen a horseshoe pounded so thoroughly into shape."

"Commendable, I'm sure." Now Valentine, too, was mostly dressed, the gardener's coat once again draped over his shoulders, and his great-coat bundled over his arm. "If you'll excuse us?"

"Of course, of course." Even though they were standing in the middle of the countryside, Sir Horley stepped aside with a flourishing bow. "I look forward to meeting up in town, Malvern. We have so much to talk about."

Valentine looked about as scornful as it was possible for a man to look after he'd been discovered in blatant flagrante. "I imagine we'll have as much to talk about as ever. Come along, Bonny."

And, to his surprise, Bonny did indeed follow without protest. Had he only known that this was the secret to the man's obedience, he would have offered to lick his arse days ago.

Except, no. Of course he wouldn't have. The notion would have been unthinkable. And now it was unforgettable.

"I hope," said Bonny as they returned to his curricle, "you're proud of the way I barely noticed that gloriously meaty blacksmith."

"I was, until you felt constrained to mention the gloriously meaty blacksmith."

Deftly, Bonny began to harness his bays. "I still like you better. Best, even."

"Are you sure? Because while there are several descriptors that could apply to me, *meaty* will never be one of them."

"*Glorious*, though," suggested Bonny. "Glorious applies."

And, just like that, being handsome had found its purpose: pleasing Bonny. "Very well. I shall take *glorious*."

"Especially," he went on, "when your tongue is up my arse."

Valentine cast a nervous glance over his shoulder, but Sir Horley and his companion seemed occupied with each other. "I'm glad I showed myself to advantage." He paused, a burgeoning worry tugging at him. "Bonny?"

"Yes, flower?"

"You don't suppose there is any likelihood that Sir Horley suspected we were . . . suspected that we are—what are we?"

"Lovers."

"Exactly that."

Bonny pondered, a finger to his chin. "No, I'm sure he didn't. Now let's go and stop my sister turning to piracy on the high seas."

"I thought"—Valentine accepted Bonny's hand without thinking about it as he stepped up onto the curricle—"you were concerned she would be captured by pirates."

A second or two later, Bonny joined him, his thigh fit neatly to Valentine's. "I was. But then, on further reflection, it occurred to me that Belle is far more likely to *be* a pirate than kidnapped by one. Don't you agree?"

"Yes," said Valentine, for there could be no other answer. "Yes, I do."

And then that same peculiar impulse he had felt in the cottage swept over him. But this time, as the laughter broke free of his lips, it brought no tears with it. Instead, it came as easily as butterflies—and spiralled, jewel-winged, into the clear sky.

Chapter 25

They travelled quickly and easily through the glossy greens of Kent. It was, Valentine was beginning to think, a rather nice part of the country. Despite the vindictive bees.

Its penchant for sudden storms.

Most of the people.

But its proximity to the southern coast meant it was mostly bright and warm. And his proximity to Bonny was . . .

Very pleasing indeed. Just the pressure of his leg against Valentine's, the gentle warmth of his body, the occasional nudge of his shoulder as the curricle swayed. Mostly, they did not converse. It did not seem necessary, even to Bonny, who was, if anything, overinclined to converse. Probably he was eager to catch up with his sister. As, for that matter, was Valentine.

He was not—he had to admit—entirely sure what would happen to his life when they did, and he was not a man to enjoy uncertainty of any kind, but now his future contained Bonny, it did not loom in quite the way it once had. Of course, there would be wedding preparations and then the wedding itself. After, though, there would be Bonny. And they would be—to use Bonny's word—lovers.

Which would mean a lot of Bonny. Being loud, getting in the way, insisting on this, that, and the other. Contriving, in his infuriating fashion, to make Valentine happy. When Valentine—whose approach to his own happiness was, at best, unambitious—hadn't the slightest notion how he was supposed to offer the same.

There was, after all, only so much you could lick a man's arse. At least, Valentine assumed that was the case. He was, however, more than willing to stand, or presumably kneel, corrected.

And now he was getting distracted. Very distracted. The sort of distracted you definitely shouldn't be in a curricle.

Books. Bonny liked books. He could show him his library. Or even perhaps the stash of gothic and romantic fiction Valentine kept under his bed and usually read in the bath. Better still, he could buy Bonny his own library. And jewels. He would like jewels, if the rainbow of paste gems upon his fingers was anything to go by. And they could travel. Valentine was not himself a see-the-world sort of person. But with Bonny? Who was so full of dreams? That, he could more than bear.

But mostly, he realised, he just wanted more of . . . this. Whatever *this* was. It felt a little bit like being chased by a bee, discomforting and wearying, leaving one at the mercy of the unpredictable impulses of an alien being. And yet it was also . . . good. It was good. Bonny made everything different. Brighter. More interesting and hopeful.

Including, perhaps, Valentine himself.

His daydreams, however, were dispelled by the reality of the man he was daydreaming about. "Look." Bonny poked him in the ribs. "Look!"

Valentine looked. Farther up the road, a gig had come to what was surely an unintended halt, given its awkward angle and the fact it was listing heavily. A familiarly undistinguished brown horse had been released from the traces, and an unfamiliarly undistinguished young man appeared to be labouring, without much success, over one of the axles. A less undistinguished young man—quite a striking one, with a rather Byronic aspect—was standing a short distance away with Miss Tarleton, his rapt gaze rarely straying from her face. Peggy was resting against a nearby curricle, which, from its modish aspect, Valentine presumed belonged to the second gentleman: the one who attended upon ladies, rather than vehicles.

"The gig's been on its last legs for years." Bonny sounded more than a little smug. "Well, wheels, I suppose. At any rate, I knew we'd catch them."

Relief crept through Valentine as hesitantly as a mouse at midnight. It would all be over soon. He would be with Bonny; Miss Tarleton would no longer hate him. He would be able to go home. However, as they drew abreast of the gig, Miss Tarleton, somewhat predictably, gave a piteous cry and fainted spectacularly into the arms of the gentleman at her side.

"This is not what you think," began Valentine, stepping down from Bonny's curricle. "I am—"

The young gentleman's dark eyes flashed. "I know exactly who you are."

"Oh, do you?" Valentine gave him a cool look. "Enlighten me. Who am I this time?"

"You," declared the young gentleman, in a tone of utter revulsion, "are the Duke of Malvern."

Valentine sighed. "Yes, yes, but I'm actually the Duke of—oh." He coughed. "Then I'm afraid you rather have the advantage of me."

The gentleman attempted to strike a pose but was somewhat hindered by the fact his arms were full of Arabella Tarleton—who had managed to remain in a swoon for longer than she was usually able. "I am Cloudesley Whelpington-Byng, Esquire. And this lady is under my protection."

Valentine sighed again. Was this what his married life was going to be like? Or would his betrothed stop treating him like the villain of a gothic novel when she knew his heart belonged to Bonny? Even if she didn't, he'd bear it. For Bonny. Anything, if he could just go home with Bonny.

"Of course she is," he said aloud. "You are, I suppose, aware that she is my fiancée?"

"That"—Mr. Whelpington-Byng, Esquire, apparently had a rather declarative way of speaking in general—"is why she is under my protection."

"About that." Having left his horses in Peggy's care, Bonny trotted over to join them. "The thing is, Valentine and I have rather—"

This was too much for Miss Tarleton. She regained consciousness abruptly. "Et tu, Brute?"

"I know about you, too, Bonaventure Tarleton," cried Mr. Whelpington-Byng, Esquire. "How you betrayed your sister's cause. Suborned through perversity—"

The other gentleman—having abandoned his struggles with the gig—hurried to his friend's side. "I say, Cloud. Steady on. Let's not go around accusing fellow-inclining fellows of perversity. Bad form, don't you know?"

Mr. Whelpington-Byng, Esquire, had the common decency to flush. "Quite right, Peter. That was too much. I apologise. This is my friend, by the way, Mr. Peter Howard."

"Marvellous to meet you," said Peter, offering his hand for everyone to shake. "Bad news about the gig, though. It's suffering from an advanced case of being busted."

"Oh." Arabella pressed both hands to her mouth, then realised she would be unable to speak and removed them quickly. "Whatever are we to do? I am doomed! *Doomed.*"

Peggy, meanwhile, had picked a dandelion clock and was blowing the seeds from its head. "I'm sure we'll come to some sort of arrangement."

"No. Oh no. No." Arabella blinked rapidly, in the manner of one who very much wished she was crying. Then hid her face against Mr. Whelpington-Byng, Esquire's, shoulder. "My life is over. I am undone. Wholly undone."

Nervously, Bonny reached out to her, only to have his hand slapped away. "Belle, Belladonna, heart of my heart. It is not nearly so terrible as you think. You see, Valentine and I have been talking, and the truth is, well, he doesn't want—"

"Unhand Miss Tarleton"—Mr. Whelpington-Byng, Esquire, interposed himself between Bonny and his sister—"you Judas. And as for you, *Malvern*"—now he rounded on Valentine—"how dare you use the advantages of your birth and sex to force matrimony upon an unwilling woman."

"He's old," put in Mr. Howard. "He's from a different time. He doesn't understand these sorts of social complexities."

This did little to soothe Valentine. "For the last *fucking* time, I am *not old*. I am eight and twenty."

Arabella emitted another woeful wail. "That's almost thirty. To think, the tender blossom of my youth shall wither upon his vine."

"What's that about my vine?" asked Valentine, appalled.

"I don't care"—Mr. Whelpington-Byng, Esquire, was still using his body to shelter Miss Tarleton—"how things were managed in your day. It is now the nineteenth century, and we respect women and treat them as equals in areas not pertaining to politics, property, warfare, finances, or the law."

"Yes," said Valentine. "And?"

Mr. Whelpington-Byng, Esquire, pulled himself to his full height, which put him to about Valentine's chin. "*And*, sir, you are a villain."

Valentine stiffened. It was not, under any circumstances, acceptable to call a gentleman of quality a villain.

"Also," added Mr. Whelpington-Byng, Esquire, "a cur."

It was still less acceptable, under any circumstances, to call a gentleman of quality a cur.

"A rapscallion," continued Mr. Whelpington-Byng, Esquire, "a scoundrel, a cad, a rogue, a knave, a miscreant, a—"

"I think"—Valentine did his best to stanch the flow of invective before the young Mr. Whelpington-Byng, Esquire, extended his insult beyond the point he could possibly withdraw it—"I can see where you're going with this."

"And," concluded Mr. Whelpington-Byng, Esquire, "a blackguard."

There was a long silence.

Mr. Howard shifted his weight uncertainly from foot to foot. "Cloud, old man. Did you just call the Duke of Malvern a villain, a cur, a rapscallion, a scoundrel, a cad, a rogue, a knave, a miscreant, and a blackguard?"

"I did." Mr. Whelpington-Byng, Esquire, folded his arms haughtily.

"Entirely appropriately," added Miss Tarleton, peeping out from behind her protector.

"Not . . . not *really* appropriately." Mr. Howard was still weaving anxiously. "You can't go around calling a duke a villain, a cur, a rapscallion, a scoundrel, a cad, a rogue, a knave, a miscreant, and a blackguard. It's not the done thing."

"It is entirely the done thing," retorted Mr. Whelpington-Byng, Esquire, "if the duke in question *is* a villain, a cur, a rapscallion, a scoundrel, a cad, a rogue, a knave, a miscreant, and a blackguard."

"Which"—that was Miss Tarleton again—"he is."

There was another long silence.

Mr. Howard's anxious weaving had escalated into vibrating. "That's as may be, but don't you see you'll be leaving him no choice but to—"

"I'm afraid," said Valentine finally, "I am going to have to ask you to retract those words."

"Which words?" Mr. Whelpington-Byng, Esquire, gave him a wide-eyed look. "The ones where I called you a villain, a cur, a rapscallion, a scoundrel, a cad, a rogue, a knave, a miscreant, and a blackguard?"

So many of the travails Valentine had overcome recently had, in retrospect, been irritations. Irritations that he was just about capable of admitting he might have ever so slightly, on occasion, overreacted to. This was not an irritation; it was affront. Worse, it was a threat. But losing his temper had improved exactly zero of the situations Valentine had found himself in recently. He grasped after his patience like it was an unruly hound. "Yes. Those words."

"Well, I shan't," Mr. Whelpington-Byng, Esquire, told him. "Now do you propose I add *coward* to them?"

"Belle." Bonny tried frantically to catch his sister's eye. "Stop this, please."

"I propose"—Valentine regarded Mr. Whelpington-Byng, Esquire, steadily—"that you do not force a situation you do not fully understand."

Mr. Whelpington-Byng, Esquire, smoothed back a wayward lock of dark hair. "Oh, I understand all too well. I understand you are a villain, a cur, a—"

"For the love of God," snapped Valentine, "stop saying that."

"Or what, sir?"

"Or . . ." There was really only one *or*. And it was the last *or* Valentine wanted, but it was the only *or* that he could take without shaming himself and his family.

Bonny seized his arm. "Valentine, don't. Please don't. This isn't a matter of honour. It's a matter of . . . of . . . silly."

"To be a matter of honour"—Mr. Whelpington-Byng, Esquire, gazed loftily towards the horizon—"the Duke of Malvern would need to possess some sense of honour in the first place. As it is, he is a villain, a cur, a rapscallion, a scoundrel, a cad, a rogue, a knave, a miscreant, a blackguard, *and a coward*. And, after this affair, all shall know it."

The worst of it was, Mr. Whelpington-Byng, Esquire, was correct. Not in his assessment of Valentine's character. But that such blandishments, if unanswered, would unmake him in the eyes of society. "Fine." Valentine threw his hands in the air. "I demand satisfaction. Name your—"

"I name Mr. Peter Howard as my second . . ."

"Pardon?" said Mr. Howard. "But I don't know anything about duelling. And it's illegal. And what if you're murdered? What will I tell your mother? Oh God, what if you murder the Duke of Malvern. What will I tell your mother *then*?"

Mr. Whelpington-Byng, Esquire, pressed on, undaunted. Valentine got the sense that pressing on undaunted was rather a cornerstone of his character. "I name the time as now and the place as here. And I choose pistols."

"Pardon?" said Mr. Howard again. "What? No. You can't duel here. We're in the middle of Kent. Nor, for that matter, now. It's nearly teatime. Nobody has duels at teatime. They have tea. And little cakes."

"Well, sir?" Mr. Whelpington-Byng, Esquire, glared at Valentine. "Will you name your friends?"

Valentine shrugged. "Tarleton, I suppose?"

To Valentine's surprise, Bonny was *also* glaring at him. "Absolutely not."

"What . . . what do you mean, 'absolutely not'?"

"I mean," Bonny said, "absolutely not."

"Bonny, whatever else we are to each other, are you not also my friend? I must defend my reputation."

Bonny plonked his hands on his hips. "By getting shot? Or shooting someone else? That's the epitome of nonsense, and I won't be party to it."

It was the strangest thing, Valentine reflected, to betray a man in the name of affection.

"But Bonbon"—Miss Tarleton clasped her hands together delightedly—"a duel. A *real* duel."

"Belle." It was Bonny's coolest tone and severest look. "I'm a bit cross about this. Someone could get hurt."

"As a matter of fact," put in Mr. Howard, "I'm not sure they could. You see, it's dashed odd of me, but I somehow left the house this morning without a pair of duelling pistols."

"Don't worry, Peter." Mr. Whelpington-Byng, Esquire, clapped his friend upon the shoulder. "I have mine. They're in my curricle."

Mr. Howard stared at him. "Cloud, that's a bit worrying. Why would you have duelling pistols in your curricle?"

Mr. Whelpington-Byng, Esquire, returned Mr. Howard's look. "Why wouldn't I? Honour waits for no man."

"Actually"—this was Peggy—"aren't you supposed to wait a day? You know, to make certain you're not just making a pair of complete arses out of yourselves."

"It is too late for that," said Mr. Whelpington-Byng, Esquire, and Valentine together.

"Mm." Peggy regarded both of them. "Good point."

There was another uncomfortable pause.

"Well," offered Mr. Howard finally. "I suppose I'd better be, um, I'd better go get the . . ." With a vague gesture in the direction of the other gentleman's curricle, he ambled off to retrieve the pistols.

Chapter 26

"Valentine?" Bonny was tugging urgently at his sleeve. "You can't do this. *Please* don't do this."

Valentine lifted his chin nobly. "I don't have a choice. I have been impugned."

"And that's worth getting shot over?"

"Why are you being like this?" Valentine demanded, turning on Bonny in frustration. "Don't you care about me at all?"

Bonny's gaze was starkly blue, and pleading. "Of *course* I care about you. That's why I don't want you to do this."

Something—perhaps Valentine's sense of betrayal—faltered slightly. "You're being ridiculous."

"I'm not the one about to get shot in Kent."

"You know," Valentine pointed out, feeling oddly stung by this lack of faith in his abilities, which only compounded the lack of regard for his honour, "I could very well shoot my opponent."

"That doesn't make it better." Bonny gave his sleeve another little tug. "I can no more be with you if you're a murderer than if you're dead."

Soothingly, Valentine covered Bonny's hand with his own. "We can flee to the continent. Isn't that quite romantic?"

"No." Bonny shoved his hand away. "There is nothing romantic about having killed someone."

"You would prefer me to stay in England and be hanged?"

"I would prefer," Bonny cried, "for you not to do this dangerous, unnecessary, and profoundly stupid thing."

Valentine's feelings were in danger of getting away from him. He was already none too happy that he was about to fight a duel. And now he appeared to be having an argument with Bonny, who should have understood the situation as well as Valentine did. "You're making too much of this. Duelling has been how men have settled their differences for centuries."

"No, it isn't." Bonny stamped his foot with even more determination than usual. "It's what men fall back on because they're too scared to talk about their feelings or admit when they're in the wrong."

Valentine wasn't sure when he'd started *listening* to Bonny, but, to his mild chagrin, he had. Except this time, Bonny was mistaken. "I'm not in the wrong. You have shown me that a man can be more things than I ever believed, but a man still does not brook this manner of insult. It is unthinkable."

By way of response, Bonny pressed his hands to Valentine's chest, as if he wasn't sure whether he wanted to cling to him or shove him away. "I will never forgive you for this," he said, and Valentine was horrified to see the tears gathering in his eyes. *"Never."*

Before Valentine could address this—though how he would have done so, he had no idea—Mr. Howard returned bearing a box which, presumably, contained Mr. Whelpington-Byng, Esquire's, duelling pistols.

"I think," he said, "the seconds are supposed to . . . inspect the weapons? Maybe?"

"Well, I don't have a second." Valentine glanced towards Bonny, hoping he would evince even the smallest degree of guilt for having caused such a mortifying situation, and was disappointed. "So you'll have to do it for both of us."

"Ah," said Mr. Howard in a tone that was probably a good deal less neutral than he had intended. He turned the box about in his hands, fumbled with the clasp, and then dropped the whole thing, causing the lid to fly open and the two firearms inside to spill onto the grass.

Mr. Whelpington-Byng, Esquire, did not look pleased. "Peter!"

"Sorry." Mr. Howard scrambled after the pistols, bundling them back into their blue velvet cradles. Then he ceremonially lifted them out again and peered at each closely. "Yes," he announced finally. "After inspecting them, I can confirm that these are certainly both guns."

"Excellent," declared Mr. Whelpington-Byng, Esquire.

"Now what?" asked Valentine.

A pause.

"Oh." Mr. Howard gave a little jump and nearly dropped the pistols again. "Me? Of course. I suppose we . . . well, the thing to do would probably be moving out of the sight of the lady, don't you know?"

"No, no," protested Miss Tarleton. "I want to watch."

Momentarily distracted from the duel he'd compelled by the woman he was supposed to be helping, Mr. Whelpington-Byng, Esquire, gazed down at her earnestly. "Miss Tarleton, you have suffered enough already. Do not let your gentle spirit tarnish itself in the violence of men."

"How about"—Mr. Howard gestured vaguely to a nearby field—"over there."

Turning, Valentine trudged in the indicated direction. "Fine. That will do."

"Wait." If this nonsense was going to be delayed by anyone, Valentine would have wished for it to be Bonny. Unfortunately, it was Peggy. "I'll be your second."

"You?" Valentine blinked. "But you're a . . ."

The look Peggy was giving him somehow made it difficult to finish the sentence. "I'm a what?"

"You're a . . ." Oh dear. "Person?"

"Thank you. Yes. I am a person. Now, do you want a second or not?"

"I . . ." Defeated, Valentine hung his head. "Yes, please."

"Good. Now—"

She was interrupted by a furious noise from Miss Tarleton. "Et tu *too*, Brute?"

"Belle"—Peggy somehow contrived to sound both irritated and conciliatory—"do you really wish this to end in bloodshed?"

"Yes," said Miss Tarleton. "Yes, I do."

Mr. Whelpington-Byng, Esquire, took her hand and kissed it tenderly. "You poor wounded creature. How desperate you must be to escape this dastardly man."

"In any case," Peggy went on doggedly, "as a challenge has been issued, the seconds have a duty to try and resolve the issue peaceably before the matter progresses."

Mr. Howard perked up visibly. "We do? Yes. Yes, we do! Um . . . how?"

"Well"—Peggy made a nebulously placating gesture—"if, hypothetically, the situation had been presented to someone in a way that might make them interpret things more negatively than, perhaps, they should have?"

"What are you talking about?" demanded Mr. Whelpington-Byng, Esquire.

Peggy gave one of her lazy, loose-limbed shrugs. "Just that misunderstandings happen. Apologies could be, you know, offered? What do you think, Belle?"

Miss Tarleton was looking at Peggy much as Bonny had previously been looking at Valentine—the same mixture of bewilderment and genuine hurt. "I think"—she twisted her neck into what seemed to be a viciously uncomfortable position—"you must do as you will, as always. And I shall do as I must. As always."

Things had gone astray. That much had been obvious for quite some time. But Valentine was starting to realise that *astray* was not so much a binary state as a spectrum of disaster along which they had not yet ceased progressing. He had somehow been provoked into issuing a challenge, which was already nonideal, but he had managed to upset Bonny in the process. And now Peggy had contrived to upset Miss Tarleton, which admittedly concerned Valentine significantly less than Bonny being upset. But an upset Miss Tarleton was an unpredictable Miss Tarleton, and that did not bode well for anyone, least of all Valentine.

"Very well," said Mr. Whelpington-Byng, Esquire, suddenly. "I shall offer my apologies."

Valentine was so startled—to say nothing of relieved—he nearly choked on his own breath. "You will?"

"Indeed." Mr. Whelpington-Byng, Esquire, drew back his shoulders. "I am sorry that you are a villain, a cur, a rapscallion, a scoundrel, a cad, a rogue, a knave, a miscreant, a blackguard, and a coward. It must be terribly inconvenient for you, sir."

For the second time in recent memory, Valentine flung his arms in the air. "Oh, for God's sake. Fine. We shall duel. I mean, why not? I didn't have anything else planned for this afternoon."

"Apart from forcibly marrying me," Miss Tarleton reminded him.

"Yes, yes. Apart from that. And"—words were happening, ill-advised words that Valentine was somehow unable hold back—"the nun I was going to blackmail, and the widow I was going to have turned out of her home, and the pack of vestal virgins I was going to carry off in my chariot."

Mr. Whelpington-Byng, Esquire's, mouth was hanging open. "By Gad. I do not know whether to condemn your iniquity or applaud your efficiency."

"Don't worry about it," Valentine told him. "Just come and shoot me."

Not quite daring to look at Bonny—though wanting to more than anything—Valentine climbed into the field Mr. Howard had . . . not so much found as noticed. He had no idea if it would make a good duelling ground. It seemed a perfectly acceptable field, being mostly grass, the occasional flower, and a large sycamore tree, its branches flung heavenward in a manner Valentine read as exasperated.

To his surprise, Peggy had fallen into step beside him, keeping pace easily despite his superior height. "I suppose," she remarked, "you know what you're doing."

"Of course I know what I'm doing."

"Good. Because otherwise you'd be in a god-awful mess right now."

Valentine digested this. It was not a pleasant morsel. "Let's say, for argument's sake, I was in a god-awful mess. What could be done to mitigate that mess?"

"We're a little past the point of mitigation. Are you at least a decent shot?"

"Probably."

A pause. "Probably?"

"I mean . . . is it hard?"

"No," said Peggy reassuringly. "Of course not. After all, it's not like anybody practices or anything."

"Ah." Valentine also digested this. It was still unpleasant. "I confess I am not overly enamoured at the prospect of dying."

"It's"—Peggy seemed to be seeking a word—"*unlikely*. That you'll die."

"Is it?"

She nodded. "Probably you'll just be maimed."

"What now?" called out Mr. Howard, who had also joined them in the field, along with Mr. Whelpington-Byng, Esquire.

"We should measure out ten yards apiece," Peggy called back.

The events that followed did so in the sort of blur that made Valentine half hope he was dreaming again. Though why his mind would hate him to the extent that it would offer such a scenario to his slumbering self, he was yet to discern. He did, however, draw some consolation from the fact Mr. Whelpington-Byng, Esquire, had gone pale to the point of chalkiness as the pistols were loaded.

"These aren't very well maintained," Peggy whispered as she handed the gun to Valentine.

He gave her a slightly wild look. "What does that mean? Is that bad?"

"Well"—she made a valiant effort to sound consoling—"it should help with the death problem."

"What about the maiming? Does it help with the maiming?"

"Not so much with the maiming, no. There could be quite a bit . . . more maiming, actually."

"But," protested Valentine, "I don't want there to be *any* maiming."

"In which case, maybe don't get involved in firefights?"

They had, by this point, marked out his ten paces. And from this very specific perspective, Valentine discovered his opponent was at once impossibly distant and far, *far* too close, wavering upon the horizon like a mirage.

"Why won't he stand still?" demanded Valentine. "Is that permitted?"

Peggy squinted down the field. "He *is* standing still. It's just your hand is shaking. Your hand is shaking a lot."

"Perhaps"—Valentine tried to take a steadying breath, but his breath was not steady either—"you could not mention this to Bonny?"

"I don't think Bonny's going to care."

"Actually . . ." For some reason it felt important to say this. To someone. In case he never got the opportunity to say it to anyone. "Actually, we've grown somewhat . . . I suppose . . . close?"

"That's why he won't care, Malvern. He's terrified you're going to be hurt."

Hardly a negligible concern for Valentine either. "He must understand—"

"All he understands is he likes you. And that he could lose you."

This was an element of the situation that Valentine had not fully considered. Of course, Bonny had made it very clear that he did not approve of what was happening, but in the pressure of the moment Valentine had responded only to his anger. He had not stopped to think about what such anger might be cloaking. Perhaps because of the simple truth that Valentine was not accustomed to being cared for.

He did not, as a general rule, allow it.

"Oh God." His hand was already perspiring around the pistol grip. "Peggy. How do I survive this?"

"You call it off."

"I . . . I can't."

"Then turn your body sideways and do your damnedest to shoot him before he shoots you."

"Fuck," said Valentine very softly. "Fuck. Fuck. Fuck."

"Remember to cock the pistol?" suggested Peggy.

After three attempts, Valentine cocked the pistol.

"And open your eyes?" suggested Peggy. "It'll make it easier to see."

Reluctantly, Valentine forced his eyes open.

"Ready?" asked Mr. Howard.

His voice seemed very loud and very slow, the word itself almost meaningless. And suddenly Valentine was very . . .

There.

The skin-warmed metal of the gun. The stir of breath upon his lips. The pulsing of his heart within his chest. Even the ceaseless, invisible tides of his blood.

He had never seen so blue a sky. Nor so green a sycamore, every leaf its own star, and on the underside a tracery of veins as intricate as the ones across his palm. It felt, in that unmoving moment, such a waste: all this impossible wonder that Valentine had never learned to see.

"Um," said Mr. Howard. "Fire?"

Valentine had a split second to realise he really, *really* did not want to fire. And then an extra second to realise he had to. So he did.

Bracing himself for noise, for recoil, for his own death.

Chapter 27

And nothing happened. He glanced at Peggy.

She shrugged. "Flint was badly maintained. It didn't strike."

Across the field, Mr. Whelpington-Byng, Esquire, was also peering at his gun. Or, rather, directly into it—as if the mystery of why it hadn't fired lay buried deep within the barrel.

"You probably shouldn't—" began Peggy at the same time Mr. Howard said, "I did tell you I didn't know how to—"

One or both sentiments were enough to make Mr. Whelpington-Byng, Esquire, lift his head, an expression of irritation etched upon his face. There followed a retort far too loud for one small pistol. Mr. Whelpington-Byng, Esquire, yelled and dropped the weapon. Mr. Howard screamed and dived into a nearby bush. Valentine—now convinced he was going to die—contributed a noise of his own, far more manly and dignified than either of the others'.

And then a pigeon tumbled from the sky with a small, sad plop.

Mr. Whelpington-Byng, Esquire, was the first to recover himself. "Did you see that?" he cried. "Did you see that? I made a point of shooting a bird from the air. I hope you realise what a lucky escape you've had today, Malvern."

"Yes," said Valentine, thoughtfully. "Yes, indeed."

At which point he was struck by a cannonball of Bonny, who was hugging him with such fervour that he knocked Valentine clean off his feet. "Don't you ever ever *ever* do anything like that again. Do you hear me? Not ever ever ever *ever*."

"You said . . ." Valentine clutched him, far beyond the point of pride, or worrying how it might look or what anyone might think. "You said you weren't going to forgive me."

"I haven't. I'm not. I'm furious at you, Valentine. Absolutely furious. I may never stop being. But, oh, oh, thank God you're alive."

Bonny dissolved into tears, and Valentine was very inclined to dissolve with him. Instead, he just whispered nonsensical things like "Yes" and "I'm sorry" and "I promise" over and over again, and tried not to drown in the unbearable sweetness of being so very cared for by someone who had far too many reasons not to care in the slightest.

The world was slipping back into everyday hues—the sycamore had faded a little, as had the sky, but Valentine knew he would never forget them. Whatever it meant, whatever it took, he would learn to deserve his bright moments. Just as he would learn to deserve the man in his arms, in whose eyes and touch and laughing he had already found the brightest colours of all.

"By Gad!" The exclamation came from Mr. Whelpington-Byng, Esquire. "What's she doing?"

Peggy followed his gaze towards the road. "I think she's stealing your curricle."

"But . . . but why?"

"I could explain, but it would take too long. Belle—" She sprinted across the field and back onto the road. "Wait! Please."

Extricating himself from Valentine's embrace, Bonny set off after Peggy. "Quick. After her."

Valentine did his best to pursue, but his legs appeared to have been replaced by blancmange. He managed a sort of weaving wobble and then collapsed to his knees in the grass. "It's possible," he conceded, "nearly getting shot has affected me somewhat."

As Peggy readied the curricle, Bonny came bouncing back and helped Valentine to his feet. "Yes, flower, you were very brave doing the needlessly dangerous thing you were in no way required to do. Come on."

Valentine was still a little shaky as he half climbed, half flopped into Bonny's curricle.

"Go," cried Peggy, who was balanced on the groom's seat. "Go. Go. Go."

"I'm going," Bonny cried back.

"Why are we shouting?" asked Valentine, plaintively.

And then they were off, thundering their way towards Dover on what—if Valentine could have had his way—would have been a road both considerably wider and considerably smoother. After the last couple of days, Bonny's bays were tired, and they were bearing three now rather than two, but Valentine realised his earlier assessment of Bonny as a decent whip had been far from just. He was *skilled*—the perfect combination of audacity and adroitness—and it wasn't long before they caught their first glimpse of Miss Tarleton ahead of them.

She had mettle of her own, but she lacked Bonny's confidence and was driving unfamiliar horses who had clearly been chosen for their style rather than their stamina. Eventually, after some jostling, and a few close calls that did nothing for Valentine's postduel nerves, they drew abreast of her.

"Come on, Belle." The wind buffeted Bonny's voice but did nothing to conceal the pleading in it. "It's been a grand old game. But it's time to call it quits."

Miss Tarleton's hair had come loose from its bindings, and it streamed behind her in rebellious waves. "Never."

"You're going to get hurt."

"I already am."

"I mean, you're going to end up in a ditch."

"Rather that than sold to a—" Whatever she had to say about Valentine was lost beneath the slap of her reins and the rattle of curricle wheels as she pushed ahead of them again.

"It's no good," said Peggy. "She won't listen. Not after everything that's happened."

Bonny gave a little growl. "Why does she always have to be so stubborn?"

"No idea." Valentine didn't have to see Peggy to know she was shrugging. "It's almost like it runs in the family or something."

"I'm only stubborn when it's sensible, though."

"Yes." That was Peggy's most sceptical voice. "Absolutely that is true."

"Oh, what are we going to do?"

It hadn't been a question so much as a despairing wail, but Peggy answered regardless. "Can you get me level?"

"I can."

Leaning forwards in his seat, Bonny coaxed a fresh burst of speed from his steeds.

"Wait." A series of unpalatable possibilities was occurring to Valentine. "Why does she need you to—what's she going to do?" He twisted round so he could see Peggy. "Surely you aren't—"

"Get ready," Bonny told her. "As the road widens."

Valentine was torn between clutching his heart and clutching the edge of the carriage. It was beginning to feel very like he had survived a duel, only to die in a cataclysmic curricle crash.

"Stay away. Don't you dare." Belle, still struggling to maintain her lead, seemed to have guessed what they were planning. "I will push you into the road, Margaret Delancey, so help me God."

"No, you won't," Peggy told her.

And then, just as Bonny had manoeuvred them alongside, she leapt. The swift motion, the unexpected loss and acquisition of weight, was enough to throw all four horses into panic.

Valentine, too, if he was being honest. "Oh God."

For a nauseating carousel of seconds, the world was nothing but wild motion, the clatter of hooves and the screech of wheels, Belle's furious cries. No time for beauty or clarity, just the splinter of wood and the crunch of bone in Valentine's head. An unyielding conviction of impending destruction. And then—

It stopped.

He opened his eyes. Only for the sky, the grass, the road to start . . . slipping past him somehow, smearing into a painter's palette of green and grey and muddy brown.

Bonny's palm landed warm and firm on the back of his neck. "Head between your knees, flower."

"Am . . ." Valentine's breath seemed to be coming and going in waves. "Am I dead?"

"No. You're just having quite a day."

Just then, Bonny's hand was the most perfect thing Valentine had ever felt. It was all he could ever imagine needing. That steady pressure, keeping him safe. "I had quite a day yesterday as well," he pointed out miserably.

"I know," murmured Bonny. "I know. But it's all over now. Everything's all right."

Valentine did his best to believe him. He sincerely wanted to. Everything being all right was beginning to feel like an unattainable state of affairs. "Where are we?"

"Exactly where we were."

"Definitely not dead?"

This made Bonny laugh, but not unkindly. "No."

"Or in a ditch?"

"No."

Slowly Valentine looked up, relieved to discover they were, indeed, neither dead nor in a ditch, and still on the road to Dover. Some short distance ahead, the other curricle had come to a less controlled halt; its passengers had both disembarked and appeared to be engaged in heated discourse. They broke off as Bonny and a still somewhat blancmangey Valentine approached.

Miss Tarleton was the first to speak, and it was not encouraging. "You're all against me."

"We're not." Bonny sounded . . . tired suddenly. Tired and slightly fragile, as if he was blancmange on the inside. It made Valentine ache to hug him. "We just want to go home."

"We don't have a home," snapped Miss Tarleton. "Or have you forgotten?"

Bonny flinched. "Belle . . ."

"Don't *Belle* me, Bonny. This isn't Arkandia. There's no happy ending here. There's just a man I don't like, and a future I don't want, and ruin if I won't submit."

"But . . ." It was one of the few occasions Valentine had seen Bonny struggling for words. "It doesn't have to be like that. I've . . . we've . . . he—"

Miss Tarleton threw her hands in the air. "I should have known you'd see it his way."

"Well," Bonny retorted, "you didn't give me any opportunity to see yours. You just left."

"I've been telling you for years how I feel. And you've never listened."

"How"—Valentine recognised the waver in Bonny's voice, the trembling of his lashes, and found it no easier to bear when he was not the direct cause—"how can you say that?"

"Because it's true. How many times have I told you I would run away to America if he ever came for me?"

"I thought you were . . . you know . . . being dramatic?"

For a moment, Miss Tarleton only stared at him. Then made a sort of *gah* noise, threw her hands in the air again, and stamped her foot. "When have I ever been dramatic?"

A pause.

"All the time?" suggested Bonny.

"Fine." She tossed her hair. "But that doesn't make what I say less true."

"Fine." He tossed his. "But that doesn't mean I want you to go to America."

It was a little bit, Valentine reflected, like watching a mirror argue with itself.

"And I"—Miss Tarleton again—"never wanted to marry *him*. And yet here we are."

"You used to like him," said Bonny softly. "I thought it would be different when you met again."

"That's because you think life is a fucking fairy tale."

His lashes fluttered once more in that pained way that had become painful to Valentine. "I don't think that. I just don't see why it can't be."

"Maybe"—Miss Tarleton had flushed, in the angry, hectic way that Bonny flushed sometimes—"I don't *want* a fairy tale. Did you ever stop to consider that?"

"So you want to go to a strange country? With nothing? And no idea what will happen when you arrive?"

"I want," cried Miss Tarleton, "something I've *chosen*. Instead of something chosen for me by two dead men. Or"—she made a wild gesture—"two living ones who think they know what's best for me."

Valentine stepped forwards. "Then we shall discuss your choices. But not by the roadside."

"How magnanimous you are, Your Grace." Miss Tarleton swept a sardonic curtsy. "In victory."

Bonny made a small sad noise. "This isn't victory. It's . . . compromise. Please, Belle."

"Think of it this way," offered Peggy. "You can still change your mind and run away to America at any point."

This did not seem to console Miss Tarleton. "I was *trying* to run away right now. No thanks to you."

"Oh, come on." Peggy's eyes—which were not given to theatrics—widened fractionally. "I stood by you all the way, Arabella. I just balked at helping you get someone killed."

"But he wasn't killed, was he?"

"And, believe me, I'm as surprised about that as you are."

"I am not surprised," Miss Tarleton said with far too much conviction. "I'm disappointed."

"Well"—Valentine sketched a bow as sincere as Miss Tarleton's curtsy had been—"grieved as I am to have disappointed you with my continued existence, allow me nevertheless to escort you back to your uncle's house."

Miss Tarleton glared at him. "No."

Keeping his temper seemed like by far the best course of action. So it was with perfect equanimity that Valentine descended upon Miss Tarleton and hoisted her over his shoulder, an act she greeted with very much the opposite of equanimity. Which was to say by screeching furiously and attempting to both punch and kick him—although her kicks involved little more than flailing her ankles in the air, and her punches were mostly futile swipes to a region she clearly felt as uncomfortable pummelling as he felt about being pummelled there. Undeterred, Valentine bore her to Mr. Whelpington-Byng, Esquire's, curricle and dumped her unceremoniously in the seat before climbing in beside her.

"I trust," he said, "you will not be so foolhardy as to fling yourself from a moving curricle."

She turned her face sulkily away. "I hate you."

"I shall take that as a yes." Gathering the reins, he shifted his attention momentarily back to Bonny and Peggy. "You'll follow?"

Bonny gave a miserable little nod. More than anything, Valentine wanted to reassure him. But it was hard to know how with Miss Tarleton seething none too quietly beside him. And, just then, it seemed too revealing—all the new things inside him too tender to be shared with anyone but their recipient.

So instead, he said nothing further. Simply urged the horses into a brisk but undemanding trot. And did not dare look back.

Chapter 28

They travelled in distinctly noncompanionable silence. Miss Tarleton sat, stiff backed and pale faced, her gaze locked on the horizon and her mouth set with the grim determination of a soldier upon the battlefield. If Valentine could have found something admirable in her resilience, at this particular juncture the only thing he was capable of experiencing was tiredness. It rolled over him in a grey haze, enlivened occasionally by ripples of frustration and renewed dread.

In Bonny's arms, everything had seemed possible. Even simple, for he had been so sure his sister would understand. Now, however, Valentine was beginning to doubt that she would. Because even a marriage to a gentleman who wished no marital interactions beyond those required by necessity was still marriage. And Miss Tarleton gave every impression of despising him, some of which he knew he had earned, and some of which he thought might perhaps be a result of the situation, rather than anything directly personal. At least, he hoped so; otherwise it was hard to see how any sort of truce might be reached between them.

Perhaps the best thing would be for them to go their separate ways. It would disappoint their families, but as Miss Tarleton had brutally pointed out, the people they would be disappointing were, for the most part, dead. Valentine's mother, of course, presumably shared the same hopes as his late father, though it wasn't something they'd ever discussed. Probably she wouldn't want him to be unhappy or for him to make someone else unhappy. Except abandoning the Tarleton twins to penury wasn't likely to make them happy either. Miss Tarleton had to understand that. Surely?

Besides, if Valentine didn't marry Miss Tarleton, he would still have to marry *someone*. Which would involve—

He shuddered.

Wooing. It would involve wooing. Something he had always previously been able to avoid on the basis of his family's arrangement with the Tarletons but would become unavoidable, even with money and status to do most of the work for him. The problem was that he had previously known himself too little, and now too much, and all because of Bonny. Bonny, who had annoyed him and endangered him and rescued him and, somehow, *wooed him*. And—still more strangely—been wooed in return.

Whether it was a quirk of Valentine's nature, or some unspoken broader truth, there was no more denying it: he could not desire where he did not like, and he would not woo where he could not like. And he liked Bonny. And even if there lurked in some distant corner of the world someone he might like just as well, he had no wish to find them. Clearly Valentine had lost his mind in its entirety because he preferred to spend his life arguing and exasperated and bewildered and happy. That is, with Bonny.

Besides, one could probably circumscribe the globe a couple of times over before finding a posterior as exquisitely formed and succulent as Bonny's . . .

Oh, good God. Valentine's thoughts had gone *severely* adrift. He returned them, with some effort of will, to the present. Really, what he needed to do was talk to Miss Tarleton. Not, of course, about her brother's assets, but about the possibility of a future together that might work for both of them. Even putting aside the *wooing* issue, it was difficult to see how Valentine could present the idea of Bonny to another bride.

Discreet affairs were one thing. A fully fledged—well, he wasn't sure what Bonny was or would be exactly. But Valentine was not a man for affairs. And discretion was not one of Bonny's more developed qualities.

Valentine opened his mouth, then closed it again. How did one even begin to broach the topic of having developed a tendre—a significant tendre—for a young lady's male twin? Perhaps it was best to wait for Bonny. The Tarletons may have currently been in conflict, but he would surely know best how to speak to his sister.

It was, however, at this moment that Miss Tarleton remarked of her own volition, "I must insist, Your Grace, that we stop at the next inn."

From the position of the sun in the sky, he had no hope of returning Miss Tarleton home that evening. But Valentine felt the more distance they put between her and Dover, the better it would be for all of them. "Well, I must insist we continue."

"N-no. You don't understand." Her voice lifted with something like alarm. "I must *insist*."

"I think you've done more than enough insisting for the time being, don't you?"

"Valentine."

His given name on her lips surprised him. She had not called him by it since they were children, and there was enough of Bonny's lilt in it— *Val-EN-tine*—to inspire an instant of appalling personal sentimentality.

"I have," she muttered, "a need. A physical need, of the sort no gentleman would require a lady to speak of."

For a second or two, Valentine was blank. He was accustomed to thinking of women's bodies as inviolable vessels: that one might need to urinate made biological sense but still fell rather outside the realm of his experience. "Can you not avail yourself of the local shrubbery?"

Her mouth formed a perfect O of dismay. "How can you even suggest such a thing?"

"Upon my honour, I will not look."

Now her lip was trembling and her lashes were fluttering. And Valentine realised that for all he'd spent the best part of three days chasing her, she'd spent three days being chased. Undoubtedly she was as tired as he was and hurt beneath her anger. Even a little frightened. It was no wonder she didn't want to piss in a bush.

"We'll stop at the next inn," he told her. "But I don't know when that will be."

Her look of gratitude seemed sincere enough that it did not occur to Valentine to question when "the next inn"—an establishment luxuriating in the name of the Wobbly Bullock—turned out to be just around the corner. It was a cheerful, rustic place with a thatched roof and its own little stream idling by—not Valentine's sort of place at all, but more than adequate for the purposes for which they sought its services.

Miss Tarleton jumped down from the curricle with such alacrity when it entered the stable yard that Valentine briefly suspected she was bolting, but it turned out she was only bolting in the direction of the taproom. He thought it best to follow her, just in case, but he was conscious of a pang of guilt. The poor girl must have been terribly uncomfortable.

Once inside, Miss Tarleton was nowhere to be seen. That, however, was to be expected—she had clearly retired to attend to herself. Somewhat wistfully, Valentine took up a place by the bar. If there was ever an occasion on which he would have dearly welcomed a drink, this was it. Unfortunately, he was still without funds, and further excavations of the assistant gardener's coat had turned up only a pencil stub and a button.

"What can I get you?" asked the innkeeper.

"Nothing for the moment. I'm just . . . resting my elbows while I wait for my companion."

The innkeeper did not look like he appreciated this answer.

"I recognise," Valentine tried, "that this might not seem, on the surface, convincing, but the fact is, I'm actually the Duke of Malvern and—"

Suddenly a hand delivered a cheerful slap to Valentine's shoulder. "Malvern," cried Sir Horley Comewithers. "We really must stop meeting like this."

Oh God. Not again. "Yes. We really must."

Sir Horley Comewithers grinned his awful grin. "What are you drinking?"

"Nothing," Valentine admitted, trying not to sound too woebegone about it.

"Nothing? Why, that's the most tragic thing I've ever heard." Sir Horley gestured to the innkeeper. "A drink, for my good friend the Duke of Malvern."

Valentine was not particularly enamoured of the way *friend* had occupied the middle of that sentence. But he was very pleased about the *drink* part.

The innkeeper gave a polite little nod. "What'll be?"

"Er . . ." Valentine cast his eye over the casks and bottles behind the bar. "A glass of your best claret?"

The innkeeper's expression wavered.

"Make that two ciders," said Sir Horley.

Two ciders were duly provided, and Valentine took a grateful gulp of his—comforted by, well, mostly the alcohol in it, to be honest. Of course, now he was obliged to converse politely with Sir Horley, but it was only until Miss Tarleton had completed her ablutions.

"Where is your blacksmith friend?" he enquired.

Sir Horley's eyes glittered. "Back at his forge, naturally. But let me tell you"—he waved an exuberant hand—"I would heartily recommend throwing a shoe or two in his vicinity."

"Noted."

"Not," Sir Horley continued, "that I suppose you'd feel the need."

As ever, there was something about talking to Sir Horley that made Valentine uncomfortable. "It seems unlikely. My stables are extremely well managed."

"And how is your lovely young man? Will he be joining us?"

"As it happens, I'm here with my fiancée."

Sir Horley's lips twitched. "So I see."

"She has gone to . . . refresh herself."

"Mm-hmm."

Not liking Sir Horley's tone—or, indeed, anything about him— Valentine occupied himself with his cider. He was not, as a general rule and unlike his peers, a big drinker, for he enjoyed activities such as having inhibitions and being in control of his own behaviour. On this occasion, however, the effect of alcohol on his relatively unaccustomed person was markedly pleasant. It was a warm, cushioning feeling, and he welcomed it.

"Malvern," said Sir Horley, after far too little silence had elapsed. "Don't you think it's time we . . . you know."

This already sounded horrifying. "Time we what?"

Sir Horley wagged a finger. "There's no need to always be so coy— not that it isn't rather adorable. And to think I used to think you such a prig . . ."

"I beg your pardon?"

"When really"—Sir Horley smirked at him—"you're a *tease*."

"No, no. I'm definitely a prig."

"Valentine. Valentine. Valentine." Bad enough that Sir Horley was laughing, but now he was using Valentine's given name. Without his permission. And three times in a row. "Shall we not come clean with each other?"

"I'm afraid," said Valentine stiffly, "you have me at a loss, as usual."

"You have your delightful Mr. Tarleton. I have my blacksmith. And my soldier. And my groom. And my priest. And my grocer. And my publican. And my fellow-whose-occupation-I-can't-for-the-life-of-me-recall. Don't you see?"

There was something at once defiant and faintly unguarded in Sir Horley's voice. And, yes, Valentine saw. Not just the truth that Sir Horley was telling him, but that the telling mattered more than the truth. It was an open hand, offered by a man Valentine had long feared could see through him. And, perhaps, if Bonny had been with him, Valentine might have found the courage to accept it. But alone, uncertain of his future, full of questions he barely knew how to articulate, let alone answer, he just offered a cool glance. "I see you consort much with the lower orders."

Sir Horley shrugged. "One consorts where one can. But one does relish a little bit of rough on occasion."

The cider was . . . Valentine should not have had the cider. His tongue had grown six sizes too large for his mouth and was thrashing in outrage. "Bonny is not . . . we are not . . . it is not *like that*."

"Of course it isn't," said Sir Horley soothingly. "It is clear even to . . . what did you call me? A reprobate. Well, it is clear even to a reprobate like me that you have something together. Something rather special."

"Something entirely fabulous," mumbled Valentine. "But I am still to be married to his sister."

"Oh, for God's sake." Entirely unprovoked, Sir Horley slammed his tankard down. "Have it your way, you incorrigibly discreet scoundrel. You are engaged to Mr. Tarleton's conveniently mysterious twin sister. I wish you joy."

Valentine offered a distracted nod. "Thank you."

"Are you now content?"

"Yes," he said. And again, "Thank you." Where was Miss Tarleton? How long had she been gone? Did ladies normally require such an extensive amount of time to address their bodily functions? Was she, perhaps, unwell?

"In which case," declared Sir Horley "let us be *friends*, you and I."

"What?" How on earth had the conversation ended up here? It was the last place Valentine wanted it to be. "And how dare you? My fiancée is not conveniently mysterious. She was here less than ten minutes ago. I just . . . I just don't know where she is at this exact moment."

"How convenient," drawled Sir Horley. "And, indeed, mysterious."

Which was entirely infuriating of him, but Valentine had other concerns. He rapped upon the bar to attract the innkeeper's attention. "The young blonde lady who came in just before I did. Where is she now?"

The innkeeper looked confused. "How should I know?"

"She . . . she did not ask for a private room to . . . for . . . reasons?"

"No." He shook his head, looking no less confused. "She went straight out the back door."

Sir Horley choked on a mouthful of cider. "Wait. She *exists*?"

"She exists," growled Valentine, "and may the devil take her."

The door to the taproom burst open—Peggy and Bonny careening over the threshold in a tangle of boots and coats and flailing limbs.

"Where's Belle?" they chorused.

"Oh, for *fuck's sake*." Valentine charged past them, the assistant gardener's coat flapping behind him and his boots clattering on the flagstones, then the cobbles, as he reached the stable yard.

He cast his gaze towards the horizon, and sure enough, on the other side of the stream, just beyond the road, he caught the gleam of golden locks against the greying twilight.

"Valentine"—Bonny stumbled out after him—"I think it would be an excellent idea, probably the very best idea possible, not to . . . um . . . lose your temper."

"Lose my temper?" roared Valentine. "I'm at the *end of my tether*."

Bonny tried to catch his arm. "I'm sure you have more tether. Find more tether."

"No." With a wrench, Valentine freed himself. "I am without tether. Wholly tetherless. Now stand aside. I'm going to murder your sister."

Thankfully, the curricle was still ready to go. Why Belle—given her usual, maddening resourcefulness—hadn't taken it, Valentine wasn't sure. But he had no intention of surrendering such an advantage himself.

Leaping onto the seat, he seized the reins and departed the Wobbly Bullock at a thunderous gallop.

He had just rattled across the bridge and onto the road that ran alongside the stream when he realised that the curricle was not handling particularly well.

In fact, it was handling quite badly—even for a vehicle the owner had clearly chosen to be flashy. It was . . . weaving. And Valentine, for all the adequacy of his driving skills, was finding it increasingly difficult to keep the horses working as a team.

Then came an ominous snap.

The sort of snap that one's traces might make if they had been partially severed by a knife in a determined hand and were now giving way entirely. A less cider-cushioned Valentine might have reacted to this with greater efficiency. As it was, he only watched in bewildered consternation as one of the horses—finding itself abruptly relieved of the weight of both vehicle and passenger—gave a surprised neigh and pranced off unhindered into the distance. Its companion, unsure how else to react to this unusual circumstance, stopped moving altogether.

These various ordeals were too much for the curricle. It swayed right, then left, then right again, listing more heavily with each undulation, while Valentine scrambled from side to side in frantic counterbalance. For a few teetering seconds, he thought he might have established an equilibrium.

But no.

Slowly—almost inevitability—the curricle tilted. Then kept tilting. Then tipped over entirely. And, finally, lay curled on its side like a salted slug.

Equally slowly—equally inevitably—Valentine tumbled out.

He rolled gently off the road, down the streambank, and into the stream itself, where he landed face-first in some frog spawn.

Chapter 29

Valentine pushed himself to his hands and knees in the chilly water, dragged a wreath of frog spawn from his hair, and spat out some algae.

"Oh my God." Bonny's worried voice drifted slowly down to him. "Are you all right?"

"Do I look," enquired Valentine, "like I'm all right?"

"I mean . . . you don't look hurt?"

"I am *in a stream.*"

"Yes, but you don't look hurt."

"There is frog spawn in this stream. The stream that I am in."

"Yes," agreed Bonny. "But you aren't hurt."

Valentine raised an arm, over which was draped a curtain of something green. "And whatever this is."

"Pond weed?" suggested Peggy. "It could be pond weed."

Valentine gazed up at them. They were standing on the bank, gazing down at him in return. They were both dry. Very dry. Mockingly dry. "It's slimy," he told them.

"I think," said Peggy carefully, "you should go back to the inn with Bonny."

"I can't go back to the inn with Bonny. I'm in a stream." No matter how many times Valentine mentioned it, the whole notion remained absurd. How could he possibly be in a stream? He was a duke. Dukes were not in streams.

Hand on chin, Peggy assessed the situation. "You could get out of the stream. Then go back to the inn with Bonny."

"No." Valentine shook his head decisively. "When I get out of the steam, I have a prior engagement to kill my affianced."

"Please"—that was Bonny—"just get out of the stream, Valentine. You'll catch a chill or something."

He dropped his knees on the bank and offered a helpful hand. Valentine stared at the hand, at once moved and mortified by the gesture. You probably had to care for someone in a very real and significant way if you still wanted to touch them when they were in a stream. But it also meant that Bonny would encounter all the ways that being in a stream made one wet and slimy. And Valentine did not want either of those adjectives to be associated with him in Bonny's mind.

"Thank you," he said awkwardly. "But I believe I can remove myself from a stream without assistance."

Peggy blew out a breath. "I don't know. Slippery buggers, streams."

"I'm *fine*," Valentine insisted.

To prove it, he rose with all the poise and authority of Poseidon from his watery domain, promptly lost his footing on some moss-slick pebbles, and this time fell into the stream backwards.

There was an endless silence.

Valentine stared at the sky. The first stars were beginning to pierce it. Very pretty.

"You know what I appreciate?" said Peggy.

"No," said Bonny. "What do you appreciate?"

"The endless variety of England's freshwater flora and fauna. Is that a water snail?"

A pause while Bonny considered. "It could be. It's cute. I like it."

"And all this greenery. Well, is *greenery* the right term? Some of it's brown. The brownery then."

Valentine was dragging himself towards the bank, across the pebbles and through the mud, trailing a cloak of green-and-brownery.

"And," Bonny went on, "the frog spawn is positively *abundant*. It's so nice to see."

The problem with the bank was that, being close to a stream, it was already wet. And Valentine, having been in a stream, was also wet. This meant his attempts to climb the bank—gently sloping though it was—were undignified at best. Futile in their worst moments. Eventually, though, by a combination of crawling, clawing, and scrabbling, he managed to ascend and then climb to his feet.

"Good evening," he said.

Bonny stared at him. It was not the way Valentine wanted to be stared at by the man he most wanted to admire and desire him. "Oh . . . oh, Valentine—"

He gave a polite bow. "Excuse me."

And then he set off in pursuit of Miss Tarleton.

Not that *set off* really did justice to the speed and intensity of that pursuit. He sprinted. He stormed. He positively *charged*. In a manner all too similar to the raging manticore to which Bonny had once, on a somewhat happier occasion, compared him. And as he sprinted, stormed, and charged along, Valentine became aware of a sort of . . . sound. A low and bestial mumbling, such as might emerge from the depths of a creature taken past the point of endurance.

Oh fuck. It was him.

Yet the knowledge was not enough to grant him composure. He had descended, like Dante, into his own personal inferno, where the Acheron was a stream made of cider, and all nine circles were filled with bees and spiders and ostlers, gossipy reprobates who wanted to be his friend, and sapphic (?) ladies who locked him in cellars, and there were no valets or baths or Bonny.

Just a terrible certainty that he was going to spend the rest of his life chasing Miss Tarleton and never feel comfortable, or in control, again.

As for Miss Tarleton herself, believing she had evaded her captor, she was proceeding along the road at a brisk and determined walk. As soon as she became aware of Valentine—soaking wet, pondweed draped, and howling like a barghest—bearing down on her, she screamed, hitched up her petticoats, and broke into a run. Perhaps hoping to lose or otherwise discourage him, she scrambled over a stile and plunged into a small wood.

It was her first tactical error of the whole adventure.

While she was initially able to put some distance between them by darting between trees, the undergrowth was far kinder to Valentine's boots than it was to her shoes, and the bracken kept snagging at her skirts, slowing her down. He was going to catch her, and they both knew it.

Of course, that didn't remotely dissuade her from trying to escape him. Indeed, such was her commitment to doing so that he was starting to worry he was going to have to physically bring her down. Which he balked from. Because—even in the midst of being quite unreasonably angry at her—it didn't feel quite gentlemanly.

Not that threatening to kill her earlier had been gentlemanly either.

Nor lifting her into a curricle when she very much did not wish to be lifted into a curricle.

But then, getting him locked in a cellar, challenged to a duel, and thrown into a stream wasn't exactly ladylike.

Thankfully, his quandary was solved by a tree root. Its position—partially disguised beneath a pile of leaves—caused Miss Tarleton to stumble over it. She landed in a heap, made a valiant effort to rise again, tripped over her own skirts, and then proceeded at a frantic crawl.

Valentine discovered his entire body was burning and he could barely breathe. He slowed to a walk. "Miss Tarleton," he said. Or rather wheezed. "E-enough . . . of . . . this."

She kept crawling.

"I am taking you home, whether you will it or no."

A tree intercepted her. She turned into a sitting position, putting her back to the trunk, and—with a disregard for propriety that

Valentine still found shocking—pulled a handgun from her stocking top. "S-stay away from me."

Since he had been threatened so often recently, pistols being pointed at him was becoming a borderline quotidian experience for Valentine. He sighed. "I have run out of patience for your nonsense, Miss Tarleton."

"You're a monster."

"I'm not a monster. I'm just a very weary man."

A click as she cocked the pistol, levelling it at him with visibly shaking hands. Miss Tarleton, too, looked weary: pale and dark eyed, muddy from her adventures in the undergrowth, and perhaps even on the verge of tears. "I want *nothing* to do with you. Can't you leave me alone?"

"I can't let you run to God knows where, with nothing, and unprotected."

"Why not?" she cried. "Why am I any of your business?"

He opened his mouth. Then closed it again. The most obvious answer was that he had come to care for Bonny, and he couldn't let anything happen to someone Bonny cared for—even if she was an obstinate and bloodthirsty hoyden who'd probably be better off as a pirate anyway. Except he didn't know how to begin to tell her that. So offered instead, "I have a duty."

"Fuck your duty. I'm *a person*."

Talking to Miss Tarleton was . . . well, Valentine had never been struck in the face repeatedly by a blunt object—thank heavens—but if he had been, he imagined it would feel much like talking to Miss Tarleton. "So am I."

"This isn't about you." She closed her free hand around her other wrist in an effort to steady the pistol. "Not everything is about you."

"I would like," said Valentine, with the bare shreds of patience that he still retained, "to have this discussion at your uncle's house when I am dry and you are reasonable, and there are no guns involved."

"Then"—her eyes glittered—"I hope you appreciate the lesson, Your Grace."

"And what lesson is that?"

"The lesson that even dukes cannot always get what they want."

He took a step towards her. "I think you will find that penniless young ladies with more spirit than sense do not get what they want either."

"That's not a lesson," she scoffed. "That's a truism."

"I'm taking you home."

"If you try, I will shoot you."

"Belle? Oh my God, Belle." It was Bonny's voice—loud, even for Bonny, in that little woodland. "What are you doing?"

He broke through the trees a second or two later, tousle haired and flushed, with Peggy—closer to flustered than Valentine had ever seen her—just behind.

"Is that my gun?" she asked. "Did you steal my gun? Friends don't steal friends' guns."

"Friends"—Miss Tarleton's eyes flicked briefly to Peggy—"don't betray friends to one's enemies."

"I didn't betray you. I just didn't want anyone getting shot. A state of affairs that continues: put my damn pistol down."

"No," said Miss Tarleton.

Bonny gave an urgent yelp. "Don't shoot Valentine. Please don't shoot Valentine. He already nearly got shot today. And he nearly got shot yesterday." He wrung his hands. "This is just too much shooting."

"She's not going to shoot me," Valentine told him reassuringly.

"I'm going to shoot him," declared Miss Tarleton, somewhat less reassuringly.

"You are not"—Valentine addressed her directly this time—"going to shoot me, Miss Tarleton."

Intending to relieve her of the gun and put a stop to these theatricals once and for all, Valentine lunged forwards.

A neat little bang.

And, in its wake, a silence like falling.

"What just happened?" asked Valentine.

He felt, he had to admit, slightly strange. There was a blank space in his body rippling outwards from his shoulder and upper arm.

Miss Tarleton looked absolutely terrified, the gun slipping from between her fingers, as slow as treacle.

"Is everyone quite well?" asked Valentine.

He was warm. No, his shoulder was warm and getting warmer, as if something with teeth, red-hot teeth, was gnawing its way through the numbness. Curious, he pulled the assistant gardener's coat aside. His clothes beneath were already partly saturated from his visit to the stream, but a fresh, dark stain was spreading rapidly through the fabric.

And still he burned. Almost itchily at first, but then just relentlessly, the pain burrowing into him, deeper than he had thought it was possible for pain to be felt, as it seeped through skin and muscle and sinew until it seemed to be scraping against his very bones.

He put his fingers to the still-expanding stain. It was a little frightening how quickly it was travelling. How sodden his garments had become.

The same wet darkness was upon his fingers now.

And then he saw it was red. The reddest red, as bright as Bonny's rings in the nascent starlight.

"Oh," he said, glad to have solved the mystery. "I've been shot."

Chapter 30

There were a lot of voices around Valentine. They seemed at once too loud and too quiet, and he was having trouble understanding any of them. It probably didn't help that he kept fainting.

Although he did wish everyone would leave him alone. They kept moving him about, and he very much did not want to be moved about.

The pain had decided it no longer dwelled in his shoulder. It had decided to be *everywhere*.

Occasionally he would try to explain—*I've been shot*—but he didn't think anyone was paying much attention.

There had, he hazily recollected, been a pleasant interval—sometime before, he wasn't sure; time was proving difficult to hold on to—when all he'd had to do was lie in the leaves, which were soft, and look at the stars, which were pretty. And Bonny had been with him, he was sure Bonny had been with him, and perhaps it had rained because water had kept landing on his face. Except too intermittently for rain. And too warm.

And he'd wanted to tell Bonny about the stars. But Bonny had been in the oddest of moods—constantly shouting at Valentine not to close his eyes and slapping him in the face when he did. Which had been fairly often because Valentine had been unaccountably tired. Or maybe not unaccountably because . . . because . . .

It was late?

He'd had a tiring few days?

Really, Bonny had no business keeping him awake, after everything he'd gone through. But Valentine had stayed awake anyway.

Because Bonny had wanted him to.

And said things like: *Don't you dare leave me, don't you dare.* And *If you think a bullet is keeping you away from me, you are sorely mistaken.* And *You are going to give me my happy ever after, Valentinian Gervase Lorimer Layton, or I'll shoot you myself.*

Except then Peggy had come running back and spoiled it.

And everything had been moving and shouting and hurting, and Valentine hadn't liked it *at all.*

Then it had got worse.

Pulling-him-out-of-his-clothes worse. Poking-at-him worse. Digging-into-his-flesh worse.

Why were people digging into his flesh? Didn't they know he'd already been shot today?

It was outrageously unfair.

Valentine would have told them so, in no uncertain terms, had he not already been preoccupied with screaming.

And then the blackness. And the redness. And the blackness again. Pulling him down, down, down like some vast and inevitable ocean.

He would have liked to keep sinking. But unfortunately, the pain followed him even there.

And watched with pin-sharp eyes.

Sometimes there were dreams. And sometimes things that felt like dreams. And sometimes things that didn't.

Like more moving. And more voices. The sear of alcohol against peeled-open skin. And the bitterness of opium upon his tongue.

Maybe he'd dreamed about getting shot.

It did seem a profoundly unlikely thing to have happened to him.

He could have dreamed it all. The gun and the stream and the duel and the cellar and the bees. And the sound of Bonny laughing. And the taste of his mouth. And the perfect heat of his body in a shared bed: realer than anything Valentine had ever believed possible.

The light was beginning to hurt. He opened his eyes.

And everywhere was glass, slick as mercury. The floor and the sky two unrelenting reflections of an infinite emptiness.

There was a path. It looked no different to its surroundings, but Valentine knew it was there. So he followed it.

And followed it.

A line that never deviated through a landscape that never changed.

Sometimes, he thought he saw shadows in the glass. The silhouettes of people, talking, laughing, passing back and forth, their outlines smudged like charcoal.

His fingertips, when he tried to touch, left nothing behind. Not a mark nor a blemish, nor even the heat of his body.

The people never stopped. Never looked at him nor spoke to him.

When he called out to them, they did not answer.

So he walked on. Down the endless path. Until he understood that he was searching for something without knowing what it was.

That he might, perhaps, never know what it was.

He stopped then. Looked around him. At the smoothly shining forever that followed him and awaited him.

And realised he was alone.

Endlessly, mercilessly, unassailably alone.

A cry clawed its way out of his scream-raw throat. The pain was back. It crouched on him, and in him, like some fanged monster, eager to rend him bloody.

But Valentine didn't care. He wasn't afraid of hurting.

He was afraid of—

He needed—

His lips couldn't seem to form the words. And he could have wept with the despair of that immovable silence.

And then.

"Bonny," he whispered. "I want Bonny."

And Bonny whispered back, "You have me."

And, through the pain and the darkness and the memory of glass, Valentine discovered his hand was safe and warm in Bonny's.

Because Bonny had been there all along.

Chapter 31

There were satyrs on the ceiling. They were doing exceptionally lewd things to nymphs. Wait. Not nymphs. Other satyrs.

Valentine thought it was probably best to start screaming.

"Nononono." A hand covered his mouth. A smooth, soft hand that, while devoid of rings, was nevertheless undoubtedly Bonny's. "You're safe. I promise you're safe."

The satyrs were not making Valentine feel very safe. He gave a sceptical croak. His throat felt appalling. As, he was slowly coming to realise, did the rest of him. Bonny's hand went away and came back, this time with a glass of water. And Valentine would have protested the indignity of having someone else—even if it was Bonny—helping him, but he was desperately thirsty.

Not that he was permitted to quench himself as he would have wished.

Apparently he lived now in a world of tiny sips.

Tiny sips and sodomitical satyrs.

"Where am I?" he finally managed to ask.

"Um." Bonny took the glass away. "Sir Horley's hunting lodge."

Valentine contemplated the ceiling. "This is . . . a hunting lodge?"

"I'm not sure he comes here to hunt animals."

Valentine contemplated the ceiling still further. From a certain perspective, it was quite educational. And the satyrs seemed to be enjoying themselves. "Why," he wondered, "am I at Sir Horley's hunting lodge?"

"I thought you might be more comfortable than at the inn. But I may have made a grave misjudgement."

Since his eyes were still the only parts of his body that Valentine felt confident about, he moved them carefully from the ceiling. The satyrs were on the walls, too, sometimes with each other, sometimes with young gentlemen, and sometimes the young gentlemen saw to their own entertainment. Not all of this entertainment, Valentine was pleased to note, was wholly wanton—including as it did strolling, reading, and cuddling—even if it was still wholly naked.

Gilt mirrors and pink marble columns interspersed the murals, with the mirrors set in such an ill-designed way that they only reflected the bed. Valentine had never seen himself from so many angles. At least, what little there was to see, for he was tucked up with such determination that his nose barely poked from beneath the blankets. As for the bed, it could—and, knowing Sir Horley, perhaps had—have taken five of him and still had room for a breakfast tray. The hangings, like the covers, were rose-pink velvet, embroidered with golden flowers.

Valentine thought it best to close his eyes again. "What . . . what happened to me?"

"What can you remember?"

It was a good question. "I was . . . everything was glass. And I was alone."

"You had a fever. Quite a bad one." Bonny's fingers drifted gently over his hair. "But you were never alone. I was here with you the whole time."

And suddenly Valentine *could* remember. Bonny's voice and his touch and, in a moment of disconnected lucidity, opening his eyes in a dim and unfamiliar room to find Bonny slumped at his bedside, his head pillowed on his folded arms. How long must he have been sitting there? How long had he been sitting here?

God, he looked so tired, heavy smudges beneath his eyes and his jaw a haze of golden fluff. Even his cheeks had grown a little gaunt.

"You . . . you need to rest," said Valentine, horrified and awkward, and inadequate and embarrassed, and utterly, utterly grateful.

But Bonny just grinned. "You're right. And now that you're awake and talking for the first time in days, I will certainly choose that time to nap."

Days? "D-days?"

"You did get shot, you know."

"Oh yes." This Valentine also recalled, but it felt strange and distant, like he'd read it in a book, or it was a story he'd heard about something that had happened to someone else. "Yes, I did."

It had become an experience of fragments. Of pain and darkness. Best not dwelled upon.

Except.

"My arm." Valentine would have thrashed, but he was too weak, and the blankets held him too securely. "Did I lose my arm?"

For a moment Bonny just stared at him. "Did you what? No. Of course not."

"But I can't move it."

"That's because you were shot in it. Well, in the shoulder mostly. I'm not a doctor, but I understand they're connected."

That seemed anatomically sound. "I'm . . . I'm not going to die then?"

"No." Bonny reached for his pillow and eased it, somehow, into an even more comfortable position. "You scared me with that fever, but you're going to be just fine."

"What if a bullet splinter travels through my bloodstream and stabs me in the heart?"

"Flower. The doctor removed the bullet. There's no infection. You need to stay in bed for at least a fortnight, and you'll be in a sling for three months or more, but you'll be all healed up in half a year. And there'll be nothing but a scar."

"A scar," repeated Valentine.

"A scar that I shall find intensely alluring and kiss very often."

"I b-bu-buh—" A huge yawn attacked Valentine out of nowhere. He had been awake but minutes, done little more than converse, and was already exhausted. "I believe," he tried again, "I can live with that."

"You should sleep," Bonny told him.

Valentine tried to look lofty through another yawn. "So should you."

"I will if you will."

A pause. "You don't look like you're intending to sleep."

"How would I look if I was intending to sleep?"

"You'd be lying down, for a start."

"Flower, the way I'm feeling right now, I could sleep on a wire in a thunderstorm."

Bedbound and physically incapacitated as he was, Valentine was reduced to giving Bonny big eyes. "Come to bed?"

"I could jostle your wound or open your stitches or—"

"Please, Bonny."

Bonny made a production of being put upon, but he hopped up beside Valentine readily enough and curled up next to Valentine's unshot shoulder. "Happy now?"

"Blissfully," said Valentine, with perfect sincerity.

❧

When Valentine next awoke, the room was garishly pink-orange with the dawn.

He felt more cogent in general, but his shoulder ached fiercely. Bonny was still fast asleep, pressed against Valentine's side. It was an odd kind of torment, having him so close, and yet being unable to touch him.

So he looked instead. And glut himself on looking.

Remembered the sycamore tree, and the stars, and thought Bonny more beautiful than either.

Proof, if anything, of the watchmaker. That a being of such intricacy and delight—of such strength and vulnerability, and so many infuriating contradictions—could exist at all was a marvel far beyond the vagaries of happenstance.

But, no. Bonny had made himself: from books and stories, and hopes and dreams. As Valentine had made himself from duty and fear and mistrust and ignorance.

"What have I been without you," he whispered. "What would I have become?"

And, just for a moment, he caught the glint of silver from one of Sir Horley's mirrors.

The thought of glass made him shiver.

❦

The next time Valentine achieved consciousness for more than a scattering of minutes, Bonny insisted on feeding him soup.

Resentful of his temporary frailty, Valentine was not minded to enjoy the experience. And Bonny was not minded to be patient with him.

"Just eat the soup, Valentine." He waved the spoon emphatically. "Or you'll die. You'll die of lack of soup."

"That is not an established medical condition."

"It will be if you don't eat the soup."

Valentine did his best to look haughty in a nightshirt. "I don't want the soup."

"How are you going to get better if you won't eat soup?"

"How are you still going to desire me if you have to feed me soup?"

"Oh, flower." At last Bonny put the spoon down, which was something of a relief to Valentine because he'd several times nearly received a poke in the eye. "Do you know the first time I wanted you to kiss me?"

"Well, of course I don't," Valentine retorted huffily, "or I would have kissed you."

Bonny giggled. "No, you wouldn't. You'd have run away and never come back. Although you sort of did that anyway."

"Wait. When was this?"

"It was the last time you visited before your father died. I think you must have been about fifteen—and you'd just put on all this *height* in all directions."

Not one of the happiest periods of Valentine's life: he had felt too long, somehow, for his own body. Had never known what to do with his hands and been constantly tripping over his feet. "So I recall."

"You had no idea how beautiful you were," Bonny told him.

"I looked like I'd been stretched."

"I know, but it was so endearing."

"Bonny, you could not have been more than seven or eight. You should not have been finding other men endearing at the age of eight."

"What can I say?" Bonny shrugged. "I've always known who I am and what I wanted."

And Valentine could hardly dispute that, when he had lived so long in complete ignorance of both.

"Anyway," Bonny went on, "it was when Belle was . . . well, you remember how Belle was."

"I remember finding her rather charming."

"You always took such pains with her. She'd hardly speak to anyone back then except me, and occasionally you."

Valentine rolled his eyes. "She's certainly made up for lost time since."

"Put your claws in, pretty kitty. I know she shot you, but I used to worry about her all the time."

"And now?" asked Valentine dryly.

"I worry about her *some* of the time. You know she had that secret den under the oak tree; sometimes she just wouldn't come out."

And suddenly Valentine remembered that day too. Impossible though it seemed now that Arabella Tarleton might ever have been shy or frightened or fond of him. "We gathered posies together."

"Yes, and she made you a flower crown of rosemary and rue."

Needless to say, it had done little to flatter him. "And that made you want to kiss me?"

"No, I wanted to kiss you afterwards. When you were still wearing it, because Belle wanted you to, and your father said you could make a spectacle of yourself or come to dinner."

"Is there a point to this story?" Valentine couldn't have said why, but he was beginning to feel oddly uncomfortable.

"The point to the story," Bonny told him, "is that you didn't come to dinner and I wanted to kiss you. Because that was the most heroic thing I'd ever seen anyone do."

"For someone who reads as much as you do, your sense of the heroic is oddly banal."

"Sometimes the truest heroism is. Now"—Bonny's tone hardened abruptly—"eat this damn soup."

"I am still not going to eat the soup."

"It's getting cold. But don't you see, Valentine. I wanted to kiss you when you were fifteen years old, with feet the size of sledges and hands the size of dinner plates, and wearing a withered flower crown my sister had made, frankly, terribly. I wanted to kiss you when you ran away from an entirely harmless bee. I wanted to kiss you when you were covered in frog spawn. I *always* want to kiss you. Soup isn't going to change that."

"It's embarrassing," Valentine muttered.

"If your twin sister had shot me in the shoulder, would you feed me soup?"

"Of course."

"And would you still want me to kiss me afterwards?"

"Of course."

"Then listen to yourself, stop arguing with me, and eat this soup, or—as God is my witness—I will force it down your throat." Bonny paused for moment to breathe. "Besides, there will be no kissing at all, ever, if you die of lack of soup."

So Valentine grudgingly gave his consent and allowed Bonny to feed him lukewarm soup that was, despite the circumstances of its consumption, delicious. Even the sting of requiring assistance faded a little; it was undignified, but it was Bonny, and had compensations—like having him sit close, and the way his free hand was resting almost idly against Valentine's leg.

"She is . . . ," Bonny began, when Valentine had taken as much as he could manage, which was a pitifully small amount. "You know. Sorry."

"Who is?"

"Belle. For shooting you."

Valentine managed a faint sneer. "That is a great consolation to me."

"*Val-EN-tine.* It was—well, not an accident because she did shoot you."

"Oddly enough, I'm aware of that."

"But she didn't . . . *want* to shoot you. She just wanted to stop you. And it was the only means she had."

"And it didn't occur to her that she could talk to me?"

Sighing, Bonny put the tray with the soup aside. "She was wrong to shoot you. She knows she was wrong to shoot you. I'm not trying to defend it, but I was there too. And you were not in a talkative mood."

Was that . . . fair? Valentine couldn't remember the evening particularly clearly, and he wasn't sure he wanted to, for it probably hadn't reflected well on either of them. "Did I really scare her so badly?"

"She'd never admit it, but yes."

Guilt and soup, as it turned out, did not go well together, and were, in fact, making Valentine feel queasy. "I would never hurt her, Bonny. You know I wouldn't."

"I know that and you know that. But you've got a sharp tongue and a nasty temper and—"

"It's not the same thing," Valentine protested.

"—and," Bonny went on gently, "you're six foot something and she—like the pocket-sized philtre before you—is five foot four. Plus, you're a man and she's a woman, and you did sort of . . . accidentally attack us with a chair that one time. All of that makes you *scary*, Valentine, even when you think you aren't."

Wilting, Valentine pressed his head to his knees. For all that it had been dangerously misguided on Miss Tarleton's part to shoot him, the fact his actions had led her to believe she had no other choice was its own condemnation. "Oh God. Maybe I *am* a monster."

"I don't think you're a monster. I think you're just a bit . . . careless sometimes."

"That's only a slight improvement."

"Oh, flower." Bonny patted his good shoulder soothingly. "The moment got away from you. From both of you. And it probably didn't help that you'd gone completely manticore."

"There was frog spawn," Valentine mumbled. "I had frog spawn in my hair."

Bonny kissed his temple, including some of the hair in question. "I know. You poor dear thing. What trials you've endured."

"I have." Valentine's glance was sulky. "Many trials."

"In any case, Belle didn't *mean* to shoot you. She panicked." Bonny's nose wrinkled. "Probably the moral here is we should all take guns a bit more seriously."

If Valentine had his way, he wouldn't encounter another firearm for the rest of his life. "I'm aware I keep saying this, but I really do owe your sister an apology for . . . well . . . several things."

"She owes you at least a couple herself." Bonny gave a rueful shrug. "Not that I imagine you'll get them. Belle isn't the best at apologising, even when she knows she should."

Valentine projected rue of his own, though shrugging was going to be very much out of the question for a while. "It's moot in any case."

"Why?"

"Well . . . we shall have no hope of finding her now."

It was hard for Valentine to tell whether the international abscondment of his wife-to-be was going to make his life more or less complicated. Possibly less in the short term, as he would not have to deal with Miss Tarleton and could indulge himself in simply being with Bonny. In the long term, though, there would be gossip, his mother's disappointment, and of course the broader question of being an unmarried duke with obligations to his lands and titles.

"Actually," said Bonny, "it shouldn't be difficult."

"Oh? Isn't she on her way to America?"

"Not exactly." Bonny gave him a nervous smile. "She's at your mother's."

Valentine coughed. "I beg your pardon?"

"It seemed a respectable explanation for the last few days."

"I was shot near Dover because we were visiting my mother in Bath?"

"Well"—a shrug—"since my sister is now with your mother in Bath, nobody seems to be asking any questions. My aunt and uncle weren't best pleased we forgot to tell them where we were going, but they did raise us. They're used to having no idea what's happening."

This was a lot of information, and Valentine was having trouble with it. "Your sister is with my mother?"

"Mm-hmm."

It was slightly hard to imagine. Valentine's poor widowed mother, being suddenly descended upon by a beautiful tyrant and her unusual companion. "Is she—how is she?"

"Your mother? Very well, according to Peggy's note. I mean, not delighted you'd been shot."

"She must have been distraught. To lose her husband and then come so close to losing her son."

Bonny blinked at him. "She was in no danger of losing her son—which we made very clear to her. And your father died over a decade ago."

"Yes, but my mother took it very hard. And she's a woman left unprotected, and the world isn't kind to women left unprotected, even when they are dowager duchesses."

"She never remarried?" Bonny asked.

Valentine shook his head. "She's devoted to my father's memory. I suppose it will be good for her to have some company. Do you think Peggy and your sister will mind living so quietly, though?"

"I don't think it'll be that quietly. Peggy said something about a party."

Probably a card party or something equally staid, but Valentine realised he was allowing himself to become distracted. "So. Miss Tarleton? She's no longer running away?"

"Not for the moment."

And there, it seemed, was Valentine's life uncomplicating itself again. He should not have been disappointed. "What about Sir Horley?"

Bonny grinned impishly. "He's not running away, either, as far as I can tell."

"That's not what I meant. He's the most indiscreet man in London."

"There are some secrets he has no problem keeping. And you should be nicer to him. He *is* letting you stay in his . . . um"—Bonny's eyes darted to the satyrs—"hunting lodge."

"He wants," said Valentine, pouting, "to lick your arse."

"Flower, everyone wants to lick my arse. My arse is absolutely divine."

"I still don't like him."

"Then"—Bonny rose and then leaned down to press a kiss to Valentine's brow—"try harder."

Valentine was about to protest that liking Sir Horley lay beyond the power of any reasonable person. But he realised he was far too tired.

"Besides," Bonny went on, "you already do like him."

That, however, he could not let pass unchallenged. "Whatever led you to such an absurd conclusion?"

"The fact it's true? You want to stop people getting close to you, so whenever you think you might like someone, you pretend *really hard* that you don't."

"I like you." The words blundered out of Valentine's mouth, slurred by sleepiness.

He sank back against the pillow, eyes closing almost against his will. Exhaustion was like another blanket being drawn over him: inescapable, but strangely soothing. It was soft and warm and dark.

But he still heard Bonny whisper, "I like you too."

Chapter 32

Time was still playing games with Valentine. Sometimes the nights were long and the pain was sharp; sometimes he lost whole days. But slowly, steadily, things improved. He was able to eat his own soup, then—oh glory be—could manage small amounts of food that wasn't soup. Bonny rarely left his side, although Valentine was relieved to see he was losing that hollow-eyed, faintly haunted look.

And then one morning he bounced into the room, wearing a smile that contrived to be at once secretive and smug. "You know," he announced. "I think you're well enough for a visitor."

A visitor? Oh no. Apart from his mother, who was at home, and Bonny, who was already there, Valentine couldn't think of anyone else he would want to see in the normal run of things—let alone when he was bedbound and unable to escape.

"I'm not well enough," he said quickly. "I'm very tired. I could be fevered again. And my arm hurts because I was shot in it."

Bonny's smile grew, if possible, even more smug. "You'll like this visitor, I promise."

"But I don't like anyone." Valentine was whining. He could hear it in his own voice. "You know that."

This did not prove to be a persuasive argument. As Bonny pulled open the door with a flourish, Valentine did his best to force his face from an expression of "Please go away" to one of "How marvellous to see you."

Although, as it turned out, this wasn't necessary. Because Valentine's startled pleasure was entirely genuine when he beheld upon the threshold none other than—

"Periwinkle," he cried.

Beholding him in return caused his valet to drop the valise he was carrying and clasp both hands to his heart. "Oh, Your Grace, what have they done to you?" He whirled to Bonny. "He's not even wearing a cravat."

Bonny flinched from the intensity of Periwinkle's ire. "He was shot."

"That's no reason," Periwinkle told him firmly, "to neglect proper attire." He risked another glance at Valentine. "Good heavens, his hair." Then back to Bonny. "He has *a beard*."

"Only a little one."

Periwinkle's nostrils flared with indignation. "That is not the point."

"You're right. I'm sorry." Bonny hung his head.

"No, no." A knife-swift motion of one of Periwinkle's hands. "*I'm sorry.* I just wasn't prepared for . . ." He made a gesture to indicate the description-defying shock of Valentine's appearance. Then sank to his knees upon the floor. "This is all my fault. I should never have let him go to Surrey alone. Why, I might as well have shot him myself."

"He's mostly fine," said Bonny.

"I'm mostly fine," agreed Valentine.

"Milord"—Periwinkle gazed at him in profound despair—"you are very much *not* fine." He inhaled deeply. "But remain calm."

Valentine nodded. "I will remain calm."

"I'm here now." Regaining his feet, Periwinkle collected the valise and approached the bed. "All will be well. I've brought your shaving kit and your hairbrushes and your favourite dressing gown, and your sec-ond-favourite dressing gown, and your third-favourite dressing gown, and several changes of clothing suitable for a gentlemen at"—another glance at Valentine, propped up on pillows—"leisure."

"And cravats?" enquired Bonny, so seriously that Valentine had to hide a smile. "I hope you brought cravats."

"Sir, what do you take me for. Of course I brought cravats. I brought everything necessary to life. Although I will require assistance carrying it upstairs."

"Sir Horley keeps a manservant." Bonny paused. "Oh God, I hope he's a manservant. I've been asking him to do things. Anyway, I'll see if he can help."

A mere four hours and eight valises later, Valentine had been shaved and groomed and had his favourite dressing gown draped tenderly over his shoulders and his sling reslung in a fabric that better matched the rest of his attire. Admittedly he had slept through some of this process, but he was awake again now, enjoying the familiar sight of Periwinkle gliding noiselessly about the room, unpacking, organising, putting Valentine's life back into its rightful order.

Bonny, meanwhile, was sitting in one of the travelling trunks.

"I'm a pirate," he said. "And this is my boat."

Periwinkle regarded him with unusual indulgence. "It's a ship, and you are crumpling His Grace's stockings."

"How can one person"—Bonny peered into the depths of the trunk—"need so many stockings?"

"A gentleman," returned Periwinkle haughtily, "can never have too many stockings." He turned to Valentine, shaking out a waistcoat. "I am concerned that Mr. Tarleton's valet has not been taking proper care of him."

"I don't have a valet."

Periwinkle nearly dropped the waistcoat, but professionalism proved stronger than his dismay. "A man's relationship with his valet is the most important in his life."

Valentine smiled at him. "You don't think you're just a little biased in that regard?"

"Not at all," retorted Periwinkle. "Look what happened to you without me."

Bonny was regarding them through narrowed eyes, hands firmly on his hips. "Is there something I need to know? About this very special and important relationship?"

"Mr. Tarleton." Periwinkle gave an exquisite shudder. "It is also a *sacrosanct* relationship. When it comes to"—a polite cough—"other matters, I happen to have an understanding with the Marquis of Canterhough's groom. He is"—another polite cough—"brawny."

"I'm sorry." Visibly reassured, Bonny climbed onto the bed and nudged under Valentine's good arm. "I'm the jealous type."

"You should never be jealous of another gentleman's valet. You may on occasion, however, be envious."

"If you say so," said Bonny, laughing.

Periwinkle only offered a lordly flick of his fingers. "Passion fades, love changes. But style, Mr. Tarleton, style is forever." Gathering up a selection of Valentine's shirts, he opened a drawer, looked startled at whatever it contained, and hastily closed it again. "I advise caution, milord. This house contains some . . . hmm . . . idiosyncrasies."

"What kind of idiosyncrasies were in that drawer?" asked Bonny, sitting up.

"Nothing His Grace needs to think about in his weakened condition."

Needless to say, Valentine did not find this reassuring. "What's in the drawer?"

"Objects," returned Periwinkle, busying himself aggressively with Valentine's waistcoats, "whose use lies quite beyond my comprehension."

Valentine watched him in rising bewilderment. "I thought no aspect of a gentleman's grooming lay beyond your comprehension, Periwinkle."

He cleared his throat. "Well, this is more a matter of . . . personal care."

Slipping away from Valentine again, Bonny went to investigate. He had been quite the perfect companion—constant, attentive, soft of touch and voice—while Valentine had been in the doldrums of recovery. But now he was on the mend, Bonny's natural inability to stay still for five seconds together had returned with a vengeance. Not that Valentine truly minded. After all, a Bonny in motion was a Bonny displaying all his best features.

On opening the caution-requiring drawer, he uttered a squeak. A squeak of multitudes: surprise and amusement, and glee and embarrassment. "I see what you mean."

"What?" demanded Valentine. "What did he mean?"

Bonny was giggling now and rummaging excitedly around in the drawer—which was causing the contents to clack softly against each other. "Probably best wait until you're feeling better."

"I insist," Valentine insisted, "on knowing what's in that drawer."

Shrugging, Bonny drew out a very strange object indeed: a smooth piece of jade with a rounded head and a gentle curve.

Valentine stared at it. "What is that for?"

Bonny grinned.

"I've never seen anything like that."

"Oh, flower. You've seen *something* like it."

"When would I have . . ." Abruptly, Valentine stopped talking. Then could not help himself: "Why would you . . ." No. He was not pursuing that thought. "I'm very tired," he said. "I need to rest."

And pulled a pillow over his face to hide his blushes.

Chapter 33

"I," announced Bonny, bounding into the room a few hours later, "have a bone to pick with you, flower."

Ostensibly, Valentine had been resting, but it had not been a completely successful endeavour. He was caught in that particular stage of convalescence wherein he felt tired and in pain for quite a lot of the time, while being neither tired nor in pain enough to not find being tired and in pain deeply frustrating. He eased himself carefully into a sitting position against the pillows Periwinkle had arranged for him with a deft and expert hand. "What manner of . . . bone?"

"A book bone." A handsome, though well-read, copy of *Northanger Abbey* sailed through the air and landed next to Valentine on the bed. Followed by *Castle Rackrent*. And would possibly have been followed by *The Libertine* except Bonny gave a squeak of alarm. "Oh God. Sorry. Your arm. Did I jostle your arm?"

"I'm quite well," Valentine reassured him. "You may continue with your . . ."

"With my bone?"

"Indeed. Though I'm hard pressed to understand what Sir Horley's taste in reading material has to do with me."

Bonny tumbled the rest of the books he was carrying onto the bed and stood with his hands on his hips. "These aren't Sir Horley's. They're *yours*."

"M-mine?"

"Yes. Periwinkle brought them with him."

"Ah." Valentine glanced away, hoping to hide an incipient blush. "I might happen to have glanced—"

"*Happen*," repeated Bonny. "*Glanced*. Periwinkle said you're *devoted* to your books. That you're an *avid reader*."

"*Devoted* seems rather a strong word. As does *avid*. And in any case," Valentine went on, hopelessly flustered, "what a gentleman does in the privacy of his own bedchamber is his own business."

"Not to his . . . not his"—Bonny seemed momentarily lost for words—"his me."

Valentine shifted awkwardly—he was not sure he could have felt more revealed had Bonny caught him with a hand on his cock. "You are making too much of this."

"Valentine, you know what I'm like. I make too much of everything." Bonny hopped onto the bed, kneeling on the covers. "But I don't understand why anytime I mentioned reading, you behaved as though I was speaking absolute gibberish."

"Well, you were. It is one thing to divert oneself with the occasional novel. Quite another to . . . to . . . try to live in them, as you do."

"I only tried to live in them," said Bonny softly, "when it seemed like I had nowhere else to go. But even if I don't need that from them anymore, they're still important to me. Those stories still feel like places I've been and the characters in them—no matter how virtuous or villainous—like old friends." He paused, grinning. "And some of them more than that. I mean"—and here Bonny fanned himself vigorously—"the things I've done with Lord Orville and he to me—"

"I would prefer, thank you very much, not to hear any more about your fictional affair with a fictional aristocrat."

Of course, this only made Bonny giggle with unabashed glee. "I love how jealous you get."

"I'm not jealous," insisted Valentine. "I'm just . . ." He sighed. "Jealous."

"Don't worry. You're so much better than Lord Orville."

Valentine considered this. "I do, at least, have the advantage of not being fictional."

"And what," declared Bonny, kissing his cheek with a flourish, "an advantage that is." Then he sat back on his heels and began sorting through the pile of books with the enthusiasm of a very literary-inclined pirate having unearthed a trove of buried treasure. And if Valentine had hoped this would be enough to distract Bonny from his original purpose, he knew him too well to count on it. "And these really mean nothing to you?" he asked.

"On the contrary, I said they were quite diverting."

"So if I . . . oh, I don't know . . ." Bonny slipped nonchalantly off the bed. "Threw your copy of *Northanger Abbey* out of the window. You wouldn't care?"

"There would be no reason for you to throw my copy of *Northanger Abbey* out of the window."

Bonny was moving towards the window. "But I could be reading on the window seat, and it could just fall out of my hands and into the water feature below."

"Please stay away from the window with my copy of *Northanger Abbey*."

"Why?" asked Bonny. "It's just a book. It doesn't matter to you."

"Bonny"—Valentine had been intending to sound commanding but unfortunately only managed plaintive—"the degree of esteem in which I hold my possessions should not be the metric by which they do or do not end up in water features."

Now Bonny was sitting on the window seat, *Northanger Abbey* balanced precariously on one upraised knee. "There's a bit of a breeze here. It's surprisingly strong. It's just whooshing right—"

"Fine fine fine fine fine." Valentine broke. "I love my books. The more romantic, the more sentimental, the better; there are pages that probably still bear the marks of privately shed tears. Now for the love of God, get the fuck away from the window, you monster."

Clasping *Northanger Abbey* to his chest, Bonny returned to the bed. "You didn't really believe I was going to drop it, did you?"

"That was a hostage situation." Relief and embarrassment were waging a private war in Valentine's heart. "It was very disquieting, and I wasn't thinking clearly."

"I'm sorry," said Bonny, with apparent sincerity. He gathered the rest of the books up carefully and stacked them on the table beside the bed before curling up next to Valentine, his head resting against his good shoulder. "But there's nothing to be ashamed of in liking to read."

It was too late now for dissembling. Valentine sighed. "It was both a comfort and torment to me. I sought closeness with fictional characters because I felt incapable of it with anyone else. After all, if someone isn't real, there are no expectations, no chance of loss. No discovery of something lacking in yourself. Are you satisfied now?"

"There is nothing lacking in you, Valentine," Bonny told him fiercely. "Not in how you feel or what you like or the way you have sex. You are perfect."

"I am very far from perfect."

Bonny smiled up at him, his eyes shining and his mouth like the promise of a kiss. "Then you are perfect *for me*. Especially now that you've admitted you read. Oh my God." He sat up again, abruptly. Because even Valentine's bullet wound wasn't enough to still, for any length of time, a Tarleton. "We are going to have so much fun."

"Fun?" asked Valentine warily.

"Yes. So much fun. I need to know *everything*. All your opinions. Your favourite writers, your favourite books, your favourite characters.

Your most nefarious villains, your most courageous heroines, and your most romantic heroes."

"I . . . I'm not sure my opinions are sufficient to this degree of scrutiny."

"They will be." Bonny was, as ever, indomitably certain. "I mean, which Jane Austen hero would you marry?"

Valentine had seen no reason to give the matter much thought. "None of them, because it's illegal and—even presupposing one of them gave their consent—everyone would surely laugh at me for making the attempt."

"In an ideal world, where it was possible, and nobody would laugh at you."

"I really don't know, Bonny. I would probably need to have some kind of . . . personal relationship with them first."

"You do have a personal relationship with them. You've read about them."

It took Valentine's mind a longish moment to agree to even contemplate the matter. It felt like the mental equivalent of expecting to walk upon clouds. But then, what were fancies but clouds themselves? Safely ephemeral. Yet as present as you needed them to be.

"Or any character," Bonny added, since Valentine's moment was lingering.

Valentine opened his mouth. Then closed it again. Then closed his eyes. Then muttered, "Henry Crawford."

"Oh, flower." Bonny sounded half-awed, half-horrified. "You have terrible taste."

"He . . . he's very charming. And adventurous."

"He'd cheat on you. And spend all your money."

"I thought," offered Valentine huffily, "that reformed rakes are supposed to make the best husbands."

Bonny flicked his hair out of his eyes. "Lies. Henry Crawford is the sort of man you fuck. Absolutely not the sort of man you marry."

"Then who is the sort of man you marry?"

"Mr. Darcy," returned Bonny, with barely a pause.

"Mr. Darcy?" repeated Valentine, in some consternation. "He's the most dreadful prig."

At this, Bonny gave a gasp of real outrage. "How dare you. He just takes some getting to know. And obviously, he's a bit proud: he's young, he's rich, he's handsome and from a fine old family, so he has every reason to be. Besides, he *changes* . . . or rather, I think, he becomes who he always was, deep down. And all for love. What could be more special?"

"Or you could, for example, take up with someone who was beguiling from the outset?"

"I could," Bonny conceded, "but where's the excitement in that?"

Valentine glanced at him in bewildered disapproval. "I might have known even your ideas about books would be absurd and questionable."

Bonny returned his look. "I might have known even *your* ideas about books would be absurd and questionable." And then rushed on in the same breath, "Oh, but Valentine. I need to borrow . . . well . . . everything you have. Sort of immediately. I've been longing to read some of these for literally *years*."

"Of course you can." Careful not to pull his stitches, Valentine leaned down to kiss Bonny's brow. "All of me is yours. Books included."

It took less than thirty seconds for Valentine to regret this offer. Bonny had fallen on Valentine's collection with shrieks of delight, hugging *The Castle of Wolfenbach* like an old friend and actually running circles round the room when he discovered Valentine's copy of Ambrosia Blaine's *Agnes Polk, or The Dread Castle of Von Schlaufenberg*. To Valentine's mind, reading was a quiet business—one that, in his pre-Bonny days, he had largely transacted in private, in bed, or, if he was feeling decadent, the bath. For Bonny it was loud, energetic, and—perhaps this went without saying—extraordinarily irritating.

It turned out he didn't read books. He *possessed* them. He carried them around with him, stuffed in a pocket, or tucked under his arm, burying himself into them whenever the whim took him—occasionally even wandering into furniture, or forgetting to stop pouring tea, because he just "had" to finish this chapter. And, even when all he was doing was reading, which ought to have been occupation enough, he would still contrive to throw himself around, rolling off the furniture or kicking his legs in the air when particularly enamoured or alarmed.

Then there were the *sounds*. The breathless little hiccoughs. The excitable yelping. The gasped-out *No*s and relishful *Oh my*s. And the inevitable moment when he would fly towards Valentine, crying: "Oh my God, have you *read this*." And Valentine would muster an uncharmed expression and say, "It's my book. Of course I've read it."

That was when the talking began, Bonny usually taking the opportunity to sit far too close, with his chin in his hands and a rapt look on his face, bombarding Valentine with a thousand "What did you think of" and "Wasn't it amazing when" and "I just didn't know what to do about" and "I'm madly in love with so and so" and "I wish such and such hadn't happened," only to stuff his fingers in his ears and run away, yelling, "Don't tell me don't tell me don't tell me" the moment Valentine could get a word in edgeways.

It was never ending. Exhausting. Utterly irresistible.

And worse was yet to come. Because a book that Bonny had read was a book that would never be the same again. It wasn't that he damaged them—the idea of hurting a book would have appalled him—but there were traces of him everywhere. Little pieces of paper sticking out of the pages. The occasional light pencil mark or underlining. The most delicate of lines down the spine, hinting at the places he'd turned to most frequently. Sometimes just the sense of touching where he might have touched, or the faintest scent of his skin layered over paper and leather.

Perhaps Valentine would be like that someday. Studied and pored over and known. Line by line. Cover to cover. Indelibly marked in ways only he could recognise. It was not, in all honesty, a thought that troubled him.

Chapter 34

Eventually Valentine was able to sit in the garden—informally but, thanks to Periwinkle, nevertheless appropriately dressed. It had only been a few weeks, but summer had laid its claim upon the world: gilded all the grass and crowned the trees with gold. The days, too, were golden things: slivers of silver mornings and soft indigo nights wrapped around sun-drenched afternoons that lingered forever beneath skies as blue as porcelain.

Valentine knew it couldn't last. That he lived in something perilously close to a dream, far from the compromises the world would require. But it was easier not to think about it. To pretend that nothing was waiting for him—no duties or responsibilities, nor the great name to which he owed so much obligation. And devote himself instead to Bonny, to slow walks along flower-swept avenues, to arguments over games of chess when neither of them could play, to evenings wrapped in each other's arms. To prising open the lockbox of his own happiness, when once he had believed it necessary to cast away the key.

Of course, this would have been easier had not Sir Horley Comewithers kept taking advantage of the fact Valentine was living in his house by paying gratuitous visits.

He claimed to be enquiring after Valentine's health, but any fool could tell he just wanted to bask in the sunlight like some kind of serpent and flirt with Bonny. Who would persist in flirting back. It was as if they were caught up in some kind of perverse conspiracy to make Valentine as grumpy as possible.

"The man is like the French distemper," a particularly disgruntled Valentine told Bonny on one occasion. "You just think you're done with him, when he comes back."

There had, however, been enough of a lull between outbreaks of Sir Horley that Valentine had misguidedly dared to hope he had gone back to London. But no. He had merely been in remission and, having let himself in by the back gate, was now tip-tapping buoyantly down the garden path to where Valentine and Bonny had been taking tea very happily without him.

Worse, he appeared to be *accompanied*. What was he thinking? Bringing people here. And now. When Valentine had been shot.

"Valentine," he called out. And, as if his only goal in life was to make Valentine scowl, "Lovely Bonny. I come bearing friends."

Valentine scowled even harder. Sir Horley knew very well that Valentine did not have friends. Which was only proven when—putting a hand to his brow to shield his eyes from the sun—Valentine recognised Miss Fairfax and Miss Evans trailing in Sir Horley's wake.

They were arm in arm, Miss Fairfax somewhat spectral in pale grey and Miss Evans radiant in buttercup yellow, and they both gave every impression of being about as pleased to see Valentine as he was to see them.

"Can you believe"—Sir Horley occupied a chair nobody had invited him to occupy and tossed his hat nonchalantly onto the table—"Ambrosia Blaine. The Ambrosia Blaine. Living so close to my little home away from home, and I would never have known."

Valentine was still scowling. He could feel it latched onto his face like an aggrieved cat. "So how do you know?"

"Our lovely Bonny told me, of course. To help me better be the agent of your worldly affairs."

"He did what? To do what?"

Sir Horley ignored him. "Ladies, ladies. Please, put yourselves at ease."

"It's hard to be at ease," said Miss Fairfax tartly, "when one may owe a duke a significant apology."

Whatever Valentine had been expecting, it was not this. It left him at a loss to respond.

Miss Fairfax pulled her shoulders back, though her eyes remained worried. "Well, Your Grace? Do we?"

Three months ago Valentine would have said no because it was easy to be gracious when you were largely indifferent. When manners were just another mask. Three weeks ago, he would have said yes because his wounded pride demanded it. But what Valentine cared about, and what he didn't, had been in the oddest state of flux lately. And while all this new caring had turned out to be riven with vulnerability, perhaps it could encompass grace too?

"No," he said. "No apology is necessary except from me to you, for you offered me shelter and I was an abominable guest."

Miss Evans was nodding. And got as far as "You weren't our fav—" before Miss Fairfax elbowed her into silence.

"Also"—the memory made Valentine wince, the indignation he felt at the time long since stifled by mortification—"I broke a chair. And a window. And possibly a table?"

It was at this juncture that Sir Horley smirked his way back into the conversation. "I have compensated Miss Fairfax and Miss Evans on your behalf. Really, Valentine, whatever had you been doing to cause so much damage?"

"I had made some errors," Valentine told him. "And that is the last that shall be said on the subject." He eyed his companions. "By anyone." If mutiny fomented in the ranks, none dared brook this ducal edict. Which should have been a relief but made Valentine feel oddly uncertain. "I shall, of course," he added, "repay you in turn, Sir Horley."

A not quite comfortable silence fell over the gathering.

"Fine." Valentine made a gesture of surrender with his free hand. "Ladies, do sit down, take tea with us. While I reluctantly regale Sir Horley with the unedifying tale of the worst night of my life, and he laughs at me."

Sir Horley made a noise like a cat being stroked. "Oh, I do love being regaled. It's my"—he counted quickly on his fingers—"seventh favourite thing."

"Please do stay." Bonny had, at last, succeeded in extricating himself from *Agnes Polk*. "It's so lovely to see you both again. We might even have cake. Valentine, do we have cake? Or did I eat it all?"

Miss Fairfax and Miss Evans exchanged glances. "We can stay," said Miss Fairfax. "I confess that, despite having lived it, I am rather intrigued to hear this story too."

While Bonny ran off to secure cake and a fresh pot of tea, Valentine fretted over what he'd agreed to, and why he'd agreed to it. He preferred—or at least had fallen into the habit of—sharing as little of himself as possible. And here he was about to embark on a lengthy reckoning of his own foolishness.

"So"—it was not, perhaps, the most original beginning, but it was, if nothing else, *a* beginning—"there are two things you need to know in advance of this story. The first is that I had given my signet ring to an ostler in a moment of . . . a moment of . . ."

"Absurd jealousy?" suggested Bonny, tumbling a new set of tea-cups and saucers onto the tabletop.

Personally Valentine thought his jealousy had been entirely justified under the circumstances, but it did not seem appropriate to discuss the matter before guests. "What matters here is that there was an ostler and to the ostler—"

Except then Sir Horley interrupted him with a, "That reminds me."

"I am quite content"—Valentine gave him a cold look—"*not* to tell this story."

"On the contrary. I am already positively agog for the story. But I thought you might like to have this back." Reaching into the interior pocket of his coat, Sir Horley produced something small, glinting, and familiar.

"My signet ring." Valentine slipped it back on his finger where it belonged, surprised by how heavy it felt, and how tight. "However did you . . . that is . . . thank you."

Sir Horley offered one of his foxiest smiles. "Believe me, it was very much my pleasure."

"Even so, I am sorry to have put you to the trouble."

"No trouble," returned Sir Horley cheerfully. "Someone had to do something about the chaos you left behind you."

"Chaos? What chaos?" When it came to Sir Horley's actions, Valentine was never sure whether he was supposed to be grateful or suspicious, so leaned suspicious on instinct. "What else have you been doing on my behalf?"

"Darling, what haven't I been doing? Not counting tracking down signet rings and visiting women whose homes you've smashed up, I've been paying off innkeepers, returning stolen curricles, replacing coats for assistant gardeners, tendering apologies to concerned relatives, and ensuring that young ladies who have promised to go to Bath actually do go to Bath. Your mother is lovely, by the way. She sends her love."

"Oh God." Since Valentine couldn't easily put his head in his hands, he put his head on the table instead. "And you've let me stay in your"—neither he nor Bonny had yet worked out how to refer to Sir Horley's hunting lodge—"residence. This is dreadful. You've been so kind to me."

"I've been having the time of my life."

"But I owe you so much. What on earth possessed you?"

"Would it make it easier," asked Sir Horley, "if we pretend I had some ulterior motive?"

"Please."

"Like secretly wanting to get into Bonny's breeches?"

Valentine's whole body quivered. "That's not secret. That's obvious to everyone."

"Perhaps I'm lonely then?" suggested Sir Horley.

"At least try to be plausible. You have so many acquaintances."

"And so very few of them know who I am."

"It is very difficult, Sir Horley"—Valentine lifted his head again—"*not* to know who you are."

"Knowing, suspecting, and assuming are very different things, dear boy. But"—and here Sir Horley heaved a sorrowful sigh—"if none of these suffice, you may have to confront the very real possibility I'm actually a good person."

"Of course you're not a good person," Valentine retorted. "You're a terrible person." He paused. Then thought again about everything Sir Horley had done for him, most of them without him even knowing, and groaned. "Please don't be a good person."

"He has good taste in books," offered Miss Fairfax.

"And chairs," added Miss Evans.

Miss Fairfax nodded. "And we were not even obliged to tie him to one."

"Well," declared Sir Horley, "now I *have* to hear this story."

Valentine put his head back on the table and groaned again.

And Sir Horley had the outright gall to pat him consolingly. "You can consider it my reward for being such a splendid friend to you."

"Friendship with me," Valentine said, straightening up, "should be its own reward."

Sir Horley raised his brows. "Valentine, you've met you. You know it isn't. So do spill your guts for my entertainment like a good fellow."

It was, in the most literal sense, the least Valentine owed him. "As I was saying, there are two important pieces of context to the tale: one, that I had given my signet ring to an ostler; and the second was that, prior to my arrival, Miss Tarleton had been quite busy presenting me to Miss Fairfax and Miss Evans as an utter villain."

"It's true," chimed in Miss Evans. "She was *lavish* about it, wasn't she, love?"

Miss Fairfax's lips turned into their mysterious smile. "Indeed. As I believe I said at the time, it was positively novelistic."

"A tricky situation, as you can see," Valentine continued, "but one easily resolved through the simple expedient of behaving like a gentleman and explaining oneself in a sensible fashion."

Sir Horley nodded reassuringly. "And that's what you did?"

"Good heavens, no. I barged in like an irate hippopotamus."

There was the slightest of pauses, as if nobody was quite certain how to react to this. Then Bonny giggled, which seemed to encourage the others, amusement travelling through the group like a ripple.

It was oddly . . . encouraging? Valentine regarded his audience severely. "Never let it be said I am a man to follow the obvious path. I mean, any fool could have *remained calm* and *initiated a conversation.* Not I, though. *I* chose to eschew such paltry ideas of social decency."

"What did you do?" asked Sir Horley. For someone who talked far too much, he was a surprisingly good listener.

"Why, I . . ." And here Valentine paused for moment. "I opted to make it worse."

This time there was no hesitation in the amusement, but there was no unkindness either. And even if they were—on this occasion—laughing at him, Valentine realised there was no reason he couldn't laugh with them.

His attempt to tell the story rather unravelled from there. The more seriously he presented it, the more absurd it sounded, and the more absurd he allowed it to be, the more he was interrupted. Miss

Fairfax had detail she wanted to add, and Miss Evans and Bonny both wanted to offer their own perspectives, and Sir Horley had an endless stream of enthusiastic questions. It culminated with Bonny and Miss Evans attempting to outdo each other on who could do the most accurate impression of Valentine's transformation into a rampaging chairbeastman. Although *accurate* was clearly code for *most ridiculous*.

"And you know what makes this all extra silly?" Bonny said finally, picking himself up off the grass, where he'd been thrashing in a way that was unflattering to Valentine but rather flattering to himself.

"Delicious boy"—Sir Horley wiped a mirthful tear from his eye—"I don't believe *anything* could have made this business sillier."

"On the contrary," Bonny told him triumphantly, "the decorative strawberry leaf on this strawberry ice cream of nonsense is that Valentine here is actually the most outrageous admirer of Ambrosia Blaine."

Miss Fairfax's teaspoon chinked in her saucer. "His Grace? Surely not."

"That's his copy of *Agnes Polk*." Bonny gestured at it, sealing his betrayal of Valentine with incontrovertible proof.

"I . . ." The heat was travelling so rapidly through Valentine's body it was a wonder his fingertips weren't blushing. "Yes. I . . . I would not take it amiss were you to . . ." He swallowed. "Sign it."

Miss Fairfax had also gone slightly pink. "Certainly, if that is something you would like."

Before they could lose themselves in an exchange of ever-increasing awkwardness, Sir Horley ambled off to find a quill, and Bonny distracted Valentine by sitting in his lap.

"Can everyone stay for supper?" he asked. "Please?"

Valentine blinked up at him. "Well, I'm sure Sir Horley has nothing better to do, but don't you think we've imposed on Miss Fairfax and Miss Evans enough?"

"But we're having the most wonderful time."

"That doesn't mean it's acceptable to—"

"What's not acceptable?" Sir Horley had returned with ink and quill, both of which he set before Miss Fairfax. "This is for you, my dear."

Bonny half turned towards him. "Valentine is deploring me because I want everyone to stay for supper, so I've suggested asking."

"I would love to stay for supper," said Sir Horley predictably. "What about you, ladies? Can you spare us a little more of your company? My carriage, of course, remains at your service."

Again an exchange of glances between Miss Fairfax and Miss Evans that suggested an understanding of such significant depth and duration to transcend words. Valentine wondered if he would reach such a point with Bonny. Truthfully, it seemed unlikely. Even if they did develop the capacity to communicate through spiritual vibrations, Bonny would probably announce every thought in his head anyway.

"We'd be happy to stay," said Miss Fairfax. "If you'd be happy to have us."

Bonny pushed his face close to Valentine's like a badly trained puppy. "Please? *Please?* Pleasepleaseplease?"

"Do recall"—that was Sir Horley, unpredictable as ever—"that poor Valentine was quite recently injured and has already been a more than generous host all afternoon. We must not exhaust him."

It was an escape route. One Valentine could have taken without dishonour nor insult to anyone. In fact, it would have been easy.

And yet.

"Please do stay," he heard himself. And then because all his secrets were already unravelled: "On one condition."

"What kind of condition?" asked Miss Fairfax, whose tendency towards wariness Valentine could not but find sympathetic.

Bonny's tendency to clamber all over him with impunity, however, was another matter entirely. Even if, on this occasion, Valentine was glad to be partially obscured. He took a deep breath. "On the condition that we play the dictionary game later. I mean, if you're willing. I wouldn't want you to—"

He got no further, because he was drowned in enthusiasm for the idea, even from Sir Horley, who had no idea what the dictionary game was, which just was so entirely typical of the man.

As far as Valentine was concerned, the way he kept being likeable was starting to feel pointed. And probably meant they were friends.

Dammit.

Chapter 35

Inside Valentine's copy of *Agnes Polk*, Miss Fairfax had written, "To Valentine, who is really a duke." He kept peeking at it when he thought nobody was paying attention.

"How many times are you going to look at that?" asked Bonny, throwing himself down on the bed next to Valentine.

Guiltily, Valentine slammed the book closed. "What? No. I wasn't."

"Thank you for tonight." Turning onto an elbow, Bonny gazed up at him, the blue of his eyes muted into something soft and secret by the candlelight. "It was such fun."

"I think you would make anything fun."

Bonny prodded him in the knee. "You're fun too."

"Only to you, my heart."

"To other people as well. When you let yourself." Bonny was still watching him. He had all this *knowledge* of Valentine. And it was such a complicated thing, being known that way. "Valentine?"

"Yes?"

"I like you so much."

"Oh, Bonny." Complicated. Wonderful. Enough to make his heart buckle with the weight of it. "I like you too. More than I have ever liked anyone. More than I can imagine ever liking anyone."

"That's because," Bonny told him, laughing, "you don't try."

"I do try. That is, I have tried. I liked . . . I like . . . your sister, after all."

"And how did that work out for you?"

"Splendidly. As you know." Valentine fell silent a moment. "I think often when you like someone . . . when you like a woman . . . there is an expectation you may feel other things as well. And I never have. There came a point when it began to seem . . . deceptive. And it was not the sort of thing I ever knew how to talk about. I'm still not sure I do."

Bonny's fingers stroked lightly over Valentine's knee. "What about men?"

"I never really thought about it. It would likely have struck me as too perverse to seek what I did not experience with women in other men. Or perhaps I was, in some unacknowledged way, afraid that I might."

"Well"—Bonny's fingers had found their way to his inner thigh, the touch incandescent even over pantaloons—"it looks like you've made peace with it."

Valentine smiled at him. "I didn't have much choice. But I also learned it didn't have to change anything. That it need not be impossible. Thanks to you."

To his surprise, Bonny uttered the strangest little groan. "Please stop smiling at me like that. It's giving me needs."

"I beg your pardon?"

"Valentine." Another groan. "You know I adore everything we do together? Especially at the end of the day, when it's just the two of us and we can hold each other and touch each other and kiss and . . . *ngh*."

"Thank you," said Valentine warily, "for confirming that. I confess, I've been working under the assumption you would tell me if I did anything to make you unhappy."

"I'm *very* happy. But"—Bonny closed his eyes tightly and rushed out the words—"I'm also desperate for you, and you've been shot, so I feel selfish."

This was nowhere near the problem Bonny apparently thought it was. "I'm much recovered from being shot. And, for your information, desperate for you in return."

Some of the anxious lines faded from between Bonny's brows. One of his eyes popped open. "Are you?"

"Certainly. Have you not recently beheld yourself?"

"I am magnificent," Bonny agreed.

"I'm almost embarrassed to tell you how often I've thought about . . . thought about what we did by the waterfall."

Bonny sat back up. "Well, I think about it all the time."

"I would love . . ." For some reason Valentine was overtaken by a sudden flood of shyness. He cleared his throat. "I would love to do it again." A pause. "I would love to do it again right now."

"Your arm, though."

"As it happens," Valentine murmured, "I have actually considered this too."

"Oh, have you?"

"Yes. I was thinking, were I to lie back, keeping my shoulder supported upon the pillows, you could . . . perhaps . . ."

"I could perhaps what?"

Bonny was teasing him. Bonny was assuredly teasing him. And Valentine was beginning to discover just how much easier it was to imagine things than describe them. "You could remove all your garments."

"That's a good start."

"And then you could . . . for example . . . lower yourself. Your . . . arse. You could kneel over me. And present your arse, your delightful arse with its hungry flower, in a fashion convenient for my mouth to reach. While I lay beneath you."

Moons waxed and waned in the silence that followed. Bonny was blinking rapidly.

"If . . . if that was agreeable to you," Valentine finished. "If you feel it would be feasible."

Bonny was still blinking. "*Val-EN-tine*. The things you've been doing to me in your head. I'm *shocked*."

"Oh dear. Are you really?"

"About . . ." Bonny held his thumb and forefinger approximately half an inch apart. "This much. But I shouldn't be."

"Why?" Valentine wasn't sure if this was going to go well for him or badly.

"Because"—Bonny leaned over and kissed him right between the eyes—"you are secretly a very wicked and creative man."

"Does that mean," asked Valentine, with unbecoming eagerness, "we can attempt the activity I suggested?"

"We can . . ." Except Bonny sounded, not doubtful exactly. A little hesitant perhaps? "But wouldn't you like to explore some of the other, um, activities we could do together?"

"I don't feel I've fully encompassed that one."

Bonny's lips twitched. "That's not how it works, flower. It's a buffet, not a sit-down dinner. You try all the things, not just the things immediately in front of you."

"What if I've found a dish I particularly enjoy?"

"The dish isn't going anywhere. You can have it served as often as you like. I just don't want you to overlook some of the other . . . *delicacies* on offer."

This was disappointing news. But Valentine did his best to take it gracefully. "As ever, you are correct." He hung his head. "I'm being selfish."

That earned another laugh. "I simply adore the way you think licking my arse is selfish."

"But the last time I chose what we would do," Valentine pointed out. "It is only fair that you should get the same opportunity."

A mischievous light flared in Bonny's eyes. "Taking turns. I like this."

"Is there something you have in mind?"

"Actually"—apparently Valentine had not been the only one imagining things—"there is. But only as long as you're comfortable with it."

Valentine sighed. "With negligible experience, it's hard to know what I'm comfortable with."

"Sometimes even the idea of something will feel wrong. You need to let me know if that ever happens."

"I will," said Valentine, with perhaps a trace too much earnestness. "But please tell me what you want to do tonight."

"Well . . ." A flush was painting the tops of Bonny's ears and the tip of his nose. Perhaps he had encountered the same chasm between inspiration and expression that Valentine had discovered. "What I would like to do tonight is . . . I would like us to choose one of the objects from the, you know, the personal-care drawer, and I would like you to put it inside me."

"Oh." Valentine considered this. And discovered he could picture all too vividly the way a piece of jade—so hard and smooth—might look as it disappeared into the glorious pink softness that was Bonny. "I think," he went on breathlessly, "I would like that too. Very much."

Bonny grinned. "Good. And then I—"

"Wait. There's more?"

"Obviously, there's more, flower. I'm me, remember?"

Valentine's nod was a little more nervous than he would have ideally preferred. "G-go on?"

"After that, I would like to arrange you very comfortably and securely upon some pillows, as you suggested. And then I'd like to . . . be inside you. And I'd like you to watch us in all these mirrors. But I understand if—"

"Yes," said Valentine. "Let's do that."

"Are you sure? Because—"

"Yes." Catching Bonny gently by the nape of his neck, Valentine drew him into a kiss. "Yes." Then another. "Yes." And then, briefly diverted by more practical concerns, "I should ring for Periwinkle."

Bonny's recently kissed mouth twisted quizzically. "Not what I was expecting to hear. Why?"

"Well, I . . ." Valentine made a clumsy gesture with his sling. "I'll need some assistance."

"I can do that."

"But," Valentine protested anxiously, "Periwinkle is a professional. What if my coat gets crumpled?"

Bonny stood, insinuating himself between Valentine's knees, necessitating their parting. It was an odd sensation, making space for someone else with your body—oddly exposing for all Valentine was fully dressed. "I think you'll be too distracted to care."

"I like this coat very much."

"And I'm"—Bonny wriggled a finger through the knot in Valentine's cravat and pulled—"very distracting."

He was. And so was *this*. The simple act of having his cravat unravelled in a fashion infinitely removed from Periwinkle's detached and efficient motions. Bonny . . . teased. Took his time. Let Valentine feel every twitch and tug upon the fabric, the occasional brush of his hands. By the time Bonny had unwound the linen and was drawing it free, Valentine was dizzy. Unbelievably aware of the two buttons holding his shirt closed.

"See," said Bonny, flicking open the top button. "Isn't this nice?"

"Murrrghlff," replied Valentine.

Bonny popped the second button free of its buttonhole, revealing Valentine's neck and a small patch of skin below. It was nothing. It should have been nothing. But Valentine might as well have been naked. And Bonny had barely touched him. Was now only looking. Intent, though, as if he could see the breath caught in Valentine's throat.

"Should . . . ," asked Valentine. "Should it feel like this?"

"I don't know. Is it bad?"

Valentine shook his head. "It's . . . it's not the same."

"The same as what?"

"As when Periwinkle . . ."

"Flower." Bonny's hand briefly covered his mouth. "I know a duke and his valet have a very special relationship. But I need you not to talk about Periwinkle when you're making love with me."

"My apologies."

"And of course it's not the same. He Who Shall Not Be Joining Us Even Verbally in the Bedroom is doing his job. I'm . . ."

Still more special than the relationship Valentine had with his valet was the occasion on which Bonaventure Tarleton was lost for words. "What?"

"I'm in heaven," he finished.

Now Valentine, too, was lost for words. "Oh."

"Yes. I'm serving you but a little bit in control of you at the same time. So it's as if you . . . all the beauty of you . . . is for me."

Valentine shivered slightly. It was, now that Bonny had drawn his attention to it, a peculiar juxtaposition of power and surrender. "That will remain true even when I regain full use of my arm."

Bonny's answer was a kiss, pressed like a seal over the place where the pulse beat in Valentine's neck. Then he dropped to his knees and began removing Valentine's boots.

"You did this for me at the inn," said Valentine.

Bonny glanced up through his lashes. "I remember. You were driving me to derangement. But I still wanted to push your legs apart and take your cock down my throat."

"Had you attempted it, I would probably have expired on the spot." One of Valentine's boots sailed over Bonny's shoulder. His toes wriggled appreciatively in their newfound freedom. "It was already the most erotic experience of my life."

"Oh, Valentine." Bonny curled a hand around Valentine's calf and pressed his cheek to the interior of Valentine's knee. "I hate thinking how lonely you must have been all these years."

Valentine smiled down at him, twining a finger through one of Bonny's too-long, too-wayward curls. "Ah yes. As a rich, powerful duke, I've had a terrible time of it."

"That doesn't discount feeling bad."

"But I cherish every bad feeling I've ever had, every regret, every moment of boredom and sorrow and uncertainty. They brought me to you, after all."

Bonny made a sound like *ack* and bit Valentine's leg.

"Ouch. What was that for?"

"For being just *too lovely*. It's more than I can bear sometimes. *You* are more than I can bear sometimes."

"If you take away the title and the wealth, I am not so very remarkable."

"Aren't you?" Bonny lifted one of Valentine's feet and settled it upon his thigh, bracing it there as he peeled down Valentine's stocking. "You could have anything in the world. And yet you chose me."

"You're the only thing I've ever truly wanted."

"And nobody has ever made me feel as wanted as you."

Valentine laughed. "That's the sheerest nonsense, Bonny. A significant number of people want you and have made no secret of it."

"In which case"—now Bonny was easing down Valentine's other stocking—"I chose you back. Remarkable enough for you?"

"You seem to be arguing, intentionally or not, that what makes me remarkable is you. Which I shall not dispute."

"What? No, I . . ." Sighing, Bonny sat back on his heels and stared up at Valentine with a comically disgruntled expression. "*Val-EN-tine.* That's not fair. I'm distracted with getting you naked. You know I didn't mean that."

This just made Valentine laugh harder. Although his mirth dissolved into a strangled gasp when Bonny retributively seized him by the ankle and dragged his tongue wantonly all the way up the arch of Valentine's foot.

"Your"—Valentine could barely articulate himself through the blaze of unexpected sensation—"point is well made."

"My points always are."

Bonny pushed himself upright and stood, contemplating Valentine, who—despite still feeling rather flustered by this kind of scrutiny—remained sitting obediently on the edge of the bed.

Apparently, his coat had been designated next for removal. This operation was simple enough, for it was only resting on his shoulders, and his waistcoat soon followed. His shirt was more complicated, for it had to be untucked from his pantaloons before being eased first past his sling and then over his head. This was hard to sit still for because, while Valentine's arm was much improved, it was still somewhat tender. Still expectant of pain.

Bonny, however, was in no rush. Leaning over Valentine, he brought only the warmth of his body, the soft ripple of his breath, and touches so delicate they fell upon his skin like the sunlight had that day by the waterfall. By the time he was shirtless, Valentine was undone, pliant in the purity of his trust, floating on a haze of warmth. Understanding, at last, what it meant to be cared for. Not, as Periwinkle did, attentively and competently for his well-earned salary. But for nothing beyond the offering of Valentine himself.

Wordlessly, Bonny took his hand and urged him to stand, so he could coax down both pantaloons and unmentionables, and then to sit again while he slid them off entirely—once again flinging them behind him to land, most likely crumpled, and who knew where. But in this, as in so many other things, Bonny was correct. Valentine was long past caring.

Instead, he just reached down to where Bonny still knelt at his feet and cupped his cheek. Struck by the way a lover's beauty could be at once so familiar and so endlessly new. He'd noticed, of course, the dance of freckles across the bridge of Bonny's nose. But that particular freckle? The one that nestled a little higher than its fellows, its colour a little darker, too, as if it wished to assert itself. And Bonny's smile—surely he knew that well? But what of the two little brackets that curved over the corners of his lips when he did? The smile of his smile. And his eyes, how long and how often had Valentine gazed into Bonny's eyes? Were they not, now, his favourite shade of blue? But what of their greens? The clandestine little flecks that danced for only the most devoted watcher, in the rarest lights?

"I cannot help but notice," he said at last, "that only one of us is devoid of garments."

Bonny pushed his cheek against Valentine's thigh, rubbing against the hair there, and making odd little growling-purring noises. "Yes, I know. But I've gone from being distracted about getting you naked to being distracted by the fact you are naked."

Of course, it was not the first time Bonny had seen Valentine unclad, nor the second, given he had rather relied upon Bonny during his recovery. But this was a whole new context—different even to the day at the waterfall, when their nudity had been more about bathing, at least initially, than it had been about each other.

Tonight, it was a baring, a sharing. A choice made in the fullness of understanding.

And Valentine did not want to be alone in it.

"Bonny?"

Whatever was in his voice made Bonny look up immediately.

"I need to see you too."

Bonny was on his feet in seconds. What followed was a blur of motion, a chaos of arms and legs and flying garments, before he emerged flushed, wild haired, and naked.

Completely, beautifully naked. In all the strength and frailty of his skin.

Chapter 36

Bonny gave a little skip. "Personal-care drawer time."

Then scampered off—gold limned, his haunches gleaming in the candlelight—to rummage. Leaving Valentine still reeling slightly: spoiled with caretaking, dazzled by loveliness, humbled by intimacy.

And, unaccustomed though he was to sharing such a thing, quite ferociously aroused.

"I'm thinking—probably a no?" Bonny held up a column of rose quartz, whose length and girth was sufficient to make Valentine's eyes water even at a distance.

"Would that even be pleasant?"

"For some people, certainly. But *this* . . ." And here Bonny slapped himself soundly on the posterior. "She's a lady. You handle her with care."

Valentine tried not to stare too avidly at the area in question. "I had no intention of doing otherwise."

"This is rather nice?" Bonny had now taken hold of the same jade object he had earlier discovered and was stroking its length with his palm in a manner Valentine found quite unaccountably stirring.

He crossed one leg over the other in the hope of retaining even a splinter of modesty. "Y-yes." It came out a croak. "I mean. Yes. Certainly. Whatever you think you would enjoy."

Then Bonny let out an "oooooooh" and pounced on something at the back of the drawer—which was already somewhat intimidating Valentine by both its capacity and its contents. "I think I'd enjoy this."

And he held out, to Valentine's nervy gaze, a piece of carved amethyst. Neither as long, nor as wide, as some of its comrades—although it did not lack for heft—it was nonetheless intriguingly shaped: tapered at one end, broad in the middle, and set upon a flared base.

Bonny was already staring at it in starry-eyed wonder. "It's purple."

"It is," Valentine agreed, "purple."

"I *love* it. But do you think it will go with my arse?"

"G-go with your arse?"

"Yes. Do you think it will look pretty? Purple can be such a difficult colour. And I'm not sure precisely what shade of pink I am back there."

"A sort of . . . dusty rose?" suggested Valentine. "About . . ." He lifted one of the bed hangings. "This colour? Oh God. Has Sir Horley decorated his room in shades of arsehole?"

Bonny came bounding back, clutching both the amethyst implement and a vial of what looked to be oil. "At this moment in time, I would like your attention, flower, to be focused strictly on my arsehole, rather than arseholes in general or the soft furnishings."

Feeling oddly emboldened, Valentine let his legs fall comfortably open and wrapped a hand about his cock. He gave it a long, firm stroke, not quite prepared for the way this act of mild physical satisfaction would ignite beneath the spark of Bonny's regard. It wrung a startled groan from him, to say nothing of some liquid enthusiasm. "You need be in no doubt of my attention."

"And you can't be expecting to just do that right in front of me without any consequences."

Before Valentine could answer, Bonny had tossed his items onto the bed, thrown himself between Valentine's knees, and had his mouth upon Valentine's cock—lapping up the taste of his excitement with eager motions of his tongue.

Valentine's world flashed white. Then broke like dandelion seeds into bliss and spun him away upon them.

"Bonny." He stifled the cry into his own hand. "Bonny. Bonny. Bonny. Please, I'm—it's . . ."

Bonny paused and peeped up at him, half repentant, half not. "Sorry."

Valentine's heart was still in frenzy. His breath in tumult. "How do people not die of this?"

"Valentine. Nobody dies. Except, I suppose, euphemistically."

"But it's . . . so much."

This was apparently too much provocation again. Bonny's lips found Valentine's cock again, though their touch was exquisitely light. "I love the way you respond to me."

Valentine panted his way through the pleasure. Letting himself trust it. Seek out the shape of it. As infinite and intricate as the sycamore leaf. Just about discernible in the flickers of heat Bonny left behind. "I will not last the night," he murmured.

"Don't worry." Bonny grinned up at him. "You're going to come on my cock, Valentine. I'll make sure of it."

Shivers were rioting up and down Valentine's spine. "Telling me things like that isn't helping."

"Would it make you feel better"—Bonny stroked his thighs soothingly, which, incidentally, also wasn't helping—"if you put that piece of amethyst inside me?"

Valentine suspected he was doomed to carnal dissolution whatever happened. "Yes, please."

It took them a couple of minutes of tangly naked wriggling to find an arrangement that kept Valentine's arm out of harm's way while still allowing him to proceed with the task before him. In the end, they settled for Valentine propped up on pillows and Bonny kneeling over him, facing away. Sliding a hand up to the nape of his neck, Valentine eased Bonny gently down until his chest was flat to the bed and his hips rose up in counterpoint.

Once he was in position, Bonny wriggled enticingly. "I'm getting a tiny bit concerned you like my arse more than my face."

"Not at all." Valentine ran his hands eagerly over Bonny's cheeks, letting their curves fill his palms. "I am just afforded fewer opportunities to see this end of you." He leaned forwards and dropped a kiss on the rosy, dimpled flesh. "I have missed you, Bonny's arse."

Bonny half laughed, half groaned. "Are you going to get all talkative again?"

"Well, you responded so positively last time."

"I did not respond positively. I—*oh*. Oh my."

Valentine had taken the opportunity to spread him open. "Ah, there you are. My sweet, hungry flower."

"Oh no."

"So beautiful and pink and *eager*." Settling a fingertip over Bonny's hole, Valentine was delighted to find it just as responsive as last time. That same supple strength that hinted at an untold capacity to yield. "You are eager, aren't you?"

"Fine," sighed Bonny. "I'm eager."

"Do you remember last time? When I kissed you"—Valentine tapped the spot—"right here?"

Bonny squealed.

"How I covered you with my mouth and sucked until you—"

"I'm eager I'm eager I'm eager." One of Bonny's hands flailed vaguely at the coverlet. "If you . . . the oil. In the vial. You can put a finger inside me."

Valentine was shaking slightly—or perhaps more than slightly. Enough to spill some of the oil, but at least it meant there was no danger of his not using enough. He let it warm upon his hands. "I won't . . . I won't hurt you?"

"I promise," Bonny told him, somewhat muffled by the way he was writhing about with his face mashed into the bed, "you won't."

Still a little uncertain, Valentine stroked him with oil-slick fingers. And then gasped. "Bonny. You're . . . you're *glistening*."

"Um. You know you don't have to describe me to me every time? You are aware of that?"

Entranced, Valentine retrieved the vial and tilted it carefully over Bonny, watching the heavy droplets slide languorously down the sweetly opened gully between his cheeks.

Bonny's spine hunched up like a cat's. His toes curled. "Ohmygodthatfeelslewd."

"It looks lewd. You're shining like honey. As wet as a painted mouth."

"W-well . . . ," Bonny choked out. "I'm sure that's lovely."

It was certainly impossible to resist, for all Valentine could have sat there all night, just stroking and talking and teasing, watching Bonny clench and quiver, and listening to his noises, his increasingly incoherent attempts to talk back. He settled the pad of his finger against Bonny's hole—between the oil and Bonny's eagerness, it took almost no pressure. There was just the sensation of sinking, of being welcomed, into heat, living heat that rippled and surged around him, responding to him. It was like being part of Bonny. And made him wonder how it would feel when it was Bonny he took into himself.

Deeply satisfying, he hoped, from the sounds that were spilling from Bonny's lips. Happy little purrs and needy growls. His head twisted back towards Valentine. "Fuck me, flower."

"L-like this?" Valentine moved within him, as smoothly as he could. "More."

Another finger just made Bonny buck more wildly, moan more fervently. Before he pulled away and flipped onto his back, spreading his legs wide. For a moment Valentine could only stare—at his sweat-tangled hair and his arousal-wide eyes, the flush upon his chest, and the way each breath shook his whole body. It was only belatedly that Valentine realised he was trembling in return, gasping, too, his own cock straining as urgently as Bonny's.

Bonny shoved the amethyst pleasure aid at Valentine. "Put it in me. So I can fuck you back."

Slick from Valentine's hands, the object positively *glided* into Bonny. He opened around it sweetly—hips arching up to meet it—and then voraciously, his fingers clawing at the bedsheets, his mouth shaping a series of harsh, hungry cries.

"You need not have worried," Valentine told him. "Purple becomes you."

Although Valentine's relationship with amethyst had been forever altered. The next time he caught a glitter of purple from a dowager's tiara, he was going to think of this instead: Bonny cast wide across the bed before him, a piece of polished stone buried deep inside him, its base nestled between his cheeks, gleaming like the most wicked piece of jewellery imaginable.

Bonny stretched an arm behind his head and slid a foot up Valentine's thigh, his smile full of knowing satisfaction. "Your turn."

"Oh *God*."

He helped Valentine onto his back—horizontally across the bed, with his legs dangling over the side, and Bonny standing between them—and then tucked a pillow beneath his shoulder. It was, as ever . . . a little strange to be looking up at someone from that position, especially when you were used to looking down at them. But then Bonny leaned over him, chest to chest, and kissed him hard, and Valentine realised that even though he couldn't embrace him back with his arms, he could wrap his legs around him, and hold him that way. Bonny pressed his hand over Valentine's, twining their fingers together upon the bed, and, all at once, Valentine found himself pinned, held, protected, helpless, his heart flying on the freedom of it.

Bonny's other hand was lost somewhere between their bodies. Then an oil-slippery finger breached him, and Valentine arched up—a cry of surprise pressed to Bonny's lips. He waited, trembling slightly, anxious on instinct, but his body was unperturbed. Really, it was no different to being kissed: just another joining, another meeting. And it felt . . . it felt so good. Bonny's tongue in his mouth, his hand on Valentine's hand, his fingers inside him. A pleasure made of many pleasures, taking him apart, until he was nothing but pleasure.

It was the same when Bonny pushed into him. A moment of uncertainty. And then just the sense of his body knowing how to give of itself. A warm stretch. Sweet internal pressure. The sense of being so very deeply touched. A cry broke from his throat like a dove.

"Open your eyes." Bonny's voice was rough. A little wild.

Valentine's eyes fluttered open. Bonny was stretched out over him, his body moving in long thrusts, his face alight and fierce, almost exultant.

"Look at yourself," Bonny told him. "Look at *us*."

For the first time, Valentine hesitated. Bonny didn't insist, and Valentine knew, in that moment, that he wouldn't. That this could be something he only felt and didn't have to see.

But why shouldn't he see it? What was there to fear in truth?

He turned his head to one of the mirrors. And there they were, two bodies, perfectly entwined, sweat gilded and heat flushed, locked in mutual rapture. Valentine met his own eyes—searching for something he recognised in the reflected man who had abandoned himself so freely, so fearlessly, in the arms of another.

The Duke of Malvern: all undone.

Valentine laughed, dazed and delighted by the discovery.

"See." Bonny straightened, drawing Valentine's legs more firmly about his waist. "See who you are. That beautiful, passionate, generous man who's all mine."

"Yes," said Valentine. "Yes."

Bonny curled a hand around Valentine's cock. "Say you're mine. Valentine, say you're mine."

"I'm yours."

It echoed through every reflection. Every Valentine and every Bonny. And then everything Valentine was feeling—everything he saw—everything Bonny had given him—coalesced into starlight: sharp and silver and eternal, shining inside him and through him. Until he shattered.

And even the breaking was beautiful.

Chapter 37

Afterwards, they lay together, still clad in the remnants of their pleasure, though Bonny had dispensed with his amethyst friend.

"That felt amazing," he said, his head tucked against Valentine's good shoulder. "It was fucking me while I was fucking you. You have to try it."

Valentine had barely remembered how to breathe. "May I have five minutes?"

Bonny just laughed and contrived to drag one of the blankets up to cover them. It occurred to Valentine that they could, perhaps, make more of an effort to right themselves: to sleep in the bed as it was designed to be slept in, with one's head at the top and one's feet at the bottom. But with breathing still in question, moving was beyond contemplation.

"I loved"—Bonny stifled an enormous yawn—"everything about that."

"As did I."

"And you're . . . well? I didn't hurt your shoulder? Or anywhere else?"

Valentine made a play of thinking about it. "Well, I'm not sure, Bonny. Your cock is so prodigious, it could have done untold damage to my interior."

"Excuse me, my cock *is* prodigious."

"I have no basis for comparison."

"Yes, you do. And mine is definitely the most prodigious."

"What?" Valentine scrabbled uselessly at the blanket. "Your vision is defective. Or your sense of scale distorted."

Pressing his face against Valentine's neck, Bonny shook with giggles. "How about," he suggested, "you demonstrate your prodigious cock to me in the morning?"

"Very well." Valentine did his best to sound dignified but unfortunately only managed huffy. "I will."

Bonny drifted off to sleep soon after and, not long after that, annexed Valentine's leg and stole most of the blanket. Thankfully, Valentine was used to this, and Bonny provided his own warmth. For some reason, however, despite being thoroughly exhausted, he was having trouble finding his own peace.

The problem was he was happier than he had ever been in his life. And the longer he dwelled in happiness, the darker the shadow cast by the uncertainties of the future. As much as he might want to, he could not stay here forever, pretending his arm was worse than it was, and Bonny must have known that too.

What they had was strong and real; Valentine truly believed that. It could survive his dukedom, it could survive the world; Bonny had said himself that Miss Tarleton would understand. So why couldn't Valentine sleep? Why, when he had everything to hope for, was dread twisting like a cobra in his gut?

It was still twisting in the colourless no-time before dawn and the chalky grey hours that followed. It twisted through the buttercup yellow of the early morning and looked set to twist through the deepening gold of noon, all while Bonny slept the easy sleep of the utterly unconcerned.

Valentine couldn't bear it.

"Bonny." He nudged him gently. "Bonny."

Nothing.

"Bonny."

A mostly still unconscious nuzzle.

"Bonny."

Bonny's eyes shot open. "Wh-what?"

"Bonny, I've been think—"

"What's happening? What time is it?"

"I don't know. But, listen"—Valentine had the oddest sense of forcing a horse to a jump he knew it would refuse—"I've been thinking we should probably visit your sister."

Half sitting up, Bonny pushed the hair out of his face and rubbed the sleep from his eyes. "Um . . . yes? We can do that?"

"Good. I'll ask Periwinkle to make the preparations."

"Wh-what's brought this on?"

"Well, I just thought it would be . . . for the best. To move forwards with our lives."

"Fair enough." Bonny yawned. Then yawned again. Gave his head a little shake. "It would probably be good for you to have a talk."

Valentine chuckled, nausea roiling senselessly inside him. "Well, yes. It would be difficult to marry her without talking to her."

A pause.

"Sorry," said Bonny. "I'm still half-asleep. I thought you just said you were going to marry my sister."

Another pause.

"Aren't I?" asked Valentine.

This time, it was Bonny who laughed, though it sounded no more convincing than Valentine's had. "I mean, I hope not? Given you're . . . with me?"

Now there was a pit of cobras. And Valentine was the pit. But this was fine. It was going to be fine. It was some kind of mistake or misapprehension. It would be resolved, and all would be well again.

"But," he tried, "you said she'd understand? That once she knew it was you I cared for, she wouldn't feel the same need to flee to the colonies?"

"Indeed. Yes." Bonny's tone was equally cautious. Equally careful. "Because if you're with me, then you won't be with Belle, and so she won't have to run away to avoid marrying you."

Oh God. Valentine couldn't breathe. Perhaps he really was going to be sick. "Bonny, I'm a duke."

"Believe me, flower. We're all aware you're a duke."

"I have to marry."

There was something happening in Bonny's eyes. It was like watching the stars flee the sky. "Wh-what? B-but . . ."

"There's my place in society to think about."

"And I don't have a place in society to think about?"

Valentine squirmed. "Not in the same way."

"Oh, wonderful. Thank you for reminding me of my own triviality."

"I didn't mean it like that," said Valentine, having blatantly meant it like that. "Besides, there's my name to think about. My legacy."

"But what"—Bonny's voice barely a whisper—"what about me?"

Wild hopes clutched at Valentine's heart. "I still want you, Bonny. I still want this."

"You just don't want me in your actual, you know, *life*?"

"If it were up to me—"

"It *is* up to you." Shoving the covers away, Bonny jumped out of bed. Then—seemingly startled by his own nakedness—grabbed for the covers again.

"I don't understand." Valentine gazed at him pleadingly. "How can this be a surprise to you?"

"Valentine." It was not a *Val-EN-tine*. It was a desert. Empty. Stark as glass. "What did you think I meant when I told you I didn't share? When I told you I was looking for someone to be my everything? When I called you mine?"

"I . . . I am yours. As completely as it is possible for me to be anyone's."

"That . . . that's not what you said last night, though, is it?" Bonny had both hands folded over his mouth, as if he could catch the pain of his words in his palms. "You didn't say, 'I'm yours except in these specific areas that are pretty important, actually.'"

Valentine reached out desperately, only for Bonny to ignore him. "They're only important to the world. They don't have to be important to us."

"They're important to me."

"Am I not also important to you?"

"Oh no." Bonny's tone sharpened. "Don't do that. Don't you dare do that. This is about your choices, not mine."

"Bonny . . ." Had some part of Valentine always known this would happen? Suddenly, it felt like it did. That this had been inevitable, and he had been a fool. A self-deceived fool. "We must compromise."

"Why?"

"Because it is the only way to be together."

Tears were spilling unchecked from Bonny's eyes, down his cheeks and over his fingers. "It was always true to you, wasn't it? When you said my life would never be what I want it to be. That I could never have what I'm looking for."

"You know I cannot marry you."

"But you can give me your heart and your fidelity and your days until death do us part."

"And I will," Valentine promised. "I will give you all those things."

Bonny looked less than reassured. "While married to someone else?"

"If it's your sister, she won't want them."

"She's my *sister*," Bonny cried. "How can I be with my sister's husband?"

When put like that, it did seem . . . inappropriate. Wrong. Fine, it seemed wrong. Valentine nodded eagerly. "You're right. Of course you're right. I'll find someone else. Someone you like too. Someone who'll—"

"No no no no no." Bonny's wail bounced from mirror to mirror to mirror, an endless echo of anguish. He paused. Stilled. Breathed painfully in and out. "I can't help the world. But I can help myself. And I deserve a man who will love me as completely as I love him."

"Do you even realise," Valentine asked, "what I will have to sacrifice—"

Before he could finish, Bonny had crossed the room in a bound and landed on his knees next to Valentine, tornadoes of fury churning through his eyes. "I am not a fucking sacrifice."

Even like this, heartbroken and impossible, he was irresistible. Everything Valentine could have ever dreamed of wanting. "I put that badly," he said, externally composed, inside nothing but tatters. "But don't force this choice on me. I beg you. I cannot be without you, Bonny. I *cannot.*"

"Then be with me." Bonny's voice broke. "Please."

"I—"

But Bonny read the rejection in Valentine's voice before he got beyond a word. "Oh no," he said. "Oh no. Don't don't don't." And he started to cry again, the helpless tears of someone who knows they've already lost. "I'm in love with you, Valentine. Don't do this to me."

"We can make it work. We can find a way."

But Bonny just folded into Valentine and sobbed and sobbed.

"Bonny . . ." How did you comfort someone you were in the middle of destroying? Helplessly, Valentine curled an arm around him, held him close, and felt—

No. He could not feel anything. Or else he could not do this.

Because, had it only been his life at stake, he would have gladly thrown away everything he possessed, all his past and all his future, for the man in his arms.

Eventually Bonny calmed. Eased himself free from Valentine's arms and wiped his face.

"I have to go," he said.

Everything that Valentine refused to feel threatened to be felt regardless. "Don't."

Bonny gazed at him, his eyes sticky and swollen half-shut from tears, his nose running. "Then tell me—how can I stay when you would have me be nothing?"

"It wouldn't be nothing," Valentine whispered, already knowing it was not enough.

Taking his hand, Bonny raised it to his lips and kissed it. He had done this once before in play. Now it was farewell. "I will not live in your margins, Valentine, when all I've ever wanted is to be your hero."

Then he heard the rustle of pulled-on clothes. The thump and clatter of hasty packing. Footsteps walking away. Hoofbeats fading into the distance.

Emptiness settled like dust in Bonny's absence. The mirrors watched Valentine in silence.

Chapter 38

Valentine arrived in Bath a ghost. Oh, he looked like Valentine, talked like Valentine; everyone assumed he was, in fact, Valentine. But he knew he was a ghost. The world moved round him, passed through him, leached of all warmth, all light.

Also, there was a strange woman in his mother's house. She was slim and elegant, with dark hair and dark eyes, clad in a morning gown of striped green—actually, Valentine didn't care.

"Oh," she said, gliding down the staircase to meet him. "Hello, Valentine."

He squinted at her through his ghost's eyes. "Who the devil are you?"

"I'm Peggy," she told him, visibly vexed.

"What? But she's a—you're a—"

"I said I'm sometimes a girl. Do you ever pay attention to anyone?"

Clearly not. "Where's Mother?"

"In the front drawing room, I think. With Mr. Peacock."

Valentine groaned. "He's here?"

"Well, obviously he's here," said Peggy. "He's—oh, you're just walking away."

Having dropped his hat, coat, and gloves in the vicinity of the butler's outstretched hands, Valentine had set off towards the drawing room. Piano music and soft voices drifted through the door as he approached.

Within he found his mother at the piano, the ubiquitous Mr. Peacock turning the pages for her, with his head unnecessarily close to hers. From his father, Valentine had inherited his height, from his mother everything else, including the smouldering eyes and chestnut hair that had made her the great beauty of her day. Made her something of a beauty still.

"Hello mother," he said. "Go away, Avery."

His mother looked up with a smile. "Darling, I wondered when we'd be seeing you."

"Malvern"—why Mr. Peacock felt bound to enter the conversation, Valentine could not imagine—"it's been too long."

"On the contrary," Valentine returned. "Now go away, Avery."

Mr. Peacock was a strikingly handsome man, some two decades his mother's junior. "Perhaps," he suggested, "I should leave?"

"Perhaps." His mother offered him a somewhat conspiratorial smile. And then, to Valentine, once the door had closed, observed—as she so often did: "I do wish you'd be a little kinder to Avery."

"I just don't understand why he's always hanging around."

"I know you don't, darling." Turning on the piano seat, his mother regarded him with a slight frown. "Are you quite well, Vali? I heard you'd been shot, but you look dreadful. Have you been sleeping? Or eating? Or taking care of yourself even the slightest bit?"

When not a ghost, Valentine had never been able to lie to his mother. Ghost Valentine found himself subject to the same weakness. "I . . . I . . ."

"Darling?" Now his mother sounded alarmed.

The next thing Valentine knew, he had fallen to his knees in front of her, buried his face in her lap, and burst into tears.

"Oh my," said his poor, startled mother.

Valentine made incoherent noises.

"Whatever's the matter?" She still sounded too astonished to be wholly consoling. "This isn't like you, Vali."

"Having feelings? I am allowed, you know."

"Well, of course you're allowed," she said, as if it had been obvious all along. "It's more that you've never been in the habit of sharing them with me."

Was that true? His mother was one of the people he loved most in the world—certainly, one of the few he felt close to. Yet even from her, he had held himself back. And, just like that, Valentine was not a ghost at all. Just a hopeless and heartbroken man.

"Mother," he sobbed. "Mother, I've fallen in love."

His mother was stroking his hair, as she had when he was a child. "Is that so very terrible?"

He sniffed. "Yes, it's very painful and inconvenient."

There was a pause. "I'm afraid I can sort of see that, darling. It's been lovely finally getting to meet Arabella Tarleton, but she has caused you quite a lot of trouble, and—to be frank—I don't think that will change after you're married. On the other hand, I don't think that matters if you love her."

"N-not," Valentine managed, "with Arabella Tarleton."

"Phew." His mother gave a relieved little laugh. "You had me worried for a moment there."

Valentine looked up, blinking through his tears. "I thought I was supposed to marry Arabella Tarleton?"

"Well, your father and her father thought it would be a nice idea. But you can't do something just because a couple of men thought it might be a nice idea."

"But . . . Miss Tarleton's prospects. Their estate. We can't let the family fall into ruin."

"Of course not," said his mother soothingly. "The Laytons and the Tarletons have been friends for generations."

This seemed to be circular. Or Valentine was too sad to actually think about anything. "So I *should* marry Miss Tarleton?"

"It has occurred to you, I suppose, that marriage need not be the solution to every problem?"

As it happened, this had not occurred to Valentine.

"Settle a dowry on Arabella yourself," suggested his mother. "Perhaps with a nice annuity so she can live on her own terms?"

"Aren't . . . ," asked Valentine uncertainly, "aren't I breaking your heart?"

"My heart?" repeated his mother. "What does my heart have to do with your marriage?"

"I . . . I thought you might care."

"Well, of course I care. I care that you are happy. But how you find that happiness is, frankly, none of my business." She gave a little laugh. "What a dull life you must think I lead, darling, that I go around caring who other people marry."

Perhaps it was all the crying he had done, but Valentine's brain felt fluffy and useless. "And what about Father?"

His mother winced. "Forgive the unseemly candour, but he's dead: I don't think he cares about anything very much."

"It was what he wanted, though."

"I told you, Vali: it was a romantic dream. And romantic dreams are lovely, and some of them absolutely deserve to be lived. But some of them are, and should remain, nothing but dreams."

"I'm letting him down," protested Valentine, hardly knowing why he was protesting—only that unhappy marriage to Arabella Tarleton had been an inevitability of his future for such a long time that he didn't know how to let go of it.

"Don't be absurd." His mother gave him a chiding poke. "Look at you. You're handsome, clever, kind—"

Recalling his recent adventures in Surrey and Kent, Valentine winced. "I . . . am not as kind as I would wish to be."

"You are my son," his mother told him sharply. "I'll think of you however I please. But any father would be proud of you, Valentine. And I know yours would. Now give that marvellous termagant of a girl some money and allow yourself to be happy."

Valentine sat back on his heels. Suddenly everything seemed terrifyingly simple. "If I can give Miss Tarleton a dowry, I can also pay the mortgage on the estate, ensure it is bequeathed to the Tarleton family in perpetuity, and Bon—I mean, Mr. Tarleton—can begin to repay the debt to me once the land is generating income again."

"There." His mother clapped her hands together. "Didn't I say you were clever?"

He gave her a look. "You don't have to patronise me, Mother. I'm well aware this was all you."

"Sorry, darling." At least she had the grace to blush. "I was trying to make you feel better." A pause. Then she started to laugh. "I can't believe you were seriously contemplating marriage to Arabella Tarleton."

"Why is that amusing to you?"

"I just don't know how you didn't immediately realise you were not right for each other."

"I was trying," said Valentine coldly, "to do right by the family and honour my father's wishes."

His mother sighed, then gently pushed a lock of hair from where it had fallen partially into his eyes. "Oh, Vali, I wish you had been able to know your father a little better. You're so like him. Almost to a fault."

"I beg your pardon?"

"He thought too much of who he was supposed to be and did not spend enough time as who he was. Which, by the way, could be very charming. He used to make me laugh."

"He . . . no. Impossible." Valentine's father had been nothing but serious. Nothing but stern. Nothing but perfectly in control.

"He wanted so badly to be a good father to you—set a proper example—that I'm afraid he made the most dreadful hash of it." She sighed again. "And I kept thinking there would be time, time for you to grow and for him to unbend, for you both to talk and know each other at last. And then he died, and—well." Her fingers fluttered, a gesture of regret and grief and the ultimate absurdity of life. "Here we are. Time's harlots. Each and every one of us."

Valentine gasped. *"Mother."*

"There, there, darling." She patted him unrepentantly upon the shoulder. "Now, this woman you've fallen in love with. I want to hear all about her."

In the deluge of revelation about his father—which Valentine was still struggling with—he'd forgotten he'd as good as confessed about Bonny. "It . . . ," he began. Only to discover he had no idea how to finish.

"Don't be shy." His mother's shoulder patting became a shoulder poking. "Whoever she is, I will love her for having believed your heart worth winning."

"Um . . ."

"All this demurral. Is she unsuitable?"

"Perhaps a little," Valentine admitted.

"Darling, this just makes me like her more." His mother gazed at him, all twinkling smiles and shining eyes. "Is she impoverished? A bluestocking? Older than you? A governess? A courtesan? French? A cat burglar? An actress. A—"

"Mother," Valentine yelled. "She's a man."

A split second of silence. "Well," said his mother, the faintest squeak in her voice. "That's certainly unusual. But do tell me about him, won't you, darling?"

Valentine was momentarily frozen. "How can I tell you about him? He's a man. Didn't you hear me? He's a man. I'm in love with a man."

"Well, yes. I did hear you. I think perhaps the boy who cleans the knives and boots heard you." She searched his face in some confusion. "Vali, you seem very upset about this?"

"And you aren't?"

"What would that accomplish?"

"I don't know," snapped Valentine. "But it would be normal."

His mother's bewildered air did not dissipate. "Why would it be normal to be upset at my son for falling in love?"

"I . . ." Valentine hid his face in her lap again. "I can't be with him."

She began, once again, to stroke his hair, which made Valentine start crying again. "He doesn't return your feelings?" she asked.

"No, he does. But I'm a duke."

"Yes, and one of the privileges of being a member of the aristocracy is being able to do whatever you damn well please. I'm sure there will be those who will laugh at you for your choices, but why would you care about such people?"

"The estate," protested Valentine.

"I'm sure you can still manage the estate while being in love, Vali." There was a touch of impatience in her voice now. "Your father coped."

"But"—Valentine, cautious of all things, but hope most of all, was still stuck in a loop of protesting—"I have to marry."

"Why?"

"To secure the line of succession."

"Darling, what's-his-name can inherit. Your uncle William's son." She snapped her fingers. "Ernest. That's it."

"Ernest?" repeated Valentine.

His mother shrugged. "He's neither a rake nor a profligate. He's happily married, so I presume his tastes run contrary to yours. And he's already got an estate of his own, so he'll know what he's doing."

"What about"—Valentine flapped a vague hand—"blood and heredity and . . . and . . . things."

"Are they more important than your happiness?"

"And my father's legacy?"

"*You're* his legacy."

"What about grandchildren? Don't you want grandchildren?"

His mother was silent for a long moment. "You're not going to like this answer, darling, but not particularly. Which is not to say I wouldn't welcome any you had. I am not, however, awaiting their arrival in order to give my existence meaning."

"Oh, Mother." Valentine's tears seemed to have at last subsided. He climbed to his feet and did his best to compose himself—as a kind of manageable first step to thinking about everything they'd talked about. "I do worry about you."

She gave him a sharp look. "Whatever for?"

"Well, you're a widow. You're all alone."

"Valentine, have I forgotten dropping you on your head as a baby? I'm not remotely alone."

"Wh-what do you mean?"

"You've met Avery. You were insulting him less than an hour ago."

"What does he have to do with anything?"

She shaded her eyes with a hand and gave her head a little shake. "He's my lover."

"He's your . . ." Valentine abruptly recalled the succession of beautiful young men who had been keeping his mother's company for as long as he could remember. "Was—"

"Probably yes."

"And—"

"Yes."

Valentine fell heavily into a chair. "All of them?"

"Well, not all together, darling. One after the other. I'm not insatiable."

"Oh God," said Valentine. "Oh God."

His mother shrugged. "I'm sorry to shock you." She did not sound very sorry. "But what did you expect?"

"I don't know. I thought you were sad."

"Well, I was sad. I loved your father. I still do. But my life didn't end with his."

"Oh God," said Valentine. "Oh God."

His mother rose, crossed the room, and kissed Valentine on his very troubled brow. "Vali, I should probably have said something years ago. It just seemed . . . easier for you, somehow. To have this story about your father and me."

"Oh God," said Valentine. "Oh God."

"I can see you have a lot to think about, and I would like to get back to Avery. But"—and here she offered him a consoling smile—"I would love to hear about the young man whenever you're ready."

Valentine offered a dazed nod.

"And in the meantime, darling, why don't you trust me with my happiness and think about caring for your own?"

The door closed behind with her with a neat, certain click.

Chapter 39

Miss Tarleton was in the stables, having just come back from a ride. This meant she had a crop but, as far as Valentine could ascertain, no gun.

She greeted him with, "So it's you."

This was undeniable. Valentine nodded.

"I suppose," she said, "I should apologise for shooting you."

"I suppose," he said, "I should apologise for trying to force you to marry me."

A long silence. Miss Tarleton kicked idly at a scrap of hay that was blowing across the stable yard. It occurred to Valentine that he had spent a lot of time pursuing Miss Tarleton through stables.

"Shall we walk?" He offered his good arm.

With the air of one visibly reluctant but trying hard to be polite, Miss Tarleton accepted. It was the closest they had come to peace since the flower crown. Valentine's sky was still gently falling—revealing a world wholly different to the one he had always believed he understood. But at least he was not a ghost.

They proceeded together into the garden, which his mother had taken some time to cultivate and Valentine hoped Miss Tarleton would appreciate. It was, after all, a rather pretty spot, with its meandering shrubbery walks and the borders ablaze with cornflowers, poppies, and marigolds: all the colours of summer, finding harmony through profusion.

"You are in good health?" enquired Miss Tarleton, making no attempt to make it sound less than stilted.

"I was recently shot," Valentine said mildly, "but otherwise, yes. Yourself?"

"Very well, thank you. And your family?"

"You are staying with my mother, so you would know better than I."

Miss Tarleton thinned her lips. "Were the roads very dry?"

"Tolerable—Miss Tarleton . . . Arabella." Valentine paused. "What happened to us?"

"You tried to wed me against my will, then chased me across the country like an absolute monster. I thought you might have noticed."

"Before that."

"Oh." Miss Tarleton struck a pose of understanding. "You mean, when you abandoned us?"

"I . . ." That was difficult to dispute. "I did not intend to abandon you."

She shrugged. "That relieves my mind."

"Arabella, I'm sorry."

She shrugged again.

"I was young and foolish, and selfish and cruel, and I did not think how my actions would affect you."

A long silence, Miss Tarleton offering only her profile, her eyes shadowed behind their lashes, her teeth digging into her lower lip. Then, in a venomous whisper, "I thought you were my friend."

"I am your friend."

"Then"—she swept one of the theatrical curtsies he was sure she practiced—"God save me from your enmity, Your Grace."

Valentine clenched his teeth on a noise of frustration. "For God's sake. Must we play these games? I am sincerely and humbly repentant."

"And what has that to do with me?"

"Will you not forgive me?" It was his softest voice, his most coaxing and hopeful.

"Why should I?" she asked. "You broke my heart, Valentine. The heart of a child who had already lost both her parents. You promised me friendship; you asked for my trust. And you forgot me the moment it was convenient."

There was nothing Valentine could say to that. The guilt had long been a pack of wolves at his heels. Today was apparently the day it caught him.

His dismay must have shown on his face, for she gave him a brittle smile. "Quite."

"You know," he said carefully, "even if I had come back, we could not have married. It's . . . complicated. But I am not suited to it."

At this, she just laughed. A feral thing, all claws and teeth. "You men, you think of nothing but matrimony. It was my friend I wanted, not a husband."

"I had no idea how alone you felt. Or how vulnerable you were."

"Why should you? When you have never been either?" Another laugh. "I am grateful, though, for the lesson you taught me."

It was a statement that begged a question. One Valentine very much did not want to ask but felt he had to. "What lesson was that?"

"That waiting to be saved is a fool's game. I shall never make that mistake again."

"You have," Valentine conceded, with a pained smile, "become rather adept at saving yourself."

Something flickered in the eyes that were so like and so unlike Bonny's. "Thank you, Your Grace."

They walked a little farther. A bee whizzed past Valentine's nose.

"Miss Tarleton," he said. "I have been thinking about the future."

She offered an indifferent "Mm-hmm?"

"Given the long-standing friendship between our families and our, I believe, mutual decision not to honour the wishes of our parents, it is only right that I settle some sum upon you for the occasion of your marriage, along with an appropriate annuity."

Her eyes narrowed. "Are you trying to buy me?"

"I'm trying to set you free. Will you let me?" The silence was already growing ominously long. "Please?" he tried.

She shrugged. "Very well."

"The estate I will buy. If Bonny will not let me give it to him outright, we will set up the most generous of repayment schedules. It will be returned fully to your family."

Another shrug. "Very well."

"And"—Valentine was sweating, partially because of the heat, but mainly with guilt and anxiety—"I should probably tell you . . . I should probably tell you . . . I'm in love with your brother."

Something amused and almost warm flashed across her features before she schooled them back to a civil blankness. "Perhaps I've underestimated you."

"In what regard?"

"Well, Bonny's been half in love with some fantasy of you for years. I'm a little surprised you managed to live up to it."

"Oh, I certainly did not live up to it," Valentine admitted. "But Bonny has somehow managed to find something worth loving in me regardless."

Or he had. Before Valentine had broken his heart.

Miss Tarleton made a noise of unladylike scepticism. "That, by contrast, isn't remotely surprising. I suppose he told you about Arkandia?"

Valentine nodded.

"He wrote nothing but love stories. He tried, occasionally, to turn his hand to other things, but it always came back to a man and a kiss and a promise of forever."

"What did you write?" asked Valentine, curious in spite of himself. In spite of the mistrust that still simmered between them.

She shrugged, somewhat self-consciously, as if she wanted very much to pretend none of this mattered to her. "Everything. Some love stories of my own, when the mood took me. Gothic horror when I was in a bad mood. I have spilled a lot of fictional blood."

"And some real blood," Valentine reminded her.

"Yes." She looked momentarily . . . Valentine might have said *remorseful*, but she quickly banished the expression. "I shall try not to do that again. In any case, I mostly wrote adventures—to places both real and imagined. And Bonny has been an incurable romantic all his life."

"What about you?"

"A cured one." Her gaze drifted over the flower beds and alighted upon a rose, dying among its fellows. A quick twist and she had snapped it from its stem. "Perhaps I shall meet someone someday. But why must everything be love?" She peeled off a pinkish-brown petal. It crackled like old parchment. "Love. Love. Love. When there is so much else in the world."

"Whatever it is that you are looking for," Valentine told her, "you may count on my help to find it."

She glanced at him, her broken rose pressed to her lips. "If you hurt Bonny, I will shoot you again. And, this time, I will aim for your heart."

"I understand, Miss Tarleton." He sketched her a bow. "Shall we shake hands?"

A contemplative pause. But then she shook her head. "Someday, Valentine. Perhaps someday."

Given everything that had passed between them—from the betrayal Valentine had barely noticed to his bungled proposal to the actual shooting—it was probably the closest they were going to come to peace. At least for the moment. And it was, Valentine thought, with some relief and no rancour, enough.

Chapter 40

When Valentine was shown into the sitting room at Toodling Grange, the home of Bonny's aunt and uncle, he was treated to a yelp and the sight of Bonny diving out of the window into the herbaceous border. Then sprinting away across the lawn and into the distant trees.

It was true that Valentine could have been, in general, more sensitive to the subtleties of other people's emotions, but he was getting the distinct sense that Bonny might be somewhat apprehensive about talking to him.

The door opened to admit Wilbur Tarleton—a solid, amiable man, whose farmerly aspect could, on very special occasions, be polished up to country squiredom. He looked from Valentine to the open window to the empty room.

"That's odd," he said. "I could've sworn young Bonny was in here."

"Perhaps," offered Valentine, "he's in the gardens?"

Wilbur Tarleton nodded. "Could be. Or on the roof. Or the moon. Those twins. You've more chance picking up water with your bare hands than figuring what they're up to from one moment to the next."

"That does sound like them."

"Which reminds me," Wilbur Tarleton went on, "I've a bone to pick with you, Your Grace."

Valentine flinched. "Do you?"

"Running off with them like that with nary a word to anyone. Now, they're a pair of flibbertigibbets and I don't expect any better. But you."

Wilbur Tarleton lifted a chastising finger. "You should know better. Begging your pardon, milord."

"No, no." Valentine waved away his apology. "You're quite right. I should have been more considerate."

"Well, that's damn—I mean, dashed mannerly of you to say." Wilbur Tarleton mimed a bridge with water running under it. "And we do know what they're like. That pair would bedevil the devil himself, given half a chance."

It was getting increasingly difficult for Valentine to pay attention to the conversation. All he wanted to do was find Bonny—even if that meant jumping out of a window himself.

And Wilbur Tarleton was still talking. "They've got good hearts, though."

"Mm," said Valentine. "Yes."

"Especially losing their parents like that. As I said to the wife, they're too young to be alone in the world. We do our best for them, but—"

"Forgive me." Valentine couldn't stay silent a moment longer. "It really is imperative I speak to Bonny. And I do believe he's in the gardens. May I go and look for him?"

Confused, as well he might be, Wilbur Tarleton did his best to accommodate his unaccountably restless guest. "There's no need for that, milord. I can send the kitchen lad."

"No," snarled Valentine. "I mean, thank you, but that's not necessary. I'm more than happy to go myself."

"If that's your wish."

"It is."

Wilbur Tarleton stepped politely aside. "Since you're heading out, you can give your regards to Boudicca. She likes a bit of company, she does."

"Of course," said Valentine, with as much patience as was left to him, which was perishingly little. "Should I encounter Mrs. Tarleton on my search for Bonny, I will be only too happy to tender my greetings."

There was a pause best described as fraught. Wilbur Tarleton didn't seem to quite know where to look or what to say. Then he gestured to the picture hanging above the fireplace. "That's Boudicca."

For some moments, Valentine regarded the portrait: it depicted a very large, very round pig, lavishly rendered in oils. "And what a magnificent animal she is," he concluded.

Before tipping his hat and running out of the room.

There was no sign of Bonny on the terrace or the lawn, or in the kitchen garden, but it didn't take much wandering before Valentine realised that he already knew where he was. His memories were a little faded, but they took him to the woods that bordered the park, and from there to the largest oak within them. A gnarled old giant of a tree, with a trunk it would have taken at least six men to encompass, and branches that had become private kingdoms.

Valentine circled it slowly. Even the light was different here, green heavy and gold tinted. "Bonny?"

No answer.

"Bonny, are you in the tree?"

Nothing.

"I know you're in the tree."

Crouching on the leafy carpet, Valentine peered between the roots into what had once been Arabella Tarleton's den. Bonny peered back at him through his own knees.

Valentine sighed. "Please talk to me."

"No." Bonny was all elbows and glares. "You don't deserve to be talked to."

"You just talked to me."

"Telling you I don't want to talk to you isn't talking to you. It's telling you I don't want to talk to you."

"That's a very specific distinction."

Bonny's lips trembled, and he pressed his face against his legs. "Go away, Malvern. I never want to see you again."

"Are you really," asked Valentine, "going to make me do this *through a tree?*"

"Do what through a tree?"

Valentine stood, brushing dirt and twigs from his pantaloons. "Very well. Just remember in our future life, you brought this on yourself." He cleared this throat. "Bonaventure Tarleton, you are the most beautiful man I've ever seen. You have filled my heart—"

"*Val-EN-tine.* What are you doing?"

"You know what I'm doing."

A scrabbling from within the trunk. "What about Belle?"

"Your sister, I'm sorry to tell you, has too much sense to marry me."

"Turned you down again, did she?" asked the tree moodily.

"I didn't ask her. I offered her a dowry and an annuity instead."

"Why?"

Valentine shrugged. "Well, it seemed the right thing to do. As did buying your estate, but we can talk about that later."

"No, I mean"—the tree seemed confused—"why didn't you ask Belle to marry you? *You bought my estate?*"

"Yes, and I would very much like to return it to you."

"You can't just give me an estate."

"Well, it is yours," Valentine pointed out.

"Yes, but—"

"Then you can pay me back from the income it generates. Or we can work together on some modernisations that I've been—Bonny, do we really have to discuss agriculture?"

The tree was now visibly sulking. "Well, since you own all my things, we might have to."

"We can spend our lives discussing agriculture, if that's what you want. But will you please ask me again why I didn't propose to your sister?"

"I suppose," sighed the tree. "Why didn't you propose to my sister?"

"Because it seems more than a little foolish to propose to someone when you're very much in love with someone else."

"But what about"—the tree was using its sarcastic voice—"your legacy and your family name and your blah blah blah."

"Well, as it happens, I already have a very suitable heir in my uncle's son. And, as it happens, I was being a goosewit."

The tree considered this. "You absolutely were."

"I've spent a lifetime with my legacy and my family name and my blah blah blah," Valentine went on, "and while I cannot deny they've made my life very comfortable, they have never once made me happy. You have very rarely made me comfortable. But you have—somehow, impossibly and undeniably—made me happy."

"I am pretty wonderful," said the tree in a small voice.

"You are." Valentine cleared his throat again. "You are also, as I've been saying, the most beautiful man I've ever—"

"I'm in a *tree*."

"Even so. And I would like to remind you it was your choice to be in a tree. Now can I please . . . not even continue. Can I start? Are you going to let me start?"

The tree radiated magnanimity. "You can start."

"Thank you." Then, with rather more impatience and rather less romance than he might have hoped, Valentine ground out, "You are the most beautiful man I've ever seen. You have filled my heart with—"

"Valentine?"

Valentine uttered a little roar. "Oh, for God's sake. What? What is it now?"

"Are you really doing this?"

"I'm *trying* to."

"Give me a moment." Another series of creaky noises from inside the trunk, and then Bonny rolled out of the tree at such high velocity he crashed straight into Valentine's legs. "I'm here," he cried, jumping to his feet.

For a second or two, Valentine was lost in looking. It had been a mere handful of days, but it had been far too long. Far too long to be without Bonny in his life and by his side. Making everything ridiculous. And perfect.

"Ahem," said Bonny, pointing downwards.

Only too happy to oblige, Valentine sank to one knee. Except . . .

"Oh God, I've forgotten what I'm supposed to be saying. I'm sorry, I'm just . . . I'm just . . ." And suddenly he was perilously close to tears. "I nearly lost you. And through my own damn foolishness."

"That's the only way you'll ever lose me."

"If I'm foolish? Bonny, that could be—"

"No, silly. By pushing me away. Now can you stop being all sad? I want my proposal."

"Sorry. Yes. Sorry. Of course." Valentine's head was still far from unfuzzy. "Um . . ."

"I'm the most beautiful . . . ," Bonny reminded him.

Then everything snapped back into place. And the dark edges of the world curled back on themselves, leaving only Valentine and Bonny, beneath an oak tree, in a world made of gold and green. Valentine smiled. "You're the most beautiful man I've ever seen."

"Yes." Bonny was blushing exquisitely—and trying to pretend he wasn't. "Good."

"You've filled my heart with laughter."

"Have I?"

"And my soul with joy."

"Really?"

"You've driven me to the brink of madness with desire. And, let's be honest, in general."

Bonny pressed his fingers to his lips, his smile all in bloom behind them.

"My life without you is a vast and empty . . . you know I still don't like this line. But fine. My life without you is a vast and empty ache."

"So was mine," Bonny whispered, "without you."

"You know I can't marry you legally . . ."

"Oddly enough, I do know that."

"But, Bonaventure Tarleton, I'm still asking for your hand. Because I will marry you, with everything I am, in every way that matters, with my heart and soul and body and mind, and forsaking all others, now and for the rest of my life. If you will only make me the happiest and most fortunate of men and say—"

"Yes," said Bonny. "Yes yes yes."

And hurled himself, half laughing, half crying into Valentine's embrace. While the oak, in all its wisdom and generosity, spread wide its ancient arms and offered them the confetti of its leaves.

ACKNOWLEDGEMENTS

Thank you, as ever, to my amazing agent, Courtney Miller-Callihan, my indispensable assistant, Mary, and, of course, the duckchildren, who feel it's about time their importance was recognised. Also my fabulous editor, Lauren Plude, for indulging me in this frankly very silly book. And, finally, to the people who copyedited and proofread this book, because you were extraordinarily helpful and super willing to meet me where I was.

ABOUT THE AUTHOR

Alexis Hall is determined to marry into money, as his grandfather drank half the family fortune and gambled the rest. He lives in a tumbledown mansion in a fictional county, and his valet doesn't even have a humorous name.